OF WEE SWEETIE
MICE & MEN

BATEMAN

headline

Copyright © 1996 Colin Bateman

The right of Colin Bateman to be identified as the Author of
the Work has been asserted by him in accordance with the
Copyright, Designs and Patents Act 1988.

First published in Great Britain in 1996 by
HarperCollins*Publishers*

First published in this paperback edition in 2012 by
HEADLINE PUBLISHING GROUP

1

Cataloguing in Publication Data is available from the British Library

ISBN 978 0 7553 7874 6

Typeset in Meridien by Palimpsest Book Production Limited,
Falkirk, Stirlingshire

Printed and bound by CPI Group (UK) Ltd, Croydon, CR0 4YY

Headline's policy is to use papers that are natural, renewable and recyclable
products and made from wood grown in sustainable forests. The logging and
manufacturing processes are expected to conform to the environmental
regulations of the country of origin.

HEADLINE PUBLISHING GROUP
An Hachette UK Company
338 Euston Road
London NW1 3BH

www.headline.co.uk
www.hachette.co.uk

For Andrea and Matthew

1

Peace had settled over the city like the skin on a rancid custard. Everybody wanted it, just not in that form. The forecast remained for rain, with widespread terrorism.

When it came, the steady drizzle forced diners off the sun deck of the *Rose-Marie*. They congregated in unhappy proximity in the hold of the old ferry, robbed of prime contact with the murky delights of a fading Belfast winter. They chatted in subdued tones, their only views through misted portholes, and picked in a desultory fashion at their food. For a while it had seemed exotic, lunching out on the river, something rich, something unusual. But now the reality of their situation was starkly apparent. They were eating burgers in the interior of an old rusty boat cemented to the side of a polluted river, and they could do better than that at home. Children were crying. Waiters were slow. The drink was warm.

I followed Cameron up top again, our drinks replenished. The tables were awash with ketchup and rain. Seagulls cried for the spring and sparrows chirped optimistically for a rainbow. We leant on the rail and looked out over the river at the rubbish on the far bank.

'This could be New Orleans,' Cameron said laconically.

'Yes, Steamboat Bill, it certainly could.'

I spat into the brackish water. It looked tastier than my pint.

'So anyway,' Cameron said casually, as if he hadn't been working his way up to it all afternoon, 'what do you know about Bobby McMaster?'

He gave me a little smile as he said it; everyone did when they mentioned McMaster.

'Fat Boy McMaster?'

He nodded. I shrugged.

'How do you rate him as a fighter?' he asked.

'Well, he's not Sugar Ray Leonard, but not many are.'

'No, he's not that.'

I knew Fat Boy McMaster well enough. I'd written a few articles about him over the years. Big, friendly guy, in the wrong profession. He'd been a heavyweight boxer for six years, the Irish champion for two. That, of course, meant nothing. It was like being in the Swiss Navy or the Dutch Mountain Rescue Team. He'd ventured outside Ireland three times, been beaten twice and drew once. A week before, his manager had somehow been able to wangle him a shot at the European title, stepping over a number of legitimate

British contenders in the process. It had more to do with money than sense. He met Fabrice Benizon in Toulouse. Fabrice was no Ali himself, but had defended the title six times. Fat Boy accidentally butted him in the second round and took the decision on cuts.

'He's the best heavyweight in Europe,' said Cameron, smiling again, 'he has the belt.'

'The belt round my trousers would be harder to win, Sam.'

I wasn't sure if I liked his smile. Too few teeth. He had a Dublin accent. I like a Dublin accent, in women, but it made Cameron sound cynical and manipulative. Shame how an accent can do that. His hair wasn't the best either, as if his mother had cut it with a broken bowl. But he wasn't a bad chap, for an editor. He was on his way to offering me an assignment for *Irish Sports World*, and he liked to lead up to offering me negligible money and abysmal working conditions by warm beering me in exotic locations.

'What is it, Sam,' I prompted, 'an afternoon in a Sandy Row gym with the new King of the Ring?'

He shook his head, then lifted his glass to his mouth and took several gulps, watching me with dark-rimmed eyes the whole time. He wiped his lips with the back of his hand. 'What would you say,' he said, 'if I were to tell you that Fat Boy McMaster was to fight for the world title in New York next month?'

I snorted. 'The world title of what, eating?'

'Boxing. The heavyweight title.'

'I'd say catch yourself on, Sam. No fucking way.'

'Yes, fucking way.'

'Aye, Jackanory, Sam.'

Cameron shook his head. 'I'm serious. I mean, it's not official, yet. Will be by the end of the week. You heard it here first. Fat Boy McMaster will fight Mike Tyson for the world heavyweight title in Madison Square Garden in three weeks' time.'

I lifted my glass and emptied it into the river. 'Pish,' I said.

'I'm serious, Starkey. I had it straight from the horse's mouth.'

'Mr Ed, the talking horse, Sam?'

'Mr McClean himself. You know he has the connections.'

'I wouldn't let him connect my Christmas lights, Sam.' I shook my head. Tutted. 'Fat Boy McMaster is going to fight Mike Tyson? He'd have a better chance against that girl Tyson raped. You know as well as I do he's invincible. And Rocky Marshmallow expects to be in shape in three weeks? Wise up.' Cameron shook his head. 'Tell me some more, Sam. Then give me the punch line. And I'm not excusing the pun.'

Cameron opened his palms sympathetically to me. 'I know it's hard to believe, Dan, but, like they say, it's a funny old game the fight business.'

'Funny as a fire in an orphanage.'

'Sure. But take Tyson. Since he got out of prison he's cleaned up the division. What is it, a year, and he's unified the four titles. Since he's the undisputed champ, there's a fairly straightforward punching order – he was signed to fight the official number two contender Marvin Simons on

17 March. Simons broke his leg in a car accident night before last, limped away from a four-million-dollar pay day in the process. Numbers three to five have all fought in the last month and don't want to take the chance at short notice. Beyond five there's no one of any real quality anyway, but Fat Boy winning the European title put him in at number eight. He may not be the greatest in the world, but he's white, and the fight's on St Patrick's Day. Any clearer to you now?'

'St Patrick's Day?'

'St Patrick's Day. Makes sense, doesn't it?'

I nodded. 'Sense to McClean.'

'Sense to McClean, sense to Tyson's people. I mean, you know his record, he's beaten everyone out of sight. It's hard to justify paying him millions of dollars every time he pulls on the gloves if he's just going to blow them away in the first round. I mean, Americans have the attention span of a midge anyway, but you can stretch a point. The fans were bored. What have they been looking for since Rocky Marciano? The Great White Hope. Make him Irish and you'll make a fuckin' fortune. You know what they're like over there. Most of them think they can trace their line back to Bernard the fuckin' leprechaun, and that's just the blacks. And see how crazy they go on St Patrick's Day? So along comes McMaster at just the right time. It's short notice, sure, but he's in shape from the European fight. Can you imagine the hype they'll put into it, Dan?'

'Sam, don't get carried away. McMaster can barely fill a

church hall here. He can't fight, he has the charisma of a bag of sugar and has more in common with tripe than hype. He is the Great Fat Hope. And you know it.'

'Ach, Dan,' Cameron exclaimed, bunching his fists, 'don't forget he has these! A puncher's chance.'

'He'll get killed, that's the chance he has.'

'He won't get killed.'

'Sam, you know as well as I do how many Tyson's put in hospital. And they were killing machines compared to Fat Boy.'

Sam shook his head. 'You don't understand, Dan. Look at McMaster. What has he got? He's semi-pro at best. He spends a couple of hours in the gym and the rest stacking shelves in one of McClean's warehouses. What he earned for the European title wouldn't keep you in drink for a month. This is his chance to earn a million. To make something of himself. Jesus, Dan, you'd do it for a million.'

'I'd have a better chance, for fuck's sake.'

The rain began to thicken up. The birds stopped singing. The Lagan had a sullen, listless look about it. Everything looked as miserable as Fat Boy McMaster's chances of landing the title. The only sound was the tump-tump-tump of the rain on the deck. Even the children down below had stopped wailing. I felt a bit sick, and it wasn't entirely the warm beer.

I was always a fight fan. I had only a handful of years on me when I listened to the Thrilla in Manila on the radio. I remember Jim Watt singing 'Flower of Scotland' every time he defended his world title. The mass hysteria that followed

Ireland's own Barry McGuigan to the featherweight crown. The sadly neglected but all-conquering flyweight king, Dave Boy McAuley. But McMaster was different. In Ireland he'd been okay, the biggest fish in a tiny pond. In the world ocean of boxing, he was less than plankton.

His mentor, Geordie McClean, built his fortune in the insurance business, no bad thing to be in during Belfast's roarin' seventies, then branched out into supermarkets and pubs. Everything he touched turned to gold. He'd always been something of a boxing fan and a move into managing and promoting boxers had been a natural progression for an otherwise faceless moneyman who fancied upping his public profile. It could just as well have been politics, but he didn't have an honest enough face to lie convincingly in public. So now, by fair means or foul, he had landed the big one: a shot at the world heavyweight crown. It didn't matter that he was about to propel a piss-poor fighter from the undercard to the undertaker.

'Imagine it though, Dan,' Cameron was saying, 'a Belfast boy fighting for the world heavyweight title.'

'Yeah,' I said, 'what a way to go.'

'Ach, Dan, there's no romance in you.'

'You might say that.'

'I don't like the sound of that.'

'Yeah, well.'

'You're still together, aren't you?'

'Mind your own business, Cameron.'

'How can you say that to me, Dan? Wasn't I best man at the wedding?'

'Worst, as I recall.'

'Ach, Dan.'

'Truth, mate. We've split up. Not much more I can say really.'

'How long?'

'A few months.'

'Ach, that's nothing. They say time's a great healer.'

'Aye, I know. I get the stitches out next week.'

'Jesus, I didn't like to say. She did that? Jesus, Dan, you're always breaking your fucking nose. What'd she do that with?'

'Her fist.'

'Fuck, maybe she should be fighting Tyson.'

'*She'd* have a better chance, Cameron.'

'Don't say that, Dan.' Cameron drained the last third of his pint. He looked behind him, then tossed the glass into the river.

'That was a bit stupid,' I said.

'What?'

'Tossing the glass overboard. It's pollution.'

'What the fuck are you, the Green Hornet, Dan? All I did was throw a glass in. It'll sink to the bottom and some dozy trout'll get a bit of double glazing for his nest. You poured most of a pint of pish in, they'll be pulling bodies out of there from now till Christmas.'

I shrugged.

'So you're surviving okay anyway? You're still at home?'

'I have a bedsit. Wonderful.'

Cameron tutted. 'It must be hard.'

'Usually is, then I think of Trish and it goes away.'

'Oh, bitch, bitch.'

'Yeah, well.'

'Humour masking a broken heart.'

'Humour masking a broken nose. Sam, I still can't get my finger right up the left nostril.'

'Of course, you could tell me to mind my own business,' he said. He looked into my face. His nose was short and turned up a fraction at the tip. His crack-bowled hair, as dank as the Lagan, was plastered onto a broad skull, and little streams of water ran down his face. I had no idea why we were standing getting soaked on the deck of a crap non-floating restaurant with only the annually reconstructed skyline of Belfast to impress us. No idea but the fact that I quite liked him and the knowledge that eventually he would get round to offering me some loose change.

'Mind your own business.'

'But did you never think of a second honeymoon?'

'No.'

'Rekindle the old love.'

'Wishful thinking, Sam.'

'Even if it was free? A good hotel, best city in the world, and a world heavyweight championship taking place down the road.'

'Sam?'

Cameron shrugged. It was a good shrug. Not up to my standards, but a good effort all the same.

'I signed a deal with McClean for a book of the fight.

Unlimited access to Fat Boy, McClean, the whole camp, the whole campaign. What do you think, Danny, could you do it?'

I turned my back to the rail, splashed my foot down into a puddle. It was the best clean my Docs had had for months. 'You're asking me to write a book about something which is at the least misguided, at worst manslaughter.'

'Yes.'

'You're asking me to spend a lot of time with a no-hoper fat lad from Belfast who's about to get brained for no good reason but cash, and write a cheap exploitative book about it? And for good measure spend a couple of weeks with a woman who has tried to kill me?'

'Yes.'

'Okay,' I said.

2

The day after I was arrested for punching my wife I was asked to write a book about boxing. My life is full of cruel little ironies like that.

Don't get the wrong impression. I didn't just punch her out of nowhere. I punched her out of self-preservation, seeing as how she'd already lamped me five or six times and I was leaking more blood than you'd get with the average shrapnel wound.

No charges were brought. She calmed down a bit and I got sewn up. And so to the reconciliation.

While Patricia was in the bathroom I slipped into her bedroom. I was looking for, but not wanting to find, evidence of some further infidelity. I was surprised by how spartan it was. The room, not the evidence. Patricia's domain was normally such a mess. But the carpet was clean, the bed was made, the walls were bare. The drawers were damp from being wiped. The only objects even vaguely out of place were a couple of paperback books by the bed. And a diary. And a pen. I . . .

I heard the toilet flush and moved quickly back into the living room. There was certainly nothing to indicate another man. Suspicious in itself, on one level. That's just it, boss . . . it's too quiet. The diary almost invited perusal. But I had called unannounced. So there was no suggestion of her deliberately leaving it there to cover her tracks by false testimony, unless she was in a state of constant readiness and then there would never be a man in the place anyway . . .

I told myself to shut up and stop worrying. I willed the knot in my stomach to disentangle. It wasn't that I didn't trust her . . . it was just that I didn't trust her.

Patricia emerged from the bathroom. She looked lovely. 'So?' she asked.

'So what?'

'To what do I owe the pleasure?'

'You're experiencing pleasure right now? That's a good sign.'

I followed her into the lounge. She sat in an armchair. Only room for one. I took a seat on the settee and tried to look inviting. It had never worked before.

'I was just passing,' I said.

'I was just going out,' she countered.

We looked at each other for a long moment. I wasn't just passing, but she was going out. 'Where?' I asked.

'Out.'

'But where to?'

'Just out.'

I nodded. I didn't want to know. I did want to know.

'So?' she asked again.

I shrugged. 'Just thought I'd call round and see what you were up to. See if you'd had any deep and meaningful thoughts about the meaning of life or marriage. You know, anything you might care to share with me.'

'No.'

'Okay.'

It had all seemed so simple in the car.

She laughed. A friendly laugh. Not mocking. She wore a nice black blouse, black stretch pants and some moderately high-heeled shoes. Her make-up was perfect. Her eyes were still a little hollow.

'Dan, you're scrunching your eyebrows up,' she purred. 'I know that look. You fear the worst. No, I'm not going out with anyone you need to know about. I'm going out with a couple of the girls from work. We've just finished a very big project and it's the first chance we've had to let our hair down in ages. Okay?'

I gave her the nonchalant shrug. 'Sure. When are you going?'

'Soon.'

'You want me to give you a lift down the street? The car's outside.'

'No, it's okay. They're calling for me.'

'It's no trouble. I don't mind. No strings attached, if that worries you. You won't have to kiss me when you get out.'

'Dan . . .' It was just a one-syllable name, but she managed to change the emphasis halfway through, from an exasperated whine to an expression of slightly muted sympathy.

'I'm sorry,' I said. 'I'm doing my best to get on with you, but it all comes out wrong.'

'I know. Don't worry. I think I'm the same way.'

The room was as bare as the other. A television, unplugged. The armchair, settee. A small coffee table, unstained. She'd had a massive clear-out. 'Not much like the house I remember,' I observed. Better, I might have added.

She shook her head slowly. 'Not at all. I'm getting rid of bad memories, Dan.' She gave me a sad kind of smile. 'How is it? How are you coping?' she asked to fill the vacuum of my silence.

'Fine. Fine. Y'know.' Jesus, it was like talking with a stranger. Right. Time for it. Talking of home, our home, led necessarily to love and marriage. 'Patricia,' I said, 'I was wanting to ask you something.'

She nodded, half suspicious, and, I fancied, half fearful. A good sign. I had rehearsed several versions in the car on the way over, although thinking at the same time how ridiculous it was to be nervous about asking a simple question of a woman I'd been married to for so many years. But it was difficult, because a turndown without good reason would be tantamount to hammering the final nail in the coffin of our relationship. I needed the second coming of the Starkeys.

I could spend ten minutes telling her how much I loved her, then mention New York. I could drop it into the conversation, see if she offered to come. I could say I was going off on holiday with someone, see if she got jealous, and then tell her she was the someone. Or I could just ask her if she wanted to go on a second honeymoon. Which is what I decided.

'Fire away,' she said.

'Do you want a divorce?'

I sat back, pleased that I had finally gotten it out. It was only after a moment that what I had actually asked sunk in. I sat forward again. But the words wouldn't come.

'You want a divorce,' she said in a monotone. Her face remained impassive, but her eyes betrayed her confusion. They darted from me to the window to the TV, back to me – like pinball, and she looked like she wasn't winning.

I shrugged. She shook her head slowly. 'I suppose I had this coming.' She bit at a nail. She slipped off her stilettos and curled her feet up under her. She shook her head again. 'Has it really come to this, Dan?'

I wanted to scream: No! Of course it hasn't, you stupid bitch! But all I could give her was the doe-eyed look of a man whose brain was sadly out of step with his tongue.

She let a wry smile slip onto her face. 'You know, me living away from you all this time was meant to give me time to make my mind up about our relationship – not you. I'm the one who was supposed to keep you waiting. Then you spring this on me. It's not fair.'

'Sorry,' I said.

'Your sorry isn't overwhelming.'

I gave her the sympathetic palms. 'I thought you were going out.'

'I am.'

'I shouldn't keep you then.'

'You're not.'

'You said they were calling for you . . .'

'They are.'

'Okay.'

We sat in silence. Patricia stared at the carpet. I stared at the wall. I closed my eyes. Concentrated. I emptied my mind as best I could of all memories: of lovers, of battles, of death, of jealousy, of alcohol; chased that bitter history down the corridors of thought; locked it in a dungeon of dulled subconscious.

'You've met someone else.'

A simple statement, not delivered with conviction.

'No,' I said.

'You must have.'

'Why?'

'Just.'

Just and because are two of the great unarguables.

There was a sudden rapping at the door. Patricia bit studiously at a fingernail.

'There's someone at the door,' I observed.

She nodded. 'They'll go away. It's probably the Mormons.'

'It's getting dark. They don't come out at night, like Apaches.'

'Apaches did come out at night. That was the whole point about them.'

'No, they didn't. They stayed round the campfire making bad medicine. That was why they were always so bloody grouchy.'

'I beg to differ.'

'It'll be your lift.'

'What?'

'It'll be your lift at the door.'

'Too early.'

The rapping came again. I got up. Patricia got up. 'It's okay,' she said, 'I'll get it.'

She walked quickly from the lounge, closing the door behind her. I followed. She opened the front door. A tall, slim-looking fella stood on the landing. He smiled at Patricia, then frowned over her shoulder at me. I frowned back. Patricia looked round at me, and joined in the frowning.

'One of the girls?' I asked.

'I'm sorry?' the fella asked. His accent was English. Smart suit, fresh-faced. He looked like he was on a first date.

'Shhh,' said Patricia and motioned him in.

I stood in the lounge doorway and tried to look threatening. My stomach was knotting up again.

'The others in the car?' Patricia asked.

'Others?'

Patricia nodded enthusiastically.

'Oh, yes, downstairs.' Liars, and the pair of them didn't even have the courtesy to redden up.

'Ahm, Dan, this is Tony, from work.'

'Hello, Tony.'

'Hi, Dan.'

I crossed to the door. I put my hand out. As he put his out I hit him with the other.

In fact, I nearly hit him with the other. He leant back and my left missed his nose by an inch. Unbalanced, I stumbled forward. Tony caught me and threw me back. He took two steps forward and hit me with his left and followed it up with a right. The blood was pumping from my nose before I hit the carpet. He'd fractured my fracture.

Patricia caught him by the arm as he loomed over me. 'Don't,' she said.

He hovered above me. I was torn between making a fight of it and sticking up for my woman, and staying on the ground looking pathetic. In practice I have found that looking pathetic usually does the trick, and is also somewhat less painful, but it generally doesn't quell dangerous passions.

He was still there. 'Don't,' Patricia said again, and this time he stepped back.

'Sorry,' he said. To Patricia. His eyes didn't leave me. I got to my feet and stared back.

'Lucky punch, fella,' I said.

'Lucky two punches, fella,' he replied. It was a fair point. Patricia stood between us.

'You've ten seconds to get out, fella,' I said.

'Don't threaten people in my house, Dan,' said Patricia.

'I'll threaten whoever the fuck I want,' I shouted.

18

Tony reached out a finger to poke me in the chest, but Patricia blocked it and pushed his hand back.

'Stop it,' she said, 'both of you.'

I swung for him again. Missed. I nearly hit the back of Patricia's head. He pivoted left, Patricia went with him, but he switched to the right, had a clear shot at me, and popped me on the nose. Another spurt of blood.

'Stop it!' Patricia screamed, and this time she whacked him on the nose. He staggered back clutching his beak, his eyes wide with shock.

'What was that for?' he demanded, blood starting to trickle through his fingers.

'It was for being a big bloody kid. Now stop it, the pair of you, please!'

Patricia wasn't beautiful when she was angry. Her face tightened up, her skin blanched, her eyes glared. She turned to me, placed her hand on my chest and pushed me back.

'Into the lounge,' she ordered. 'Stay there.'

She guided me through the door and closed it after me. I stood staring at it. A real man would be out there, at it hammer and tongs. She was flaunting this man in my bloody face. The door could do with a lick of paint, I thought.

In a minute I heard the front door close. Patricia entered the lounge. She shook her head. Tutted. She took a handful of tissues from a box on top of the TV and handed them to me.

'I think it's stopped bleeding,' I said. 'I've run out of blood.'

'What a pity.'

I shrugged.

'There was no need for that,' she said.

'Well, what do you expect? Jesus, Patricia, you're my wife still.'

'I know. I'm sorry. Look, you probably won't believe me, but Tony is just a . . . date . . . Nothing's going on. Honestly.'

'You expect me to believe that?'

'No.'

'Okay.'

Patricia sat down on the settee. I went and stood by the window. There wasn't much to look at in the gathering gloom beyond a couple of pine trees and an elderly Labrador. My nose was about to fall off. Why did everyone always go for my nose? I wanted a drink. I wanted away.

'I'm going to New York.'

Silence.

'I'd like you to come with me.'

Silence.

'Kind of a second honeymoon.'

'No.' A pause. Dramatic. 'Honeymoon suggests too much.'

'Just a holiday then?'

'After all this . . . blood and jealousy?'

'And deceit.'

'Yeah.'

'Yeah. No strings attached.'

'Okay.'

'Really?'

'Why not? We should make the effort.'

'Okay.'

'Dan?'

'What?'

'I'm sorry.'

I shrugged.

'Dan?'

'What?'

'Can Tony come?'

3

Fat Boy McMaster stood in one corner of the ring, drinking from a can of Coke. He held it between two big red finger-less paws like one of those cute but unsatisfactory baby cans you get on aeroplanes. He wore a scarlet headguard. He'd spat his white plastic gumshield on the floor. In the opposite corner his sparring partner slumped on a stool. I recognized the pallor of defeat and humiliation. He looked like he'd been in a scrap with Patricia. His breaths came in great whoops and he grimaced at each intake; there were big red weals about his torso where McMaster had caught him and punished him with his favoured left fist.

Still, it wasn't exactly impressive. His victim was at most a bloated middleweight. He'd been hired ostensibly to get McMaster to work on his speed, but also because there were no half-decent heavyweights in the country to give him some serious sparring at such short notice. He'd given the Fat Boy the runabout for three rounds, picking him off easily with lengthy jabs, until he'd been caught himself by a left to the ribs which slowed him down long enough to secure a proper hiding. It doesn't matter how good a fighter you are, how nimble you are on your feet, if you're light and you get caught by a heavyweight, you know all about it.

McMaster tossed the can out of the ring. 'Ready for more, Ronnie?' he called across.

Ronnie shook his head.

'Thank fuck for that.' McMaster grinned. 'I'm knackered. Get these bloody things off me, wouldja?'

Jackie Campbell, his trainer, climbed under the ropes and began to unlace the gloves. His moonbeam skin had an elastic look, courtesy of sixty years of chewing gum sixteen hours a day. His greased hair had a greeny-grey sheen. He pulled impatiently at the laces. 'I don't see why you have to drink that piggin' stuff, Bobby. It's fulla piggin' rubbish.'

Fat Boy looked down on Campbell, fully a foot below him, like a freak son on a dwarf father. 'Don't I follow everything else to the letter, Jackie? Don't I get up and run? Do I touch alcohol? Do I stay up late at night? Do I dodge training? No.'

'No.'

'So let me have one little thing, eh?'

'You didn't mention sex, Bobby,' growled Campbell.

'What?'

'Didn't I tell you there hasn't been a heavyweight

23

champion of the world yet who didn't lay off the sex for three months before a fight?'

A big sheepish grin spread across McMaster's face. 'Ach, Jackie, c'mon, I'm only married, what do you expect me to do?'

'I expect you to lay off the sex!' shouted Campbell, yanking off one of the gloves. 'It saps your strength! You'll go weak at the knees!'

'Ach, Jackie, wise up. I don't even use my knees.'

There was a nudge on my elbow. I turned and looked at Geordie McClean. He went to hand me a cup of coffee, but I put my hand up. 'Sorry,' I said, 'I'm with the champ there, strictly a Coke man.'

'Yo!' shouted Fat Boy from the ring.

The sparring partner let out a little groan as he bent under the ropes and shuffled past us. Geordie clapped him on the shoulders. 'Great show, Ronnie, you'll be a contender yet.'

'I'll be a fuckin' bar tender.'

'Ah, you're not beat yet, son. Have a shower there and I'll sort you out.'

'Sort me out with a fuckin' ambulance,' Ronnie said dryly as he moved towards the locker room.

Laughing, Geordie McClean turned back to me. He set one of the plastic cups on the edge of the ring and took a sip from the other. 'So,' he said, 'you'll be the famous Dan Starkey.' He held out his hand, the wrong hand for shaking in polite company.

'And you're the infamous Geordie McClean.' I put out my

wrong hand as well, and we just rubbed knuckles for a moment.

'Infamous? I wouldn't go that far.'

'What about notorious?'

McClean gave me a thin smile. 'Cameron did say you were a bit on the cheeky side. Still, you get used to that round here, as long as you don't mind gettin' a hidin' once in a while, eh?'

I shrugged.

'So you're gonna write me a book about all this, are ye?'

It was one to nail right from the start. 'I'm going to write Cameron a book.'

McClean nodded. 'But you'll be expectin' my cooperation.'

'You've been paid for your cooperation.'

'Aye, there's that, of course, but there's cooperation, and cooperation, if you see what I mean.'

'I see what you mean.'

McClean laughed down his nose. It wasn't a pleasant sound. It wasn't a pleasant nose for that matter, but I was no one to talk noses with. It sat in the middle of a squarish, well-tanned face, and beneath bushy eyebrows which, taken all together, made him look a bit like an owl. Despite the heat in the gym he wore a tan-coloured cashmere coat half buttoned up, a white button-down shirt and a thin grey tie.

'You ever do any boxing yourself?' he asked. 'That nose looks like it's been through a few wars.'

I shook my head. 'Car accident. Nose hit the front window.'

'Sorry to hear it.'

'Yeah, well.'

'So what got you this job? I've read your stuff, Starkey, good'n'all, but I don't recall seein' nothin' about boxin'.'

'I'd say I'm more of a boxing fan than a boxing writer. Cameron's not lookin' for a boxing book as such. The sports pages will do that for you. I'm more of a people man.'

'More of a people man? That's novel. So what do you make of our boy here, people man?'

I glanced at Fat Boy, blowing in the corner, his hair matted, drenched in sweat, the bulge of his stomach.

'He's lost a bit of weight,' was the best I could muster.

'He's lost more than a bit.'

'But still has some more to go.'

'Of course.'

McClean lifted the other cup of coffee and signalled for me to follow him. We threaded our way through the other boxers, about a dozen of them, mostly amateurs, with a few Panamanian imports. McClean kicked open a door and ushered me into a small, cluttered office with a slant of his head. He put both cups down on a desk and pulled a seat back for himself. I lifted a couple of magazines off another and sat down.

'This,' he said, sweeping his arm before him, 'is my home.'

I'd seen his home. It was a millionaire's mansion on the County Down coast, with a covered pool and a tarted-up pigeon loft with white doves, but I let it go.

'All the money, all the deals, mean nothing to me,

compared to this place. Boxing – boxing is something in the soul, people man. I mean, I couldn't punch my way out of a paper bag, but I'm a boxer at heart. I care about these people. I mean, I don't need to be in this business. It costs me a fortune every year. But I can't help it. Boxing's like that . . . can you imagine someone getting this worked up over badminton or bowls or something?'

I shrugged.

'This phone,' he said, tapping an old-fashioned round-dial black telephone, 'is the one I did the deal on. Imagine it – the heavyweight championship of the world!'

Yeah. I cleared my throat. 'You weren't put off by the press conference this morning, were you? They seemed to take your man less than seriously.'

'Naaaah,' he wheezed, scrunching up his face, 'I expected that. I mean, give me some credit. I know none of yousens think Bobby has a dog's chance, but youse are only basing that on his past record.'

'It's what all boxers are judged on . . .'

'Only up to the point where they make a breakthrough.' I nodded as if he was making sense. 'You see, I've known Bobby since he was an amateur . . .'

'A bad amateur . . .'

'A reasonable amateur . . . I've known that he's had potential all along, because I watched him train. Or not train as the case may be. Yeah, sure, he's Fat Boy McMaster. He's not proud of that name, but he knows why it's there. He never trained a day in his life, not properly. When he was an amateur, just a young lad, all he did was turn up and fight. No running, no sparring, no weights. The only kind of practising he did was at the bar, and I'm not talkin' legal shit here. Jesus, he's fought a couple of times with a skinful on him. He eats shit, drinks like a fish, and yet he becomes the heavyweight champ of Ireland.'

'Yeah, well . . .'

'Okay, okay, big deal, I know what you're thinking. But it's a big enough deal for a dedicated non-sportsman, just a big fat git who thinks it's a bit of a laugh to go and have a fight and get paid for it. Do you see what I'm getting at?'

'No.'

'Ach. Look, put it this way. You know the Irish League is full of crap footballers, right?'

'Right.'

'Okay. So you're at the Irish Cup Final and the manager of Linfield suddenly drops his prize centre forward and picks big Sammy the Lump from behind the hamburger stand to lead the attack. Sammy the Lump lumbers onto the pitch, runs circles round the other side, scores a hat-trick, wins the cup. What does that say to you?'

'That Irish League football is crap.'

'Naaaah, you're not gettin' my drift. If Sammy the Lump, never kicked a serious ball in his life, can do that against footballers with at least some pretensions of professionalism, what would he be capable of if he was fully fit, properly trained, agile, everything?'

'I hesitate to think.'

McClean noticed the smirk. 'You're not taking this very seriously,' he said. 'Fair enough. It'll make your wee book that much more interesting in the end. But I tell you, I'm taking this very seriously.'

'Because there's serious money involved . . .'

'Yes, of course there's serious money involved . . . but that's not the point . . .'

'Isn't it?'

'No, it bloody well isn't! The point is I believe Bobby has a realistic chance of taking the world title!'

McClean sat back; he was starting to sweat up, something he'd managed to avoid in the heat of the gym.

'Look,' he began again, 'if you're going to be around us all the way up to the fight, you should understand why I'm doing this, okay?'

'Okay.'

'Of course there's the money . . . but I've got money. I don't need any more. There's the glory. Sure, I could do with some of that. But I'll tell you this, if there's glory to be had, it'll all be his . . . Bobby's not even under contract to me. That's how interested I am in the money. I get a percentage, sure, but it's as fair as any you'll find in the fight game. Ask around, be my guest.'

'I know there's no contract, Mr McClean.' I'd done some research, which was a rarity. It consisted of a phone call, but it was a start.

'Okay. Forget the money, let's get back to Bobby. So he's Irish champ. He's just married, but on the dole. I give him

29

a job. I say to him, Bobby, come into my stable, let me train you properly, I promise to turn him into something . . .'

'A corpse, quite possibly . . .'

'Ach, there's no need for that, Starkey. It won't come to that. I know. Believe me. I've paid him a considerable sum of money just to get into shape. Now he's getting a million for just one fight. He's fast, he's powerful . . .'

'And he's fought no one . . .'

'The important thing is, Starkey, he knows he's different, he knows what he's capable of. He had no ambition before. He strolled the Irish title. It gave him a bit of a kick. Then we had six months to work on him before the European fight. We deliberately kept him out of the spotlight during that time. We deliberately kept him away from other heavy-weights, kept him in with middles to build up his speed. We know what we're doing. You think I would waste my money getting him the European title fight if I thought I was sticking a big barrel of lard in there? No chance. You any idea how many heads I had to stand on to get that fight? I'm talking real money. But he was ready for it. Was it my fault they clashed heads in the second round? He never had the chance to show what he could do, Starkey. But he's the European champ, he deserves it, and he deserves his shot at the world title.'

You hear so much crap before a fight, before any fight of any importance. He's a real contender. He's in perfect shape. He has a puncher's chance. I don't care about the money, I care about him. He's like a second son to me. Yeah.

I left McClean in his office after shaking hands. He wished me luck with the book and promised to be cooperative. I wished him luck with the fight and promised not to get in the way. I didn't believe him and he didn't believe me, but we respected each other's lies.

Outside I met Cameron. He was chomping on a Paris bun and leaning across the bonnet of his BMW. 'Well?'

I shrugged.

'How's McClean?'

'He thinks that fat shite can take the title.'

4

Cameron took me for a drink. There was a pub about a hundred yards up from the gym. Sixty yards away he would have been in trouble over his accent. Belfast's funny that way. Dead funny. I had a pint of Harp and he got a bottle of Corona with a slice of lemon wedged in the top. I tried not to look too embarrassed.

We spent a while discussing money for the book. I told him what I wanted and he told me what he was prepared to give me. We settled somewhere in the middle. After six Coronas I got him to admit that McMaster didn't have a chance and I was halfway to talking him out of doing the book at all before I realized I was cutting my own throat. I re-sold it to him as a study in failure. The English would be sure to go for it. I think he fell for it. He didn't ask for his cash advance back. At least I think it was an advance. He could have been leaving a tip for the barman. At about four Cameron stood and lifted his keys from the table.

'I'm due back in Dublin,' he slurred.

'You're not driving, are you?'

'Only till I'm stopped.'

'You'll kill yourself.'

'Possibly.'

We shook hands like adults and he left. I got another pint and sat back. I wanted to think about the book. No – I wanted to drink. Thinking about the book was a good cover. I had no shifts on the paper, there was no Patricia to go home and annoy, and it was too early in the week to entice any of my friends out for a binge. Sad, really.

For a moment I didn't recognize Bobby McMaster with his clothes on. The bar door swung inwards, McMaster stuck his head in, peered round the mostly empty lounge, and then nodded behind him to a smaller, dumpier guy. They came in and sat at the end of the bar. McMaster caught my eye, but there was no hint of recognition. I could put bad eyesight with all the other advantages he would carry into the ring with Tyson.

There was no doubting he was a big fella. He wore a zipped-up leather jacket, stretched tight across his chest, and black jeans. His companion had cropped hair, verging on a skinhead, looked a bit of a fighter too but without much of a notion of the Queensberry rules. He had a flat nose, was pink round the eyes, big hands. It wasn't till he went to the toilet after his second pint, then stopped at my table on the way back, that I recognized him. McMaster remained at the bar, sipping at an orange juice and studying the racing form in a paper.

'Hello, Stanley,' I said.

'Thought I recognized your ugly bake, Starkey.'

'I must admit I had to give you a second glance, Stanley. I thought you were in the Crum.'

'Finger on the pulse as ever, Starkey.'

'At least I have one.'

'Very funny. Use that in your column, son, it could do with brightening up.'

I raised my glass to him. 'I write better than you sail, Stanley.'

He shook his head slowly. 'Wanker,' he said quietly and went back to McMaster. They exchanged a few words and then Stanley turned for the door. As he passed my table he winked.

I finished what was left of my pint and approached McMaster. 'Mind if I join you?'

He looked at me, head down, eyes up, as if he was peering over a pair of bifocals. He shook his head slightly. It was an ambiguous shake, I thought, so I sat down and ordered a drink.

'You're off the drink, I presume,' I said. I thought it would be a nice, light opening.

'Of course I'm off the drink,' he said dryly.

I nodded. 'An orange?'

'An orange what?'

'You want another orange juice?'

He shook his head and returned his attention to the paper.

'You won't need to do that much longer,' I said.

'Do what?' He didn't bother looking up.

'The gee-gees. What you'll be earning, you'll be able to buy your own bloody horse.'

'I don't want my own horse.'

I nodded and took a sip of my beer. 'You looked pretty sharp in the ring today.'

His head moved slowly towards me. Blue eyes, very blue, sea blue and sea cold, bore into me. Menacing. He maybe wouldn't become world champion, but he could punch my lights out in his sleep.

'Explain to me,' he said quietly, 'the difference between cynicism and sarcasm, Starkey.'

'I wasn't . . .'

'Explain to me . . .'

'I'd rather explain to you why I don't think you should take this fight.'

He pulled himself up to his full height in the chair, his back ramrod straight. Now, here, there, inches from my face, I couldn't see any fat on his body at all.

'You know, I could pull your head off right here and eat the insides out with a spoon if I wanted to. What do you think of that?'

'That's neither sarcasm nor cynicism, that's a threat.'

'I could give you a cynical hook to the ribs, Starkey, a sarcastic crack to the nose.'

'Someone's beaten you to the nose.'

'So I see. You must make friends everywhere you go.'

I thought about taking a drink, but I wasn't sure if my hand would be shaking. Besides, he'd probably think I was going to whack him with the glass and kill me as a precaution. I tried the appeasement line. It worked wonderfully for Chamberlain.

'Have I done something to annoy you, Bobby? I mean, I'm supposed to be writing a book about you.'

'Stan says you're a wanker. Are you a wanker, Starkey?'

'Metaphorically or literally?' It was a desperate attempt to blind him with a lot of syllables.

'Both,' he said.

I gave the question due consideration. Out of the corner of my eye I could see the barman hovering nervously by the phone. The door was about ten yards away. After seven pints it might as well have been a mile, with hurdles.

'Well, yes, I suppose I am then.'

Abruptly he laughed. A big hearty laugh. It warmed my heart. 'You are a sketch, Starkey. You know, the wife's a big fan of your column.'

Gulp. Metaphorically and physically. I eased up on the stool. 'Really?'

'Yeah. Loves it.'

'What about you?'

'Oh, I like it too, but I wouldn't tell you that. You want another drink?'

'If you insist.'

The barman, all smiles, brought me another pint. 'It was only my say that got you doing the book, y'know? McClean wasn't the least interested really, but I thought it would be good to have something solid to remember it all by, y'know? And something funny as well.'

'You want something funny?'

'How else would you approach it? I've never seen you write a serious thing yet. Besides, there's something intrinsically funny about a fat bastard like me going for the world title, isn't there?'

Later he told me how he'd come to know Stanley Matchitt, or Matchitt the Hatchet as he'd been known for many years, or Snatchit Matchitt as he was now known on a hundred graffitied walls around the city.

'We both grew up in Crossmaheart, y'know?'

'Jesus, that must have been fun.'

'What is it they say about Tyson? You can take the man out of the ghetto, but you can't take the ghetto out of the man.'

'You think that applies to you?'

'A bit of it, maybe. Crossmaheart's not Butlin's, put it that way.'

'There've been more liberal concentration camps.'

'When I was growing up I thought concentration camps were, like, places intellectuals went to think about things.'

'I don't see much of the ghetto in you, maybe in your friend, Snatchit, but not you. How come you hang about with him?'

'I don't. Not much anyway. I can't say I agree with everything he does, but we've been through a lot together. A lot
of fights when we were growing up. But we both got out.
I met a girl, graduated to Belfast. Stanley never met a girl.
He learnt how to use a gun.'

'And a hatchet.'

'And a hatchet.'

Stanley had been a high-up in the Red Hand Commandos,
a Loyalist terror group with a penchant for hacking up innocent Catholics. Of course they didn't think there were any
innocent Catholics. A messy business. Everyone knew he
was involved, but nobody could pin it on him. The IRA, the
INLA, even the UDA, had made a couple of attempts on
him, but he always managed to keep one step ahead of them.

Then he took a job as a bouncer in a pub down the coast
and kept out of view for a year or two. One memorable
night he got plastered, recruited a crew of equally inebriated
locals and stole the *Golden Hind*.

The *Hind*, a full-scale replica of Drake's ship, had been on
a round-the-world trip and stopped off overnight in the
harbour as the top attraction at an annual festival. At least
one member of Stanley's crew had once been on a yacht
and managed to pilot it out into Belfast Lough, but that was
about the extent of the seafaring. By the time the coastguard
and police caught up with them, dawn was coming and so
was a mighty swell. A police photographer captured Stanley
being sick over the side seconds before he was arrested, and
released it to the papers. From that day on the fearsome

monster that was Matchitt the Hatchet was dead and Snatchit Matchitt was born. He wasn't too pleased. He wasn't too pleased about going to prison either.

'You visit him in the Crum, Bobby?'

McMaster shook his head. 'Nah,' he added.

'Any reason?'

'The wife.'

I nodded. I'd been there.

'I mean,' he continued, leaning closer, voice low, 'she's . . . well, she's not Protestant.'

'You tell Stanley?'

He shook his head. 'But he's probably guessed. With a name like Mary Mairaid Muldoon she's hardly likely to be donning an accordion for the Twelfth.'

He laughed, took a sip of his orange. 'Y'know, I grew up hating Catholics, fighting them, beating them, being beaten up by them. I never really knew why. When I was about six my dad tried to explain to me the difference between us and them. I remember I kept asking, why, why, why? In the end he just said, son, it's as simple as this: we're the goodies and they're the baddies. That's the sort of B-movie Western philosophy a six-year-old can really get a grasp of.'

He stood up and drained his glass. 'I must go.'

'Walking?'

He nodded.

'Mind if I walk with you?'

He shrugged. 'I'm only round the corner. Stagger along if you can.'

Outside it was cool and après-bar bright. We walked in silence for a while, McMaster occasionally nodding at people who nodded at him. We began to crisscross alleys as he took me on a shortcut to his home. In one I stopped to relieve myself up against a bin.

'Do you ever worry about getting killed?' I asked.

'I worry more about getting caught up an alley with a man with his balls out,' he said, and when I looked round his head was darting nervously this way and that.

I finished off and he marched quickly ahead. 'I mean in the ring.'

'Not so far.'

'But against Tyson.'

'Not especially.'

'But why not?'

He stopped. Pushed a finger into my chest. 'Because,' he said, and walked on.

Britannia Avenue. A small terraced house. He showed me into a compact front room. A small set of pristine dumbbells in the corner were the only concession to sport. There was a framed poster of pre-army Elvis on the wall. A video and TV. Three untidy piles of CDs, two of them topped by Elvis, one by Shakin' Stevens. Two out of three ain't bad. A battered acoustic guitar. A small library of books in a wooden case – paperbacks of Hemingway, Steinbeck, Bukowski and Dickens.

'Read these?' I asked, running my fingers down the spines.

He nodded.

I smiled by accident.

'What?'

'Nothing.'

'What?'

I shook my head. He shook his.

'Starkey, your problem is you go round with too many preconceptions in your head. You're presuming that because I beat people up I can't read. You're a mind bigot, Starkey, bad as any other kind.'

'Sorry,' I said.

'Okay.'

For a couple of hours we sat and watched videos of Tyson in action. McMaster pointed out weaknesses in his defence I couldn't see. 'All there is of me on video is two rounds for the European belt. I'd like to see Tyson suss me out from that,' he said.

He made coffee, some sandwiches, strummed a bit on the guitar. I nodded politely, though it sounded like he was still wearing his boxing gloves.

When it was time to go I said: 'It's time to go.'

'You're not staying to see the wife?'

'Things to do.'

'She'll be sorry to have missed you. Still, plenty of time for that in the States.'

'She's coming as well?'

'Of course.'

'I thought wives were always banned . . .'

'Where I go, she goes.'

I shrugged. 'Yeah, just right.'

At the door I turned to him and said, 'Bobby, I'm sorry about the books. I expected you to be as thick as champ. I must admit I'm pleasantly surprised.'

I put my hand out and we shook.

'Maybe you'll be pleasantly surprised by my boxing.'

'I doubt it.'

He laughed.

5

Seven a.m. Mary McMaster set the plate in front of me and smiled. 'Enjoy,' she said.

It was a good kitchen, clean, lived in, old but well maintained. A nice house, bearing in mind the neighbourhood. The house said, we care about this place, even if we haven't the money to do much with it.

'He's not an early riser then?'

'Not for training, no.' I just caught a wicked glint in her eye before she darted from the kitchen and hollered for Bobby from the bottom of the stairs. A muffled groan came in reply. She re-entered, shaking her head. 'He's getting worse.'

She was nice. Petite. Blond hair, dyed, pulled back, the roots just showing, no make-up, sharp face, baby crow's feet, teeth slightly spaced, ready smile, educated accent. Even on a damp winter morning she was bird-chirpy, polite, inquisitive, chatty, but not flirty.

I'm not really a breakfast man, but it seemed impolite to refuse. I picked up the knife and fork. 'Should I start without him?'

'God, yes. You wouldn't get him eating a chicken omelette anyway. First and last time I made it for him he took one look at it and said it was the only time he'd ever been asked to eat a mother and child in one meal. Culinary incest, he called it. I'll join you though. Gets you going for the day.' She brought hers over from the cooker and sat opposite me. 'He'll eat when he gets back from his run. Doesn't take much though. A bowl of Rice Krispies usually.'

'It's hardly straight from the training manual.'

'It's not, but it's what he likes, and he says that's what's important. Jesus, it's not long since I got him to cut out the Opal Fruits for breakfast. He took a lot of convincing that they weren't really concentrated fruit juice.'

'Seriously?'

'What do you think?'

'I think not.'

'No, well, maybe not.'

'But he is a little weird, like, for a fighter.'

'I wouldn't know.'

'What do you know?'

'That I love him.'

'That's sweet.'

'That's true.'

'And you're not worried about this fight?'

'Of course I'm worried.'

'But you won't talk him out of it?'

'Why should I?'

'Because of what might happen to him.'

'His decision.'

'But if you love . . .'

'I do love . . .'

'Yes, of course, but . . .'

'But nothing. He happens to think he can do it, and that's what's important. Not what journalists think. Not what McClean thinks. Not what Tyson thinks.'

'Fair enough.'

'Is this an interview?'

'No. Yes. Not really. Background stuff.'

'Are you recording it?'

'No. Of course not.'

I was, in fact, but the tape recorder was small enough not to bulge anywhere. It wasn't subterfuge, as such, I just have a memory like a sieve and notebooks make me lose concentration. Visible tape recorders make other people lose concentration.

'You don't mind me asking you some questions?'

'Not at all. I suppose in the end we're profiting from the book. And, like, well, I'm proud of him. Whatever happens.'

I'd brought the morning papers with me. They lay folded beside my plate. I'd glanced at them on the way from the shop. The headlines said it all. Predictable really.

I nodded at them. 'I didn't know whether to bring them or not,' I said.

Mary shrugged. 'Might as well.'

'How does he cope with negative press?'

'I don't know. He hasn't really had any.'

'He'll have to get used to it.'

'I suppose so.'

She set her knife and fork down. 'You want some tea?'

'No. Thanks. I don't.'

'Mormon?'

'Coke addict.'

'Bit early for that.'

'Never too early.'

'That tracksuit looks like it's seen better days.'

'It has. I used to play a bit of football.'

'How're you going to keep up with him with all that chicken in you anyway?'

'I didn't think he'd be going that fast.'

'You'd be surprised.'

'And I brought a bike.'

'Smart move. What do you do, shout questions to him as he runs?'

'Something like that. You always get up this early for him?'

'I get up this early for me. I've a job to go to. It keeps us in Rice Krispies. What McClean pays him wouldn't.'

'No advance on your million?'

'We get paid after the fight.'

'Smart. On McClean's part.'

'Why'd you say that?'

'No reason.'

'You don't think he'll be around to collect it?'

I shrugged.

'I will,' she said.

Something was moving around upstairs. Chances were it wasn't a baby elephant. A voice from the top of the stairs, thick with sleep: 'Mary, d'y'see ma gutties anywhere?'

'Where you left them.'

'Thanks.'

Clump. Clump. Clump.

Mary shook her head. 'He gets worse.'

'I can relate to that. Where'd you meet him?'

She rested her chin on her hand and she got a faraway look in her eyes for a moment. Bobby McMaster didn't seem the type to get all romantic over, but I wasn't much of an expert in that department. 'Virginity Hill, April 1988. 17 April. Three-forty p.m. Sky blue. Slight wind.'

'You've only a vague recollection then.'

She smiled. 'I remember it all. Right down to the . . . well, I remember it all.'

'Where's Virginity Hill? It's not in Belfast, is it?'

'Aye. St Louisa's Collegiate. The girls' school on the Falls Road. Known locally as Virginity Hill.'

'A sarcastic nickname then?'

'Of course . . . then . . . loose women used to be

fashionable. You think it's strange remembering a first meeting like that, don't you?'

'No. Not at all. Maybe a little.'

'You remember where you met your wife, don't you?'

'No.'

'Not at all?'

'Well, vaguely. I was plastered. I woke up one morning and there she was. She just didn't go away again. It must have been a killer chat-up line. So you were at Virginity Hill?'

'Sad that really, you should remember things like that. I dare say she remembers okay?' I shook my head. She shook hers. 'Well, anyway, yeah, Virginity Hill. Believe it or not, I was considered quite bright in those days, top of the class and all that, head girl. It didn't go down too well. I mean, this was in the middle of all the rioting back then and a lot of the girls were staying away from school to join in. I was never politically minded – I mean, neither were they, they just loved a good riot. I'm no lady, like, but they were a rough lot and when they saw me still going to school and still doing well, despite all the trouble, well, they kind of had it in for me.'

I nodded sympathetically. Cod sympathy, of course; I was trying to imagine what she would have looked like in a school uniform.

'Anyway,' she continued, tracing a circle with her index finger on the table top, 'one day after school they pounced on me, about ten of them. The idea was to tar and feather me, but the gypsies hadn't been for a while and tar was in short supply, so they started cutting my hair off and covering me in flour and eggs and all that shit, and giving me a hiding besides. Then Bobby came round the corner. He wasn't exactly a knight in shining armour. I mean, if he hadn't rescued me and I'd just seen him in the street I would have described him as a big fat spotty git, but he ploughed into them. He took a bit of a beating as well; they were vicious, really vicious, but eventually he chased them off. Now, I was in a bit of a state by that stage, but he took me under his wing, took me home, got me sorted out. And he just turned out to be such a nice fella as well. A wee sweetie, really. Funny how things work out, eh?'

'Yeah, I know. What brought him there anyway? The Falls is hardly the place a young Protestant wants to go wandering, even if he can take care of himself.'

'He wasn't living that far away, just inside Proddie land really, but he was a member of the Holy Redeemer Boxing Club. I'm told it is, or was, the best in the city. He used to spend a lot of his time there, and he'd pass the school on the way home.'

'So he took you back to your house. What did your mum say?'

'Well, no, he took me back to his house. I couldn't go back to my house the way I was, my mum would have been straight down to the school creating blue murder, and that would hardly have done my popularity much good. My hair was all ragged, I was bleeding, I was covered in all that, well, shite . . . he took me home to his mum and she sorted me out.'

'What was she like?'

'Great. Great-ish. She's a bit like him, big shy thing. I mean, she didn't know who I was, didn't recognize the uniform, didn't realize I was a Catholic. I don't think she'd even spoken to one up till then. To break the ice, to cheer me up, she told me a joke – how do you know ET's a Catholic, 'cause he looks like one. Yeah, I know, ha-ha, but I didn't know where to look. She wasn't even right, 'cause he looks like a Prod.' She smiled sheepishly. 'Sorry,' she said, 'you're not sensitive about things like that, are you?'

I shook my head.

'Anyway, that's how we got started. I mean, he was shy, but he was interested without ever having the courage to ask me out. I think I ended up asking him out – he kept calling round to see me, to see if I was okay.'

'What'd your mum say about it all?'

'What, about him or the fight?'

'Both.'

'Well, like, I told her I fell off my bike. That explained the cuts. The hair, well, once I'd played about with it a bit, I managed to persuade her it was the latest fashion. I'm not sure if she quite fell for that one, but what could she do? Yeah, she liked Bobby immediately. Who wouldn't?'

'She didn't mind him being a Protestant?'

'She never said. Never has said. So I suppose she didn't. She was a bit more concerned about the fact that he was a boxer. Not the sort of security a mother looks for in a son-in-law.'

'How'd you get round that one then?'

'Didn't really, what could she do? It was either a big friendly boxer or a hit man for the IRA.'

'Seriously?'

'Nah, not really, but most everyone I knew back then had connections in that direction, and who wants to end up hitched to a murderer?'

'As opposed to someone who tries to kill his opponent in the ring?'

'He's never tried to do that.'

'Do you not think you need the killer instinct? Particularly against someone like Tyson.'

'No.'

'Seriously?'

'He's a sportsman. He'll go out there and do his best and enjoy it. That's all there is to it. If he wins, he wins; if he doesn't, he doesn't.'

'You really think it's as simple as that? For him?'

'Yeah.'

'But it's not as simple as that for Geordie McClean.'

'No, of course not.'

'What do you make of him?'

'I don't make anything.'

'Do you trust him?'

'Ish.'

'That's hardly a vote of confidence.'

'Well, put it this way. He hasn't ripped us off. He's given Bobby a crap job, he's paid some bills, and he's promised to give us a million. Nobody else has done anything for us. The chance of getting a million pounds isn't something that comes along every day, why not go for it?'

'That's easy for you to say.' I didn't mean it to come out quite so sharp. Her eyes fixed on mine. She looked hurt, but steely too.

'That's uncalled for. This is entirely Bobby's decision. It's what he wants to do. I've nothing to do with it.'

'He must have talked it over with you.'

'Of course.'

'And?'

'He said he wanted to go for it, but wouldn't if I didn't want him to. So I told him to go for it. You think I was wrong?'

I shrugged. 'Who's to say? I'll tell you after the fight.'

'You can't really lose then.'

'No.'

'You said earlier about your footballing days – I mean, if you just played locally, thought you were quite good, but were then suddenly offered the chance to play in the World Cup final, wouldn't you take it? Just to be able to say, I did that?'

'No. I wouldn't.'

'Scared?'

I nodded. 'Scared of the whole world laughing at me.'

Mary shook her head. 'That won't happen.'

'I hope not.'

The kitchen door opened. Bobby McMaster filled the void. His hair was tousled, his cheeks pink. He clutched his guitar in his hand. 'Mornin',' he said.

I nodded.

'Do you want to hear a song before we go?'

Mary stood and lifted our plates. 'Please, Bobby, no.' She looked at me and shook her head. 'He only knows three chords, and two of them are his trousers.'

Bobby smiled warmly at her, then set the guitar down. He puffed out his cheeks and aimed his thumb at the back door. 'Let's go then,' he said.

6

A fine rain was falling when we finally left the house, but it was a good rain, not cold, no wind to back it up. Mary kissed her husband at the door and smiled at me.

We made for Belvoir Forest Park. It was about a mile up the road, a pleasant enough little enclave in which McMaster could stretch his muscles without being poisoned by exhaust fumes. He said he normally made three or four circuits of it, which didn't seem much. He liked the trees and the quiet and spotting the occasional squirrel. The nearest I'd been to nature in the last decade was the can of Pine Fresh I kept in the bog.

We hit the rush hour square on. No horns were pumped at him. No one shouted encouragement. No kids ran after him for autographs. It wasn't because he was well happed up or because of the drizzly rain and depressing grey skies. It was because no one had any idea who he was.

The press conference the day before had been muted. Most of the journalists were in shock. McClean had already explained to me his . . . ahem . . . master plan. He knew the press would crucify him, and of course McMaster, if he really tried to hype the fight on this side of the Atlantic. He would leave the real hype to the Americans. They are, after all, the masters of hype. Reaction to the fight in Britain or Ireland didn't matter to him or to Tyson's people; boxing revolves around America. The only place the hype mattered was America. That's where the tickets were sold for the arena, where the tickets were sold for pay-per-view television, where the advertising deals went down. The task on this side of the Atlantic was damage limitation, on the other side, damage exploitation. So a handful of reporters were invited to the press conference, a press release, short, the briefest of announcements, was handed out, and photos were taken. McClean said a few words, McMaster a few less, in and out. No time to answer the important questions like how, or why, or what if.

Still, I'd expected at least one camera crew in tow for this first training run after the announcement, but McClean was keeping a tight rein on all the publicity and wouldn't let anyone near. I suppose I should have felt honoured, but all I felt was damp.

McMaster kept to the side of the road, the hood on his grey tracksuit pulled tight around his face. I didn't have his faith in the traffic, so I kept to the edge of the kerb, jinking between the telegraph poles and schoolkids. He set a fair pace, head bowed, shoulders hunched, hood pointing up, looking for all the world like a druid on manoeuvres.

The good thing about telegraph poles is that they tend to stay in the one place. You can't say the same about school-kids. The way you expect them to go, they invariably go the other; try taking that into consideration, and they'll go the way you expected them to go in the first place, so you lose both ways. After driving a car for so long, I'd forgotten how effeminate a bike's bell sounded. I was embarrassed ringing it. By the time I'd failed to dodge the kids, stopping, starting, shouting, apologizing, McMaster was a hundred yards up on me and disappearing through the park gates.

I freewheeled through the entrance and peered down the path. No sign of him. I braked, caught my breath. There were a few people about, miserable-looking in the rain; their dogs were the enthusiasts.

'Hey, slow coach!'

Bobby was sitting on a green wooden bench off to my right. I pushed the bike over to him using my toes. His face was red, his tracksuit dark with the rain.

'Stacks of fun, eh?' he said.

'Taking a breather already, champ?'

'That was a bit of a climb. Won't be no hills in the ring with Tyson.'

'That's hardly the point.'

He smiled and stood up. 'Just letting you catch up, sunshine, didn't want to lose you on these wee paths. You ready?'

'Always.' He set off. A slower pace. I eased along beside him. 'Do you mind talking while you run?'

He didn't reply, which I took for a yes. You have to really.

'Does your trainer never come with you on these runs? Isn't that what he's meant to do? Y'know, inspire you?'

'Jackie? Nah, he's not up to it.' He turned abruptly to the left, took a downward path, rougher terrain. I braked and turned after him, thumping through potholes as I tried to regain ground. As I caught him he shouted back, 'Jackie can't train with me any more. He has one of those consonant bags. I think he has a vowel problem.'

He turned his head back to me, puffed out and smiled. 'Joking. He's not too well though. He's too old for all this anyway. He trusts me to do the work.'

'I was thinking last night,' I shouted back, 'that this is not unlike the plot of *Rocky*, y'know: no-hoper white guy given the chance of his life against an invincible champion. Done more for the publicity and the hype than any sense of competition or sporting achievement. What do you think?'

'Shite.'

'But you see the similarities?'

'No.'

'I mean, *Rocky* was . . .'

He stopped. I skidded. He put his hand on the handlebars and lifted. He took the wheel about three feet in the air while I hung on, suspended like a rodeo rider on a frozen horse. 'I don't need you to be so fucking negative round me all the time,' he said, his face snarled. 'It doesn't do me any good. I need to think positive.'

'I . . .'

'So either learn to be positive, or learn to speak with your jaw wired shut. Understand?'

I nodded. 'I'm sorry,' I said, 'I'm not trying to be negative.' He nodded and eased the wheel down.

'Okay,' he said. 'Listen. Observe. Ask if you have to. But keep your negativity to yourself. Save it for the book, okay?'

'Okay, champ.'

'And don't call me "champ". I'm the contender.'

'Well, I can hardly call you "cont". It's a bit close for comfort.'

'We're getting back to wired jaws here, Starkey.'

'Sorry.'

He turned back to the track and set off again. I pushed off after him and tried to muster a more positive attitude.

'Can you get insurance for a fight like this?' I shouted after him. They were the questions any honest-to-God reporter had to ask, and I was the only one with access.

'For fuck's sake, Starkey, will you fuck up?' He broke suddenly from the track, cut into a bunch of pines. By the time I'd recovered from another skid in the loose gravel he'd disappeared.

I stopped and spat. I was soaked, I was exhausted, I had

a truculent, missing subject and I could feel the chicken fighting the egg in my stomach. I felt miserable.

Ten minutes later I caught a flash of him through the trees. I suppose 'flash' is not a word that is often used in connection with McMaster, but catching a lumber of someone doesn't hang right. He was a good bit off, maybe two hundred yards through the trees, and at a lower level. I turned the bike off the track and began negotiating my way towards him, angling my descent based on a calculation of how far you can reasonably expect a fat man to run on a muddy track against how much ground a stick insect with the sense of balance of a befuddled baby giraffe can expect to cover, and my calculation came out spot on, if I'd been hoping to come out a hundred yards behind him.

By the time I'd pulled the bike back up onto the track and looked up after him, McMaster had stopped, his hooded figure motionless on a curve of the track. I thought maybe he'd heard me careering through the trees and had had a change of heart about my company, but as I moved forward I saw through the drizzle four dark figures emerge from the trees, two on either side of him. They were too far off for me to pick out any detail on them, save that two appeared to be carrying baseball bats. It seemed an unlikely place for autograph hunters. Or for baseball.

The journalist is supposed to be a non-participant in conflict, to observe objectively and report. Yet despite McMaster's apparent antipathy towards me, it seemed a bit churlish to leave him to tackle four hoods by himself. I pushed forward on the bike. I don't know what was propelling it, adrenaline probably, because my jelly legs weren't. Perhaps the unheralded arrival of a stranger would help heal what appeared to be a festering situation. Or perhaps they would kill me. My posthumous biography, *Requiem for a Pixieweight*, would contain all the answers.

Fifty yards short, my way was blocked. A young fella, maybe twenty-five, stepped out from the trees and held his hand up. He wore a green bomber jacket, black jeans, mud-spattered red DM boots and a scowl. He was thickset, and either a skinhead or prematurely bald under his cap.

I braked. When he dropped his hand I caught a glimpse of the letters UVF tattooed across his fingers. He couldn't do much undercover work for them.

'Sorry,' he said, 'the path's closed.'

I looked over his shoulder. McMaster was engaged in animated conversation. His shoulders were moving left and right, but he kept his arms well tucked in. The two with the baseball bats held them lazily over their shoulders. They would find it difficult to swing them quickly if McMaster made a sudden move. Sudden move and McMaster are words rarely found in the same sentence.

'What's the problem?' I asked, dismounting.

'Subsidence,' he said, his lip curling up in seeming distaste at the length of the word.

'I'll be careful,' I said, and started to push past him.

He put his hand on the handlebars. 'Dangerous subsidence,' he said firmly.

'How dangerous?'

He slipped his other hand inside his jacket and produced a revolver and stuck the muzzle into my chest. 'This dangerous.'

I nodded sagely. 'The National Trust's sure getting protective of its pathways,' I said, 'and I'm glad to assist them.'

I turned the bike. My first instinct was to ride away, so was my second and third, but as I set to pedalling there was a shout from down the track and we both turned to see McMaster clatter into one of the baseballers. He went flying into the undergrowth. Two of the hoods jumped at McMaster and he hugged them tight, swinging them round, their arms and legs flailing helplessly, while the second batsman swung at McMaster's legs, but he moved sweetly, avoiding contact and forcing the batsman back using his own comrades like animated clubs.

My gunman turned quickly back to me. 'You fuck off!' he shouted and made to join the fray, but in the second he turned I was a step behind him and my foot had snaked under his and pulled back and he was on his face in the mud. It was an assault honed in primary school but still admirably efficient. He hit the track with a splat and the gun fired as it hit the ground. I dropped the bike on him and jumped on it. He let out a squeal. I flattened his hand in the mud with the heel of my shoe and picked up the gun.

The shot had momentarily stopped the commotion down the track, but as I ran towards them they resumed.

McMaster dumped the first, then the second of his passengers onto the path. Winded, they lay there for a moment while he advanced on his third assailant. The batsman swung forward, McMaster leant back almost imperceptibly. If it had been me, the curve of the bat through the air would have ended with a severed nose, but it just whisked past McMaster's face, either a fine judgement or very good luck. As the batsman followed round with the force of his swing the heavyweight contender stepped forward and punched him full in the face. He dropped. The other two, now back on their feet, looked at each other, nodded, and moved forward again, one left, one right. They were big enough, well built, looked like they worked out.

I stopped ten yards away. I shot a tree. All three turned to look at me. Two groans came from the undergrowth.

'Do you want me to shoot them, champ?' I asked, waving the gun at them.

He shook his head, then smiled at the two hoods.

'Okay, boys,' he said, 'ding ding.'

I looked back up the track. The former gunman was making off on my bike. It was a shooting offence in most parts of Belfast, but I was happy to let him go.

Meanwhile McMaster stepped forward. He ducked down low then brought up his right. It glanced off the skull of the hood to his left, staggered him, but the hood on the right slipped in and threw a punch into McMaster's kidneys;

McMaster dropped his shoulder and swung round with his left, connecting with the hood's nose, breaking it with a crack audible in Dublin. McMaster straightened and smiled as the hood dropped to the ground. The other hood, showing impressive powers of recovery, was suddenly before him again, and threw a lovely arcing left which landed in the centre of McMaster's gob. The contender staggered back and spat out one of his front teeth, but the hood was in no condition to take advantage; he let out a scream, his hand split across the knuckles, blood spraying everywhere. He looked at the gash for a shocked few seconds. Then he ran away.

McMaster started after him, went twenty yards into the undergrowth, then stopped and stared after his rapidly disappearing foe. I stood and marvelled at him for a moment, standing there amongst the mizzled trees with his fists clenched by his sides, erect, supreme, primeval, vanquished bodies littering the murky undergrowth about him. Then he opened his mouth and guldered: 'Away ya go, ya fuckin' wee fuckin' fucker!'

Three hundred years of Protestant culture distilled in one man.

7

We wandered on down the track, leaving the fallen to drag themselves back into the murk from which they had come.

As he slopped along the puddled track McMaster shook his head in bewilderment. 'In all the years I've been fighting,' he said, wistfully poking at the gap in his top row, 'that's the first time I've lost a tooth.'

He'd a thick lip as well, some scratches about the face, and he was splattered in mud thanks to the contortionistic attempts of his assailants to free themselves from his grasp.

When we'd rounded the curve in the track I looked back quickly, saw that we weren't being followed, then wiped the gun with the unfulfilled width of my tracksuit top and threw it into the undergrowth. Doubtless it had a story to tell, but it wasn't one I wanted to pursue. There had been too many guns in the past, and they were seldom happy stories.

'Do you mind telling me what that was all about?' I asked.

'Just a bit of a disagreement.'

'I gathered that.'

'Nothing to worry about.'

He gave the impression of moving slowly, but I had to work to keep pace with him. Odd, that, I thought. Worth remembering. 'Bobby, listen. Those guys just tried to kill you,' I said, telling him nothing he didn't know already. 'Worry about it.'

'If they'd wanted to kill me they'd have shot me, Starkey, you know that.'

'Well, what'd they want then? Did you know them?'

He shook his head. 'I know their type. They don't worry me.'

'Bobby, you're fighting for the world title in a couple of weeks. You can't afford to go losing teeth.'

'It's unfortunate, I agree, but it did expose a weakness in my defence. It hasn't been an entirely worthless experience.'

As we walked the sun began to wink warily at us through the clouds and it started to look as if the miserable hangover of wintry rain might be slowly transformed into a hint of early spring. As we approached the park gates a Labrador, damp and old, waddled towards us, tail wagging. McMaster knelt down to pet it. A man, damp and old, waddled up after him. McMaster straightened, still patting the dog's head.

'Sorry,' said the old man.

'Nice dog,' said McMaster, smiling. It wasn't a very pleasant smile.

'You're Bobby McMaster, aren't you?'

McMaster nodded. The smile faded.

The old man put out his hand. 'Good luck in the fight, son. I'll be cheering for you.'

McMaster clasped it.

'Thanks,' he said. 'I'll do my best.'

'Can't do more than that.' The old man nodded and moved on. After a few seconds the dog followed him.

McMaster shook his head slowly. 'Almost makes it all worthwhile, doesn't it?'

I shrugged. 'Better than letting the UVF have a go at you.'

'How do you know it was the UVF?'

'I'm a knuckle reader from way back.'

McMaster nodded. 'They don't worry me.'

'So you say. Do you mind telling me what exactly they wanted?'

McMaster gave me the gap-toothed smile. 'They wanted me to throw the fight.'

I snorted.

'I know,' he said, 'crazy, isn't it? They wanted me to take a dive in the third. As if I'm going to last that long.'

'So what did you say to them?'

'I said the best I could offer was a dive at the weigh-in, but they didn't appreciate it.'

'That's seriously what they were after?'

'Honest. They were just hoods, Starkey, out to make some

money. They're thick as shite and they thought they could pressure me into a few quid. They don't know any better.'

We walked through the gates. McMaster stood on the side of the pavement and tried to flag down a taxi. There was no shortage of them passing and several slowed, but they didn't appear to fancy letting a muddy giant into their cabs. After ten minutes McMaster stepped back into the shadow of the gates and I tried my luck. The third one along stopped and we were both in the back before he had a chance to change his mind.

'McClean's gym, Sandy Row.'

The car edged out into the traffic. I could see the driver eyeing McMaster up in the mirror.

'Shouldn't you go and get that sorted out?' I said, nodding at his mouth.

McMaster shook his head. 'Later.'

'You don't want to go home and get cleaned up?'

He shook his head again. 'I'll get cleaned up down at the gym.'

I shrugged. The driver looked back and said: 'You're that boxer, aren't you?'

McMaster nodded wearily.

'Been in a fight?'

'There'll be another one if you don't fuck up,' McMaster said testily. The driver nodded and returned his attention to the traffic.

It was early yet, but the gym was already packed and sweating up. McMaster led the way in. We had to pass through the aspiring fighters working on the bags, skipping, shadow-boxing on the floor of the gym, then along the side of the empty ring, to reach the changing rooms. Silence fell as one by one the fighters spotted the mud-spattered giant lumbering across. McMaster kept his eyes down and pushed through the swing doors into the changing area. I followed through, but the doors had barely swung shut before they opened again and Jackie Campbell came in.

McMaster, seated on a bench, looked up at his elderly trainer, but kept his mouth closed.

Campbell, hands on hips, looked at his boxer and shook his head. 'What happened to you?' His voice was ill-raspy.

The heels of my trainers clipped the base of the locker stack as I leant back against them and Campbell looked round at me for the first time. He nodded slightly.

'He took a tumble out running, that's all,' I said.

Campbell looked back at McMaster. 'That all, Bobby?'

McMaster nodded.

'You look like you've been in a fight.'

McMaster looked up. He reached up to scratch his nose, his massive hand shielding his mouth as he said: 'I took a tumble.' He dropped his hand and was tight-lipped again.

'Where's the rest of your gear?'

McMaster scratched his nose again. 'Forgot it.'

'Jesus Christ.' Campbell shook his head again. 'You forgot it? You're telling me you forgot your gear? Jesus Christ,' he said it again, louder. He rattled his hand against one of the metal lockers. 'Jesus H. Christ!' he shouted.

McMaster turned his head away. 'Take it easy, Jackie. I forgot. I'm sorry.'

'Jesus Christ!'

'I'm sorry.'

'Jesus Christ!'

'I'm sorry, Jackie.'

'Jesus Christ!' He turned to me. 'He's fighting for the world title in a couple of weeks, and he can't remember to bring his gear with him to the gym?' I shrugged. McMaster stared resolutely at the far wall. 'What's the matter, Bobby, got too important all of a sudden to bring your own gear? You expect it to be all sitting ready for you here like some fucking Maradona? Jesus Christ!'

'Jackie, I forgot my gear, that's all. Calm down. I can borrow somebody else's.'

'Aye, aye, aye, Bobby, fuck, aye.' He shook his head again. Clattered the locker again. He was trembling with rage. 'Do you think Christiaan Barnard forgot his scalpel when he was about to do the first heart transplant?'

McMaster shook his head.

'Do you think Newton forgot the apple when he was about to invent gravity?'

McMaster shook his head

'Do you think Bismarck refused to sign the fucking armistice because he'd forgotten his pen? Well? Well?'

McMaster turned his head slightly towards Campbell, spoke quietly, barely moving his lips.

'Bismarck didn't sign the armistice.'

'Yes, he did.'

'No, he didn't.'

'Yes, he did. He signed the fucking armistice.'

'No, he didn't.'

'I tell you he fucking did. I was fucking there.'

'No, you fucking weren't.'

I decided to add my tuppence worth. 'I think it was Marshal Foch. For the French. I don't know who it was for the Germans. Von someone.'

'Von fucking Bismarck.'

'I don't think it was Bismarck,' I said. 'Von something.'

'Who the fuck asked you anyway? I don't care if it was Frankie fucking Vaughan!'

McMaster stood up and opened a locker. He lifted out a groin protector. He sniffed it and put it back. Campbell stood with one hand on the lockers, drumming with his fingers. I could see the rapid pulse beat on the side of his temple. He shook his head.

'It was Marshal Foch, for the French,' said McMaster, 'General von Winterfeldt and Captain Vanselow for the Germans. I have the First World War on video.' He closed his locker and sat down again.

'You're one fucking smart biscuit, Bobby,' sneered Campbell. He turned to me. 'Isn't it just like a fucking big barrel of lard like him to know everything there is to know about fucking surrender.' I shrugged. 'What're you gonna do, Bobby, sign an armistice with Tyson?'

McMaster looked at me. 'Don't worry about this, Starkey,

it's straight from the textbook. He pretends to hate me just to make me angry in the ring. Water off a duck's back.'

'I do fuckin' hate you, McMaster.'

'How could you hate a smile like this?' For the first time McMaster turned and faced him full on. It was a wicked smile.

What little colour there was drained from Campbell's face. 'What the fuck happened to your mouth?' he screamed.

McMaster burst into laughter.

'What the fuck happened?' Campbell surged forward, McMaster took off round the back of the lockers. 'What the fuck happened?'

McMaster appeared round the other side. 'I took a tumble, Jackie, that's all.'

Campbell laboured round behind him; McMaster kept his distance. 'Slow down there, Jackie,' he said, 'you'll have a coronary.'

'Don't bloody coronary me, you big galoot! Now stand still and tell me what happened!'

McMaster let the smile fade, then took his seat again on the bench. 'Sorry, Jackie. I got in a fight. Not my fault.'

'It wasn't his fault,' I said.

'You were there?'

'I went along with him on his run this morning. Some hoods jumped him. He sorted them out.'

'Jesus Christ!' Campbell slammed his fist into the lockers again. 'Biggest night in your life coming up and you get in a fight! Fuck!'

'What the hell did you expect me to do?' McMaster shouted.

The doors swung inwards. Geordie McClean came through; behind him I could see the fighters grouped in the doorway, enjoying the argument. 'What the bloody hell is going on?' McClean snapped.

'Look at the champ there,' said Campbell, 'look at his lovely smile.'

Now McMaster looked a bit sheepish. 'Sorry, Mr McClean,' he said, 'but I've lost a tooth.'

'And been in a fight!'

McClean turned to the elderly trainer. 'Okay, Jackie, okay. Calm down. I'll sort this out. Go away on out there and sort that lot out. Never mind about Bobby, I'll get to the bottom of it . . .'

Campbell turned for the door. '"Never mind about Bobby,"' he mimicked, pushing his way out. In a moment I could hear another rush of swearing and then the steady beat of skipping returned.

'Don't worry about Jackie there, Starkey, he's the best trainer there is. Just has a bit of a temper on him. He's been like that since I was in nappies.'

'Kind of depends when you got out of nappies.'

'Very funny, people man, very funny.' I gave him a smile. 'Right, Bobby,' he said, 'into my office.'

Bobby stood up and moved forward. I went with him.

'And where do you think you're going?' McClean asked.

'With you.'

'Oh yeah?'

'If you don't mind.'

'And if I do?'

'I'm supposed to have access. We've paid for it.'

'We?'

'Someone has.'

'What do you think, Bobby?'

'May as well let him come. He was there this morning, for the fight. You might appreciate his perspective on it, seeing as how I'm just a big dumb fighter.'

McClean looked at his boxer for a moment, eyes searching for the sarcastic glint. Then he nodded. 'Okay then, Starkey, come to my parlour.'

McClean pushed through the doors. McMaster followed him, holding the door open for me. 'That's one interesting chapter for you anyway,' he said quietly.

'You think?'

8

In my younger and more vulnerable years my father gave me some advice that I've been turning over in my mind ever since.

'Whenever you feel like criticizing anyone,' he told me, 'just remember that all the people in this world haven't had the advantages that you've had.'

Actually, that's a direct lift from *The Great Gatsby*. I would like to be able to say something like that about my dad, to remember him as an old philosopher sitting on the verandah, quietly rocking in his chair, puffing on his pipe and being magnanimous to those less fortunate, but the fact is he sat in the old armchair in our poky front room, staring at the box, wasting his money on a string of losers and the most profound thing he ever managed was, 'Away down to the shops for a packet of fags, son.'

Actually that's not strictly true either. He said some profoundly bigoted things.

Let me take that again.

In my younger and more vulnerable years my father gave me some advice that I've been turning over in my mind ever since.

'Never trust a Catholic,' he told me, 'and never trust a woman.'

Even when you're only seven or eight, when your father is your God, you don't accept those things carte blanche. You ask why. And your dad shakes his head like he's talking to a fool and mumbles beerily, 'Fenians and women, Fenians and women. Away down to the shops for a packet of fags, son.'

Fenians. I wonder if he knew about the Fenians. I wonder what he would have done if this little man, short trousers, cropped hair, Action Man in one hand, cheese and onion crisps in the other, had said, 'Actually, Father, did you know that the Fenian Brotherhood was an organization active in the nineteenth century in Britain and North America fighting British rule in Ireland? It had as many Protestant as Catholic members.'

I expect he would have sat back in his chair, nodded thoughtfully, then stubbed his cigarette out in my eye.

And women, what did they ever do to him? Surely not Mother, dead but not forgotten, always there in a dozen photographs about the house. There seemed no bitterness towards her. Perhaps she stood apart from her sex. An honorary man. Which woman, which women, had treated him badly, to so jaundice his view?

I never did ask, but the question came back to me as I sat in my car outside Patricia's flat and watched her kiss Tony From Work.

A long, lingering kiss. It wasn't just saying good night to a colleague.

I sat, I seethed. I gripped the wheel like it was her throat. I sat and watched and after five minutes he left, and I sat and watched as he drove off, and I sat and watched as she went in, and then I sat and watched some more: the midnight traffic, the cats skulking in the streetlight shadows, my breath on the window. I tried to quell the shaking in my hand. It wasn't the cold.

I thought of the way hope can rush out of a body, a dam-breach of the soul. Hopes of the trip to America bringing us back together. Hopes of living together again. Hopes of sex. Sucked out in the seconds it takes to park a car, to reach into the back seat to pick up the chocolates and the flowers, to turn and confront your private hell.

I took ten minutes to compose myself, then locked up the car and knocked at the door to her apartment.

'Yes?' A short word, but short enough to reveal a tremor in her voice.

I lifted the letter box and peered in. She was in her pink dressing gown; it was loosely tied in the middle, which was about all I could see. She took a step back.

'Tony?'

'No,' I said sharply, and let the box fall.

The door opened quickly. Patricia looked pale-faced and damp about the eyes.

'Hello, Spaghetti Legs,' I said.

'Hello, you.'

'Sorry to call round so late.'

She shook her head. 'Doesn't matter.'

'Just I got the tickets for America. Just earlier there. Thought we could maybe chat about the holiday.'

She held my eyes for a moment, then her face started to crease up and tears began to run. I stepped into the hall and she threw her arms round me and held me tight. I put my arms round her and patted her back. 'It's okay,' I said, but it wasn't; I knew it, she knew it, Tony probably knew it.

After a couple of minutes she slowly extricated herself. She stood back and put a hand to my face and patted it softly. 'I'm sorry,' she said. 'Come on up.'

She turned and led me up the stairs into the apartment proper. Not much had changed. It was as tidy as ever, save the damp tissues littered about the lounge.

She sat me down on the settee, let her hand linger on mine for a moment and then set herself down carefully in an armchair. Patricia wasn't one of those women who bloomed in adversity. Her eyes were puffy, her hair dank, her skin blotchy.

'Stop looking at me,' she said abruptly.

'Sorry,' I said, but there was really nowhere else. I reached out to her, but she was too far away for me to touch her leg, and my hand just kind of flopped helplessly a few inches short before I retrieved it. 'Have I come at a bad time?'

'That's a stupid bloody question.'

'I'm just trying to be diplomatic.'

'Well, there's a first.'

'Sorry for trying to be nice.'

'Ach, Dan, stop it, be yourself.'

The anger – no, the hurt – was welling up. 'Really?' I snapped. 'No sympathy? No caring enquiry? No shoulder to cry on?' She shook her head. The tears were still falling. I shrugged. 'Get dropped again, did you?'

She bit at a finger. There were no nails to chew on. She shook her head again. Her eyes were set on the far wall, on a colour photograph of a tusky walrus. It was a new one on me.

I let it flow. The breach was made. 'I didn't think so. I saw you outside. You didn't look like youse had come to the end of the road. I didn't think youse had got much beyond the start of the road, seeing as how he was only meant to be a work colleague. He didn't seem like a bad sort that night I met him and tried to punch his lights out, but I knew there was something going on. He was just a bit too protective of you – so was I, of course, but that's my prerogative as I'm the husband – but when you agreed on a holiday with me to the States I thought there might be the chance of us getting back together on a permanent basis . . . then I saw you slobbering over him out there . . . I don't know, maybe my office is different, but I don't often say good night to my colleagues like that. Maybe you have a more open approach to—'

'Dan, will you shut up?'

'Of course.'

She reached down to the carpet and picked another tissue out of a half-empty box of Kleenex. She stood with it and wiped at her face, then walked out of the lounge to the kitchen.

'Do you want a drink?' she called.

'Sure.'

'What's your poison?'

'You should know that.'

'People change.'

'Don't they just?'

'Dan . . .'

'Sorry.'

'What'll you have?'

'Whatever's easy.'

'Dan, they're all easy.'

'It doesn't matter. Whatever's handy.'

'Dan, they're all handy.' She appeared in the doorway. 'Dan, I've had you nice, I've had you horrid, and now you're back to being nice. Can you be yourself?'

'Of course.'

She gave me a half-smile. 'Good. Now what's your poison?'

'I'll have a Harp. And fix a Paraquat for yourself.'

Her smile widened. She turned for the kitchen. 'That's more like it,' she said. A moment later she returned with two tins of beer and handed me one; we popped them together. For a minute we sipped and watched each other. The tears had stopped, for the moment anyway.

Eventually I let my can creep as low as my lap. 'Forgetting for the moment that I am the cruelly spurned husband and you the deceitful, disloyal wife, what's got you into such a state?'

'I'm pregnant,' she said.

'Fuck,' I said.

I stood by the window. It had started to rain. Most of the city was laid out before me, but the little rivulets on the glass made it look all distorted, like I was looking at it through English eyes. We'd had three cans of silence each.

I could see Patricia's reflection in the window. She watched me. Occasionally she dabbed at an eye. No TV. No CD. Not even the occasional car outside. The people of Belfast were sleeping, or plotting quietly. The only noise was the slight tap of the rain and the occasional sniffle from behind.

Finally she said, 'Aren't you going to say anything?'

'My silence speaks volumes.'

'Jesus. Dan. Say something.'

'Congratulations.'

'Really?'

'What do you think?' I turned to her. She shook her head. 'I take it, seeing as we haven't been to bed together in months, that it isn't mine.'

'Maybe it was delayed reaction.'

'I think not.'

'No.'

'Tony? Tony from work?'

She nodded.

'I'm very happy for you two.'

'Don't, Dan.'

I shrugged. 'Is he happy for you two?'

She shook her head. 'He's married.'

I gave an involuntary snort.

'It's not funny.'

'Of course it is. He just had to be married. It stands to reason. You knew he was married, of course?'

'Of course. It was only meant to be a bit of fun. It just got out of hand.'

'Out of hand and into the womb.'

'There's no need to be crude.'

'The only crudeness is you fucking around.'

'Don't be like that, Dan.'

'What do you expect, sympathy?'

She gave me a slight nod. Her eyes narrowed. Tears again. I started towards her. She put her hand out to stop me. 'You can stick your sympathy up your hole,' she said. But there was no stopping me.

We ended up lying in the bed in her neat bedroom. Arms around each other, touching, but not sexually. I couldn't.

She didn't say much. We kissed a bit. She cried some more. I asked her why she didn't take precautions; she always had with me, even if it was just locking her bedroom door in her parents' house. She didn't know. She'd gotten careless. She'd gotten horny, but not for me. She said she was two months gone. Hadn't decided whether to keep it. I suggested a bottle of brandy and a hot bath. She said that's what had got her into trouble in the first place. Ha-ha.

'We have a habit of getting ourselves into situations like this, haven't we?'

'It's me, Dan, not you. You're on the outside, looking in.'

'I'm on the outside wanting in. You've kept me there.'

'I know.'

'Because you couldn't make up your mind whether you wanted me back.' Her head nodded gently against my chest. 'Then you slept with someone while you were making your mind up.'

'I know. I'm sorry.'

'Is it a sex thing?'

'Is what a sex thing?'

'Tony.'

'It involves sex. It has to.'

'I mean, is it because he's something sensational in bed? And I'm not.'

'No. Of course not.'

'I mean, he hasn't got some ginormous walrus cock or anything, has he?'

'Dan, what size is a walrus cock?'

'I've no idea. I'm sure I could find out.'

'What, like, in a book or something? The Penguin Book of Walrus Cocks?'

'I think there's one like that. Or was it the Walrus Book of Penguin Cocks?'

She snorted.

I plucked up the courage. 'Do you love him?'

Pause. A long pause. My heart tom-tomming away, scared to death of the answer, scared to death of asking whether she loved me.

'I don't know,' came eventually, murmured, not convincing either way.

I stroked her hair, massaged her temples with one hand. 'You know,' I said, 'we were always chalk and cheese.'

A little rush of air from her nose. 'Weren't we just?'

'You never liked the pictures.'

'I liked soap operas.'

'You never liked The Clash.'

'I liked the Beatles.'

'I liked walking in the forest.'

'I liked lying on the beach. I liked big fat blockbusters.'

'I liked the classics. Dickens. Hardy. Dalglish.'

'I hated football.'

'I loved boxing.'

'The Grand National was cruel.'

'It was brilliant. I couldn't stand tennis. All those lesbians.'

'You never danced with me.'

'At the wedding I did.'

'You were forced to. The only time.'

'It wasn't the dancing. It was the music.'

'You never liked my friends.'

'They never liked me.'

'You never gave them a chance. I gave your friends a chance.'

'They gave you a chance. I like kissing with tongues.'

'I prefer it with lips.'

'I like the missionary position.'

'I like to be on top. Dan?'

'Mmmmmm?'

'Why did we ever get together?'

'Because I fell absolutely and completely in love with you. And I still absolutely and completely love you.'

And that set her off again.

9

I was drunk for three days. I spoke to no one. I ate nothing. I neither washed nor shaved. I listened to my music. When my eyes could focus, I read my books. I listened, I read, I thought, all of it suffused by images of Patricia. Images of her making love with another man. Images of her having a baby, another man's baby.

I thought about Tony From Work. I thought about following him home, stalking him to his lair . . . setting fire to his car . . . setting fire to his house . . . setting fire to his wife . . . thought about being able to say: see how you like it now, Tony. I wondered about him, what was he playing at – what was Patricia to him, a bit of extra-marital sex, or was it the real thing, the discovery of true love while trapped in a sterile marriage? If it was true love, who was I to intervene, besides the husband? Would I have let that get in my way? No. What excuse did I have? None. I had true love, and let it slip away.

Twice the police called to get me to turn the music down. The record that seemed to set them off was 'Flying Saucer Attack' by the Rezillos. They were quite pleasant really. Didn't threaten me at all.

On the fourth morning I got up, showered, shaved and burnt a twelve-inch hole in one of my favourite shirts.

I phoned Patricia at work, but she was off; I phoned her at home, but there was no reply. Then I set off for Aldergrove International with a rucksack, a hangover and a broken heart.

I spotted Geordie McClean and Mary McMaster in the bar, standing, ordering drinks. I walked up and set my rucksack down behind them.

'Mine's a pint,' I said. They looked round. Mary smiled, McClean nodded.

'You look rough,' McClean said.

'I'm fine. Where's Bobby?'

'He's in Eason's looking through the *Economist*. Or the *Beano*.'

McClean leant over the bar and called for an extra pint.

'I'm sorry to hear your wife isn't coming,' said Mary. She rested her hand briefly on my arm. 'I was looking forward to some female company. Boxing's very much a man's game.'

'Couldn't be helped. She's not well.'

'Nothing too serious I hope.'

'Nah. Just picked up a bug. Just takes a while to run its course.' About nine months.

'Pity.'

'Yeah.'

McClean handed me a pint of Harp I didn't need. 'Get that down ya,' he said. 'Might put some colour back in your cheeks.'

'Thanks.' I took a slurp and set it on the bar. 'I'm sorry about the wife's ticket. It couldn't be avoided.'

'Never worry. It wasn't wasted.'

A shadow fell over the bar, and its name was Bobby McMaster. He was taller than I remembered, bulkier. He wore a sleek black tracksuit, Ray-Bans, black trainers, his face looked tanned, his haircut short, eyes keen, lips mercifully normal, open enough to reveal a full set of teeth; you'd only have noticed a very slight difference in colour in the false one if you were really searching for it. He looked impressive.

'You clean up well,' I said.

McMaster nodded. 'Orange juice,' he said.

'I must try some. It works wonders.'

'From the bar. Orange juice.'

'Ah.'

'I'll get it, Bobby,' said McClean. 'Sit yourself down there.'

McMaster moved and unnatural light once again lit the bar and revealed not only a lot of curious punters looking the big man up and down – and wondering no doubt who he was – but also another familiar figure standing just a couple of feet in front of me. Stanley Matchitt, King of the High Seas.

He gave me what should by all rights have been a weasely little smile, but to be honest it was quite normal. 'Hello, Starkey. I heard you'd be here,' he said warmly.

McClean stepped forward and put his hand out to Stanley. 'Glad you could make it, son,' he said. They shook. I shook my head, but held my tongue, which is difficult to do at the same time. It was hardly good PR to be seen off by a notorious killer, but it was none of my business.

I lifted my pint and joined McMaster and his wife at their table. 'Nice of him to come and see you off,' I said.

'He's not seeing me off.'

'What's he up to then, jetting off to a high-powered business meeting?'

McMaster turned to his wife. 'You know, Mary, even in a country famed for its sarcasm, I don't think I've ever heard anyone as sarky as Starkey here.'

Mary took a drink. 'It does grate after a while,' she said quietly.

'Sorry.'

'There he goes again.'

'Aw, c'mon,' I said.

McClean and Stanley joined us with their drinks. 'Starkey,' began McClean, 'you should know that Stanley here will be travelling with us. He's part of the team.'

'What're you planning to do, cut Tyson's throat before he gets in the ring? It's hardly Marquess of Queensberry.'

'No need for that, Starkey,' said McClean. 'Stanley here's a reformed character these days. Aren't you, Stanley?' Stanley nodded. 'But still a force to be reckoned with. After what happened the other day I think it's in all our interests to have a bit of muscle around.'

'I thought there were a few muscles on Bobby.'

'You know what I mean, Starkey. We need to keep the shit away from Bobby.'

'Isn't it a bit like asking the wolf to guard the sheep?'

'I'm no fucking sheep,' McMaster growled.

'Sorry. No offence. But you know what I mean.'

'Starkey, why don't you get your pencil out and write something down?' said Stanley. 'That's what you're here for.'

I shrugged.

'It's not like I need your approval,' he continued, 'it's not like you matter in the slightest.'

'Stanley's a friend from way back, Starkey,' said McMaster, 'and I'd trust him with my life. And with my wife's.'

I shrugged. 'Fair enough. I just hope he flies better than he sails.'

'I don't know, Starkey,' said Stanley, 'I've never flown before. But if I get sick you'll be the first to find out; I'm sitting beside you.'

Five minutes before we were due to go through security to our gate, Jackie Campbell arrived. He looked tired and hassled. He puffed across to the check-in desk, riffled through his wallet for his ticket and then turned to scan for us. Mary waved across to him. He didn't see her, though he was looking right at her. I walked across to him. It was a relief to get away, even for a moment, from our little ensemble. Things were a little frosty.

'Hi, Jackie,' I said. His small blue eyes homed in on me. He didn't know me from Adam. 'Starkey. Dan. I'm doing the book on Bobby.'

He nodded. 'I can't stop. I've a plane to catch. Bastards took my car apart on the way in. I mean, do I look like I'm the sort to carry a fuckin' bomb?'

I shook my head. 'You're okay, Jackie. The others are just over there. We're just about to board. And your boy's looking good.'

'If looks could kill,' he croaked, 'they probably will.'

I laughed. 'Deep, man. That's a Peter Gabriel song. You don't look the type, Jackie.'

He shook his head. 'I'm not the fucking type. My fucking son's forty and he's still listening to shite like that. Plays it all fucking day. At least I grew out of Glenn Miller.'

'Now there's a name to conjure with just as you're about to get on a plane.'

'Yeah, whatever.' Campbell lifted his bags, two over-the-shoulder holdalls, and puffed off towards the rest of the team.

McClean clapped him on the shoulder. 'Thought you weren't going to make it there, Jackie.'

'You know what thought did.'

McClean smiled weakly. 'Take the bags there,' he said to Stanley.

'I'm no fucking bag man.'

'I'll carry my own bags, thank you. I'm not that decrepit yet.'

'Don't you want to check them in, Jackie?' asked Mary.

'They stay with me. Last time I flew out to a fight I went to London and my bags went to Paris. Anyone tries to take them off me, they get flattened.'

I was disappointed. I wanted Snatchit Matchitt to be scared. I wanted him to freeze. I wanted his clothes to stick to him with cold sweat. I wanted him to be sick over himself. I wanted him to scream. I wanted him to stick his knuckles in his eyes. I wanted him to cling to me. I wanted to pat him on the head and say, 'There, there, son, you'll be okay.'

Ten minutes into the flight Stanley sat there with a big smile on his face, his earphones on, drinking a double, eyeing up the air hostesses.

'Beautiful,' he said, loud enough to compensate for the maelstrom in his ear and for the hostesses to hear. They looked daggers at him, and he grinned back. 'Beautiful,' he said again. 'You know,' he bellowed in my ear, 'they're just like waitresses, save that waitresses don't run much risk of crashing into a mountain from forty thousand feet.' He cackled in my ear.

'Very good, Stanley,' I said, but he didn't hear me.

McClean, McMaster and Mary were cosseted in first class. I thought if they'd decided in their wisdom to put a nationally renowned journalist like myself in economy class, at the very least they might have continued with the pecking order by putting a seasoned killer like Stanley on a deckchair in the hold instead of sticking him next to me.

'This is class,' bellowed Stanley again as he drained his glass. He lifted his earphones off and tipped the empty glass towards me. 'Do you want another?'

I shook my head. It was time for a dry-out.

'You might as well, they're free.'

'I know they're free, Stanley.'

He shook his own head, then snagged one of the hostesses' sleeves as she passed. 'Fill that for us, wouldja?' he said. 'Whiskey and Coke. And he'll have a double vodka and orange.'

The hostess nodded glumly and moved on. She reached the drinks trolley and said something to a colleague. They both looked back up at Stanley.

'I said I didn't want one.'

'But you didn't say you didn't want two.'

'I suppose there's a flawed kind of logic in there somewhere.'

'Waste not, want not, Starkey.'

'Shouldn't you be up front with McMaster being muscular rather than getting pished back here?'

'Sure he's fine up there. Nothing's going to happen to him up there in upper class. Nothing ever happens to the upper class.' Suddenly he giggled. 'Except for Lord Mountbatten. Did you know he had dandruff?'

I nodded, but it didn't deter him.

'They found his head and shoulders on the beach.' He cackled again, like a hyena having a caesarean.

'Very droll.'

'Do you get it – head and shoulders? Head and . . .'

'I get it, Stanley. Most of the passengers get it.'

Stanley shook his head disdainfully. 'Take it easy, Starkey. Are you scared of flying or something? You're very edgy.'

'Sitting beside you makes me edgy.'

'Ach, sure I'm just a big cuddly bear.'

'I know what you are, Stanley. I'm just worried that someone might try to kill you during the flight and I'm sitting next to you.'

Stanley sniggered and accepted the drinks from the hostess. 'Thanks, honey,' he said. He kept both glasses and the mixers on his table. 'Cheers,' he said as he mixed the whiskey; the mix was more fascist than liberal.

'Cheers,' I said, and closed my eyes.

The restorative powers of sleep somehow passed me by. I woke up tired. I woke up sweaty. I woke up with a sore head. I woke up and that bastard was still beside me. Drinking. Smiling. Annoying people.

We were four hours into the flight. He had a couple of fresh drinks in front of him. I looked at my watch, did a quick calculation, then switched it to New York time. Stanley watched me with an expression of benign bemusement on his face.

'Aren't you going to change your watch?' I asked.

'It's a Rolex. I'm perfectly happy with it.'

'No. I mean, change the time.'

'It's the correct time.'

'I mean, for New York.' I was regretting bothering already. 'To New York time,' I added, to clarify things.

Stanley shook his head.

'It'll still be the correct time in New York. Rolexes don't lose time.'

I nodded. He was silent for a couple of minutes. I watched the clouds below.

'How much would I need to change it by?' he asked.

I turned, surprised – I hadn't heard any cogs moving – and showed him my time. He nodded and started to footer with his Rolex. 'My uncle used to fly all over the world,' he said, 'all over, east, west, north, south, all over the place.'

I nodded.

'He said he used to fly through so many time zones in the course of a single trip that he could start off clean shaven, and by the time he finally got off the plane he'd have a full beard.'

I nodded some more.

'He said on one trip a woman at the back of the plane conceived, gave birth to a boy and had him all dressed and ready for prep school by the time they landed.'

'Really,' I said, dryly.

He nodded and took a sip of his whiskey.

'What was your uncle?'

'A nut.'

After a moment of due reflection I said, 'I asked for that.'

'You did,' said Stanley, and took another drink.

10

We were all a little stunned.

First there were the forty wailing men in the green skirts. Then out into the speckling snow and the steaming chariot.

The 43rd Hibernian lads, forty-three sons of the oul' sod, forty-three me-me men pressing their elbows on sheep bladders and puffing like their lives depended on it, made Kennedy Airport sound like a giant beehive, one crying out to be smoked. None of us knew where to look; the flashing cameras only served to confuse us further. A chauffeur, giant, black, dressed incongruously in a bright-green uniform, holding a sign which carried McMaster's name and four crudely painted shamrocks, collected us from arrivals and cut a path through the photographers to the longest, sleekest car any of us had ever seen.

'Welcome to America, folks,' our driver said, ramming a

huge cigar in his mouth. If I'd been filing it, it would have gone in under American cliché number one.

Even McClean, who liked to control things, looked a bit stunned. 'Clay sure knows how to put on a show,' was all he could say.

Marvin 'Poodle' Clay, as bald as an egg and with a head not that different in shape, rapped on the microphone on the top table of the New York Mirage conference centre, and slowly silence fell over the assembled press corps. Clay smiled. It made his face look like there was a gash in it.

Clay was a Harlem fraudster from way back. He'd moved into boxing in prison and emerged into freedom with a ready-made stable of fighters and enough money stashed away to ensure they won a lot of fights. He'd built his powerbase in Manhattan and Atlantic City, distrusting the flash and distance of Las Vegas, and signed fighters by the dozen until he was almost a rival to Don King, the electric-haired promoter who'd dominated the fight scene for decades. Almost a rival, but not quite. The difference between them was the heavyweights. Where the real money was. King had Tyson in his camp and just about every contender you cared to name. King had done time for manslaughter. Clay thought King was too nice.

King had the division sewn up nicely. As promoter, like every promoter in every sport, he took the lion's share of the cash – box office, cable, promotional. As manager of the champ – albeit through his son – he was able to negotiate with himself for the fee Tyson was paid, and then take a cut of it. Invariably he was manager of the challenger, so he was able to negotiate with himself for a reduced fee, and then take a bigger cut of that for giving his challenger the opportunity to fight his champion. It was the most perfect cartel in the business. And he thought he had enough money to stop anyone breaking it up. Sign for me or you don't get anywhere in the business was the bottom line. He seemed to have every black man in America over fourteen stone on his books, just to cover all contingencies. Who could conceive of there being a good white boxer? King could. King signed them. There were a couple. But who would ever think of making a fat Irishman sign on the dotted line? Marvin Clay would. And Marvin Clay had Bobby McMaster, through McClean, sign on the dotted line even before he picked up the European title. Some cynics might say that he even arranged for McMaster to win the title, but who could foresee a clash of heads and cuts stopping a fight? Mmmm. Whatever, Clay had enough clout, just, to get the WBC to insist on a mandatory defence of the heavyweight title despite the unforeseen (mmmmmmm) injury to Tyson's scheduled opponent, and the WBC and the IBF had little choice but to fall into line. For once King had been outmanoeuvred. But it would be back to normal after the fight.

'Ladies and gentlemen,' Clay proclaimed out of courtesy, for there were no women present – Mary was sleeping off the flight upstairs – 'welcome to the fight of the century!'

I sat at the back of the hall. An elderly gent, notebook in

hand, duly noted Clay's opening remark, then whispered, 'Bullshit,' out of the side of his mouth.

Clay smiled down at Don King beside him, and Tyson one place up, then turned and nodded at Geordie McClean and Bobby McMaster on the other side. Then he launched into a spiel about the fight. My neighbour was right, it was bullshit. It was all duly noted by the press, recorded by the cameras and microphones, but there was a tangible lack of excitement.

Clay threw the floor open to questions.

After a few moments of motionless embarrassment, a couple of hands slowly snaked into the air. Clay pointed.

'Matt Bronski, *The Ring*. Mr Clay – who the hell is Bobby McMaster?'

'Bobby McMaster is the European champion and the nearest ranked contender available for Mike Tyson to make a mandatory defence. You know that, Matt.'

'But who the hell has he fought?'

'He's fought plenty. He'll give Mike the fight of his life.'

'What do you base that on?'

'Take my word for it, Matt.'

Matt sat down, muttering under his breath, 'That'll be the day.'

Clay pointed. 'Bernie Gold, *Boxing World* – Mr Clay, allegations are being made in some quarters that this is a cynical attempt to exploit St Patrick's Day.'

Clay banged his fist on the table. 'Show me those alligators!' Anger glared briefly in his eyes and the wide set of his mouth, but then he swallowed and pushed the smile back onto his face. '"Cynical" and "exploit" are two words which don't even figure in my vocabulary, Bernie. Two good fighters are being matched at just the right time, one champion who's proved himself time and again, and a hungry contender on the way up. It's the story of boxing, Bernie. Who gave Ali a chance against Liston? Leonard against Hagler? Of course there's a marketing angle to it, I'd be a fool to deny that, but we have a genuine fighting Irishman here and what better way to celebrate St Patrick's Day than have him fight for the world title?'

'Alec Cowan, NBC – Mr Clay, is this an attempt to wrest control of the heavyweight division from Mr King?'

'Yes.'

Clay turned to King. They both laughed.

'How do you feel about that, Mr King?'

'Marvin Clay has two hopes of winning the title. Bob Hope and No Hope.'

They both laughed again.

'So you don't rate Bobby McMaster's chances?'

King laughed again and shook his head, the mad brush of hair waving like wheat in the wind. 'We're not worried about him.'

'Mike – do you expect any trouble from Bobby McMaster?'

'I've met Bobby, and he seems like a sweet guy, but no, I don't expect any trouble from him.'

'What will your tactics be?'

'I intend to go out in round one, sound him out, then drive his nose up into his brain.'

An ominous silence settled on the room. A dozen heads

nodded, almost imperceptibly. I looked at Tyson, and I could see death written all over him. Bloody, painful death. McClean looked across at Tyson. His head nodded too. McMaster, eyes down, studied his fists. His paleness was way beyond simple lack of pigmentation.

The old guy beside me stood up. 'Patrick O'Brien, *New York Irish News*. I'd like to ask Bobby McMaster what his tactics will be.'

A couple of nervous snorts.

McMaster looked up, scanned the room until he saw the diminutive figure on my right. He looked down at his fists again, then up. 'I plan to run away,' he said quietly.

The silence was almost complete. A couple of clicks, camera flashes. All eyes now on McMaster.

'Is that it?' O'Brien asked.

'Naw,' said McMaster, a cherubic smile slipping across his face, 'at the end of round six my trainer, Jackie Campbell, plans to slip a horseshoe into my glove. Then Mike'll know all about punching power.'

It started with a giggle at the back. It spread along the row, then down towards the top table. Suddenly everyone was laughing. Even Tyson had a smile on his face.

'Evan Ward, *Boston Globe*. Bobby – where do you stand on the Irish question?'

'What Irish question?'

'About the British in Ireland?'

'I'm British and I'm Irish. It's a conundrum, Evan, but I don't much mind who supports me, British or Irish. It's only a fight.'

Evan Ward took his seat again. He turned to his neighbour. 'What's a conundrum?' he asked.

'David Alexander, CNN – what star sign are you, Bobby?'

'Taurus, David. The Bull.'

'Mario Fidelli, *New York Times* – where in Ireland are you from, Bobby?'

'I'm from a small town in Northern Ireland called Crossmaheart. You may not have heard of it, but it's twinned with Beirut.'

More laughter. Bobby was starting to enjoy himself.

'You still live there, Bobby?'

'No. I live in the Holy Land.'

'Really? Israel?'

'No, Holy Land, Belfast. It's a district of the city, but it's God's own city. So popular, people keep fighting over it.'

Don King stood up. 'Mike's taking this fight as seriously as any, he's been in solid training for six weeks. No socializing.'

'That's very good, Mike. Mike Lebowitz, *New York Newsday*. I'd like to ask Bobby McMaster about his first impressions of America.'

'Well,' said McMaster, scratching at his chin, 'I'm only just here really. But I suppose my first impression is the number of black people there are.'

A black reporter, halfway down the hall, jumped to his feet. 'Martin King, *Amsterdam Review*. Do you have a problem with black people?'

'Only with one.'

More laughter. King persisted. 'Can you explain your comment then?'

'It wasn't a comment, it was an observation. I come from Ireland, Martin; there aren't any black people in Ireland. Maybe five or six.'

'Is that because Ireland operates a form of apartheid?'

'I don't know why that is, Mr King. Perhaps St Patrick threw them out.'

'I'm aware of the St Patrick myth, Mr McMaster. Are you comparing black people with snakes and vipers?'

'Vipers are snakes, Martin.'

'That's not my point.'

Geordie McClean was on his feet, pulling the microphone away from McMaster. 'I think this gentleman is missing the point. There are genuinely very few black people in Ireland, it's a question of simple demographics. Bobby made an innocent comment about his first observations of America. I think this gentleman is taking Bobby's comment out of context.'

McMaster pulled the microphone back. 'You don't need to apologize for me,' he said.

'Do you even know any black people?' shouted King.

'I can't say I do, but I have all of Al Jolson's records.'

Half the floor erupted in laughter, the other half shifted uneasily.

McMaster waved his hand, shook his head. 'Nah, I'm only taking the piss. No, I don't know any black people, but that's only because I've only been out of Ireland once, and that was to fight for the title in France. So Mike here is just about the first black guy I've ever met. He's been a great champion, he's had his problems but he seems to be getting over those, and he seems like a genuinely nice guy. I'm sure he's looking forward to retiring.'

Tyson bent forward to his mike. 'I'll come to your funeral.'

Another voice from the front. 'Stuart Adamson, *Sports Illustrated*. Bobby, we know Mike Tyson as Iron Mike. Any nicknames lurking in your corner?'

McMaster looked at McClean. He put his hand over the microphone and whispered something. Even from the back I could read his lips: Fat Boy? McClean shook his head.

'Nothing springs to mind, Stuart. How about you lot coming up with something?' He glanced at Clay. 'Something better than the Fighting Irishman.'

'How about the Racist Irishman?' shouted Martin King.

'How about a mouth clamp for my friend here?' retorted McMaster.

'How about the Quiet Man?' suggested Don King.

'How about the Big Potato?' came a shout from the floor.

'The what?'

'Y'know, New York's the Big Apple. You being from Ireland, eating potatoes and all, you could be the Big Potato.'

'I think Martin King there should interview you about racial stereotyping. How about it, Martin?'

'Racial stereotyping is no laughing matter!' King shouted.

'Who's laughing?'

Most of the reporters were.

'Rankin, Ulster Television – Bobby, hi!'

'Hello, Mark. Good to see you.'

'Bobby – what flag will you be coming into the ring under – British or Irish?'

'That's a good question, Mark. I have no idea. I've made no decision on that yet. I may come in under a flag of convenience, you know, like one of those dodgy ships that get registered in Panama.'

'Barry McGuigan used to come in under the United Nations flag.'

'What, after Somalia and Bosnia? I'd get lynched.'

'What about the national anthem then? British or Irish? McGuigan used to get his dad to sing "Danny Boy" and have done with it.'

'I may sing that, seeing as how it's St Patrick's Day and I can pick out the notes on my guitar.'

'Do you have a theme song? Remember McGuigan came in to the *Rocky* theme. I believe Mr Tyson comes in to the latest rap.'

'Uh, Mark, the nearest thing I've ever had to a theme song is a hundred and fifty drunks singing "Up Your Hole with a Big Jam Roll" every time I appear in the Ulster Hall. Will that do?'

I left them to it. I slipped out of the hall and took the lift up to my room. Bobby McMaster had won the press conference, but it was about as important as winning the toss at a football match. I took a beer out of the minibar and lay back on the bed and thought about Patricia and her baby.

11

I thought about Patricia for three hours, during which I emptied the contents of the minibar. It didn't seem like three hours, and it didn't seem like that much alcohol, being in tiny cans and handy measures, but I did a lot of thinking and a lot of drinking, and at the end of it I couldn't remember a single bloody thing and the room was starting to spin. It seemed the right time to give Patricia a call.

It took me a while to work out the codes, because I'd trouble focusing on the directory. But I finally mastered it and tapped in the number. It was picked up on the fourth ring. Maybe the fifth. Sometimes you don't hear the first ring at the other end. Like it matters.

'Trish?'

'No.'

A man's voice. A bloody man's voice. A bloody familiar man's voice.

Forgive me, but love is blind and love is angry, and I'd forgotten the subtlety pills. 'You fucker,' I said.

'I'm sorry?'

'I'm going to fucking kill you, you fucker.'

He cleared his throat.

'You're fucking my fucking wife, and I'm going to kill you. You fucker.'

'Is that you, Dan?'

'Yes. You fuck.'

'Dan, this is Patricia's father.'

'Ah, hello, how are you?'

'I'm fine.'

'Is Patricia there?'

'Not just now, no.'

'Okay, well, could you tell her I called?'

'Certainly.'

'Fine. Thank you. I'm sorry. Good night.'

I put the phone down, and thought about putting myself down. Briefly.

I needed a drink. I didn't need a drink, but you know how it is. I took the lift down to the hotel bar, but it was too nice, all squeaky clean and cocktails. Jackie Campbell was in one corner, talking to the elderly reporter from the *New York Irish News*. A couple of tables up Geordie McClean sat with Stanley Matchitt; Stanley waved me over; I nodded and left. I needed a proper bar.

I like New York away from the glitz. Dirty old Manhattan has an air of cultivated seediness which is hard to beat. I'd once brought Patricia here on a freebie holiday. I wanted her there again, wanted to hold her hand and walk down Broadway, marvel at the lights in Times Square, to get dizzy with her up inside the Statue of Liberty and get pissed in Chinatown. But she was at home contemplating a baby and a lover. Maybe her dad was round discussing it with her; if he'd ever been in my camp the chances were he was now picking up his pegs.

I found an Irish bar on 44th Street. Big surprise. The only bars you can find in America are Irish, stage Irish at any rate. All shamrocks and Gaelic slogans; I wouldn't have set foot in one decked out like it at home, it would be like asking for a bullet, but then I suppose I was being a bit optimistic in holding out for a New York pub catering solely for British Unionist Loyalists with a healthy disregard for all living politicians. Mike's Bar was small, poky; there was an air of viciousness about it despite the fact that it was mostly empty. The toilet door could only be opened by means of a security buzzer behind the bar, which was a nice touch.

I got the third drink into me, sitting on my stool, tapping my foot idly to the folk music blasting from the jukebox. Some things should be played at high volume, Irish folk music isn't one of them. I don't know who they were playing it for – it was gone midnight and the only customers were three elderly black guys and a middle-aged couple conversing animatedly in Spanish. The barman was German, so it was hardly his choice of music. I took a look at the jukebox. In amongst the fiddlee-dee trash there were a couple of gems – Van singing 'Gloria' and U2's 'I Will Follow'. I slipped two quarters in and took my stool again – I'd to wait fifteen minutes and another drink for my selection to come round but then, ah, the opening strains of the Edge's guitar, ecstatically brash and then whoosh – from behind the bar the German turned the sound down to the barely audible.

I tried complaining, but either his English wasn't that good or he was pretending not to understand or perhaps my Northern accent was drunk thick; it didn't matter. I slouched out of the bar and headed back up into Times Square.

I stood mesmerized by the neon for five minutes until I started getting hassled by a couple of crackheads and moved on into 42nd Street. Here the rows of old cinemas and theatres had long been claimed by the sex shops. Patricia and I had giggled through them one cold December day – how many years before? Five, six? – bent double at the plastic and rubber, the magazines and videos, all honestly displayed like so many groceries. Even the little video booths at the back of the shops had America written all over them, little rooms where grown men masturbated over twenty-five-cent-a-minute videos: quick, clean, tasteless, fulfilling while they lasted but ultimately unsatisfying; the McDonald's of wank. Or so I'd heard.

'Live sex show, sir?'

I turned at the voice. An Indian. In a tux.

'Is there a bar?'

His brows furrowed.

'Live sex show, sir?'

I shrugged. Temptation. How long had it been since I'd seen a naked woman?

I walked into the shop. Magazines. Videos. A lot of middle-aged men shuffling about trying to disguise the bulges in their trousers. At the back of the shop there was another Indian in another tux; he stood at the foot of some stairs; he wore a leather pouch round his waist.

'Live show upstairs,' he said. 'Five dollars.'

I took out some notes and dropped them. I picked them up and studied them. The printing seemed to be impossibly faint. I looked up at the Indian. He shook his head. I offered them up to him. He extracted a note. Maybe it was a five. Maybe it was a ten. It could have been a three. He handed me a small round token then stepped aside and I carefully mounted the stairs.

A strong smell of disinfectant. Darkness. Too dark at first, then as my eyes grew accustomed to the gloom I could make out figures moving about in the glow of the faintest of creamy neon strips. I was standing in a long hall, with doors running up each side of it perhaps ten feet apart.

'Are you interested in me, sir?'

I turned, squinted. A tall girl, blond hair, wearing a two-piece bathing suit, dark blue or black, stilettos.

'Uuuuuh . . .'

Suddenly it didn't seem such a good idea.

'Go into the room, sir . . .' She smiled. Nice teeth. Brighter than the lights. She opened a door. More of a cupboard than a room. Four blank walls. Two foot square. Brightly lit. A telephone attached to one wall. She took my arm and led me in, then stepped back to the door. 'Put your token in the slot, sir,' she said, smiled, and closed the door behind her.

The cupboard stank of cleaning fluid, if that isn't a contradiction in terms. I suddenly felt claustrophobic and reached for the door again, opened it and stepped out. The girl was just entering the next cupboard. She stopped.

'Is everything okay, sir?'

I nodded.

'You're sure?'

I nodded and held up the token. 'In the slot?'

'Yes, sir, in the slot.'

I nodded again and backed into the cupboard. I shook my head.

I closed the door and rested my head against the far wall for a moment. Either it was sticky or I was. I took a deep breath. The spins, the horrible, killer bokey spins wouldn't be long in coming now, the promise to give up the drink to follow. The hollow man: emptied of sick, emptied of spirit. Blame it on Patricia, blame it on women, blame it on . . .

I put the token in the slot and the wall to my left slowly rose. The girl stood in front of me. Still smiling. Her room was much the same, but for a wooden bench behind her. She lifted her phone and indicated that I should lift mine.

I lifted the receiver. 'Is that the Samaritans?' I asked.

Her brows furrowed. 'Sir?'

I shook my head.

'Hi,' I said.

'Hi.' Accent – New York; quite cultivated really.

'What's your name?'

'Lauren.'

'How old are you, Lauren?'

'Twenty-one.'

She was beautiful. Her hair was clearly dyed. She had on a little too much make-up. She had the sallowness you get with working under fluorescent lights for too long. But she was beautiful. She took her top off.

Even mad drunk, a topless stranger is bizarre. I looked at her face for as long as I could, then looked at her breasts. They were large. They had to be, really, in this business. Larger than Patricia's. Fleshy. Soft, Jaffa Cake nipples.

'Would you like to see some more?'

I nodded.

'It's normal to give a girl a tip.'

I nodded.

'Would you like to see some more, sir?'

I nodded some more.

'It's normal to give a girl a tip.'

'Don't sleep in the subway.'

'Sir?'

'How much?'

She shrugged. Her breasts wobbled. Her smile stayed

fixed, but her eyes coolly evaluated me. Blue eyes, slowly taking in the sophisticated international reporter doing his research.

'Five dollars.'

Yeah, well.

I took the money from my pocket and showed it to her.

'Just wait there, sir, I'll come and get it.' She had her top clipped back on and was out of her room and into mine in a couple of seconds. I gave her the money. She grasped it deftly, taking care not to touch me. In another couple of seconds she was back in front of me, phone in hand, bikini top on the floor, still smiling. Then she slipped down her briefs. She'd shaved her pubic hair. She swivelled on her heels, bent to retrieve her costume, then walked to the bench, turned, sat down and spread her legs.

She was beautiful and she'd bright, keen eyes, but looking at her there, bent uncomfortably back on the bench, she was as erotic as a bucket of cod. She wasn't Patricia, she wasn't a Patricia substitute, she was a body, just a body, without spirit, without love or romance, just an exposed body with a pale valley of flesh, a penis fly trap, glowering at me in the harsh light.

I shook my head.

'Is anything wrong, sir?'

'No.'

'Don't you want to touch yourself?'

'No. I'm sorry.'

Her smile widened. 'No need to be sorry.'

'Yeah, well.'

'You still have two minutes left. Is there anything you want me to do?'

'Put your clothes on.'

She didn't take much persuasion. She was ready for the beach in seconds.

'Are you on vacation?'

I nodded. 'Sort of.'

'Where are you from?'

'Ireland. No. Sorry. That's too much of a simplification. The United Kingdom. No. Sorry. Northern Ireland. The six counties of Ireland that will always be British.'

She nodded in a detached kind of way. The smile slipped a little. 'I'm sorry,' I said. 'I'm not a nut. I'm just a bit drunk. I miss my wife.'

'A lot of men who come here do. Miss their wives. Hate their wives. All sorts.'

'Does it not put you off men completely, all this?'

'It puts me off the sort of men who would come here.'

'That's understandable.'

We stood looking at each other uncomfortably for a moment. I felt foolish and sober. 'I'm sorry,' I said. 'It's not you. You're very attractive.'

'It doesn't matter. It's your money.'

'I know it is. But I don't want you to think . . .' I shook my head. 'This must sound pretty pathetic.'

She shook her head and smiled. Her eyes darted to the

wall above her. Doubtless a clock, telling her to hurry her client towards climax.

'I don't suppose I could persuade you to go for a drink?'

She shook her head and smiled.

'You must get asked out all the time.'

She shook her head and smiled.

'Latvia is one of the most interesting of the Baltic States.'

She shook her head and smiled. Not even listening. Of course. Who would?

I didn't know how to leave. Whether just to walk straight out. Wave goodbye. Apologize again. Wish her all the best. Offer her tickets for the fight. In the end my mind was made up for me. The wall slid silently down and the light in my little room blinked suddenly brighter.

I opened the door and walked into the gloom. Her door remained resolutely closed. She would remain there until the weirdo was safely gone. I shook my head. Maybe I had made a fool of myself, but not as big a fool as someone who would have masturbated in front of her. And I'd proved a point: that it wasn't just sex with Patricia that I was missing; it was her spirit and her love. A silly, obvious point, perhaps, but one that made perfect sense, to a drunk seeking self-justification for staring between the spread legs of a beautiful woman for ten dollars.

At the top of the stairs I paused for a moment, steadied myself against the rail and then made a resolution: one more drink, then sleep, and a new, sober beginning tomorrow and a heart-on-sleeve phone call to Patricia, promising anything.

12

Many studies have been made of time travel. Well, actually, not that many, but certainly some. Three or four, maybe. Equally, many studies have been made of how to travel great distances in the minimum of time. Probably it amounts to the same thing. I know nothing about physics. I don't even know if it concerns physics. Let me put it another way: how the bloody hell does that transporter on *Star Trek* work?

What scientists (physicists?) have always failed to take into account in their otherwise learned studies is the importance of alcohol to time travel and geographical displacement. Even a fledgling drunk will appreciate the important role alcohol plays in covering great distances and squeezing long hours into seconds. A drunk can move effortlessly from one place to another: he may not know how, he can remember leaving, he can remember arriving, but has no knowledge of what went on in between, but that is scarcely important. He can find his way from one place to another through a maze that would confound the most intrepid explorer, and he can do it while shuffling along like a crab and vomiting at every intersection. It is a wonder of science, and one which too few people appreciate.

I was able to ponder all this, although not for the first time, as I lay in the double bed, torn between worshipping the giant-sized poster of Debbie Harry on one wall and investigating the blonde lying beside me. Of course one of them was more accessible and, doubtless, younger, but ultimately more troublesome. Usually it is best not to enquire, but to slip away and figure out what you can later, or, best of all, leave it mysterious. What you don't know can't hurt you, unless it turns out to be a distressing sexual disease.

I decided this was the best course of action. Beat a retreat. Thin curtains allowed a little light into the room: a double bed, dusty mirror, dressing table with a minimum of womanly sprays and ointments, hand basin, air conditioner, large TV, video, big ghetto blaster, clothes piled everywhere. I slipped from the bed. I only had on my underpants. I had charmed someone and she wasn't a thousand miles away.

Lauren. The stripper. Her back was to me, her long hair dishevelled on the pillow beside her. Bare shoulders, strap of something showing on her upper arm. Two or three colour snaps of her with young kids, presumably relatives of some description, were taped to the bottom corner of the mirror. She looked younger, fresher, than I vaguely remembered.

Clothes may have been everywhere, but none of them were mine. Doubtless they had been ripped off in a frenzy in another room. I stepped quietly to the door and opened it: I peered out into a bright hallway. I blinked for a second in the light and then checked the time – two hairs past a freckle, as they say. The watch had gone in the heat of passion as well. But the hall wasn't a hall, it was a corridor, and the rooms off it weren't another part of Lauren's home, but appeared to be studio apartments. I cursed silently. It meant the chances of my making a clean getaway were much reduced. I would have to go poking through her gear for my clothes, and the chances of doing that without waking her seemed remote.

Extremely remote, in fact, as she was sitting up in bed when I closed the door.

I smiled and said good morning. Sort of smiled. My lip hurt, felt thick, and my voice sounded like it had been dragged screaming through a mangle.

Lauren smiled back. It was a more human smile than I remembered. Perhaps I had humanized her. Clawed her back from the sordid underbelly. For all the summer's-pond serenity of her face she might well have breathed through little gills hidden beneath her flowing locks.

'That'll hurt some,' she said as I fingered my lip.

'That must have been some lovemaking,' I said, and tried not to sound too impressed with myself.

'Excuse me?' she said, only half a smile now.

'Uh. My lip.'

She nodded slightly. 'How do you feel?'

Hung over? Gloriously fulfilled? In love? Guilty? Frightened? Macho? Unfaithful? Vengeful? It was too much to contemplate.

'Uh. Okay.'

'You look awful.'

I nodded. Par for the course. 'Someone once said I looked a bit like James Stewart in black and white.'

'I never saw *Black and White*. Who else was in it?'

'Nah, I . . . Listen, no disrespect, like, but did you bite my lip?'

'You don't remember?'

I shook my head. 'Sorry. I'm sure it was wonderful, but I seem . . .'

'You don't remember falling down the stairs?'

'What stairs? Here?'

'No. At the club. You remember me in the booth?'

'Yes. Of course.' I felt my face redden. Suddenly I was thirteen again peering at my first naked woman in a dirty magazine, and being caught in the act. I felt the need for protection. 'Are my clothes about?'

She shook her head ruefully. 'You really don't remember, do you?'

I shook mine too.

'You poor man.'

'Uh . . .'

'You were my last trick of the night. When I came out of the club you were lying face down on the footpath. You'd fallen down the stairs drunk, and then the bouncers threw you out. There was a crowd of jackals round you. A cop chased them off and for whatever reason I laid claim to you and walked you back here until you could sober up. Remember?'

'No. Sorry.'

'You weren't wearing much more than you have on now.'

'Jesus. My wallet.'

'Your trousers.'

'My shoes.'

'Your socks.'

'Jesus. I could have been killed.'

'You very nearly were.'

'Jesus. I don't believe they took my shoes.'

'Shoes are a valuable commodity.'

'I don't believe they took my socks.'

'Socks are a valuable commodity too.'

'Thank God they didn't take my underpants.'

'They aren't that desperate.'

I had nowhere to put my hands. In awkward situations I like to put my hands in my pockets. Someone had stolen my pockets. I bit at a thumbnail that wasn't there.

'I have a lot to thank you for.'

She shrugged, which was normally my speciality.

'A hooker with a heart of gold,' I said.

Her eyes blazed. She reared up out of the bed, blue slip falling about her breasts, and aimed a stiletto at my head. It clattered off the door, which had more to do with her aim than my powers of evasion. 'I'm no whore!' she thundered.

I shot out a placatory hand, and kept the other defensively about my crotch. 'I'm sorry! I know! Jesus. Sorry. I must be in shock.'

'I know what I do isn't very respectable. But I'm no whore.'

'I know. I'm sorry. And I can't thank you enough.'

The angry hurricane subsided, leaving her face serene again. She sat back on the bed. She snorted, looked up at me. 'I'm sorry too. I've a bit of a temper. I forgot you were on vacation. You weren't to know whether I was a hooker or not. I suppose it's a fine difference in most people's eyes.'

I sat on the edge of the bed. 'It's a big difference. Of course it is. I'm just happy you looked out for me. You took a big chance. What possessed you to bring me back here at all?'

'I don't know. It's not something I would normally dream of doing.'

'Maybe you have some Irish blood in you.'

She shook her head.

'Would you like some?' Furrowed brow. 'Sorry. It's an old joke. A nervous joke. I must thank you. I always get myself in these awful situations and people pull me out of them out of the goodness of their hearts. I suppose I'm blessed that way.'

'I tried to get you back to your hotel, but you wouldn't tell me its name.'

'I probably thought I could seduce you. I have these sexual delusions when I'm drunk. My wife said when we were courting – there's an old-fashioned word for you – that my idea of a romantic four-course dinner was a bowl of soup, "of course, of course, of course I love you" and straight into bed. Sober, I'm really quite responsible. Did I try anything I shouldn't have?'

'You didn't get the chance.'

'But you trusted a stranger to sleep beside you?'

'Not really. I only brought you back long enough to sober up so that you'd be able to find your way home, but you were unconscious virtually by the time you hit the bed. And besides, I keep a gun under the pillow that could blow your balls off.'

Lauren wasn't called Lauren and she wasn't twenty-one. Lauren was nineteen, and Lauren was Paula. By day she was a student at New York University, by night she paid for it by dropping her shorts for sad people. She wasn't a hooker, but, like she said, it was a fine line, particularly to a Presbyterian. Her studio flat, her bedsit, was part of a large apartment block in Greenwich Village.

Paula got dressed and went out to get us some coffee. I didn't have the heart to tell her that I was a Coke man, or worse, that I was now a Diet Coke man, a small but significant tugging of the forelock to the new health sensibilities of my generation. She brought back two paper cups and a couple of chocolate doughnuts from her friend Duncan.

We supped in silence for a while, then, wiping a crumb from her mouth – beautiful mouth – she said, 'You talked about your wife a lot last night.'

'In the booth.'

'On the way home. And back here. You must love her a lot.'

'I keep trying to tell her.'

'But she won't listen.'

'She listens. I just say the wrong things. Do the wrong things.'

'You say you're a journalist.'

'Do I?'

'You did last night. Are you? Or was it a line?'

'Who would ever use that as a line? It's like saying, hey, I'm a leper, take my arm for this dance.'

'So you are a journalist?'

'Mmmm. Sort of. I was for a long time. I'm trying to be a writer. Of the old school. Big, epic works. My wife calls me a literary dinosaur, a thesaurus. I keep the money coming in with the odd bit of journalism. Right now I'm writing a book about a boxer. It's hardly literature, but it keeps the wolves from the door.'

She smiled kindly. 'You're very sweet, y'know?'

'Thank you. That's an awful thing to say to a man sitting on your bed with two-day-old underpants on.'

'Have you ever written to your wife?'

'Written? No. My solicitor has, will that do?'

'Of course not. Have you never sat down and written her a proper letter?'

'No.'

'Why not?'

'I've never thought of it. You phone your wife. You don't write to her.'

'But you can say so much more in a letter.'

'My solicitor told me not to put anything in writing.'

'I don't mean that kind of a letter. You say you always say the wrong thing to her. But why say it? You say what you do best is write. A thesaurus, whatever. Why don't you write to her and tell her how much you love her? Spell it all out to her.'

'You think?'

'Any woman would appreciate it.'

'She's not any woman.'

'Have you tried everything else?'

'I've tried everything else.'

'So do it.'

'I haven't got a pen.'

She shook her head. 'You're scared, aren't you?'

I nodded.

'It takes a lot of guts for a man to expose himself on a page.'

'But not very many to expose himself in a sex club.'

'You were scared of that too, weren't you?'

I nodded.

'What are you?'

'A pathetic little man scared of life.'

'And what are you going to do?'

'Learn to expose myself in sex clubs.'

'No.'

'Write to my wife and tell her how much I love her and beg her to come back so that we can have the happiest marriage in the world and forget all our past mistakes.'

'Yup.'

'Okay.'

'I'll even furnish a pen.'

'Deal.'

I've walked the streets in some crazy-looking things before, but it has most always been to do with fashion. This time I got to walk up Broadway in a pair of yellow ski pants and a pink T-shirt. It wasn't Paula's fault that she was a fair bit smaller than me and those were about the only things that would fit. She wanted to lend me the money, but I wouldn't have it. She had done enough. More than enough. I was alive, and I had a mission. Patricia wouldn't know what had hit her. She'd fall for me hook, line and sinker once I'd reminded her what we were all about. There was optimism in the air and a crazy-looking nut on Broadway, but that's what New York is all about.

13

'Incredible, eh?'

Bobby McMaster's awe-filled face looked out over the Madison Square Garden arena, five floors up on Seventh Avenue. From where we stood, in a $210,000-a-year suite, the arena looked deceptively small, but our guide assured us that it would hold twenty thousand fans.

'Should accommodate both of your followers too, eh, Bobby?' Stanley Matchitt said, smiling across at his friend.

'Yeah, Stanley. Looks good though, doesn't it?'

We all nodded – Geordie McClean, the contender himself, me and the guide, a rotund chap with a glint in his eye which suggested he was a sport's fan who had landed his dream job. It was a beautiful morning and most everything was well with the world. I had fresh clothes on, I'd made arrangements to get replacement traveller's cheques, a new

Visa card, and I'd already recovered some of my dignity and composed half my letter to Patricia, albeit in my head. Putting pen to paper was never an easy task, even if it was my chosen profession. Bobby McMaster had put in sixteen rounds of sparring in a luxurious gym on Central Park West and didn't look too bad, considering his talent. My swollen mouth gave a curl to my lip that made me look more like Humphrey Bogart than James Stewart, which was no bad thing in a tough-guy business like boxing.

'Yes, sir,' continued the guide, 'they've all been here – Muhammad Ali, of course, Smokin' Joe Frazier, Joe Louis . . . and soon we'll be adding your name to the list, sir. Bobby McMaster fighting for the world title at Madison Square Garden. We don't get that much boxing at the Garden any more, sir, so we're more than glad to be hosting your fight. Already looks like a sell-out too, you'll be pleased to know.'

McMaster had a faraway look in his eye. 'Say that again, that stuff about me fighting for the title.'

The guide smiled. He upped the voice a bit, like he was announcing to the entire arena, threw out his arms. 'Bobby McMaster fighting for the world heavyweight title at Madison Square Garden!'

We all smiled. McMaster glowed with pride. 'This is what it's all about,' he said, his voice near breaking. 'Jesus, Muhammad Ali fought here. Muhammad Ali. Jesus.'

'Why's there no ring?' Matchitt asked.

'Early days yet, Stanley,' said McClean.

'We have several events going on here daily, sir,' said the

guide. 'Basketball, rock concerts, conventions – we've a highly efficient team which ensures all events run smoothly. The boxing ring itself won't go up until the evening of the fight.' He pointed out over the arena. 'Those guys down there are putting up a stage for Bruce Springsteen. He's playing here tonight.'

Matchitt nodded.

'Can we get some tickets?' McMaster asked. 'Mary would love to see him.'

'I'll see what I can do,' said McClean.

'Ah! Gentlemen!'

We all turned. The voice was distinctive. Marvin 'Poodle' Clay stood at the suite door, flanked by a couple of heavies.

'Impressed, are we?'

McClean shrugged. 'It'll do,' he said, not very convincingly.

Clay advanced regally down the steps. Beautiful silk suit, not the trashy backstreet Thai job you'd expect. Despite the fact that he was a hustling ex-con, he looked well. The nearest I'd ever come to something that expensive was a libel suit. He put a bejewelled hand out to McClean, shook, then grasped McMaster's hand and held it. 'Your boy here certainly has a flair for publicity,' he said, smiling expansively and staring intently at Bobby. 'Have you seen this yet?'

He turned back and accepted a neatly folded newspaper from one of his heavies. He unfolded it carefully and held it up for us all to see. The paper was the *Amsterdam Review*. The headline took up most of the front page: SONS OF MUHAMMAD THREAT TO WHITE BOXER.

McClean grabbed the paper. McMaster snatched it from him. He pulled it close to his face. He shook his head a couple of times, then looked up, then down, and read aloud:

'The Sons of Muhammad, the military arm of the Brothers of Muhammad, the militant Afro-American organization, today issued a death threat against the white boxer Robert McMaster, alleging that he had made anti-Afro-American comments during a press conference in New York. The Sons of Muhammad, who are believed to have been behind the bombing of the *New York Times* building in July and the fatal stabbing of the television star Rabbi Lionel Black in October, allege that the boxer, from Crossmaheart, Ireland, insulted the entire Afro-American population by comparing them to snakes and vipers at a press conference for his world title fight with African-American hero Mike Tyson.'

McMaster shook his head. 'Snakes are vipers,' he said quietly.

McClean grabbed the paper back. 'What is this shite?' He read on down the story, then looked up at Clay. 'Is this worth worrying about?'

'I never ignore a threat,' Clay said, putting his arm about McClean's shoulders, 'but I wouldn't worry unduly. I have a certain influence with the Afro-American community, as you might imagine.'

'But if they bombed the *New York Times* . . .'

'They claim to have bombed the *New York Times*. Certainly

somebody bombed it, but whether it was the Sons of Muhammad . . .'

'And this rabbi . . .'

'More likely a Palestinian . . .'

McClean passed the paper along to me. It was tabloid. At first glance it looked badly designed, which was hardly relevant, but one likes to keep a professional hand in. 'Does this have much of a circulation?'

Clay shook his head. 'It's free, so there are plenty of copies about. No real way of knowing if anyone reads them. It's bankrolled by the same people who bankroll the Brothers and Sons of Muhammad, so it's hardly an objective piece of reporting. They like to whip up a bit of fear in Harlem. Paranoia. It's good for the collection plate. They're viciously anti-white, but I don't think they're a real menace. Amateurs, really. Don't worry. I have it under control. Besides, it's good publicity. I'll put on a couple of guards, get them to pose with some artillery and the contender here. The TV news teams will love it.'

'Shouldn't you just play it down?' I suggested. 'Deny the accusations of racism and leave it at that. I mean, maybe the Sons of Muhammad aren't a real threat, but there's the off-chance that the publicity might inspire someone to really have a go at Bobby.' I nodded at McClean. 'You know what it's like in Belfast, all organizations have splinter groups they farm out their nuttier members to. The UDA has the UFF, the IRA has the INLA, the Presbyterians have the Boys' Brigade. The Sons of Muhammad might have the same.'

Matchitt touched my shoulder. He nodded at McClean. 'He's right.'

McMaster rubbed at his chin. 'You mean like the Sons of the Sons of Muhammad? Wouldn't that make them the Grandsons of Muhammad?'

McClean snorted. 'I don't think this is a time for levity, Bobby.'

McMaster shook his head. 'Why not? I can't change what they think about me. I'll issue a statement and go about my business as normal. It's up to you and Poodle here to protect me. Right now the thought of getting my head knocked off by Tyson is a bigger worry. I wouldn't tell Mary about this either, she'll only fret.'

McMaster turned for the steps that led back up out of the suite. McClean stepped after him and Clay and his heavies followed.

'Did I tell you you've been invited to take part in the St Patrick's Day parade?' Clay called.

'Brilliant,' said McMaster, sarkily.

Matchitt spat over the side of the suite, watched as the spittle hit a purple plastic seat below.

'Charming,' I said.

'Are you really worried?'

'Constantly,' I said.

I turned to follow the rest of the team. Matchitt snagged my arm. 'Did you see this yet?' he said, and from inside his jacket he produced a pistol. He brandished it with the pride of an eight-year-old.

'Jesus,' I said. I've no idea what kind of a pistol. A black one. One that kills. The make doesn't matter much. 'That's all we need.'

There was an annoying smirk on his face. 'To protect, one must have the means of protection,' he said.

'Jesus,' I said, and pulled away from him.

'What is wrong with you, Starkey?'

'I just don't fancy the idea of you with a gun, Stanley. You've never exactly been reluctant about using violence.'

'Ach, stop coming over the fucking saint, Starkey. This is New York. Everyone has guns.'

'You're not everyone. You're a nut.'

'Ex-nut, if you please.'

'Aye, sure.'

'Wait and see, Starkey. Don't prejudge.'

'Aye, they prejudged Hitler too. Lovely man.'

'Starkey, just because I have a gun doesn't mean I'm going to kill anyone. I have a job to do and I'm going to do it.' He slipped the gun back into his pocket and zipped up his jacket. 'Still,' he added, with a malicious gleam in his eyes, 'I couldn't believe how easy it was to get. Just walked into the shop, signed a piece of paper, and Bob's your uncle. If it had been that easy in Belfast in the old days there wouldn't have been so many Fenians running about, I'll tell you that.'

'Ah, the voice of reason again.'

Matchitt tutted. 'I've changed, Starkey.'

'Yeah. Sure. The proof is in the pudding, Stanley.'

'The proof of the pudding is in the eating.'

131

'The proof is in the pudding.'

'The proof of the pudding is in the eating.'

'The proof is in the pudding, Stanley, that's the saying.'

'It's not. The saying is, the proof of the pudding is in the eating.'

'It's fucking not.'

'It fuckin' is.'

'It fucking well isn't.'

'Does it fucking matter?'

'No, it doesn't fucking matter.'

'Okay.'

'I was just worried you might shoot me if I didn't agree with you.'

'I tell you, Starkey, I'm a changed man.'

'Aye, the proof is in the pudding.'

'The proof of the fucking pudding is in the fucking eating, Starkey.'

'You're wrong.'

'I'm not wrong.'

He had a light grip on my jacket. I pulled sharply away and mounted the steps. I heard him curse behind me. I tensed, just slightly. There was always the possibility of a bullet. It would, at the very least, prove my point, although it probably wouldn't be worth it.

The rest of the team was just disappearing down an escalator beside the Play by Play Bar, and I debated very quickly whether to catch them up or go in for a drink. It wasn't much of a debate, seeing as how I'd sworn off alcohol, but it was made undeniably easier by the fact that when I reached it the bar was closed.

Stanley came up behind me as I stepped onto the escalator. I kept my back to him.

'We'll see,' he said quietly over my shoulder. I continued to ignore him and increased my speed to rejoin the group as a couple of security men ushered them out of the locked gate at the top of the foyer. As we emerged onto Seventh Avenue, three camera crews converged on us from different directions.

Clay didn't look unduly surprised. He turned to McClean. 'I'll do the talking, shall I?'

McClean nodded, but didn't appear to be too happy about it. I'd once thought of McMaster as a big fish in a small pond, but less than plankton in the world ocean of boxing. Now I could see that McClean was much the same, a hustler and an organizer par excellence within the headline-weary but defiantly tiny confines of Northern Ireland; in the wider world, and especially in the centre of all hustles, New York, he really wasn't up to much. Clay was calling the shots and McClean knew his place.

Clay pulled McMaster forward and together they faced the cameras. An earnest young woman, short black hair, beige trouser suit, thrust a microphone in the contender's face.

'Bobby, any reaction to the death threat issued by the Sons of Muhammad?'

'Doesn't worry me in the slightest.'

Clay pulled the microphone round to him. 'Ruth, you

were at the press conference the other day, you know there was no racism in anything Bobby McMaster said. I believe this threat can be traced back to a third party running scared at the possible outcome of this fight.'

'Would you care to explain that, Mr Clay?' another reporter said, thrusting his microphone forward.

'No.'

'Are you suggesting that the Tyson camp might be behind this death threat?'

Clay smiled benignly. 'Of course not.'

The third reporter muscled in. 'Will you be providing any extra security for the contender, Mr Clay?'

'We will be providing some extra security, yes, but mostly to keep all of you reporters away from Bobby – he needs to prepare for this fight in peace and tranquillity – he doesn't need all this extra pressure.'

'Is the pressure getting to you, Bobby?'

'No, the pressure isn't getting to me.'

'Do you regret making any comments at the press conference?'

'No.'

'Do you wish to clarify any of your comments?'

'Only insofar as to say that if anyone was able to take anything of a racist nature from what I said, then, well, they've got wee sweetie mice in their heads.'

And that shut them up.

14

Dear Patricia

Where to start, eh? Immediately you will realize this is a bit unorthodox for me, in fact I'll be pleasantly surprised if you even recognize the handwriting. Perhaps you have already flicked to the end to see who it's from?

Well, hello! There we go, starting with a misplaced sense of joviality when I feel like my heart has been ripped out and pumped full of lead and then replaced; like my ribs are being whacked continuously with a toffee hammer and someone has lodged a three-month-old Brussels sprout in amongst my taste buds. Is this what being lovesick does for you? I should remember. Who am I lovesick for? As if you didn't know. You, of course. I only pray to God that you will find it in your heart somewhere to forgive me and take me back and love me again, because I've been a silly bugger for too long and it is time to take my life in hand, our life in hand and start again.

So, how are you? Silly question. Of course. The sort of question I should reserve for a phone call. But phone calls were never my strong point, something I have come to realize during the long hours of lonely contemplation I have undertaken since we parted. Hotel rooms are good for contemplation. There are distractions, of course, particularly in a city like New York, but I have been largely immune to them, save for one bout with alcohol which resulted in a somewhat vague phone call to you, which ended up with your dad. I'm sorry. If he hasn't told you about it, well, don't ask, but I'm mentioning it to you anyway because it is part of my new philosophy – complete honesty, trust, abstinence from alcohol, faithfulness. Quite a list, you'll agree, and I know you'll be thinking, God, here we go again, I've heard this all before. Of course you have. But I mean it this time. And I've said that before as well. I don't blame you if you don't believe me, but if all our years together mean anything at all to you, please give me this chance.

In the past I have made promises to you and I have broken those promises, not deliberately, not unconsciously exactly, but through my own weak character, always believing that you would forgive me, take me back, because you loved me. It is only since we truly separated and you refused to take me back that I have come to realize the depth of my feelings for you, the depth of my love, and ponder upon how I threw it all away.

Usually marriages fall apart through an over-familiarity which breeds boredom or lack of togetherness which leads to the establishment of new relationships and ultimately unfaithfulness. With us, I suppose, it was both – from the debacle of my job attempting to be an information officer for the Government, for which I was patently unsuited, and our mutual affairs caused by the disenchantment of that period, to our ultimate separation caused by my continued affair with alcohol, which ushered in your affair with Tony.

You may be cringing at all this. You may be hopelessly in love with Tony. Any feelings you had for me may have long gone. Certainly you are carrying his child. But I think in the end that although I have been a complete bastard to you, you will realize how much I love you, and that you, too, love me back.

We can be great again!

Do you remember how we met? Neither do I. Even I, an acknowledged authority on the many states of drunkenness, failed to match you in drinking capacity on that fateful night. I do remember the next night though, when the hangover from hell stopped me going out. I remember sitting in the front room feeling sorry for myself and wishing you were there, but we'd parted sick, without the capacity even to exchange numbers. I was watching TV – no, it was on, but I was staring out the window, and the next thing I saw was you bouncing up the road on a space hopper you'd stolen from someone's front garden and I knew immediately I was in love.

And then talking to you, enjoying your sharpness. Do you know, right from the start, I kept a notebook of all the things you said to me, all the bright, witty, loving things you said to me, things that I've thus far been scared to use in any of my own writing in case you thought I wasn't a literary genius in my own right.

Knowing you, you won't believe me – you always did undervalue your own talents, thinking because I was a journalist I could write, but that because you were 'only' a tax inspector you couldn't. What shite. The only thing being a tax inspector stops you from being is a normal human being. (Joke.)

I don't have the notebook with me, but in the months since we split up I have looked at it from time to time and it has always brought a smile to my face, not just at the lines themselves, but the memories that go with them.

I think it was the second night together, when I was lying in your arms, you said, 'I feel like I've known you for a maternity,' and I, being me, even in such a romantic moment sought to correct you with 'Eternity', and you said, 'No, maternity, about nine months.'

Or the first time (I think, I hope!) you had an orgasm (with me) you said: 'I like going to bed with Liverpool fans, they're so used to coming second.'

Remember? Those early days when we didn't argue, at all. How could we do that, having so many different interests; what you liked I hated, what you hated I liked.

Remember when you were on another of those bloody silly diets you used to get so serious about, and you phoned me up in tears and it took me ages to get you to speak properly and when you did you said you'd been arrested by the diet police for unlawful caramel knowledge.

And it's not all funny either. I've made notes about you angry as well, not just with me – there's plenty of them – but with others, out in public. Remember that restaurant in London with all the airs and graces where you bawled out that waiter with the stutter for messing up our order and then trying to say it was our fault for ordering incorrectly and you saying we weren't the ones with the embarrassing stutter. And after he'd gone you sat there with tears in your eyes and the whole restaurant looking at you and you just said quietly, but with that wee way you have of making yourself heard, 'I don't mind people with stutters, I have all the time in the world for people with stutters, but if they turn out to be sleekit fuckers as well I'll take the pish out of them as I see fit.' And I just wanted to get up and throw my arms round you and tell you I loved you, but couldn't because I'd had too much drink and my legs wouldn't work. Did I ever tell you I was proud of you then? Because you know how I am, they could serve me a fried dictionary in a restaurant and I'd feel bad about complaining.

During my contemplations I've thought about that restaurant quite a lot, and my own reactions to it. I had always thought I didn't complain myself because, well, because I was such a laid-back person it didn't matter much, that any problem would just wash over me. I've gone through life like that, thinking of myself as laid-back, thinking I was the archetypal tranquil port in the midst of a stormy ocean. It is only since I've been here that I've come to realize that I'm not like that at all, that in reality I am just one big ball of emotions that I've been afraid to unleash, not even to you. It has been a revelation, this self-examination. Not quite on a par with Saul on the road to Damascus, perhaps, but pretty damn important to me, and, hopefully, to you. Because I never treated you the way you deserved. Of course I told you that I loved you, but it was a flippant kind of love, I might as well have been saying good morning or good night. Instead of lavishing love upon you, I took you for granted; I realize now that having achieved the state of marriage, I thought I had done everything expected of me, that I could go about concentrating on myself and my career; one half of me with my head stuck in the clouds dreaming of literary greatness, the other half with my journalism and my drinking, which is one and the same really; and as you know, there are no third halves in life, which meant that you were excluded. I'm sorry. I was wrong.

Some of it was your fault, of course. Neither of us are perfect. But even though we are chalk and cheese, and always will be, I believe with all my heart that we are perfect for each other. Look back to our good days, then when next you laugh with Tony, presuming that you do, is it the same, or is there something missing, and is that something me?

I know you always wanted children. Although we did all the practical work, nothing ever arrived. We took the precautions, mostly, but you always had that little hope that from those nights when we forgot or you were off the pill for whatever reason you might get pregnant; I could always tell, even if you never said it. I don't know why it never happened. Perhaps my sperm were crap swimmers. If you had had a baby sure it probably would have been born wearing armbands.

Whatever my deficiencies were, or are, Tony clearly does not share them, at least in that department. Perhaps in others, but that's just my jealousy coming through. I know nothing about him, besides the fact that he can throw a decent punch. I don't know what your feelings for him really are because I have been too scared to delve too deeply; because I love you, any protestations of love for another man bring me one step closer to . . .

I don't know . . . I should cross that bit out, but I'm just writing this as it comes so that it's completely honest . . . okay, I don't know what I'll do if you love him.

But what if he doesn't love you? What if he wants nothing to do with the baby? You must be tearing yourself apart worrying about it. You probably don't need your long-departed husband bending your ear on lost love while you try to figure out what to do with your baby.

Perhaps you've thought about getting rid of it. Don't. No matter what your thoughts on Tony, or his decision, it/he/she is your baby. It's a little you. It may be a little bit him as well, but sure you can beat that out of him/her/it.

Let me make you an offer. Come back to me and have the baby. Be mine and he/she/it will be mine as well. I won't even say it'll be as if it's my child, it will be my child; I will never think of it in any other way; even in the depths of our worst argument I will not cast it up, for there is nothing to cast up.

Come to me here in New York.

Do you remember we always hated those Hollywood love stories? Hated the idea of people's lives being ruined all over the world because they were pursuing a mythical idea of true love they had fallen for in the cinema. And then we went to see *When Harry Met Sally* and cried our eyes out and it turned out we were old Hollywood romantics after all, that we thought in those tough cynical times we needed the Hollywood idea of love to hope for in the midst of the grim realities of life. Remember we went through our hopelessly romantic phase after that – we bought the little puppy, and for months neither of us had the guts to say that we didn't like it for fear of hurting each other and it just absolutely ruled our lives. Jesus, remember the day we found ourselves hiding upstairs so that we wouldn't have to play with it? It wasn't the pup's fault; we were suffering from first love laziness and wanted to recline in each other's arms in front of the box and maybe occasionally pet a laconic puppy, not to have to sit with our feet up on the couch so that it wouldn't eat our toes or spend every night wiping slabbers off the glass table. There was such a relief when your dad finally took it away. He said he had a good home for it, but I've always had a sneaking suspicion that the Mr Watters he talked about had more to do with a plastic bin bag, a couple of bricks and the River Lagan than a home for unwanted puppies.

Still, it was the thought that counted, and we thought a good puppy.

Remember the Magic Settee? How long since we made love on that? Is it my imagination, or did something go out of our marriage once we stored it away? Why did we store it away? Was it covered in dog hairs?

Jesus, I could go on like this for ever – happy memories. You could too, of course – but maybe they aren't happy memories for you. Maybe the things that make me glow in the dark make you shiver; perhaps you were never happy. Oh, I know it's just me being doomy-gloomy, but you can't expect much more; after all, my wife's having another man's child.

Yes, come to New York. Remember that woman's other film – *Sleepless in Seattle*? We're hardly the same as those characters, but perhaps we could end up the same – meeting at midnight at the top of the Empire State Building and proclaiming true love for each other. Maybe not the Empire State, you know the way my nose bleeds at great heights, but somewhere just as romantic – what about a horse and trap round Central Park? I'm told it's absolutely beautiful if you can avoid the crackheads, the beggars and the film-makers making documentaries about the crackheads and the beggars. I'm told half the crackheads have agents now. I wouldn't know, of course, as the closest I've ever come to an agent is an estate agent. Ho-ho. Humour, once again, masking a broken heart.

Okay, it's time to wind this up. There's so much else I could write, but I know it's stupid trying to bludgeon you back into love with me with something the size of *War and Peace*. Suffice to say, I can be a better person than I have been, I can kick the booze, I can treat you like the lady you are, I can accept you and love you as you are, with or without child.

You know when I'm coming back, but it would be so much nicer to have you here, to start our relationship again away from it all. And we did love New York together, didn't we?

Of course I have some work to do, but if you want I can take some time after he's lost the fight and spend it entirely with you. I can't anticipate Cameron being in a desperate rush for the book – studies in failure need time to mature, and besides, a look at McMaster in his sad twilight years (not that he had much time in the limelight) will be a fitting end to a book which I think will expose what a crazy charade this whole boxing business is, rather than the sports biography Cameron thinks he's getting.

So call me or write to me. I'll lay off using the phone for a while. The address and phone number are at the top of the first page – I hope you like the headed paper. The hotel also has some girlie pink paper, but I thought that was pushing things a bit.

I'll send you a ticket.

I'll give you my love.

Love

Dan

xxxx

15

I had a drink to celebrate my new-found sobriety.

I knew it was pretty stupid, but I was happy in myself and in my capacity to withstand it; I was happyish with the letter, but drained by the work I'd put into it. I needed a lift, just a little one. I felt lonely. It was dark outside and there were flecks of snow drifting slowly past the window.

I sipped at a beer and re-read the letter. I wasn't so sure about it when I got to the end. Half of me loved it, the other half thought it might cause her to run a million miles, or at least as far as an unfaithful woman who's an indeterminate number of months pregnant can run.

I needed a second opinion. I have always thrived on second opinions, on disagreeing with them, thus reassuring myself. I needed an editor, and it had to be a woman, a woman's reaction. I thought of letting Mary McMaster read it. She seemed the sensitive but sensible type. But I decided it would be a mistake to let someone I was meant to be examining closely for a book get such an inside line on me. I didn't want her telling the world what a sad wreck her husband's biographer was if they didn't approve of the book. And I doubted that they would. There was no one else in the McMaster camp I could turn to.

Actually, I knew exactly who I wanted to advise me on it, and the thought worried me. But worries have a habit of dissipating with a couple of drinks and gradually it didn't seem like such a bad idea. It certainly couldn't do any harm; besides I had her clothes to return.

I called Paula's apartment block in Greenwich Village. An elderly-sounding woman answered the phone in the foyer and was kind enough to buzz her room, but there was no reply. She was probably at work with the sad people. If I was serious about getting her opinion it meant a return to 42nd Street. I weighed it up in my mind while I had another couple of drinks and decided to chance it; it was worth the embarrassment if anyone saw me; I was trying to save my marriage. I found a plastic bag and gathered up the clothes she had lent me for my ridiculous walk up Broadway.

The walk, the bite of the wind as it swirled up Broadway and the snow assaulting my face had a fairly sobering effect. By the time I reached the sex club I was having second thoughts. Maybe it would be better to wait until she got back to her apartment than to hassle her at work, but then

I considered the letter and its importance and decided to press ahead.

I walked through a neon-lit archway. There were only a couple of customers. They didn't look up as I entered. It wasn't the sort of place you struck up idle conversation. I skirted a table piled high with magazines and approached the stairs at the back of the club. I nodded at the Indian in the tux.

'Is Paula in tonight?'

He shook his head. 'No Paula.'

'Night off?'

'No Paula.'

I turned, then turned back. 'Lauren?'

'Lauren upstairs.'

They don't call me Sherlock Holmes . . . at all, but still. I started for the next floor. The Indian put his hand out. I began to protest and then thought better of it and purchased a token. Then he stopped me again.

'What's in the bag?'

I opened it up. I shrugged. He shook his head. Each unto their own.

Upstairs, things were quiet. Eight or nine girls milled about in their bikinis and stilettos, looking bored and cold. Three of them homed in on me as soon as I appeared over the horizon and, momentarily taken aback, I withdrew again to the top of the stairs. I mumbled Lauren's name; a black girl pointed back down the hall behind them and I hesitantly moved forward. It was an odd feeling passing through them, for even though I knew that for ten dollars I could see inside any of their knickers, I felt that for no dollars at all each and any one of them could just as easily turn on me and savage me like a wolf tearing into an injured deer. A door opened ten yards up the hall and a young man came out, pulling hurriedly at his zipper. We passed. He kept his eyes to the ground. A few seconds later the next door along opened and Paula stepped out.

The fake smile was in place and she started into her greeting. Then she twigged and the smile faded slightly.

'Hi,' she said, and looked nervously over her shoulders at the other girls.

'Hello, Paula,' I said.

She hissed at me: 'Lauren.'

'Sorry. Of course.'

She didn't meet my eyes. 'I didn't expect to see you again.'

'No. Neither did I.'

'You're not going to turn into one of those weirdos who gets attached to me, are you?'

I reddened. 'No. Of course not.' As if.

She nodded, then turned and opened one of the doors on her left. 'Do you have a token?'

I nodded. I entered the room. The air inside was so much more pungent in relative sobriety. I slotted the token. Up went the wall, like a drawbridge being raised on a castle where morals are for sale. Paula removed her top.

I watched her chest, perhaps for longer than I should if my intentions were purely editorial. But I shook my head. I reached for the telephone, she reached for hers.

'I'm not here for that,' I said.

She nodded.

'What are you here for?'

'Put your top on.' She nodded again and replaced the garment. I cleared my throat. 'The other day you advised me to write a letter to my wife.'

'I know. We had a deal.'

'I wanted you to read it, tell me if you thought it was okay. I need a woman's perspective.'

'It's usual to give a girl a tip.'

'I'm sorry?'

'I need a tip. It's the only job I have. Time is money.'

'Yes. Of course. I'm sorry.' I fumbled in my pocket. I produced a twenty-dollar note. I added another twenty dollars. 'Will you come and get it, or will you trust me?'

'I'll come and get it.'

Out. In. Out.

She was away before I had time to think of the bag. 'I still have some clothes of yours. I brought them with me.' I held the bag up for her to see.

'Thanks. Leave them there when you go.'

'Okay. You don't seem as friendly now as you did the other morning.' Maybe it came out like I was a little hurt. It wasn't meant to.

Her face softened. Slightly. 'I'm working.'

'Okay. Sorry.' I couldn't expect anything else. She had saved my bacon, she owed me nothing. 'Will I read this to you?'

'Sure.'

'And you'll give me an honest opinion?'

'Sure.'

'An honest opinion not coloured by the fact that I've just given you forty dollars?'

'Honest as I can make it.' The smile was back, almost entirely human.

'Okay.'

So I read her the letter.

The wall started to move down. Paula touched something on her side and it moved up again. Maybe it was some sort of quality control device to encourage clients on the verge of climax.

My letter hardly had much in the way of climax, but I could tell by the way her eyes moistened that at least some of what I'd written had gotten to her. I folded the letter, put it back in the envelope and replaced it in my jacket.

'Well?'

'You really do love her, don't you?'

I nodded. 'Do you think it'll do the trick?'

Paula pulled at her lower lip. 'It should. She'll either fall in love with you all over again, or she'll throw up.'

I shrugged. 'Yeah. I suppose it could work like that. What would you think if you received a letter like that?'

'I don't think I'd ever inspire anyone to that level of devotion.'

'Of course you would.'

151

'My man would never write like that. You don't know Chinese Elvis.'

'Excuse me?'

'Excuse you what?'

'Ahm. Chinese Elvis?'

'Chinese Elvis. My man.'

I nodded. 'This may seem like a silly question, but . . .'

'Because he's not Chinese and he doesn't look like Elvis. The perfect nickname. Everyone asks, and I never get tired of telling.'

I nodded some more. New York.

'I'm going to post it in the morning. It should only take two or three days.'

Paula smiled, a good, homely smile. 'You do that. I hope it all works out.'

I gave her a little wave. 'So long,' I said, 'and thanks for the ski pants.'

'No trouble.'

I left the cupboard. Paula's door remained closed. The other girls parted as I passed. I felt like I should stop and explain that I wasn't a customer, that I had done nothing wrong and had nothing to hide, but I was a customer, I had paid for it like any other sad person even if the masturbation was mental rather than physical. I couldn't expect them to understand, because I didn't really understand.

The air was sharp, uncomfortable. In the old days I would have thought deeply, for a second, about where to get a decent hot whiskey to chase the chill from my bones, but I was a new man now. I'd had a few drinks earlier, parched by creation, but now I had excised those demons by reading the letter to Paula. The performance had purged me in a way actually writing it had not. I felt clean again now that I was out in the New York night and ready to challenge life. I would go back to the hotel and settle in front of the TV with a club sandwich and a bottle of Diet Coke and watch re-runs of *Cheers* until dawn. Then I'd sleep for a few hours and wake blessedly free of hangover and go and watch Bobby do some sparring. Then I'd get down to some serious work on the book.

I hadn't taken more than twenty steps when I bumped into someone. Or maybe it was the other way round. I said sorry anyway. With New York politeness the man said excuse me and then held a knife to my throat.

I took a step back, and the point of the knife went with me. Only a little further. I could feel the blood. Only a nick. But blood all the same.

'Gimme the wallet,' the man said. He wore a grimy black tracksuit, with the hood pulled up; his face looked ashen in the neon glow, his eyes hollow.

I tried to hold my head back, but the point stuck resolutely. 'I don't have a wallet,' I gasped. 'Someone stole it. I have some cash in my trouser pocket . . . here . . . take it.'

I rustled. Produced some notes, about sixty dollars and a snarled-up paper tissue.

He took the lot with his left hand and stuffed them into his pocket without examining them.

'Gimme the wallet,' he said again.

'I don't . . .'

He stepped forward and moved his left hand to the back of my trousers and felt the empty pocket, then moved it to my jacket zipper and pulled it down. His hand slipped inside, feeling first right, then left. He pulled out Patricia's letter.

'Please,' I said, 'don't take that.'

He turned it over in his hand. 'What's inside?'

'Nothing. Nothing valuable. Just a letter.'

'But valuable to you.'

'Yes, valuable to me.'

'Maybe you pay to have it back.'

'You've just taken my money.'

'But I ain't taken your shoes.'

He'd a wicked gleam in his eyes and a scraggy ginger growth on his chin, a bad combination.

'You wouldn't take my shoes. It's freezing.'

'Watch me.'

He moved the knife slightly to one side. Not deeper. Longer.

'Okay,' I said.

'Just slip them off.'

I would have nodded, but it might have sliced my jugular. I pushed off my left shoe, then my right, then nudged them both towards him.

His mouth widened in a gummy approximation of a smile. 'I hope they're my size.' For the first time I looked at his feet. Or, indeed, his foot. His left foot was about the size of mine; five dirt-black toes pushed out of a trainer; his right

154

foot was, well, somewhere else; missing in action. He had no wooden foot, just a stump that ended where his ankle should have been, in a street-soiled bandage. Nor had he a crutch. I had been mugged by a man who hopped.

As if he could tell what I was thinking he said quickly: 'I'm not alone.'

He nodded to his side, into the doorways of two boarded shops, barely lit by 42nd Street's neon. Dark figures. Three or four. There was no way of telling how many feet they had between them, but it seemed pretty silly to try and find out.

'Beat it,' he said, and withdrew the knife. He bent down and picked up the shoes, balancing nicely.

I hesitated. 'The letter.'

'Fuck the letter,' he snapped and stuck it inside his track-suit jacket. He turned and hopped into the shadows.

God had spoken. He didn't want Patricia and me ever to get back together. We were finished, and I had to accept it. I returned to the hotel. I returned to the hotel bar.

16

Fog.

Fog that lurks behind the eyes. You can't see it, obviously, but it's there. Hugging every thought. Censoring every sensory perception.

Sooner or later it goes, but you have to give it time. You have to lie there with your eyes shut so that it thinks it's trapped, it'll panic and your head will vibrate until you think it will come apart and then it'll slowly work its way out, warily easing out of your ears, leaving only a trace, the merest flavour of it ever having been there at all. Oddly, the flavour is very like that of old beer.

About 11 am I was finally able to shift out of bed. I stood in the shower and let the water boil me for ten minutes, then shaved, then let the shower boil me some more. I dried myself off, then pulled on some fresh underwear and socks, a pair of black jeans, a black sweatshirt and a denim jacket. I pulled on a pair of black leather gloves to guard against my valuable writing hands getting cold and hoped they didn't look too posy. Then I remembered a couple of important things. I called room service and ordered four bacon sandwiches and a pair of trainers to go. It was a good hotel. They arrived within twenty minutes. They were tough-looking, but surprisingly light. The trainers weren't bad either.

Laced up and feeling pretty damn good, considering the fact that I was now defiantly single, I strode out onto Broadway and made my way up towards Central Park. I'd put Patricia out of my mind. There was nothing more I could achieve from this side of the Atlantic. I'd put my heart and soul into the letter and it was gone now, my heart and soul with it. There was nothing more to put down in writing. Now I'd concentrate on the job at hand. Maybe I'd been running around for too long looking for a reconciliation when what I really should have been doing was looking for a new woman. Maybe.

The previous night's snow had not hung around too long and there was a surprising warmth in the air. I took a detour down 42nd Street on the off-chance that I might encounter my friend with the one foot, but there was no sign of him. Too bright. Still, I would keep an eye out for him and even if it was too late to recover the cash, my shoes or the letter I would exact some revenge, even if it was just pushing him into the traffic.

I took my chances with the hell-for-leather yellow taxis racing round Columbus Circle, then stood for a moment patting the horses as they waited lazily with their traps for passengers at the edge of Central Park. They looked okay, but their manure smelt incongruous with the greater metropolitan stench.

I skirted the park's western side. The Dakota building, where Lennon had been shot, was surrounded by scaffolding. Yoko was probably in there somewhere, still wailing over his loss, or maybe she was just recording another record. Somewhere along this street Woody Allen lived as well. Maybe they got together sometimes and discussed persecution complexes. At any rate, neither of them did much training at the Westside Bodyshape Gym. And right then not too many other people were either.

I heard them before I saw them. Chanting.

I rounded a corner and found about forty people, some of them carrying placards, making a big noise outside Bodyshape. They weren't exactly choral, so I'd some difficulty in making out what they were singing about, but I heard McMaster's name and a clear reference to racism. It didn't take much in the way of brains to guess what they were on about. Banners bearing the slogans MCMASTER IS THE VIPER and GO HOME WHITE RACIST were other pointers in the right direction which only a trained journalist like myself would pick up on. Eight cops formed a half-circle around the entrance to the gym; behind them, wedged in the doorway, was Stanley Matchitt. He looked tense, but in his element. Twenty yards further down the street four or five women in tracksuits stood chatting, nodding at the protest, debating whether or not to attempt entry.

A gap in the traffic presented itself and I crossed at a trot, then kept it up as I pressed through the gathering. The first few people made room for me, but then when they saw that I was actually heading for the gym, and that I was the wrong colour, they began to close ranks. They were mostly middle-aged women, but bulky with it; it was like trying to fight my way through a bag of animated marshmallows. They weren't too serious about hindering my progress. I got called a couple of names and someone slapped me round the back of the head, but I eventually emerged safe and sound by the doorway.

A young cop put out his hand, palm up. 'Do you have business here, sir?' he asked.

I nodded and pointed behind him to Stanley. 'Ask him.'

Stanley nodded at the cop and he let me through. Hissing came from the crowd.

'Hi, Stanley,' I said. 'Shot anyone yet?'

Stanley shook his head. 'Nice gloves,' he said, then suddenly he moved to one side. I felt something warm brush my ear and then the door behind him shattered. The policemen ducked as one, their hands moving to their guns in one smooth movement, like a better version of Pan's People, then as an approving cheer rippled through the protesters, the cops relaxed and raised themselves. It was only a rock.

Stanley stepped back into the foyer and ushered me in.

'The natives are a bit restless,' he said.

I nodded. I touched my ear. 'They been here long?'

'About the same time as us. They just appeared out of the park. We didn't know what the fuck was going on. Bobby had his pen out ready to sign autographs when someone whacked him round the head with a placard. We had to hold them out of the gym ourselves till the cops arrived.'

I shrugged. 'Still, it's good publicity.'

'Yeah. Sure.'

'Bobby okay?'

'Take a look.'

There were three gyms in the club. Bobby had one on the top floor for himself and his sparring partners, two of whom were draped over the ropes on the far side of a makeshift ring. They looked like they'd been hung out to dry. They were big, bigger than Bobby, more muscular. Their head-guards lay discarded on the floor behind them. They'd been beaten up. Geordie McClean and some fat guy I didn't recognize stood chatting further down the room. McClean smiled across. The other guy nodded. I nodded at McMaster. He ignored me, or probably couldn't see me. Jackie Campbell, wearing an Aran pompom cap, watched intently from McMaster's corner. The third sparring partner, another black guy, stood in the opposite corner. He moved hesitantly forward. His eyes darted to his two colleagues on the side of the ring, then centred on McMaster again. The contender strode purposefully towards him: there was no art to it, no

160

stalking like Chavez or dancing like Leonard, he just walked right up to the guy and popped him on the nose. And the guy fell. Just like that. One punch and a dead weight. It wasn't the McMaster I knew and feared for.

I skirted the ring and stood beside Jackie Campbell while the other two sparring partners ducked wearily under the ropes to retrieve their fallen comrade.

'What's come over him?' I whispered. McMaster leant against the ropes on the far side of the ring and spoke quietly to McClean and the fat bloke.

Campbell shook his head slightly. 'Ask him,' he said and moved off the corner to tend to the sparring partner; his friends were having some difficulty rousing him.

As I moved round the ring McClean and his friend turned and walked to a door at the far end of the gym and disappeared.

'Nice punch, Bobby.'

I expected him to smile and say something bright. He just nodded sullenly.

'Repeat that against . . .'

'Fuck up, Starkey.'

'Sure.'

The door opened again and McClean's head popped out. 'Starkey,' he called, 'you wouldn't join us for a second, would you?'

I nodded. I walked. McMaster wasn't much company and the other side of the ring looked like a battlefield dressing station. Maybe I'd misjudged the man. Maybe he wasn't the big hunk of useless lard I'd thought. Of course it might just have been that his sparring partners were particularly crap, but they certainly looked the part.

McClean ushered me into the room. It was used to store weights and other gym equipment. The fat bloke had perched himself on an exercise bike and was slowly turning the pedals. He nodded as I came in; McClean put his arm round me in a fatherly way and squeezed, which was a bit unsettling.

I smiled as best I could and freed myself. 'So what's up?'

I didn't like the set of his face. Mock confident. 'We have a wee problem, people man.'

I nodded and looked at the fat bloke. Remembering his manners, McClean stepped over to the exercise bike and put his palm out towards him. 'I'm sorry. Dan Starkey, this . . .'

The fat bloke put his hand out. '. . . Peter Smith.' Sweaty hand, firm shake. He looked fifty. Very black skin. His hair was flecked with white. It made him look like a baker.

'Pete's a private detective.'

I nodded. 'Oh yeah? What's up?'

'Do you mind telling me where you were last night?'

'Yes.'

I looked from Smith to McClean. McClean reached out to me again. I shrugged his hand off. 'Please, Starkey, don't be awkward, this is important.'

There was just a hint of pleading in his voice. Smith looked intently at me. I looked intently back. 'I went down to Times Square to score some crack.' He held my gaze. 'But I came back with a pair of fluffy bunny slippers.' He looked at McClean.

He said it quietly. 'Mary McMaster has disappeared.'

I'd been too preoccupied with my own problems even to notice. She'd gone out shopping and hadn't come back. The police were looking into it. The FBI had expressed an interest but hadn't done much about it. Geordie McClean, millionaire, had expressed his concern and displayed his largesse by hiring an overfed ex-cop eking out a living as a private eye on the mean streets of New York.

Smith continued his luxuriant pedalling. At the rate he was going it would take him forty-eight years to get down to his fighting weight. He wore a trench coat, unbuttoned, a pair of wire-framed spectacles, fawn trousers and a pair of brown brogues. He didn't look like much, but then nobody had me pegged as a Booker-Prize-winning novelist. I told them I hadn't seen her. Told them I went to a few pubs to get the New York flavour for my book. They didn't seem too concerned. I asked Smith how far he'd gotten with his investigation.

He raised an eyebrow. 'Last thing we have on her is a Visa card used in Macy's. She bought three shirts and a pair of sunglasses. Hasn't been seen since. Nothing's been touched at the hotel.'

McClean mopped at his brow with the sleeve of his buttoned cashmere coat. 'I'm trying to keep the publicity on this down to the absolute minimum, Starkey. In fact, we weren't going to tell you at all, but I decided honesty was the best policy. As the journalist in the party we would appreciate your cooperation on this. We have to approach it as a team.'

'What're you worried about, Geordie, the fight going down the tubes or Mary turning up safe?'

'Both, Starkey.'

'Of course. I take it you think the two are connected.'

'We haven't heard anything. Certainly no ransom demands or anything like that. The police are treating it simply as a missing person at the moment. And a missing person who hasn't been missing that long. That's why I hired Pete here. To get things really moving.'

I thumbed back towards the ring. 'I see Bobby's taking it well.'

McClean scratched his neck and looked uncomfortable. 'I know . . . almost makes you wish . . . nah . . . of course not. It's just so bloody unfair! Everything was going so well. Then those bloody heathens . . .'

'Aha. The jigsaw thickens.'

'Starkey. Use your head. Of course it's the Sons of Muhammad. Who else could it be?'

Smith stopped his pedalling. He freewheeled. 'This is New York, Mr McClean. It could be anyone. Or anything. You're thinking of the Sons of Muhammad because they've threatened your boxer. But there's a hundred different groups out there could be involved. She might have been taken for a reason totally unconnected with the fight. She might have been murdered for the sheer hell of it, raped, been knocked down by a car. She might have amnesia. It happens, believe me. I wouldn't rule out the Teenage Ninja Mutant Turtles having her.'

'Are you trying to cheer me up?'

'Mr McClean, if she's out there, I'll find her.'

It was admirable confidence. I could see how McClean was approaching it. A black terror group had her. So he thought by hiring a black detective he would immediately get an inside track on it. Sure. Like hiring PC Plod in whitest Hampstead when you needed Sherlock Holmes.

Maybe I was prejudging him. Frank Cannon hadn't looked like much either, but had always come up with the goods. And then eaten them.

'So,' I said, 'now that I'm in on the secret, what can I do to help?'

'Keep your trap shut, for a start,' said McClean, a little too quickly. 'I'm sorry. Of course you will. But I'd like you to stick with Bobby as much as you can. Stop him doing anything silly or saying anything dumb.'

'I thought Stanley was his bosom buddy.'

'Stanley can stop him getting shot, but he's hardly a member of the diplomatic corps. You'll need to handle the press with kid gloves. Keep them away from Bobby until we get this sorted out, but keep them on our side. Can you do that?'

I nodded.

Smith clambered off the bike. 'Of course,' he said slowly,

even slightly breathlessly, 'she might just have run off with someone else.'

McClean looked round sharply. 'She wouldn't do that. You haven't seen them together. They love each other.'

'Doesn't always keep people together, Geordie,' I said and turned for the door.

Someone who didn't know me might have taken it as the cynical observation of a bitter man.

17

'Did I ever tell you how I met her?'

I shook my head and looked at my steak. He hadn't, but it still felt like a lie. He wanted to talk.

I'd made little impression on my food. Bobby, on the other hand, hadn't let his obvious concern for his missing wife interfere with his prodigious appetite; he had laid waste to a small cow.

'Like, I was only a wee lad, walking home. She was getting beaten up by these other girls and I chased them off. I suppose she was grateful, and she went out with me.' He shook his head and grinned at me. 'I'd never had a girlfriend before. We started seeing each other all the time, everything was going great, then for a couple of days she went all quiet and I thought I was going to get dumped. I kept asking her what was wrong, and she kept saying nothing, but I knew there was, and I'd more or less resigned myself to losing her. I mean, it wasn't a question of pregnancy or anything, I knew that much. But she took so long telling me I lost my temper and stormed off and she came running after me crying and finally blurted out what had been worrying her. She said she was embarrassed with me walking about in a pair of flares. She said they never had and never would be in fashion and could I please get rid of them because they were killing her. I know it seems a bit superficial now, but I've seen photographs of myself then and I did look daft. Have you ever seen a hundredweight of spuds in a pair of flares? Sexy or what?'

He laughed, a warm laugh of love. I'd had laughs like that. I felt for him. I'd been in his situation before: a missing wife, possibly dead. But there was nothing much I could say. I hated the inanities of reassurance. She'll be okay. She'll turn up. It's something quite simple. Never you worry, get on with your training. Neither was it a time for brutal honesty: she'll turn up, Bobby – in bits. It was a time for nodding and being there.

Stanley was there, ish. He lounged in a seat by the hotel restaurant door, looking deceptively sleepy, like Switzerland. The butt of his pistol protruded from his jacket; it was meant to be seen, and those guests who opted to stay in the restaurant once they saw it and his casual but still somehow threatening demeanour kept a wary eye on him.

When the death threat became public knowledge the hotel management had briefly considered asking the McMaster camp to decamp, particularly with the arrival of a hundred or so rowdy protesters on the sidewalk outside. Then they'd negotiated with Poodle Clay for a guaranteed number of positive mentions for the hotel during the pre-fight build-up in exchange for allowing us to stay on. They'd even provided some security guards on the front doors to keep the protesters out, and a couple outside McMaster's rooms. Stanley didn't like the idea of being superfluous and had set about being super-conscientious.

I played with a tomato. I could picture Bobby being the hero. Mary had told me. A big fat spotty git who was transformed into a knight in shining armour, with flares.

'Yeah, dead sexy,' I said. 'I never had time for flares myself. I was always a drainpipe and winklepicker man myself.'

Bobby nodded and took another mammoth bite. Or bite of a mammoth. It could have been.

'Is she strong, Bobby? Could she withstand being held by someone, some group?'

Bobby chewed on for a few moments. Swallowed. Began to cut another piece of steak, then stopped and looked up. 'She's as hard as nails and as soft as butter. She's as harsh as a gale, as soft as a summer's breeze. She's Arctic ice and Ballygowan Spring Water.'

Satisfied with his response, he cut, chewed, swallowed.

In the afternoon the contender slept for a few hours. We weren't that close that he wanted me in his room. I stood outside for a while with the guards the hotel had posted and then wandered on down to the end of the corridor. Round the bend, resting against the wall by the elevators, Stanley sat on what appeared to be a bar stool.

'You going to shoot everyone who comes through those doors, Stanley?'

'Why don't you find out, Starkey? Away down to the bottom and ride up again.'

I nodded and pressed the button. I stood with my back to him. After half a minute of silence, he said: 'How is he?'

'He's okay.'

'If I knew where to find them, I'd go and get her back myself.'

I turned, slightly. 'I'm sure you would, Stanley.'

'What about this fella Smith? What d'ya reckon?'

'Early days. He knows the city better than us.'

'He doesn't look like much.'

'Which of us do? Who of us does?'

'If I knew where to find them, I'd go down there and blow them away myself.'

'So you say.'

'It's them're the fuckin' racists. Takin' her like that.'

The snigger came, before I even thought about it. 'That's rich, Stanley, coming from someone so adept at cutting the throats of Catholics.'

'In a different life, Starkey. A different world.'

'Sure, Stanley.'

And then he thumped me in the back and sent me crashing

against the elevator doors. I managed a stifled 'Fuck!' before he pushed my face into the cold metal.

'Fuck, Starkey,' he hissed, 'I really am getting sick of you and your fuckin' innuendo.'

He rapped my head once more against the door then stepped back. I turned quickly, fists bunched . . . I counted to ten in the time it takes most people to get to one. Calm and control were required. Calm and control. Calm and control. He was, after all, a notorious killer, and if the pen was ever mightier than the sword, on this occasion I had managed to run out of ink.

'Stanley,' I said, calm and in control, but with a sore head, 'I was not innuendoing anything, if such a word exists. I just don't see much change in you. Your propensity for violence does not seem to have diminished any as far as I can see. Save for your choice of more legitimate targets, like the Sons of Muhammad, you're the man I wrote about all those years ago. That's all.'

It was maybe a bit wordy, but it filled a gap which might otherwise have been filled by further violence against me.

Stanley shook his head sadly. 'You just don't understand, do you? You think if I hadn't changed I'd be so keen on trying to save Mary from those bastards? She is a fucking Fenian after all.'

'Stanley,' I began, and then spread my palms to him. It wasn't worth bothering with. We looked at each other in silence, then the elevator doors opened and I stepped in.

When the doors had six inches left to close, I gave him the fingers. I'm not a total coward.

My head was sore, but my pride was damaged. I went to the downstairs bar and got hold of a couple of glasses of something which could cure my head and plaster over the damage. Just a couple. The bar was well inside the hotel but I could still hear the protesters outside. Not distinctly, not what they were ranting on about, but it was there, like the persistently annoying hum of a swarm of tsetse flies. And they carried with them the disease of racism they thought they were protesting about.

I was starting my third, pacing myself, when Jackie Campbell came in. He perched himself on a stool beside me and ordered an Irish whiskey. I nodded to him and he nodded back.

'How's it going, Jackie?' I asked.

'Okay,' he said.

'Bobby was looking good today, wasn't he?'

He fixed his eyes on me. They crossed a little. 'Do I know you?' he asked.

I snorted. I shook my head. 'Doesn't matter.'

'No, wait, hold on.' He fished in his tracksuit pocket and produced a pair of glasses. He slipped them on, then looked warily about the bar. 'I hate these bloody things,' he said, then focused on me. The lenses were dusty. He nodded. 'Dan, isn't it?'

'Yes, Jackie. Do you want another?'

'Sure. If you're buying. What McClean's paying me doesn't allow me to buy rounds.'

'I thought he'd be looking after you okay.'

'Like getting blood out of a stone. If I was only here for the money, I wouldn't be here. Except for the money. The only reason I'm here is to make sure that big eejit does his best against Tyson.'

I nodded to the barman to replenish our drinks. Jackie licked his lips. 'I've never seen him punch better than he did this morning,' I said. 'He looked lethal.' Jackie didn't reply. He swirled the whiskey. 'You think he'll win?' I prompted.

'No. But that doesn't matter.'

'It's the taking part that matters.'

'No, it's being able to get out of the ring with your head held high, and without the use of a life-support machine.'

'You think he'll manage that?'

'All things being equal.'

'And all things being equal isn't helped by Mary disappearing.'

He nodded his head for a second, then looked sharply up. 'What?'

'Mary's disappearance doesn't help things.'

'What the fuck are you talking about?'

'Mary. Mary McMaster.'

'I know who the fuck Mary is. What about her?'

'She's been missing for two days, Jackie. The police are looking for her. The FBI are looking for her. Geordie has a private eye on the trail as well.'

Jackie slammed a brittle-looking hand down on the bar. 'Why the fuck am I always the last to know?' he demanded. I shrugged, helplessly. 'Jesus!' He drained his second glass in one gulp and slipped off the stool. 'I'm going to find that fucker McClean and punch his fuckin' lights out!'

He hurried out the door. I finished my drink, then found a call box and called Smith. I needed to get involved. Something about it all was getting to me. Déjà vu, maybe, or maybe it just reminded me of something that had happened before.

He answered on the sixth ring. There was a lot of background noise. Traffic.

I introduced myself. He remembered me.

'The reporter,' he said.

'Absolutely. How goes it?'

'Fine.'

'I don't wish to put you down or anything,' I said, 'but from the noise around you I'd say your office phone is a call box. Can't you even afford an office?'

'You're not putting me down at all, Starkey. I appreciate your concern over the success of my chosen profession. I also realize that you're from Ireland.'

'Which is supposed to mean what?'

'Well, you probably haven't heard of car phones before.'

'Ah, yes. Well.'

'Starkey, you strike me as a man with a habit of opening his mouth before he knows what he really wants to say.'

'True.'

'I don't know where that kind of attitude gets you at home, but it's liable to get you into trouble here.'

'No, well, it kind of gets me in trouble at home as well.'

'I thought as much.'

We were silent for a minute, while I thought about how best to rectify the situation.

'So did you phone me for a particular reason or just to draw attention to me?' he asked. 'I am working.'

'On the McMaster case?'

'Yes.'

'What're you up to?'

'That's my concern, Starkey.'

'Ach, come on. We're part of a team, aren't we?'

'No, you're part of a team.'

'But you're employed by us.'

'No, I'm employed by Mr McClean.'

It was time to talk tough. And lie. 'And I'm employed by Mr McClean to report on every aspect of this fight. This disappearance is a very important part of that reporting.'

He pondered that. 'So?' he said eventually.

'I had a word with Geordie, and he said it would be okay for me to follow you about for a bit, just to get a flavour of how you work.'

'He didn't say anything to me.'

'He said it would be at your discretion.'

'You don't think your following me about would somehow draw attention to what I'm trying to do?'

'Why should it?'

'Well, right now I'm sitting in a car in Harlem, staking out a house. You think you'll blend in here?'

'Okay, so you're in Harlem. It's not a no-go area for whites, is it?'

'No, but . . .'

'Mr Smith, I've lived in the heart of one of the worst trouble spots in the world for thirty years. Harlem doesn't exactly scare the pants off me.'

He cleared his throat into the receiver. 'It should,' he said wearily.

18

Marcus Savant lived in a gentrified apartment block off Morningside in Harlem. By all accounts it was a perfect little palace. Quite why he therefore chose to spend the best part of his days sitting on the front stoop, even frosty March afternoons, was anyone's guess. Maybe, like Tyson, you could take the man out of the ghetto, but not the ghetto out of the man. Maybe he felt he had to be out on the street, keeping a constant eye on the world. He was thirty-four years old, tall, rake thin. His clothes were top of the range. He wore a little jewellery, but nothing too flashy. Tortoiseshell glasses. He played dippy MOR ballads I was proud not to recognize from a portable CD, but not so loud that they annoyed anyone else, and read the *New Yorker*, although probably just the cartoons. He hadn't quite made the transition to drinking cool white wine of certain vintage. He slurped at a can of Budweiser. He showed his class by not hiding it in a brown paper sack. He had a plastic bag from Saks. Marcus Savant was a Son of Muhammad.

At least, he was according to Peter Smith. The inflatable detective sat on the hood of a '74 Oldsmobile the size of a small trawler, chomping on his third McChicken Sandwich in an hour. I thought it lacked something as undercover surveillance. Two or three times I caught Savant glancing in our direction. Not for long, but interested. Smith munched on. I sat beside him, notebook open, pretending to take down his life story.

'You come along here, day or night, you sit in your car for any length of time, people notice,' was what he'd said. 'The police come by, check you out, people come by, try to buy drugs off you, try to sell you crack. Hell, they take your wheels while you're watching someone and you don't know a damn thing about it. The trick is, get out in the open, sit on your hood, you become part of the landscape. Act like you own the place. Then nobody messes with you.'

'But Savant knows we're not part of the landscape.'

'Savant knows nothing. Look at him up there. He's got money, but he hasn't a clue what to do with it. He feels outta place. You can't buy class, Starkey. He's bought himself out of the real Harlem into this fairy-tale version, and he's not sure whether he likes it. He's restless.'

'He might be restless because we're here.'

'He's restless because he's got ants in his pants. He'll be

over here before long, wondering what we're up to. Curiosity'll get the better of him.'

I accepted a solitary French fry. It was cold and there was no vinegar on it, and I thought of home. And Patricia. Patricia liked her chips swimming in it. It would be early evening at home; she'd be curled up in front of a fire with her baby, and maybe her lover.

To give him his due, Smith had done his homework. His contacts in the area were obviously good. From whatever source, he'd managed to put together a list of some twenty-five employees at the Shabazz, a silver-domed mosque eight blocks away which served as the headquarters of the Brothers of Muhammad. He'd checked out a number of them and reckoned if anyone was making good money moonlighting as a Son of Muhammad, then it was Savant. Janitors just didn't live in apartments in Morningside.

'Maybe he has family money,' I ventured.

Smith shook his head. 'Not unless his dad's the local drug baron.'

'You're very cynical about your own people, aren't you?'

'My own people? You make me sound like Kunta Kinte. You try living here for fifty years. You'd get cynical about a box of Cheerios.'

He thought Savant was probably a minor player in the organization, he reasoned that if he was going to watch anyone it was better to watch someone relatively unimportant than a prime mover who'd be more likely to watch his tail.

I chanced another look up towards Savant. He caught my eye. I tried to make it seem like I was just panning round. I turned back to Smith. 'I take it you don't think Mary is in there.'

He shook his head. A little piece of batter flew off his upper lip. 'No, if they have her she'll be in a safe house somewhere. It would be too obvious to keep her in one of their own places. If I can get hold of their membership list, then I suspect the police can, though it might take them a little longer.'

'So what's the point in watching him?'

'Nothing else to do,' he said simply. He cast his eyes up towards Savant. He nodded. 'If you're going to take part in this charade,' he said dryly, 'at least pretend to write something. He may be dumb, but he's not blind.'

'You think he's dumb?'

I wrote BULLSHIT in capital letters.

'I think he's dumb.'

'Based on what?'

'Instinct. I never met a smart foot soldier yet.'

I wrote DOUBLE BULLSHIT. I showed him my notes. I didn't think he'd risen much above the level of foot soldier in the police.

He shrugged. As a speciality of mine, I regretted the fact that it was beginning to catch on so widely. Maybe I should have patented it in the early days and made some money. Then he nodded again. 'Make your own mind up. Look at him, he never made it out of Moomin Valley.'

I turned. Savant was off the stoop and halfway across the road towards us in big, easy strides. I flipped the page in my notebook and studied Smith for a moment. Then in my best reporter's voice: 'And you were born in this very street? It must have been a tough childhood?'

'Tough but happy.'

'Tough but happy,' came a none too good mimic from behind me.

I looked round at Savant. I pretended to be nervous. I gave him a half-smile. 'Hello,' I said. A little tremulous.

'Can I help you, son?' Smith asked, mock weary.

'I'm kinda insatiable to know just what you guys are up to.' He nodded at Smith. 'You someone famous?' One hand rested inside his jacket, like there might be a gun in there.

Smith had a gun, but he looked far from concerned. 'You don't recognize me?'

Savant shook his head slowly. He looked at me. 'Who is he?'

'Don't you know?'

He kept shaking.

'Did you ever see *Lifestyles of the Rich and Famous*?' said Smith.

'Sure.'

Smith pointed at me. 'Well, he's a researcher for *Lifestyles of the Rich and Famous*.'

'And you?'

'I'm just rich and famous.'

'You don't look rich and famous.'

Smith rubbed at his chin. 'Son, clothes and jewellery and a big flashy car don't make you a man, they just make you a slave to the consumer society. I keep my feet on the ground and my head outta the clouds.' He smiled paternally at Savant, who looked confused. 'I never lost touch with my roots, son. In fact that building over there, that one where you been wastin' the day sunning yourself in the clouds, that's where I was born. Before they all went and gen-tri-fied it all up.'

'Better now than it ever was,' said Savant defensively.

Smith shook his head. 'Shouldn't mess with the past, son. Let it stand as a monument to our mistakes.'

He nodded sagely. I nodded at him and at Savant. I wrote ABSOLUTE BOLLOCKS in shorthand.

'Me and seven other kids shared a room in that block, son. I'll bet you got more room than that.'

'I've a duplex apartment, man, top floor, all the luxuries you could ever want.' Said with pride.

'You done well for yourself then. Where'd you make your money then, drugs?'

'You insultin' me, man.'

His hand slipped further into his jacket. I tensed up, ready to dive out of the line of fire, or wrestle him to the ground. I hadn't quite decided.

Smith raised his palms. 'No insult intended, my friend. In my day, you saw a rich brother round here, he either running the numbers or running the dope. What you in, son, computers?'

Savant shook his head. 'I'm in religion, man.'

Smith smiled. 'Well, that figures. Muhammad looks after his own.' He nodded and extended his hand. Savant hesitated for a moment, then nodded and grasped it. 'You'll have to excuse me, son, busy schedule. You understand?'

'Sure.' He went to walk on, then stopped. 'What you rich and famous for anyway, man?'

'You ever see *Roots*?'

Savant nodded. His eyes appraised Smith more keenly. The portly detective raised his palms, turned his face to profile, left it for a second, then turned it back to Savant and smiled. 'Chicken George,' he purred.

'You sure gone to seed,' said Savant, and walked on down the block.

It was just edging towards darkness when we locked the car and walked quickly across the road to the apartment block. I said, 'I still don't think this is a very good idea.'

'Wait in the car then.'

It wasn't so gentrified that the owners had got round to providing a security man. There was an old buzzer system in operation. There were no name tags posted on the door, so using common sense, Smith pressed the bottom button. In a second a tired-sounding voice crackled over the intercom.

'Press the damn button, man, I'm freezing my balls off out here,' said Savant, or the closest approximation to him I was ever likely to hear.

'Fuck you, man.'

'Please, just this one time.'

'Savant, you betta get yo'self another key. This the last time.'

The buzzer sounded and we were in. The foyer was well lit. We moved quickly across to the stairs. Smith, instigator and investigator, led. I, being the procrastinator and agitator, shuffled along nervously behind. For a fat bloke he mounted the stairs almost with grace, like he was floating rather than pulling a couple of tons. He didn't even seem to be breathing hard when we hit the landing five floors up. There was just the one door. Smith knocked on it.

'He hasn't any family, but it's always good to check,' he said.

We waited another thirty seconds then Smith produced a screwdriver and a couple of long pieces of thin metal piping from the folds of his coat and started playing with the lock. I stepped across and looked back down the stairs. Nothing happening. I turned back and the door was open.

'You're sure this is a good idea?'

He nodded and stepped into the apartment. I followed him into a small hallway. Stairs ran off it immediately to the right, up to the top floor. A lounge and kitchen were ahead of us.

'Close the curtains so no light gets out,' said Smith.

I moved, but said: 'But if he see the curtains closed . . .'

'Will you just do it?'

I gave him a shrug. 'Of course.'

I pulled the curtains. Smith closed the front door and switched on the lights.

Of Wee Sweetie Mice and Men

As my old dad used to say, Savant's taste was right up his hole.

If it clashed, he had it. If it looked cheap and gaudy but cost the earth, he had it. He had excellent picture frames, with cheap posters of Michael Jordan and Magic Johnson in them. He had original oil paintings sellotaped to the wall. He had CDs by Barry Manilow, with covers which he hadn't even bothered to deface.

'Money to burn,' I said.

Smith nodded. 'Let's get lookin',' he said.

'For what?'

'Evidence.'

'Evidence of what?'

'Anything.'

He held my gaze for a moment. Then I nodded. 'Shouldn't be hard to find now that you've spelt it out.'

'I'll go upstairs,' he said.

He glided up the stairs. I started in the kitchen. Through the cupboards. All the right equipment, but none of it looked overused. The fridge had a fair selection of vegetables, no meat, some Coke, some Dr Pepper, some CDs. I'd read in a magazine that keeping CDs in the ice-making compartment was supposed to give them a longer life, but Savant had missed the point. His approach to cryogenics ensured that not only did his CDs avoid the life-extending ice but that they would also smell almost indefinitely of cauliflower on the turn. Yum.

The bathroom was clean. There was one bedroom downstairs, plainly furnished. One cupboard full of expensive clothes. A bottle of perfume sat on a bedside table. I moved on to the lounge. One massive television set dominated the room. The right wall was partly hidden behind a large bookcase. It was half full. Most of the books seemed to be of a religious nature. Along the left wall, beneath the basketball posters, there was a CD system and a stack of CDs. Beside them in a cardboard box there were about a hundred long players. I flicked through them: a lot of seventies disco, several good Motown compilations, Italian and German opera, early rap; not a power chord amongst them. There was a big black leather sofa. I pulled the cushions out of it and checked down the back and sides: an assortment of pens and candy wrappers, a few dimes and nickels. I did the same with both armchairs. More bits and pieces.

Smith appeared at the bottom of the stairs, having descended in almost total silence. He shook his head. 'Clean up there,' he said. 'I'll do the bathroom.'

'Done,' I said.

He nodded and went into the bathroom. He emerged a minute later.

'See?' I said.

'We'll see.'

He began moving around the lounge, his fingers extended before him like a blind man on a crazy golf course. I stood back and let him search. He was the professional. I went to the window and pulled the curtain back a little. I watched the street for a couple of minutes. Cars, plenty of life; it would be difficult to see Savant returning.

I looked over my shoulder. Smith stood in the lounge doorway, finger on lips, looking thoughtful. 'You think there's something worth finding here?' I asked.

He nodded slowly. 'When you were a kid, a teenager, and had something to hide from your folks, where would you hide it?'

'Depends what it was.'

'Something they'd hate you for having.'

I thought back. 'Like porn mags.'

Smith nodded.

'I used to keep them inside my album covers. The ones they'd never look in in a million years.'

'Been there,' he replied and crossed to the box of long players. He began flicking through them, his fingers slipping inside the covers. After a while he looked up. A smile slit his face. He produced a hardback envelope. He held it up for me to see, then twirled it in his fingers. 'A thrilla in Manila,' he purred.

'Open it,' I said.

He nodded and pulled back the tongue.

'Well, I'll be a Son of Muhammad,' said Smith.

19

Smith asked me to be quiet. He had work to do. Savant, tied to a chair with some handy electric flex, watched him intently. He was coping rather well. There had been no hysterics once he had picked himself up off the floor after Smith flattened him, no attempt to flee. He had sat patiently while Smith tied him and I covered him with the gun.

His wallet contained three hundred dollars in cash, an American Express card, driver's licence, several restaurant receipts and some concert ticket stubs. Smith took the cash and stuffed it into his pocket. I said nothing. He took his coat off and then fished into an inside pocket. He withdrew a set of rose clippers, held them up to the light, squeezed the action, then, satisfied, set them on the arm of the sofa. He folded his coat neatly along the sofa cushions. Then he rolled his sleeves up.

He stood in front of Savant, towering over him. Savant looked up at him. Smith slapped him hard across the face. Savant let out a surprised grunt and his kitchen chair rocked to the right, but didn't topple. When the movement stopped, Smith put a finger to his lips, his own lips. Savant nodded. There was a little crack of blood on his upper lip.

'I'm going to ask you some questions. If you tell the truth, and you tell it quickly, things won't get much worse than this. Mess me around and I'll hurt you bad. Understand?'

Savant nodded. His eyes darted to me. I tried to look steely in repose.

'Your name is Marcus Savant.'

He nodded.

'You're a janitor at the Shabazz.'

Savant nodded.

'You're a Muslim.'

Savant nodded.

'And a Brother of Muhammad.'

He nodded again. His eyes held Smith's.

'And a Son of Muhammad.'

Savant shook his head.

Smith slapped him again. This time he rocked to the left.

'I know you're a Son of Muhammad.'

Savant shook again. His nose was bleeding.

'Save yourself some trouble, son.'

Big eyes. Another shake. Another slap.

'You're a Brother of Muhammad?'

Nod.

'And you've heard of the Sons of Muhammad?'

Nod.

'And you're a janitor and you have this expensive apartment and all this lovely furniture, and you're telling me you're not a Son of Muhammad?'

Savant opened his mouth for the first time. His voice was strong. 'I'm well paid. Shabazz a big place. Just me to look after it.'

'Ain't no janitor in history this well paid, son.'

Savant shrugged. That was a mistake. Smith whopped him one on the nose and the chair shot backwards, toppling him onto the floor. He lay there, helpless. He kept admirably quiet. I would have been crying for my mummy. Then Smith kicked him in the stomach.

He let him lie there for a couple of minutes while he lit a cigarette. He puffed on it for a little, then jammed it in his mouth and bent down to right the chair. I went over to help. I said quietly: 'You know what you're doing?'

'Shut the fuck up,' he said sharply.

I raised my eyebrows and returned to the door.

'Now, Marcus, the Sons of Muhammad. They've kidnapped a lady, have they not?'

No reaction.

'A white lady. The wife of a boxer. You've seen her?'

Savant shook his head.

Smith went back to his coat and removed the manila envelope and slipped three photographs out. He showed the top one to Savant. Bobby and Mary McMaster, kissing, in Central Park. Savant nodded.

'Now, I'd like you to tell me where she is. Plain and simple. You tell me, no one else has to know. It'll be a little secret just between us, okay?

Savant shook his head. 'I don't know anything.'

'Of course you do. Where are you keeping her?'

'I . . .'

Smith whacked him again, but this time kept one foot on the leg of the chair so that it wouldn't fly back. It also served to harden the blow. Savant's head shot back. Blood flowed. Smith spent a couple of seconds examining the teeth marks on his knuckles, then punched him again.

Groggy, Savant's head tipped forward. Smith gently lifted it up. 'Hello,' he said. Savant groaned. Smith turned. 'Get some water, would you?'

I nodded and filled a cup from the kitchen sink. I gave it to Smith. He drank it.

'Now,' he said, taking Savant by the hair and shaking his head into full consciousness, 'about Mary McMaster. Why would you have photographs of her if you weren't involved in her kidnapping?'

Savant spat some blood. 'I just have them. They gave them out at the Shabazz. Pictures of the racists. That's all, man. Honest. If I'd known it was illegal, I'd've given them back.'

Smith shook his head and sighed. 'Not good enough, Marcus,' he said and turned back to the sofa. He lifted the rose clippers. 'Ever do any gardening, son?'

Savant shook his head. Droplets of blood peppered the carpet.

'The good thing about pruning roses,' said Smith, lifting Savant's left hand, 'is that eventually they grow back.'

He took hold of the little finger. Savant curled it back as tight as he could. Smith tried to get a fresh grip on it. Savant squirmed his hand away as far as he could in the confines of the electric flex, but Smith had it in a second; he squeezed the little finger hard.

'Okay, okay,' Savant spat, a little high-pitched, releasing the finger.

Smith placed the digit between the teeth of the pruner and closed it, just hard enough to keep it in place.

'You don't type, do you, son?'

Savant shook.

'You'll hardly miss it then.'

He looked his prisoner hard in the eye. 'Your last chance, son.'

Savant shook.

Smith pulled a handkerchief from his pocket and stuffed it into Savant's mouth. It quickly turned red.

Then he started squeezing the handles together.

I turned away. I walked to the kitchen. I ran the cold water. I washed my face. There was a muffled scream and then silence. I opened the fridge door. I took a carton of orange juice from behind the CDs. I checked the date, then drank. Voices came from the lounge again: Smith's aggressive questioning, murmured replies from Savant I couldn't pick up.

I leant back against the sink and closed my eyes. My head throbbed. I needed air. Presently Smith appeared at the kitchen door, shaking his head.

'That was a bit out of hand,' I said. Under lighter circumstances I would have been proud of the pun. But I felt sick.

Smith crossed the tiled floor and stepped on the pedal of a small bin. He dropped Savant's little finger into it.

'Well,' he said, 'horses for courses.'

'Meaning?'

'Meaning I'm paid to do a job and it's in my interests to do it to the best of my ability. In the great scheme of things, a small finger doesn't amount to very much.'

'That's easy to say when it isn't your finger.'

He shrugged. I passed him the juice. He took a long drink.

'Was it worth it?'

Smith returned the carton to me, then wiped his mouth with the back of his hand. He shook his head. 'He's either very brave, or he knows nothing.'

'Which do you think?'

'At this stage I really don't know. There are still seven fingers and two thumbs to go.'

Smith went back to work.

I opened the fridge to replace the remains of the juice. Then I had a thought. They don't come very often so I decided I'd better exploit it to the maximum.

I went back to the lounge. Smith stood over Savant, rose

pruners in hand. Savant was ashen-faced, but his eyes burnt courageously.

'Smith,' I said, simply.

He looked round, annoyed. I was beginning to think he might be enjoying it. 'What?'

'Stop for a minute.'

'Starkey, butt out.'

'No. Seriously. Stop.'

'Starkey . . .'

'Let me speak to him. Let me ask him.'

'Starkey, take notes, you're the reporter. Let me do my job.'

'That isn't anyone's job. It's torture.'

'You catch on quick.'

'Yeah.' I walked towards him. 'I'll make you a deal. Give me ten minutes with him. If I don't get the information we need, then you can have him back and pluck the rest of his fuckin' fingers. Ten minutes isn't much.'

Smith stepped back. He wiped the pruners on Savant's shirt. 'Okay. Ten minutes. I'll see if I can find something to eat.' He looked at Savant, then shook his head. 'Jesus, he'll probably bleed to death before I get back.'

He went to the kitchen. I stood in front of Savant. He was in a real mess. There was a bloody stump, tiny, like a twig snap. Blood oozed from it steadily.

'How're ya doin', Marcus?' I asked.

Savant looked me up and down disdainfully. 'How the fuck do you think I'm doin'? What're you, the good guy?'

I shook my head. 'I just want you to answer some questions.'

He held up his complete hand, wiggled the little finger he had left. 'Ask away.'

'I couldn't help but notice that you have a good record collection.'

Savant nodded hesitantly.

'But hardly one you would expect a black fella like yourself to have. I mean, there are a few concessions there, some rap, some Motown, but I couldn't help but notice . . .'

'I have wide and varied tastes. I'm not a prisoner of my race.'

'Quite. But I couldn't help but notice that you have an affinity for one particular artiste.'

'That's my p'rogative.'

'I heard him this afternoon, out on the porch. I found him in your record collection. In your CD stack. I found concert ticket stubs in your wallet. Then I found him in your fridge. You're a devoted fan.'

'Barry Manilow is the greatest entertainer of the modern era.'

'Mmmm.'

'He's the greatest singer of popular ballads in history.'

'Mmmmm.'

'And he's a lovely, lovely man.'

'And you've met him.'

Savant nodded again, warily, something dawning on him. For the first time he looked a little shaken.

'Where did you meet him, Marcus?'

'Back stage at Madison. I won a competition with the fan club. He was so gracious.'

'And he signed this for you, didn't he?' I produced a CD from the fridge. *Barry Manilow Live at the Cocacobana*. It felt creepy holding it. '"To Marcus, my number one fan, love Barry."'

'Yeah.' He drawled it out. Still awestruck.

'How much is it worth, Marcus?'

'It ain't worth money.'

We looked at each other for a moment. He knew what I was thinking.

'Don't do this, man.'

'You leave me no choice, Marcus.'

'Please, man.'

I lifted Smith's lighter from the sofa. I held the CD box up to the naked flame. Barry smiled at me. 'Mankind will thank me in later years, Marcus.'

'Don't do it, man, do anything else. Here, take another finger. Have a thumb. Have two. Leave him be. Leave me that, man.'

'I take your thumbs, Marcus, you won't be able to pick it up.'

'Doesn't matter.'

I held the flame a little closer.

'Please.'

I sang softly to him. '"Her name was Lola . . ."'

'Please.'

'How important is it to you, Marcus?'

'Please.'

'More important than the Shabazz?'

'Please.'

'More important than Muhammad?'

'Please.'

'You're a Son of Muhammad, aren't you, Marcus?'

He nodded.

We left him tied to the chair with the bloody rag in his mouth, blood dripping from his finger and Barry Manilow in his lap. It was a cruel way to leave him but it was better than killing him.

Three flights down, Smith said: 'Shit! Forgot my lighter.' He turned back. He tossed me the car keys. 'Only be a second,' he called after him. I hurried on down the stairs and crossed the road. I sat in the car. Smith appeared again after a couple of minutes. He opened the driver's door and squeezed in.

'Here,' he said, 'a souvenir.'

He tossed Barry into my lap and started the car.

I examined the box. There was the faintest of scorch marks on Barry's lips. It didn't matter much.

'You killed him, didn't you?'

He grunted and pulled out into the traffic.

20

We tracked the Three Amigos down to an art house cinema
in Greenwich Village. Smith hesitated; I paid. An old trick I
should have been wise to. The show had yet to begin and
the lights were still up. There were only around a dozen
people in the theatre. Bobby McMaster and Geordie McClean
sat together about halfway down; Stanley Matchitt was three
rows behind them in splendid isolation. He looked round as
we pushed through the doors and watched as we came down
the aisle. He nodded. We ignored him.

Geordie McClean looked up, then tutted. 'It used to be,'
he said quietly as we took seats in the row behind him, 'that
the cinema was my escape.'

'Sorry,' I said.

'In Belfast, when I want to be alone, this is where I go.
No one phones you at the cinema. No one talks to you. I

thought I might get away with the same here.' He tutted again. 'First Bobby insists on coming, which means Stanley trails along, which means Poodle's boys are about somewhere and now you two come after me. I won't be surprised if the Sons of Muhammad appear before the first reel and start bombarding me with popcorn.'

Bobby turned. 'Any word?'

'Not specifically,' said Smith.

Stanley joined us. 'Hopeless,' he said, easing in beside me and pushing my elbow off the arm of the seat.

'Not specifically,' Smith repeated, 'but I've a fair idea where she might be.'

'Brill,' beamed Bobby.

'A fair idea,' repeated McClean, staring at the blank screen. 'Tell me more.'

'You want the whole place to know, or should I tell you in private?'

'We're all friends here.'

Smith shrugged and leant forward. 'According to my source,' he began, catching my eye and holding it for a second, 'the Sons of Muhammad have got something curious going on at their headquarters.'

'Something curious,' said McClean.

Smith nodded. 'Yeah. The Brothers and Sons of Muhammad both have their headquarters in a mosque called the Shabazz. It's a big place. Dominates the Harlem skyline. It's popular too, a lot of people go through it every day, for prayer and that, but there's also a part of it which is strictly off limits to the public. Okay, understandable. But within that private section there's an isolated room which has become strictly off limits over the last few days. Only the highest ranking Sons are allowed access – and none of the Brothers. Guarded twenty-four hours a day. I reckon if she's anywhere, she's in there.'

'But has anyone seen her?' asked Bobby.

Smith shook his head. 'My source hasn't seen anything.'

'Can he not find out?'

'He's done as much as he can.'

'I could persuade him,' said Stanley.

'I doubt it,' said Smith.

'Well, if she's in there,' said Bobby, 'let's get on to the police, get them in, get her out.'

Smith shook his head. 'It doesn't work like that, Bobby. They need good evidence before they go into somewhere like the Shabazz. A mysterious room isn't good evidence. And if they tried to storm it, the likelihood is things would get messy, people would get hurt, then they'd have a race riot on their hands. And this is election year, so the Mayor's hardly likely to sanction it.'

'Okay,' said Geordie, still not turning, 'so the police are out. What about sending a crew of Poodle Clay's boys in? They look like they can handle themselves.'

'That,' said Smith, 'wouldn't help much either.'

'Poodle's been seen at the mosque three or four times in the past week,' I said.

This time Geordie looked round. 'You say what?'

'Poodle's been rubbing noses at the Shabazz.'

'You're positive?'

'Our source is positive.'

Geordie blew out some air and shook his head. 'The jigsaw thickens,' he said.

McMaster fixed his eyes on Smith. 'I don't understand.'

'What's there to understand?' snarled Stanley. 'Those cunts have Mary poked up in a room, and this cunt Poodle is involved.'

'Charmingly put, Stanley,' I said. 'On the other hand we could be barking completely up the wrong tree. They might just have a secret room. Some places do. And why shouldn't Poodle visit? He might be religious himself. He might be trying to track her down himself. Negotiate for her himself. Or just trying to get the threat against Bobby lifted.'

McClean shook his head. 'I don't think he even knows she's gone, Starkey. She's still technically just missing. The police are hardly bothering. We five are the only ones convinced that she's been kidnapped.'

'We six. Jackie Campbell knows.'

'Aye, Jackie knows now. You told him.'

'I thought . . .'

'You know what thought did.'

'Sorry.'

'Never worry. As far as I'm aware the story's still in-house.'

The cinema began to darken. We sat back. The trailers came on. 'So what next?' asked McClean.

Smith leant further forward, until his arm rested on the back of McClean's seat. 'We go in and look for her.'

'Isn't that dangerous?'

'Yes.'

I bent towards Smith. 'When you say, we go in, who exactly do you mean?'

'Anyone who cares to volunteer.'

'I'll go,' said McMaster quickly.

'You'll stay where you are,' snapped McClean.

'I bloody . . .'

'You'll bloody stay where you are, I haven't invested millions in this to . . .'

'She's my wife . . .'

'You'll serve no purpose being there, Bobby. You concentrate on the boxing. Let Smith handle it. He can take Stanley and Starkey with him for back-up.'

'Class,' said Stanley.

'Shite,' I said.

'Starkey . . .'

'You're not getting me in there.'

'Starkey, we need your help.'

'What the hell could I do?'

'Safety in numbers,' said Smith. He clapped his hand on my leg. I removed it. Not my leg. His hand. 'You did well today, Starkey. Build on that.'

'I'm a reporter.'

'Hey,' said McClean, 'Wilfred Owen didn't chicken out.'

'Who the fuck's Wilfred Owen?' asked Stanley.

'War poet,' said McMaster.

'"Dulce et decorum est . . ." whatever,' said McClean.

'It is good to die for one's country,' translated McMaster.

'But not very smart to get shot on the last day of the war,' I said. 'No, thanks.'

'He only got shot because he didn't duck,' said McMaster.

'Very comforting, Bobby. No, thanks for the flattery, lads, but I don't think this quite equates with Wilfred Bloody Owen. He was a soldier for one thing. I'm not. For another he would have been shot for desertion if he'd tried to run away.'

'And you think you won't?' asked Stanley.

'Oh, you scare me, Stanley.'

An irritated voice called from the back of the cinema. 'Could you guys keep it down, please? The movie's starting.'

I looked up at the screen. A motorbike was racing along an English country lane. Peter O'Toole was barely recognizable behind an old-fashioned helmet.

'Derek of Arabia,' said Stanley. 'Class.'

'Lawrence,' McMaster corrected.

'Could you guys keep it down up there?' came the voice again, a little higher pitched. 'The movie's started.'

Stanley reared up in his seat. 'Ah, keep your hair on, wouldja?' he shouted back. 'Sure hasn't it been on TV a hundred million times? And he dies at the start, doesn't he? So you bloody well know he's dead by the end, don't you?'

'I haven't seen it before!'

'Well, shut the fuck up and watch it then!'

Stanley sat back in his seat. 'Stupid cunt,' he said.

McMaster whispered something in McClean's ear. McClean nodded and turned back to Smith. 'Should we be wasting time here?' he asked quietly.

'No point in rushing it. I'll need to get a ground plan of the Shabazz so that we know where we're going, and I can't get that until City Hall opens. Sit back and enjoy the movie, boys. I'll go and get some hot dogs. Let's relax while we can.'

He raised himself with some effort and headed back up the aisle.

'You know,' said McClean, 'I saw this for the first time way back in '69 when I was at Queen's University. It had been around for a good few years then, like, but we had this cinema club, a real fleabag joint. A brilliant film, brilliant, I was really enjoying it, but I couldn't for the life of me understand why David Lean had this little black bush in the bottom corner of every frame. It intrigued me for the whole of the – what was it – three hours? This was the late sixties, like, the age of experimental film. I had dreams of being a film-maker myself.'

'A bit different from insurance, eh?' said McMaster.

'Yeah, well, boyhood dreams. But I thought Lean was such a master. I mean, there he was with this epic picture, millions and millions of dollars to make, looked like heaven, yet he has the balls to put a little black bush in the corner of every frame. I spent ages trying to work it out, the symbolism, the hidden meaning. It was a real enigma. Then it was over, the lights went up, and there was this bastard with a huge Afro sitting in the front row.' He shook his head. 'I should have killed him.'

'PHILISTINES!'

It came from the back row. Stanley turned quickly, his hand diving into his inside pocket, but all he saw was a rotund figure exiting quickly through the doors at the back of the theatre.

I turned back to the screen. I felt a tap on my leg. Bobby McMaster, thin-lipped but giant-faced scary in the flickering light, whispered plaintively, 'You'll help get her back, won't you, Starkey? I love her.'

'Of course,' I said.

It got to the torture scene and I left. I had been involved in torture and murder only a few hours before. Torture and murder. Then I was sitting in a cinema munching on a hot dog. And it tasted like a hot dog. It tasted good. But it was meant to taste like wood; torture and death were meant to have removed my appetite, left me hollow.

Smith had carried out the murder with a nonchalance which was chilling. I had asked for details. He had just grunted some more and said Mary's life was more important than pricks like Savant. I didn't know. Who was to say what made one life important, another not? Who was to say that the wife and lover of a man about to fight for the heavyweight title was more important than a man with a Barry Manilow fixation? You couldn't weigh up lives like that. Murder was murder was murder.

And now I was being asked to take part in a raid on the headquarters of the Sons of Muhammad. Me. Dan Starkey. Ace fucker upper. Now was the time to stop a taxi, go to the airport, fly home, start sorting out my life, start sorting out the things which were important. What was a book? What was someone else's missing wife? What were the Sons of Muhammad? What were any of them compared to my wife? If I'd stopped to ask those questions years ago when I first lost her, then my life would have been so different, so much better. Not the shell it was now.

Then I thought: but I had stopped to ask those questions back then; I'd known the answers and accepted the repercussions, and gone ahead with my foolish actions because I was so sure of myself that I believed everything would work out for the best; and even when I saw things weren't working out for the best I'd pressed ahead because I was a glutton for punishment and I couldn't suppress my own desires. So, tough.

The rain, cold, spat in my face. Taxis splashed past. Across the road young folk spoke animatedly over drinks in a rock bar. What I would have given to be amongst them, talking nonsense and not giving a damn. An old woman shuffled past me, head down, pulled along by a pink poodle on a long lead.

'Can I give you a ride?'

I turned. Smith. Buttoning his coat. I shook my head.

'Are you okay?'

I nodded.

'You're thinking about Savant, aren't you?'

I nodded.

'About cutting his finger off, and then shooting him.'

I nodded.

'What would you have done if it had been your wife being held captive?'

'I'd have pushed him off the balcony of a block of flats.'

'So?'

I shrugged. 'I know. It was for the best. It doesn't mean I have to be happy about it.'

'Who of us are? Which of us is?'

He nodded and moved up the street towards his car. I watched him get in and pull out into the traffic with a screech of tyres.

I crossed the road to the bar.

21

Some time after midnight there was a light rap on the door. I was just starting to drift, propped up on a pillow, Deep Space Nine casting alien shadows across the room. I rolled off the bed, stretched, then moved to the door. I hesitated for a moment. It had been a night of death. Maybe it wasn't the done thing to answer the door in the wee small hours. Then I thought that if a terrorist was standing outside with a bazooka, he wasn't going to be dissuaded by impoliteness. It takes thirty years of Belfast life to understand terrorist etiquette.

Bobby McMaster stood there, once nobody's idea of a terrorist but now starting to shape up in the ring, even if only in response to near tragedy. He had a mini-can from his mini-bar in each of his giant hands. They looked ridiculously small.

'Join me in a drink?' he asked. Doleful eyes. The lonely big eejit.

It was hardly straight from the training manual, but I nodded and ushered him in. 'You're welcome. My minibar has unaccountably run dry.'

He handed me a can as he passed. He didn't seem to notice the mess of the room. He crossed to the window. I joined him. We flipped cans together and slurped as we looked out over the lights of New York.

'She's out there somewhere,' he said.

'Alcohol is a depressant,' I said.

'No, having your wife stolen from you and not knowing whether she's alive or dead is a depressant. Alcohol is a drink.'

'I won't argue with that.'

He nodded.

'Can't you sleep?' I asked.

He shook his head.

'You're worried about tomorrow night, aren't you?' I touched his arm with my can. It was a sympathetic touch, but done in an all-men-together way that wouldn't make him, or me, feel like a softie. 'Of course you are. You think you should be going along. You think something might go wrong, that she might get hurt, that you should be there to protect her. It's natural, Bobby. I'd be the same. Jesus, I am the same, and I'm going on the fuckin' raid. But don't worry. It'll be okay. I've seen Smith in action, he's very thorough, very efficient, he'll get the job done. And I'm sure Stanley's the same, providing he doesn't have to get on a boat. We'll be fine. She'll be fine.'

He looked me in the eye. His mouth opened, he started to say something, but then it closed again and he shook his head slightly and returned his gaze to the neon city. He took another drink. 'Do you think much about Irish politics, Starkey?'

I took a drink. 'As little as possible.'

'What would you describe yourself as, British?'

I shrugged. One of my better ones, the kind of thoroughbred shrug I reserved for genuinely perplexing situations. 'On hijacked aeroplanes they always shoot the British third, just after the Americans and the Jews. No, not British.'

'But not Irish?'

'No. Not unless I'm in trouble abroad. I have an Irish passport, but I wouldn't produce it in public at home.'

'So would you say you were mostly ambivalent about the whole British/Irish thing?'

'Ambivalent? No. I'm from Northern Ireland, Bobby, same as you, not England, not Ireland, it's home, I couldn't much be bothered fighting to make it one thing or the other, but if someone walked in and forced me into one thing or another, then I might get more protective about it. And by the way, you haven't been taking any mind-altering drugs lately, have you?'

He laughed. 'No, Starkey.'

'Then why the sudden interest in politics?'

'Nothing. Just thinking.'

'I would have marked you down as a staunch Loyalist, anyway. Didn't you used to beat up Catholics with Stanley?'

'Used to, yeah.'

'I know you've changed. Obviously you've changed. But a man's politics don't change that easily, do they? You grew out of senseless violence, but you're still from the Protestant ghetto in Crossmaheart, aren't you? You're still for God and Ulster, whether you're married to a Catholic or not.'

McMaster shrugged. 'I thought I was. I got to thinking that maybe none of it mattered much. Religion. Politics. As long as you're happy with your lot and your family, it's not that important who you pray to or who you pay your taxes to. I was thinking that.'

'And worthy thoughts they are too, Bobby. We'll get you into the Peace People at this rate. My, you're getting profound in your old age.'

'Yeah. Keeps my mind off other things.'

'I can understand that. But don't worry. It'll go okay.'

'I don't think we should even attempt it. This raid.' He put his hand up against the window, rubbed it slowly round. 'It's too dangerous. If we know anything from home, it's how volatile religious types can be. We should leave it up to the police or the FBI.'

'Aye, they did well at Waco.'

'I'd just hate to see anyone get hurt for no good reason.'

'Mary isn't a good reason?'

He shook his head wistfully. 'Of course she is.'

The alcohol was gone. I lay back on the bed, sipping my way through the soft drinks. The TV flickered silently. I meandered through the radio dial. It was like politics at home. Fifty-seven different stations, all playing the same record.

Until . . . until I heard The Clash. The saving grace. 'London

Calling.' The DJ, slow, cool, asked, 'Whatever did happen to The Clash?'

I listened for a while, heard what station it was, traced them in the phone book. A squawky girl on the switchboard.

'I want to talk to the DJ.'

'On air?'

'On air.'

'What about?'

'The Clash.'

'Hold the line, sir.' She put me on hold for thirty seconds. 'Putting you through, sir. I should remind you that when speaking on air no bad language is permitted, no advertising without prior written consent from the station, no comments calculated to stir up racial tension, no appeals for money, no espousing of political causes. The station takes no responsibility for anything you may say, do or incite while on air . . . you accept all of the conditions I have outlined, sir?'

'I do.'

'Enjoy your airtime, sir.'

'Thank you.'

The Cure. 'Love Cats.' Just starting to fade. The DJ. 'Hi there. We go on air in ten seconds. And don't pay any attention to anything Sandra says, our air is your air.'

'Cheers,' I said.

'Welcome back,' he said. 'We have a guy on the line wants to talk about The Clash. Where you from, sir?'

'Belfast. I'm calling from the Mirage Hotel. I'm sorry, that's advertising, isn't it?'

'Never mind. We play The Clash, we sell some more Clash records, that's advertising too, you see?'

'I suppose. You asked whatever happened to The Clash.'

'Great English band. Great English band. Whatever happened to The Clash?'

'Joe Strummer still sings. He had a solo album out. Didn't do much. He's done some singing with the Pogues.'

'The Pogues. Great band. Great Irish band.'

'Mick Jones. He's in Big Audio Dynamite. They've had five or six albums out. Excellent albums. Haven't done much. Paul Simonon, he had Havana 3am. Had an album out. Not bad. Didn't do much.'

'What about that drummer? Great roll at the start of "I Fought the Law".' He beat it out with what sounded like a couple of pencils.

'Topper Headon. Had a drug problem. Been in prison. I think he drives a taxi now.'

'Shame, shame. What a talent. What a wasted talent.'

'Yeah. Yeah.'

I held the phone to my ear and looked out over the city again. I wondered how many people were listening. I wondered how many had heard of The Clash. Patricia always hated The Clash. Had heard more melodic cement mixers. Chalk and cheese.

'So what are you doing here . . . uh, Gary, is it?'

'Dan. Daniel. I'm on vacation. Here to see a fight actually. Mike Tyson and . . .'

'That racist guy from Ireland . . .'

'He's not racist. Not racist at all. One of the nicest guys you could hope to meet.'

'Really? Word on the street . . .'

'The word on the street is wrong. He's a nice guy, a nice guy who's gonna give Tyson a run for his money.'

'And you travelled all the way from Ireland to see him?'

'Sure did.'

'Well, Gary, a pleasure talking to you. Enjoy New York. I just know it'll enjoy you. Anyone you want to say hello to on this cold and frosty March morning?'

'No. Yeah. Just to say hi to Mary if she's listening out there, and we're all thinking of you.'

'This one's for you, Mary, the sound of the Cars . . .'

The city that never sleeps. Yeah, well, it was doing a bloody good impression.

There had been a frost. As the starry black of night soothed into the grey of dawn I walked along Broadway, deserted but for the occasional cab, the occasional destitute slumped in a doorway, the occasional burger box floating amiably along in the slightest of breezes. A Vietnam vet lay unconscious beside his begging card and cup in the entrance to the theatre which housed *Miss Saigon*. Maybe in his more lucid moments he laughed at the irony. His skin was blue. A couple of Times Square cops chatted over steaming coffee beside him, unconcerned.

I was cold to the bone. I had my leather jacket on, my black jeans, my new trainers. I'd money in my pocket and love in my heart, but no one to waste it on. I had three women in my life: Patricia at home with someone else; Paula, with Chinese Elvis or at least a whole load of willies; and Mary, missing. Later in the day I would attempt to liberate Mary. Storm the stronghold like the hero I wasn't. Maybe die in the effort. What for? For someone else's love.

Earlier I had made a list of my possessions, the personal stuff I wanted someone to have in the event of my death, not the married stuff we'd always argue over.

In no particular order:

The photo album of all the gang when we were young, teens and twenties, discovering alcohol. I looked at our faces, spotty, fresh, bright-eyed or drink-dulled. God, we had consumed some booze between us. The devil's vomit, my dad had warned us, told us where it would lead us. What harm had it done? None at all. Three of those faces were now in prison, two started supporting Celtic and one ended up in a hippie drug train to Nepal, but it had nothing to do with alcohol.

The signed photo of Mark Brinn, shortest reigning Northern Irish prime minister of all time. I'd had dinner with him and chatted about capital punishment, and then he'd exploded.

The bootleg cassette of The Clash live at the Ulster Hall. My first exposure to live music. An eye-opener.

My first love letter (never sent to Patricia, what would she make of it now?).

My first love letter (from Patricia, Jesus, how wonderful she thought I was in those early days).

Casablanca.

My first novel (unrecognized classic, never published).

Beer mats from 727 different pubs.

A photo of Patricia in Paris.

A naked photo of Patricia in Paris.

It didn't amount to much. No one would race into the street and thank God for being remembered in my will. Maybe if I was lucky they would shed a tear and think about old times and say what a good guy I was.

Joke. Who would 'they' be? Patricia, of course, there was no one else.

I phoned her.

'Dan, that's a pathetic little list.'

'But it's all I've got.'

'God, you're pathetic.'

'But I'm lost without you.'

'You're lost with me. Get a life, Dan. Do something worthwhile.'

'I'm writing a book.'

'You're running away.'

'I'm doing the only thing I know how to do. I'm writing.'

'You haven't written a word.'

'But I know what I'm writing.'

'You haven't a clue, Dan. Grand ideas. Little substance. Such a waste.'

'I may not survive tonight.'

'Of course you will.'

'I have this chill sense of foreboding.'

'What a line. You're scared.'

'Of course I'm scared.'

'But you rescued me once before.'

'But I couldn't keep you.'

'No. You won the battle, lost the war.'

'Is there no hope for me?'

'There's always hope, Dan. Make me proud.'

'I'll do my best.'

'No, Dan, not your best. Just do it. No excuses.'

'Okay. Love.'

'Love.'

There was no reply.

22

Smith led us by shuddery elevator to the third floor. Black lettering on a frosted-glass door halfway along a dusty corridor read: PETER SMITH, INVESTIGATIONS. He unlocked the door and let us into the outer office. A large black woman sat behind a desk. She wore a big flowery shirt, pink-rimmed spectacles. She looked up and nodded. Smith smiled. 'Coffee and doughnuts, Sissy, please.'

Sissy pushed her seat back and stood. She was as wide as her desk. Her face was all crinkly laughter lines and bright eyes. She was probably locked in for her own protection. Smith's office appeared to be located in the Crack World Trade Center. 'I'll go and see Duncan,' she said.

'Any messages?'

She gave Smith a look that said, are you joking?

Smith led us on through to his office, which was virtually

the same as Sissy's: big untidy desk, old-fashioned heavy black phone and a pile of out-of-date directories, green filing cabinets, an assortment of calendars.

Sissy closed the outside door. Matchitt was still nodding appreciatively. 'She's a big girl,' he said.

'She's my wife,' said Smith, sitting himself behind his desk. He indicated two chairs at the back of the office. I lifted them over.

'She's a beautiful big girl,' adjusted Matchitt.

'I think so,' said Smith laconically. He lifted the directories off his desk and set them on the floor beside him, tidied together the cluttered papers before him and put them on the floor also. Then he pulled open a drawer and produced a rolled-up document. He spread it on the desk. Matchitt and I craned forward.

'The floor plan of the Shabazz,' he said, 'courtesy of City Hall.'

We gave it a couple of minutes of studied silence. I suppose it looked like a mosque, insofar as anything one-dimensional can, but as it hadn't been that long since I'd mastered left from right I wasn't about to go promoting any ambitious plans for the taking of the headquarters of the Sons of Muhammad. I nodded a couple of times and said, 'Hmmmm.'

Matchitt was the first to sit back. 'I don't know about you, but I get lost in Woolworth's,' he said with refreshing honesty, while failing miserably to stifle a yawn. 'I'll just follow you two.'

'It's not that complicated,' Smith said, flattening the

rolled-up edges of the plan with his elbows, then pointing down with his index fingers. 'You can see the dome of the mosque, right?' We nodded. 'The main entrance, the rooms here, here and here, that are used by the flock. Then across here is the private block, with its separate entrance, here. It's a fairly straight route to the top of the building, here.'

'And that's the secret room,' I said.

'Well, no, not there exactly. A little beyond, a little above. The value of having a secret room is not having it on floor plans like this.'

I nodded.

Matchitt leant forward. 'So all we have to do is get from here, to here, then get her out, then get us out.'

Smith nodded.

'Using only our charm,' I contributed.

'I think not,' said Smith. He pulled open another drawer. The gas masks I recognized. They're hard to mistake. The other things I wasn't so sure about. He set them on the desk. Matchitt's hands darted to them greedily.

'Class,' he said, 'absolute class.'

'Would you care to explain?' I asked.

Smith picked up a small, black, rounded thing, like a headache pill for a giant. 'Stun grenade,' he said.

'For?'

'Stunning,' said Matchitt.

'The guards on the door,' said Smith.

I nodded. 'The rest?'

'Tear gas.'

I nodded.

'Class,' said Matchitt, 'fucking class.'

An anxious sigh came unbidden. I covered up, badly, by having a go at Matchitt. 'You're in your element, aren't you, Stanley?'

'Absolute class. Can't get these at home, I'll tell ya.'

'This is like Disneyland to you, isn't it, Stanley?'

'Too right.' He pulled his gas mask on, then started juggling with the stun grenades.

I shook my head. Tutted. 'It begs the question, of course, is this a Mickey Mouse operation?'

Matchitt shook his alien head. 'Lllllnn uh Sahy.'

'I beg your pardon?'

He pulled the mask up. 'I said, lighten up, Starkey. We'll need this stuff.'

Smith picked up one of the tear gas canisters and turned it lightly in his hand. 'Disney,' he said, 'is actually one of the most efficiently run organizations in the world. If I could run a Mickey Mouse operation like theirs, well, I wouldn't be stuck here.'

'Are you saying then that you're inefficient?'

'No, I'm complimenting Disney on their efficiency.'

'Are you saying that Disney have the capacity to storm the Shabazz using stun grenades and tear gas and God knows what else?'

'No, of course not. I was only making a point.'

Matchitt set the gas mask back on the desk. 'You know what I think? I think you're scared, Starkey.'

I tutted again. Rolled my eyes. 'Of course I'm scared. It's not what I do, this, this nonsense. This is more up your street than mine, Stanley.'

Matchitt nodded at Smith. 'What do you think, Smithy, would it be more efficient to have three or two people involved in this raid? What would Walt Disney do?'

'I think we're overplaying this Walt Disney thing. I think Starkey will be fine. He just needs a kick in the ass.'

'I can do that,' said Matchitt.

'You keep your fucking feet to yourself, Stanley.'

'Oh, please, no threats, Starkey.'

'Yeah,' I said.

Smith lifted a pencil and pointed at the entrance to the private block. 'What I'm suggesting,' he said, 'is that we enter here. From what I've observed things get pretty quiet around the Shabazz from about 10.30 p.m. on. There are between two and four guards on duty through the night, but there's not much activity, which suggests that they won't be that alert. The door's always open so they can keep an eye on the street.'

'No hi-tech surveillance?' asked Matchitt.

'Not according to Savant,' I said.

'But can he be trusted?'

I shrugged.

'The stun grenades will put the doormen down and out for a couple of minutes. Then some tear gas. Then I suggest we storm straight up the stairs to the top. We ignore the elevator. Too much can go wrong with it.'

Matchitt sniggered. 'Yeah, it'd be a shame if someone wanted to get on halfway up.'

Smith ignored him. 'If we're lucky we'll get to the fifth floor without too much trouble, we'll fire some more tear gas up to the next floor, disable the guards outside Mary's room one way or another, and then get into the room and get her out. Then we go back down the stairs and out.'

'Simple,' I said.

'No offence,' said Matchitt, resting his elbows on the desk, 'I've voiced my concerns about Starkey here, but what about yourself? You're not what I would call in the peak of physical condition.'

'And you are?'

'Compared to you. I genuinely don't mean it as an insult, but can you see yourself racing up five flights of stairs in your gas mask?'

'Don't be misled by what you perceive to be my physical state, Stanley. I think you'll find I measure up.'

'I'd hate to find out otherwise when it mattered most.'

'Well, we'll just have to trust each other, won't we? All I know about you is what Starkey here tells me. You may not be the psycho he says you are. You might be a wimp. I'm not saying you are, but you might be.'

'I'm no psycho.'

'Whatever you say. I'm just making a point. We're all three of us very different, but we're working together for a common aim and that aim is to get that poor woman away from the Sons of Muhammad.'

'Do I take it,' I ventured hopefully, 'that my role in this is restricted to sitting in the car outside, for the quick getaway?'

'No,' they said together.

'One for all,' added Matchitt helpfully, 'one for all. *The Three Musketeers.*'

The office door opened. Sissy entered carrying a tray and three cartons of coffee and three chocolate doughnuts. Smith pushed the assorted weaponry out of the way with his forearm. She didn't give it a second glance as she set the tray down.

'How's Duncan?' asked Smith.

'Profitable.'

'Who do you love?'

'You.'

It had an air of ritual about it. They smiled warmly at each other. Smith put an entire doughnut in his mouth. 'Helff yourselllf,' he spat out round it.

I picked a doughnut, left the coffee. Matchitt did the same. 'Not a coffee man?' he asked.

I shook my head.

'More in common than you think, Starkey.'

I shook my head. Swallowed. 'I doubt it.'

Smith took Sissy home for dinner. We went back to the hotel and got changed into our darkest clothes. It seemed the thing to do. McMaster was asleep. McClean was jumpy. Now he wasn't sure if any of it was a good idea. While we were storming the Shabazz he was to shepherd the big man to

224

CBS Studios for a TV interview to be beamed live across the nation. Some chat show. David Letterbox. Jay Lemon. Whatever. The idea was to repair some of the damage caused by McMaster's perceived racism. He was to be Mr Nice Guy.

About eight I took Matchitt to the Broadway Grill just off Columbus Circle. We got a couple of cheeseburgers and waited for Smith.

Stanley looked like a struggling poet: cropped hair, a black sweater baggy enough to hide the little pot belly, black jeans, some off-the-rack stubble. He flicked some salt off the table.

'There really isn't that much to worry about, Starkey,' he said.

'That's easy for you to say.'

'Just go in there and do it. It'll come easy, once the adrenaline gets going. I remember the first time . . .'

'I don't want to know, Stanley.'

He shrugged.

I nodded and sipped at my Diet Coke. I was trying to fool myself that it was the antidote for cheeseburger. As if it mattered. I was about to get shot and I was worried about my cholesterol level. I shook my head and snorted. Maybe I would get lucky and have a stroke on my way to the raid. Or possibly during it. And get left behind.

'Are you married, Stanley?'

'No.'

'Family?'

'Oh, I'm sure there's wee ones dotted about the place. None I'm going to pay for.'

'So who'll miss you when you die?'

'If they miss me, I won't die.'

'It's good of you to do this for Bobby.'

'I'm being paid.'

'It's more than that.'

'Yeah, well. What can I say?'

'And she's a Catholic.'

'Who is?'

'Mary.'

'Seriously?' He kept the serious look up for ten seconds, then a smile slipped onto his face. 'She's his wife, isn't she?'

'Wouldn't go down with your old company.'

'No, I don't suppose it would. But things change. People change.' He nodded absently, momentarily lost in thought, then his eyes focused again. 'How's your wife, Starkey?'

'Okay,' I said.

'She's a bit of a good looker.'

I shrugged. Then thought out loud: 'How would you know?'

'Oh, you'd be surprised what I know. Still in the tax office, is she? Still do her shopping at Bloomers on a Thursday night? Still a Smirnoff and Diet Coker?'

Someone walked over my grave. 'What're you saying, Stanley?'

'We had you checked out once, Starkey. The boys, y'know?'

'Checked out for . . . ?'

'What do the boys do, Starkey?'

'You cut throats. You shoot people.'

Of Wee Sweetie Mice and Men

Matchitt nodded. 'So we had you checked out. One too many sarky comments in the paper. So your name got added to the list. Fortunately for you it was a long list. Mind you, as far as I recall, we did do a couple of dry runs. It's amazing what can upset a murder plan. Traffic lights. Double parking. A traffic warden. Someone forgetting the gun. It was only a matter of time, though.' He ran a finger across his jugular.

I sat back. The walker had become a dancer.

'You look a little pale.'

'I'm always a little pale. What happened I never made the top of the list?'

'Don't know. Priorities change. Maybe you made a couple of digs at the IRA and you got a second chance. Maybe we all went to prison. I can't remember. I just thought you'd like to know.'

'Thanks,' I said.

'Once I might have slit your throat, and not thought twice about it, and here we are sharing cheeseburgers in New York. Funny old world, isn't it?'

'Hilarious,' I said.

23

Somewhere on Led Zeppelin's 'The Song Remains the Same' there's a twenty-minute drum solo by John Bonham. It's as annoying as most drum solos, but it's damn loud and there's a murderous beat. My heart was playing pretty much to the same rhythm as we parked the fishing boat a block from the Shabazz and did the Harlem shuffle up Morningside towards our date with destiny. Matchitt and I walked in Smith's wake. His black trench coat flapped about him in the icy wind. Observed from the front, we wouldn't have been observed at all.

When we were twenty yards from the rear entrance to the Shabazz, Smith said simply, 'Masks.'

Like the team we weren't, we produced the gas masks on cue. I'd practised the quick application of the mask five or six times in the course of the afternoon and felt only moderately uncomfortable, but although I slipped it on with ease, it still felt like someone had pounced on me with a roll of clingfilm and was winding it round and round and would only stop when all life had been extinguished. I stopped for a moment, just to steady myself, but Matchitt caught my arm and propelled me forward with a muffled grunt. He had a pistol in his other hand. In the shadow of the Shabazz, with the wind cut off, Smith produced a shotgun from the folds of his coat, swinging the barrel up towards the open doors. I put my hand in my pocket and took out a revolver. I'd practised with it as well. I could hit a stationary target at fifty yards, lifting, aiming, squeezing the trigger and saying bang. Maybe having to use bullets would be different.

A half-finished cigarette was thrown out the door. An exchange of voices, one commanding, one subservient, then a tall, thin fella in a bobble hat and tracksuit appeared, descended the four steps with one stride and bent to retrieve the butt. Then he looked up at us. Eyes widened. Words failed him. Smith shot him. He flew backwards through the door. Smith stopped, Matchitt behind him. They both threw stun grenades through the gap, then crouched down. I joined them. Crack. Bang. Flash. Wallop. Smith waved us on.

Matchitt beat him to the door. He rushed in, pistol out in front. We crowded in behind. Four men lay on the floor, out of it; a fifth had a huge hole in his chest.

We hit the stairs, Matchitt first, then Smith, I brought up the rear. On the fourth step Smith turned and tossed the tear gas back into the lobby. I'd forgotten to do it.

Smith was fast, but not fast enough. The stairs were wide, but not wide enough. Now that I was in the action, I wanted to be racing up, keeping fast, bobbing and weaving, not having to continually check back as Smith pulled his considerable girth onwards and upwards at a steady but gratingly lugubrious pace. I was stuck behind him, a Ford Fiesta in a back alley behind a bin lorry. I turned, my pistol trained on the stairs behind, but there was no movement.

The first floor was clear, so was the second. We stopped on the third-floor landing. A muffled clatter of descending footsteps and anxious babble. Amateurish. Professionals would have stood their ground, made use of the height advantage. Smith shook his horse's head and laced a couple of stun grenades up the stairs, then wheeled, a small planet on its axis, into the shelter of the wall until the crash-bang-wallop had laid the guards low as well.

Then on up the stairs. This time I slipped ahead of Smith and in behind Matchitt. Four guards lay prostrate on the fourth-floor landing. I flipped a gas canister towards them. We moved on.

Matchitt hit the fifth-floor landing first. He put a hand out behind him to stall us as he peered forward, then waved us on. The landing was clear. A long corridor led off it. He held up his hand. Three fingers. Third room. Smith grunted. We raced onward. I dropped my gun. It slipped through the sweat. I retrieved it. Smith and Matchitt were at the door. Matchitt pushed the handle down. Locked. Smith raised his gun and blasted a hole in it. Matchitt kicked it in. The shotgun blast had destroyed the lock and taken most of the head off the fella standing behind it. A gun lay beside him. Otherwise the room was bare. Matchitt nodded at a door on the other side of the room. Smith shook his head and nodded at a filing cabinet against the left wall. Matchitt nodded and they both moved towards it. I stood in the doorway, keeping an eye on the corridor and trying to keep my shoes out of the advancing puddle of blood.

As an exercise in camouflaging a secret room it was pathetic. My comrades in arms shifted the empty filing cabinet. An ordinary door. Unlocked. Smith pushed the handle down, then they both moved to either side of the door as he opened it.

A tremulous voice said, 'Don't hurt me.'

If it was Mary, she'd been at the hormones.

Matchitt and Smith moved in. I followed.

A small fat white man, bald-headed, thick glasses, white coat, stood shaking in the centre of the room. 'I'll come peaceably,' he said.

There were trestle tables on three sides of the room. Each supported a range of quietly bubbling flasks and test tubes. Maybe he was a scientist looking for the secret of life. Maybe he was producing designer drugs for the great unwashed. Maybe they were one and the same thing. There were a lot of maybes, but the one certainty was that he wasn't Mary McMaster.

'Werafugishe?' snarled Matchitt.

Smith raised his gun menacingly. 'WeraMarMasha?'

The whitecoat's brows furrowed. He pulled his glasses off and rubbed at his eyes. He coughed. 'I don't . . .'

'WERAFUG?' Matchitt screamed.

'ITZAFUGGINCRAKDEN!' Smith wailed.

The whitecoat threw up his arms. 'FBI?'

He spluttered.

I pulled up my mask. 'What the fuck now?' I shouted.

Matchitt ran forward and pushed his gun into the white-coat's face. 'WERAFUG . . . ?' he demanded.

'Stanley!' I shouted. 'Pull up the mask. He can't under-stand . . .'

Matchitt yanked at it. I coughed. I spluttered. Smith shook his head. Someone appeared at the door. Smith shot him. He fell.

'WHERE'S MARY McMASTER?'

Whitecoat took a step back. The gun went with him. 'I don't know who . . .'

'WHERE IS SHE?'

'I don't know . . .'

Matchitt shot him. He crumpled. 'Fuck it!' Matchitt said. He turned to Smith. 'What the fuck is this?'

Smith looked round him. He pulled his mask up. A look of grim resignation on his face. He turned to me. 'Fuck Barry Manilow,' he said.

More footsteps outside. I turned for the door. Without looking I tossed three stun grenades through the gap. They hit the far wall and bounced back into the doorway. CRACK. BANG. WALLOP.

*　　*　　*

. . . I was on the stairs. Matchitt was screaming in my ear, 'Move, you fucker!' I stumbled on. My mask was gone. So was his. Choking. Crying. Gagging. More than tear gas. I looked back. A great black cloud swarming towards us . . . no . . . only Smith, Smith moving backwards down the stairs, shooting . . . flames licking out around him . . . like a descent into hell . . . before us more smoky gloom . . . my head pounding . . . Matchitt had me by the arm . . . I stumbled on the steps . . . forward . . . flopping about, anchored only by Matchitt's iron grip . . . more figures in the mist . . . Matchitt fired twice, three times . . . we hit the ground floor, a hint of neon through the door, I fell again, looked down . . . a bloody corpse . . . Smith behind us then, his giant form propelling us through the door and out into the blessed night air. I fell to the ground, coughed something up. Matchitt was on his knees beside me, heaving. We looked up into the faces of a teenage gang, as surprised by us as we were by them. Bang-bang from behind. Smith fell, slowly, a barrage balloon deflating, his shotgun clattering. Matchitt pushed himself up off the ground and fired three times towards the doorway. Smith was on his back. Blood bubbled briefly at his mouth and then his head fell to the side, eyes open. Fuck . . . fuck . . . fuck . . . I pulled at him, pulled at the lapels of his trench coat . . . couldn't budge an . . . Matchitt grabbed me. 'Leave him!' he yelled. I held on. 'Fuckin' leave him, Starkey!' He got me away. We ran. We ran like fuck. Shots trailed after us. Round a corner. Round another. The car. Four wheels missing. 'Fuuuuckkk!' yelled Matchitt. He stepped into the middle of the road. A yellow car was cruising by. Matchitt raised his gun. The car screeched to a standstill. Matchitt ran to the driver's window. 'OUT THE FUCK!' An elderly woman opened her door and climbed out. Matchitt jumped in. He leant across and opened the passenger door. I collapsed in. 'I'm sorry,' I said to her, then closed the door. We shot forward. 'Jesus,' I said.

Head pounding. Neon blinding. Police sirens like wild animals.

'Starkey?'

'What.'

'I'm shot.'

'Good.'

'Thanks.'

'Don't mention it.'

'I'm serious. My sleeve's red.'

'You've probably been shot.'

'You're probably right.'

'Does it hurt?'

'A bit.'

'Good.'

'Thanks.'

'Don't mention it.'

'I should see a doctor.'

'You'd get arrested.'

'Jackie Campbell's a cuts man. He could patch me up.'

'Jackie's a boxer's cuts man. How many boxers get shot?'

'Bobby, maybe, after this.'

'Smith's dead.'

'I know.'

'What are we going to do about it?'

'Nothing. I'm sorry he's dead. He's a casualty of war.'

'What are we going to tell his wife?'

'Nothing. Geordie can do that. It was his idea to hire him.'

'I couldn't face her.'

'She'd have our guts for garters.'

Matchitt flexed his fingers above the steering wheel. Bunched them up. Spread them out. 'I couldn't do this if I was badly wounded, could I?'

'Give it time to work its way in.'

He shook his head. 'All those years back home, never got so much as a nick. Now look at me.'

'All those years picking on defenceless Catholics. Must be an eye-opener coming across someone with more sophisticated weaponry than a hurley stick.'

'Your bedside-manner leaves a lot to be desired, Starkey.'

We pulled into a petrol station. Matchitt gave me ten dollars and asked me to get as much gas as I could with it. Another time I would have argued which to use, gas or petrol, but I was beyond that; another time I would have refused point-blank to do anything at all for him, but I was beyond that as well. I went in, put down some cash, and filled a handy plastic container.

We drove back to the hotel. A couple of blocks short of

it we found a back alley. Matchitt pushed himself out of the driver's seat with a grunt. I handed him the container. He flipped up the lid, then sprinkled the inside of the car liberally. Using just the one hand, he flicked a match and tossed it into the back seat. We stood back as the car burst into flames. In a couple of seconds any evidence linking us to the stolen vehicle was gone. It was standard Belfast practice.

Back at the hotel we went straight to McMaster's room, but there was no sign of him. McClean wasn't back yet either. Matchitt tutted and kicked Geordie's door. 'You think they'd show some fucking interest, wouldn't you?'

I followed him to his room. He pulled off his jacket. The shirt was a mess. But the bullet had done more harm to his clothes than his body; it wasn't much more than a gash. He washed in the bathroom. I took four baby spirits from the minibar and beheaded them all. I gave him one. He splashed it on his arm. I went back into the bedroom and drank the other three, one after the other. He called to me as I flipped the TV on. 'Don't worry, Starkey, it might only look like a graze, but I'll probably get a blood clot before morning.'

I didn't reply. The Shabazz was on the Channel 4 news. It was burning well. 'You'll probably want to see this,' I called and turned up the volume. He appeared in the doorway with a small towel wrapped around his arm.

The reporter's voice was slightly whiny, like he'd been called out of bed. '. . . It's too early to say, John, but certainly from talking to eye-witnesses, there was a gun battle, there were bodies on the ground, and the fire followed soon after.'

'Any indication, Jerome, as to who was involved in this gun battle?'

'Nothing yet, John, but according to my police sources, the mosque, besides serving the local community, was also the headquarters of the Sons of Muhammad terrorist organization. And if that's the case, the possibility is that the fighting may have been between rival factions within that organization.'

'Yeah, sure,' said Matchitt. He turned back to the bathroom.

'Stanley,' I said.

He stopped, raised his eyebrows questioningly. I nodded at the TV. There was a photo of Bobby McMaster on the screen.

'What the fuck has he done now?' Matchitt growled.

A plastic blonde had replaced John and Jerome. '. . . has done it again. The controversial Irish boxer whose comments last week angered the Afro-American community apologized for his words on the David Letterman show tonight – and then appealed to the President to withhold financial help for the north of Ireland until the British Government makes clear its intention to withdraw. Mark Sawyer reports . . .'

Matchitt sat beside me on the bed. He shook his head. 'Well, I'll be a fuckin' Fenian,' he said.

24

We had a board meeting. Or maybe we had a bored meeting. Poodle Clay yawned at one end of the table, flanked by two heavies. He flicked through some papers and generally gave every indication of preferring to be somewhere else. Geordie McClean sat hollow-eyed at the other end, drumming his fingers on the table. I sat opposite Stanley Matchitt. We'd been waiting on Bobby McMaster for ten minutes. Ten minutes of silence. Love wasn't in the air. The Mirage had provided its own boardroom for our use. It wasn't so much a magnanimous gesture on their part as a desire to hide us in the most private and remote part of the hotel. One of their security men assigned to guard the contender had been stabbed earlier in the morning. The size of the protest outside the hotel had doubled since the fire in the Shabazz. The management wasn't happy.

McMaster, suddenly the champion of Irish unity, hadn't yet explained himself. He'd come straight back from the TV show, sullen-faced, lips sealed, and locked himself in his room with Geordie McClean. All McClean would say was, 'I'll sort it, I'll sort it,' but hadn't. I was left to deal with the press. The Americans weren't showing that much interest, but the British pack, who until now had virtually ignored us, was suddenly rabidly keen. McMaster was no longer the joky Irishman, good for a funny quote on a quiet day, but public enemy number, well, forty-three, for the sake of argument. I spent most of the night giving non-committal answers to questions I was dying to ask myself. Those who weren't persuaded by my quiet, self-effacing manner were punched by Matchitt.

I didn't even manage to give Smith a second thought.

McMaster eventually arrived, sweat-soaked. He grunted hello to the room and took a seat beside me. Matchitt stared at him. McMaster avoided his gaze. Jackie Campbell stood at the door for a moment, observing, then shook his head. 'I can't be bothered with any of this shite,' he muttered and left. One of Poodle's heavies closed the door.

'Well,' said McClean, after a further minute's silence, 'I don't know whether to laugh or cry.'

'Cry,' said Matchitt, sullenly.

Poodle Clay set his papers down. 'Gentlemen, what is the problem?'

Matchitt stabbed a finger across at McMaster. 'He's the problem.'

McMaster tutted and sat back in his chair. His eyes wandered round the room.

'Gentlemen, Madison is sold out; our man's the most talked-about guy in town; since last night's interview alone we've signed up another three hundred closed-circuit outlets and trebled our sponsorship deals. Our boy's been promoted from marcher to the guest of honour of the St Patrick's Day parade. New York's gonna salute him! Now what's the problem? I'm a busy man. I love you all, but I haven't got the time to nursemaid you through these blips.'

McClean jumped out of his seat, waving his finger vigorously at Poodle. '*Blips!* Jesus! A man was killed last night because of us! Half the Muslims in New York are trying to kill us for burning down their temple! Bobby's wife is missing!' He sat down just as quickly, breathing heavily. He took a deeper breath. Another. Calmed himself. 'You're right,' he said, 'there's no problem.'

Clay shook his head. 'Minor crisis, gentlemen, minor crisis. Do you not think that if you'd thought to come to me in the first place some of this might have been avoided?'

'You're a busy man,' said Matchitt, heavy on the sarcasm.

Poodle, being American, missed it. 'Yes, I'm a busy man, but your concerns in New York are my concerns. I know it sounds ridiculous, but this city answers to me. I get things done. You didn't tell me about Bobby's woman disappearing. I had to find out for myself. You didn't tell me about hiring that detective. I had to find out for myself. You didn't tell me that you were mounting some kind of rescue mission. I had to watch the news to work that one out.'

'We didn't tell you because we heard you were brown-nosing with the Sons of Muhammad.'

'Brown-nosing?' Poodle smiled. 'Is that a term of endearment?'

'Work it out for yourself.'

One of the heavies shifted slightly. Matchitt glared at him.

I put my tuppence worth in. 'We were told you were a regular visitor at the Shabazz. We feared the worst. We thought it better to work independently.'

Clay shook his head. 'And look where it got you. Gentlemen, you don't know New York. You should have put your faith in me. Of course I'm a regular visitor at the Shabazz. You'll find me at a dozen mosques. A dozen cathedrals. Two dozen synagogues. You'd find me at a Klan rally if I could get away with it. I talk, I mix, I connect. Always have, always will. I've been talking to the Brothers of Muhammad for years. They're mostly harmless. They talk big, that's all. I talk big too. So we get together, try to work things out. I've been negotiating to get this threat on Bobby lifted. And they were coming round, until you crashed in there last night. Now they won't even come to the phone.'

'It probably melted,' said McMaster.

'Who're you to say anything?' snapped Matchitt. 'Fuckin' turncoat.'

'I'm what this is all about, Stanley. The contender.'

He said it quietly. He examined his nails. It calmed Matchitt, a bit.

'I just don't understand,' Matchitt said, 'why you had to go and say something like that. After everything we've been through.'

A little exasperated, but still quiet, McMaster said, 'Use your brain, Stanley.'

Matchitt picked up on the tone. 'I'll use your fuckin' brain . . .'

Clay raised his hands. 'Gentlemen, please . . .' He laughed. A fake laugh, meant to jolly up the proceedings. 'I always told you, George, your boy is a genius when it comes to publicity. I don't know where he got it from, but that plea for Irish freedom was inspired. Bobby, if you lose this fight – you won't, but if you do – you just come and work for me. A genius!' He laughed again. It wasn't infectious.

'What this genius did,' said Matchitt, through grated teeth, 'was give up his birthright just so that he could make some more money.'

A pained expression crept onto McClean's face. 'Stanley, don't,' he said, half weary, half annoyed. 'He's been under a lot of pressure. Mary's missing.'

'There's no call for that. None at all.'

McMaster blew air out of his nose, shook his head.

'If she's out there, I'll find her,' said Clay.

'Where have I heard that before?' said Matchitt.

'You have to trust me. I need a little time to get them talking again. If they have her, they have her for a reason – it's just a question of finding the reason. If it's money, fine. If it's political, fine. We can sort it out.'

McClean stood. He placed four fingers on the table, looped his thumbs underneath. He drummed the fingers for a moment. Everyone looked at him, even the heavies shifted their steady gaze off Matchitt.

'I'm thinking,' he said, his eyes flitting quickly to McMaster and then on to Clay, 'of taking Bobby home. Calling the whole thing off.'

'Jesus,' said McMaster.

'What?' said Matchitt.

Clay's cool eyes appraised McClean. He shook his head slightly, but said nothing.

'I've had enough. It's getting too dangerous. Mary's missing. Smith's dead. People are getting shot. People are getting stabbed. Did you see the crowd outside this morning? It's just not worth it.'

'It's worth it to me,' said McMaster.

'Bobby, we can do it again. Some other time. Some other place. This one isn't for us. Jesus, Bobby, they have your wife. I thought we could battle on through it. I saw you sparring, I never saw you so good, I caught myself thinking, yeah, I hope they hold on to her until the fight's over because he's bound to win. Imagine thinking that.'

'Jesus, Geordie,' I said, 'I do believe you're turning into a human being.'

Clay stood up. He and McClean faced each other across the table. 'Nobody walks out on me.'

'I can. I will.'

'I'm telling you now. I have too much invested in this

fight for anyone to walk away from it. You have signed on the dotted line. Your fighter has. Either of you back out of it I'll not even think about taking every penny you have. That would be too easy. I'll just have you killed. Killed.'

'That's not a threat, that's a promise,' said Matchitt, helpfully.

Clay kept his stare on McClean. 'That's a threat and a promise.'

'It's too dangerous to stay. The hotel wants us out.'

'That isn't a problem.' Clay sat down again. 'I've already thought about this. Okay. I understand your fears for your safety. For Bobby's safety. I'll tell you what I'll do. I have a place up on Cape Cod. Town called Princetown. Beautiful place. Quiet. Let me fly you up there. Make that your head-quarters until the fight. It'll take the pressure off. I'll get a gym rigged up. It's no problem. Take my private jet. You'll be there in twenty minutes.'

McClean sat down. He put his elbows on the table and lowered his chin into his hands. 'What do you think, Bobby?'

'I don't much mind where I am, as long as I get to fight for the title.'

Matchitt shook his head at the contender. 'You're one callous cunt,' he said.

'Have to be to be a fighter, Stanley. Maybe you just don't have the killer instinct.'

'That's a laugh,' I contributed.

'And you shut the fuck up or I'll show you all about killer fucking instincts.'

'Gentlemen, please!' Clay stood again. 'Relax. Chill out. Everything will be okay. Now, I must go. Be ready to leave at five. I'll have you picked up. I'll set my team to work on finding Mary. Now loosen up! We've a world title to win!' He gathered up his papers quickly and swept down the side of the table. His heavies swept with him. He patted McMaster on the shoulder as he passed, then put his hand out to McClean. Geordie hesitated for a moment. 'Keep your nerve, George, keep your nerve!'

They shook hands. McClean gave Clay an unconvincing nod of the head and quickly let go of his hand. 'Have it your way. We'll go to Princetown. But I'm keeping my options open. If there's any more trouble, or Mary doesn't appear before the fight, we're out, we're home.'

Clay smiled paternally. 'Don't worry!' He laughed. 'Options!' He laughed again.

A heavy opened the door. Clay left. The heavies followed. One of them winked back at Matchitt. He gave the fingers back. Stanley and I had been to the same finishing school, and never known it.

After the storm, the lull was missing. Maybe it was with Mary. Matchitt glared at McMaster. McClean, pale-faced, counted his fingers and shook his head. McMaster stood at the window, looking at the back end of another hotel.

I could see McClean's point. It was getting dangerous. I thought if we went home there was an outside chance it might improve my love life, but it would make the end of my book something of an anticlimax. But I could see McMaster's point as well. Even Matchitt's. Maybe it would fall to me to explain it all again to Jackie Campbell.

'I just don't understand why you did it,' Matchitt said, turning in his seat and looking at McMaster's back.

'Do we have to go on about this?' McClean snapped. 'It's done.'

'But why?'

'Because.'

'That's brilliant. Bloody brilliant.' Matchitt pushed his seat back. It toppled over. He bent to retrieve it. He crossed to McMaster. I thought there might be some violence, but he put a surprisingly restrained hand on his old friend's shoulder. 'What's happened to you, Bobby? Jesus, we used to hate those bastards so much. I mean, if I'd told you a couple of years ago, Jesus, a couple of days ago, that you'd go on live television promoting a fucking British withdrawal you'd'd've lamped me.' McMaster turned his head towards Matchitt. 'Wouldn't you?' McMaster nodded. 'I mean, I know you've changed a bit, Mary being a Catholic and all that, but this much? We've been through so much together. What got into you, son?'

McMaster sucked on a lip. For a moment the muscles in his face kind of gave way, like he might be about to cry. When the reply came, it was only a whisper. 'Mary told me to,' he said, and looked back to the window. I don't know, maybe there was a tear.

Certainly there were enough furrowed brows in the room

for a mental ploughing championship, although if any of us had the brain power to think about it, it made perfect sense.

McClean rose from the table and crossed to his fighter. He put a hand on his free shoulder. It was quite touching. They looked like a family. I stayed where I was. 'Tell us, Bobby,' he said.

'I got a call. Yesterday. Irish voice. Irishman. Asked me if I was concerned about my wife. I said I was. He asked me if I wanted to speak to her. I said I did. He put her on. Simple as that.'

'And she said what?'

'She said hello. Hello, I'm okay, I'm fine, but they won't let me go. That was all. They said they'd talk to me later, not to mention it to anyone, then hung up. So they called back just before I went to the TV studio. First the man, then Mary was put on. She told me I had to attack the British. I don't know who the fuck they are. Some sort of offshoot of the IRA. They want to start the war up again. They said they'd let her go if I said it. It didn't seem like much to say. Not for her life. Do you understand?'

'Fuck,' said Matchitt. He squeezed McMaster's shoulder.

'But they haven't let her go,' I said.

McMaster shook his head.

'You should have told us earlier, Bobby,' said Matchitt. 'You should have trusted us.'

'I didn't know what to do. My first duty is to Mary.'

'I know that. I understand that. But . . . I don't know. You should have said. We could have gotten Clay on the case.'

McMaster shook his head again. 'He may know his own people, but he knows bugger all about Ireland. That's our territory. We can deal with our own sort.'

I shook my head too, and gave a little snort. 'You're not thinking about getting the A team back together again, are you, Bobby?'

Matchitt gave a grim laugh. 'All for one,' he said, 'and all for one.'

'Jesus,' said McClean. 'If some real hardliners have her, that means Smith died for nothing.'

'I couldn't warn you.'

'I know. I know. But, Jesus, the Sons of Muhammad will be . . .'

'Livid,' I suggested.

25

The McMaster training camp left for Princetown, Cape Cod. The McMaster training camp save for its dynamic young press agent left for Princetown, Cape Cod. Dan Starkey, erstwhile objective reporter but lately failed commando, was left to hold the fort, man the barricades and generally be last man at the Alamo.

Geordie McClean explained it as best he could. I had become a valued member of the team; they wanted to entrust me with the vital job of manning the phone in case whoever had Mary called back; they needed a connection in the city other than Poodle Clay, someone they could trust; they needed someone with a background in investigative reporting to get on the trail of Mary and her captors; they needed someone to deal with the press; I could be the difference between Bobby fighting for the title and going home in shame, considered a coward, or worse, going home as a widower. Also, he added, there weren't enough seats on the plane.

I could have argued contracts. I could have argued my past miserable record at, well, everything. I didn't. I don't know why. Maybe I was beginning to feel some sort of loyalty to them all. Maybe.

Stanley Matchitt, touchingly, promised to come back and help me out. 'I want to see that Poodle's boys really know what they're doing up there,' he said. 'Once I see the security's tight, I'll come back and give you a hand.'

'I'm happier working on my own,' I said.

'No, I insist.'

'There's no need. Bobby's safety is paramount.'

'Like I say, that's what I'm checking on. Then I'll come down and start looking for Mary.'

'Geordie's already asked me to do that, Stanley. There's no need.'

Matchitt gave me a disdainful shake of his head. 'What're you gonna do, start writing letters?'

'What're you gonna do, start cutting throats?'

'I told you I've changed.'

'Aye, I saw that at the Shabazz.'

'That had to be done. It was a life-or-death situation.'

'But you didn't need to enjoy it. You'd a big grin on your face the whole time.'

'Aye, you could see through a gas mask.'

'I could see through yours.'

250

'I'm telling you I'm not like that any more.'

'Aye, the proof is in the pudding.'

'Don't start me, Starkey.'

He bent, picked up his bag, and started for the lift. He looked back once, a slight grin on his face. I didn't see it for long enough to judge whether it was the cold-hearted grin of a murderer, or something much more whimsical, like an executioner.

Matchitt and the rest of the camp left under cover of darkness, using the proverbial tradesman's entrance. Even so, there were a dozen protesters shivering out back, but Poodle's heavies threw a ring round the team as it piled into the stretch for the journey to Newark airport.

I watched them go, then returned to my room for a drink. I only had a couple. I slept. I dreamt of Smith. Saw his corpse. Saw the others lying dead in the mosque, dead for no good reason other than the ineptitude of a bunch of amateur commandos. I woke bathed in sweat. Slept. Dreamt of Patricia. Dreamt of her in bed with Tony, them making love, me crashing into the room, pulling him off her, then realizing it wasn't him at all, but Smith, and he'd blood coming out of his mouth.

I woke with a start. Dawn was on the way. I lay on top of the covers for a while, thinking about Smith. I hardly knew him. I didn't know his wife Sissy at all, save for a nod or two, yet I felt heartbroken for her, for the loss of their obvious love. Maybe it wasn't lost, it was still there, just intangible. It wasn't thousands of miles away, like mine, it was beyond the edge of the universe, and then some. I didn't even know when his funeral was. I didn't know if the police were investigating his death. I'd no idea where Smith lived, so hearing his voice was pretty strange. I called his office on the off-chance and got his answering machine. As soon as I heard his throaty growl I slammed the receiver down and shivered. Uhhhhh.

I got up. Showered. Got into a pair of fading blue denims, a black sweatshirt, my new trainers. Then I ordered breakfast in the room. I wolfed it down, and after a while I started to feel better. Yeah, I was doing okay. Geordie McClean was right. I could achieve more in the city. Start some serious writing, for one thing. Wean myself slowly off the alcohol without the temptations of a new town, even if it was only an out-of-season holiday resort. I could maybe even do some sightseeing if my attempts to track Mary down proved fruitless. At least on that point, Stanley wasn't far off. What could I do, besides write Mary an interesting obituary? I could make some enquiries, try to mix a bit with the Irish community, put out some feelers. But the Irish community wasn't some tiny, tight stronghold where everyone knew everyone and struggled by at odds with the greater city, cut off by language and tradition like so many other nationalities in New York; it was a massive, pulsating city within a city, bigger, in fact, than Ireland itself. I was looking for an emerald in a haystack.

The phone rang. I hesitated before answering. I had a crazy feeling that Smith might be on the other end. Looking for revenge, or maybe just hoping to get paid.

I was relieved to recognize a voice from home, or an accent at any rate; then I remembered I shouldn't be relieved, that I should be a little excited and a little afraid, so I got that way instead.

'I'm looking for Bobby McMaster.'

The accent wasn't Belfast. More like Derry mixed in with a couple of years at a mainland university.

'He's not here right now. Can I take a message?'

'Who're you, FBI?'

'NUJ.'

'I'm sorry?'

'Nothing. Do you want to leave your number and I'll get him to ring you back?'

'Are you trying to be fucking funny?'

'No. Not at all. I'm sorry.'

'Do you know what this is all about?'

'I think so, yeah.' It would be a shame to go through the whole rigmarole if it was only Bobby's long-lost brother on the phone. 'It's about Mary, right?'

'Right.'

'The training camp has moved up the coast. For safety. They left me behind to take your call.'

'I need to speak to Bobby personally.'

'I can pass . . .'

'Personally.'

'Is she okay?'

'Personally.'

He wasn't in chatty form. I gave him the number McClean

had left with me. He hung up. I lay on my bed for thirty minutes, then phoned Princetown. Matchitt answered.

'Did you hear from the boys, then?' I asked.

'No. Did you?'

'I gave them your number half an hour ago. They seemed in a bit of a hurry.'

'Well, they didn't call here. You sure you gave them the right number?'

'Yes, Stanley.'

'Well, I've been here the whole time and no one's phoned.'

'Maybe they need a little time to discuss your move up to Cape Cod amongst themselves. Maybe they think we're trying to pull a flanker. How's Bobby?'

'Morose, but knocking people out of the ring with it.'

'And how's the weather?'

'Sunny, with widespread terr—'

'I get the picture, Stanley. What about the set-up there? Poodle's boys up to scratch?'

'I've seen worse. It's this place is a bugger. Nice house, but an old wooden number, would go up in flames in seconds. Nice neighbourhood, but it's all higgledy-piggledy, impossible to keep an eye on everything at once. We haven't been round the town yet. It looks sleepy enough, but you never know. Look at Crossmaheart.'

'I try not to. Still, you have your work cut out, I won't be seeing you for a while.'

'Don't bank on it.'

* * *

Of Wee Sweetie Mice and Men

It was time to forget literature and do some old-fashioned leg work. I was never a great phone user. I always found liars easier to detect face to red face. I pulled on a denim jacket, buttoned it up to the collar, then donned the leather gloves and left my room. It felt slightly odd out in the corridor: no guards by McMaster's room; no Matchitt lurking by the lift. It wasn't that I felt unprotected, just somehow alone. Imagine, lonely for Stanley Matchitt. I managed a laugh and made for the Great White Way. There were still some die-hards left holding banners outside the Mirage. The contender's departure had been well publicized, his destination described as mystery, but then some people never did believe what they saw on the telly. I managed to keep the look of mild disdain off my face as I left. I hated blind loyalty like that. We had enough of it at home. They were the sort thought Elvis was still alive, that he was rocking around somewhere with Sid and Nancy and Eddie and Gene.

I put my head down and brushed past them mid-chant. It was still all vipers and snakes. I was on the trail of a different type of viper, the poisonous ones St Patrick hadn't managed to drive out of Ireland. I'd thought about starting the trail by picking a few brains on one of the Irish papers in New York and had managed to traverse all of four blocks when I realized I was being followed.

Now, God knows, I'm no expert on professional surveillance, but this lady was right up with the worst. It wasn't so much that the ground shook when she moved, but that everyone's eyes homed in on her. As I walked along I couldn't help but notice people's eyes widen as they saw her advancing towards me. I glanced back, once, quickly, and it was enough. Her eyes bore into mine for just a second, then danced away, too quickly, too nervously, too obviously trying not to look. She was enormous. Her hair was pulled brutally back. Her dress, black, billowing in the wind, had less form than a circus tent. She'd been at the hotel when I'd been leaving. I'd seen her at reception, talking animatedly at the desk. I knew from the first that she was a Grandmother of Muhammad. She had the glassy-eyed look of a woman who had lost a son or a husband and needed some form of revenge before she could stop her mourning. And if you couldn't get the white devil, get the white devil's press agent.

There were a couple of ways I could play it. I could dive into a shop, just to be a hundred per cent certain that it was me she was following. But with that I ran the risk of getting cornered. I could turn and confront her, but that had the risk of getting flattened, or shot, or at least being drawn into an unwinnable argument about race. Or I could forget my casual saunter up Broadway, break into a sprint and lose her within a block. This last seemed the most appealing, if least dignified, escape.

And I had my left, new sneaker poised to bounce me athletically forward when her voice rolled up the pavement and slammed into my back, 'YO!' and instead of ignoring it and getting going like a wise man should, I turned.

'You talkin' to me?' I asked in my best De Niro.

She moved right on up until she towered over me. 'I know you.'

I shook my head. 'I think not.'

'You're with the boxer, aren't you?'

'Boxer?'

'Don't fuck with me, son. You're one of the boxer's men. I seen you before.'

I gave a half-hearted shrug. She didn't look like she had any concealed weapons. Just obvious ones. 'Maybe,' I said.

'Sure I did. You came to my husband's office coupla days ago.'

Gulp. I peered into her face. Tried to picture it with a smile and make-up. 'Sissy?' I asked, half incredulous.

She nodded.

It was a face you could only get by draining blood out of it. The face of true love in mourning. I put my hand out. 'Jesus,' I said, 'I'm sorry, I didn't recognize you.'

She took my hand and squeezed it gently, quickly, and let go. 'That all you got to say?'

I nodded. I was speechless. What do you say to someone whose husband you've helped get killed for no good reason?

'You want to know what I'm doing here, instead of crying at home?'

I nodded again.

'I can't stand all that nonsense. He's gone and that's that. God got him now. I'm here because he was working for you when he died, and he died with the job only half done. I'd like to help finish it.'

'Honestly, there's no need . . .'

'Sure, there's a need. He promised to get that woman back, and as far as I know she ain't back yet. That right?' I nodded. 'His promise is my promise.'

'It's very kind of you, Sissy, but really there's no need. If it's a matter of the money I'm sure Mr McClean would be glad . . .'

'It's nothing to do with the money. I've been paid for the work that was done, plus there's the insurance coming my way. But I still got a business to run. A family to feed. A job to finish.'

I took a step back. I needed my own air space. 'I'm not trying to be unkind, Sissy, but what could you do?'

'Chop you in two, for a start.'

I took another step back.

'Please, Sissy, it's a nice thought, but . . .'

She took a step towards me. It was worth two of mine. She forced her face down into mine. 'You know why we were asked to leave the New York Police Department?' she growled, and suddenly she was neither the mourning widow nor the happy-go-lucky pink-spectacled jolly wife, but the mother of all menace, as capable with a pair of garden clippers as her late husband.

'I didn't know you were . . .'

'We were two of the best . . . you know why they made us leave?'

I shook my head. I thought about Smith's interrogation technique.

''Cause we were too heavy.'

Savant's grilling had been the heaviest I'd ever sat through, and then some.

'Told us we were a disgrace to the uniform.'

I could see Smith nonchalantly dropping Savant's little finger into the wastebasket in his apartment.

'Told us we ate so much, they didn't have uniforms to fit us any more. Told us to diet or get out. We were the best in that damn department! We took it as a fundamental infringement of our rights as American citizens and we got out. We set up in business ourselves, doin' what half those motherfuckers'll never know how to do, and doin' it damn well at that, even if we didn't make no money to speak of. And now some motherfucker's shot him dead and the job's left not half done, and, goddamnit, I got something to prove.'

Tears sprang from her eyes and her huge shoulders began to vibrate and for a second I feared she might topple over on top of me and I would die flat, but she held on, swaying gently from side to side like the biggest tree in the forest dancing with the slightest of breezes. 'I'm sorry,' she said, her voice shaky.

I reached up and patted her on the elbow. 'Can I buy you lunch, Sissy?' I asked.

26

The higher up you go in the Mirage, the finer the restaurants get. Needless to say we had grown used to eating on the ground floor, where quantity ruled over quality. Sissy, despite her size and doughnuts aside, was a connoisseur of the finer things in life – either that or she wanted to exploit my invitation to the limit, which was fine by me. I felt guilty enough about her husband's unwarranted demise and a slap-up meal was the least I could do. Besides, Geordie McClean was paying for it.

She rejected one menu after the other as we gradually made our way to the enclosed rooftop restaurant. It was small, surprisingly unstuffy. We were shown to a window table set for four. We ordered drinks immediately, she a Martini, me an imported Harp, then hid behind the menus for a while to think about food and how best to move the conversation onto a less gloomy subject than her recent descent into widowhood. I was still happily scanning the entrées when Sissy's head appeared over the top of my menu.

'What about the hostage?' she asked.

'I've heard nothing.'

'Very expensive,' she said, her head nodding appreciatively.

'Could turn out that way.'

'I expect it depends on how it's done,' said Sissy. 'Fried, do you think?'

I looked up. 'That might be a bit rash,' I said, 'they've only had her a few days.'

She nodded. 'Not very healthy,' she said and sank back below the horizon. Just for a second. Her head popped up again. 'How do you know she's female?'

I lowered my menu. Maybe there was more than just tears to her mourning. Maybe she was doped up with Valium. Or dope, for that matter. 'She's McMaster's wife. Of course she's female.'

She closed her menu and set it down. She looked a little confused. Her jaw hung just a little too low, her eyes a little bit wide. 'This is very strange,' she said and took a gulp of her drink. When she replaced it it clinked against the cutlery and she looked anxiously round.

'It's okay,' I said, 'take your time.'

She gave me a little unsure smile and re-opened her menu. 'Maybe it wasn't such a good idea,' she said.

'It's okay,' I said. 'It's good to get out.'

'No, I mean about the ostrich.'

I closed my own menu. 'Which ostrich?' I said it softly. With care. I let my eyes wander lazily about the restaurant.

'The one your boxer is married to.'

'Are you feeling okay, Sissy? Would you prefer to leave?'

'I'm fine. You said Bobby McMaster was married to an ostrich.'

'I did not. I said he was married to Mary. You said he was married to an ostrich.'

'Mary the ostrich.'

'Mary McMaster. The human. Are you feeling okay?'

'I'm feeling fine. Are you sure you're feeling okay?'

'I'm absolutely positive.'

'Then what are we talking about?'

'I don't know. You asked me about Mary . . .'

'I asked you about the ostrich.'

'What ostrich?'

'The ostrich on the menu.'

She opened her menu and pointed. I followed the approximate direction of her finger as I re-opened my own.

'Right enough,' I said. Ostrich was listed. Plain as day. 'I thought you said something else.'

'Like what?'

I thought back. There was the possibility that I had misheard. It wasn't unknown. 'I thought you said hostage. But you said ostrich. I'm sorry.'

'Never mind. It's an easy mistake to make. Maybe I said hostage by mistake.'

We sipped our drinks in silence and avoided each other's

262

eyes. Outside it was getting gloomy. Winter was showing little enthusiasm about giving way to spring.

'I understand it's relatively inexpensive to have one's ears syringed,' said Sissy.

And we both burst into laughter. Big ripply laughs cascaded through her, like her body was billowing in the wind. She wiped a tear from her eye. 'I'm sorry,' she said when she finally regained control. She raised her glass. I raised mine. We clinked.

'To what?' I asked.

She thought for a moment, then raised her glass again. 'To Terry Anderson and Terry Waite.'

'To Terry Anderson and Terry Waite,' I repeated, then added, 'Why?'

'They were Beirut ostriches.'

And off we went again. She was for the moment the lovely big woman with the smile on her face, the way she should be. Maybe I could work with her. Maybe it would do us both good. I took another sip. 'And to Mary McMaster, the New York ostrich. May she soon be free.'

'And not fried.'

'Cheers.'

The waiter must have been used to it, but he still allowed a mildly irritated look to drift across his angular face when we enquired about the ostrich. 'From Scotland, sir,' he said.

'Not Australia?'

'No, sir, Scotland, sir. We buy all of our ostrich from an ostrich farm in Scotland. I'm sure there's a good reason for it.'

Sissy was less interested in the country of origin than the taste. 'Our ostrich is pan-fried in fresh herbs and served with wholegrain mustard. You have a choice after that, madam. If you remove it from the pan in the early stages of cooking, when it has just been sealed and is still pink, it will taste like beef or pork. However, if it is allowed to cook longer the meat will taste more gamey, a cross between wood pigeon and venison.'

'So it never actually tastes like ostrich?'

'Yes, of course it does, madam. I was only suggesting what range of meats it falls into. It does, of course, have its own very distinct taste.'

Sissy was keen. I was less sure. There was something vaguely unsettling about eating an ostrich. I was never one for experimenting with food anyway, but there seemed to be something particularly taboo about eating an ostrich; maybe it was the beak and the deceptively skinny legs; of course you didn't eat either, or so I presumed, but they sprang to mind as I pictured an ostrich on my plate. Maybe it was the fact that an ostrich could run at forty-five miles per hour. Or that it was well capable of killing a man. It wasn't a claim you could make about many other animals that eventually ended their days on a dinner table. I mean, no one was ever killed by a cow, unless it fell on them from a great height, and sheep aren't famed for putting up much of a fight. Pigs are feisty enough creatures, but they've never killed anyone, unless you count the kind that race around in green uniforms. I scanned the menu again. Maybe there was a way around the ostrich question without appearing unadventurous. I looked for an ostrich egg. An ostrich egg in a cup. A bloody big cup. It wouldn't be a question of having a few soldiers with a boiled ostrich egg, but an entire battalion. And what about Ireland, what did we have there with our eggs, soldiers or terrorists? Ireland, God, I hadn't . . .

'Sir?'

'Hamburger and fries, please.'

'Chicken,' said Sissy.

'Chicken?' asked the waiter.

'Ostrich,' said Sissy, 'rare, please.' She nodded at me. 'He's the chicken.'

I shrugged. I was.

'You loved him very much, didn't you?'

'More than anything on this earth.'

'I thought that. I only saw you together the once. But I thought that.'

'We were so similar. Like two halves of the one person. We did everything together. Worked together. Ate together. Slept together. Read together. Gardened together.'

'He said he was a bit of a gardener. I saw his rose pruners.'

'He was very proud of his garden. He was very proud of his work. We both were. That's why we took it so hard when we were asked to leave the department. We both had excellent arrest records. No discipline problems. Both popular. We just liked eating. That's no crime in anyone's eyes, 'cept for the NYPD.'

'How did you find out he was dead?'

'Officer came to see me. He knew Pete from way back. He asked me straight out, you want me to find out who killed him, or do you want me to write it off like we do most of the black boys? He didn't mean any offence by it. I said no, leave him be, he's gone now, ain't gonna do any good stirring up more trouble.'

'You have a family.'

'I have two boys.'

'What're they like?'

'They're fat too.'

'I don't mean like that.'

'I'm sure you don't, but that's just the way they are. They're good kids.'

'How're they taking it?'

'On the chin. They're strong boys.'

'It'll maybe hit them later.'

'Something will. That's our lot in this city.'

'That's a bit profound.'

'That's realistic. I wouldn't expect you to know what it's like.'

'Maybe not. You said you had insurance.'

'I have insurance. It'll see me through, won't make me rich. Besides, I want to work. I'd go mad if I didn't work. And this is the only business I know. You have a problem with me replacing Pete?'

'None at all. I'm just not sure about Geordie McClean. He's more of a mind to go home than spend a lot of money trying to track down Bobby's wife.'

'I wouldn't call it a lot of money.'

'No. I know. Any money then.'

'What if I just turn up with the girl? He'd pay me a reward?'

'I'm sure he would. Are you likely to just turn up with the girl?'

'I might.'

'Is there something I should know?'

'No. Just enquiring.'

'You're not holding anything back?'

'No. I just want to know where I stand. Can you have a word with him? Get me a retainer, or an agreed reward?'

'I can try. He might take some convincing.'

'Because I'm a woman?'

'Probably. Because you don't look like a detective.'

'Surely that's a plus.'

'In some ways. In others, I'm not so sure. I mean, he's going to say to me, what's she going to do that her husband didn't already do? He'll say, sure we know it's not the Sons of Muhammad have Mary after all, it's the IRA, what the hell does she know about the IRA? That's what he'll say. What do you know about the IRA?'

'Nothing.'

'His point exactly.'

'Surely the point isn't what I know about the IRA, but whether I can get Mary McMaster back.'

'It's maybe one and the same thing.'

'I want the chance to find out.'

'I'll ask. It's all I can do.'

'My husband died working for you.'

'I know.'

'You owe me.'

'I know.'

So I asked. I got Geordie on the phone. I buttered him up for a while, then I called her over and she hit him with the guilt thing. By the time she hung up she had a promise of a small retainer, plus a lot more if she managed to turn Mary up; he'd probably throw in two tickets to the fight as well, he was that kind of a guy. When we got back to the table we decided to celebrate with a tanker full of drink. It was an odd sort of party: two lonely souls, baring souls. By the end of the afternoon Sissy knew more about me than perhaps any woman on the planet, bar one. I probably knew more about Sissy than any damn man on this mortal coil, but if I did, I'd forgotten it by the time I got to the lift.

I could barely stand. Maybe my resistance to alcohol was lessening. Maybe import Harp is stronger than the indigenous variety. Maybe it was the burger. I leant on Sissy as we waited for the doors to open. She was a rock. A soft rock. A veritable REO Speedwagon of rock. 'I'm very sorry about your husband,' I said.

'Thank you.'

'When's the funeral? Maybe I could send some flowers.'

'Cremated. Already. No point in him lying around.'

'Really? Cremated. What about the ashes?'

'They're at home.'

'Spooky.'

'Doesn't worry me.'

'Where are you going to scatter them?'

'I'm not.'

'Spooky.'

The doors opened. We stepped in. She pushed for ground, my finger wandered up and down the panel. Someone had unaccountably stolen the eighth floor.

'Which floor?' Sissy asked.

'Eight.'

She pushed a button.

'I thought that was three.'

She shook her head.

'But now that I look at it, it is in fact, eight.' She smiled. 'But now I can't find three.'

'You don't need three.'

'I know. I need a drink.'

'You don't need a drink.'

'I know. Need and want are two different things. I've lost my wife, you know.'

'I've lost my husband.'

'United in grief.'

It dinged. The doors opened. 'I've work to do, Starkey. I'll call for you tomorrow. At nine – a.m. You'll be sober?'

I stepped out. I nodded. 'Nine,' I said and turned left for my room. I would be sober. By then.

27

Sissy cut a swathe through the morning crush like a juggernaut in suede boots.

There was at last a hint of spring in the air, which I might have appreciated if my head hadn't felt like some very small person was chiselling away inside it, trying to reshape it into a tombstone. My mood was not good. Sissy had been true to her word and had banged on my door on the stroke of nine, larger than life and full of enthusiasm. She said she had had a break. I wanted her to give me one, at least another three hours in the glorious confines of a continental quilt. I had to admire her. Well, I thought about having to admire her, but no one likes a swot.

There was no need to dress. Dressing has a presumption about it I have never cared for. A drinking man never undresses. The wrinkly, stubbly, beery look is a fashion which ignores fashion. Sissy, jabbering, piloted me to the lift. I was about to congratulate her on taking to her task with such relish, but then decided she might take it as an allusion to her prodigious appetite and changed tack. Besides, even the thought of relish made me feel sick. I got her to stop while I bought a can of full-fat Coke from a newsstand and drained it in two. I waited a moment while it decided to stay down, then said, 'Tell me why we're going shopping again?'

Her eyes crossed in frustration, then she shouted something back, but it was lost in a blast of horns from a gridlocked Times Square. I gave up. She ploughed on through the rush-hour crowds and I struggled along in her wake, much as I had once trailed her husband's coat-tails in that ill-fated raid on the Shabazz.

Finally we turned into Macy's. Some call it the biggest store in the world. Mary had shopped here before the Republicans had snagged her. Doubtless they had been with her at the time. While she innocently chose shirts for her husband, they measured her up for a kidnapping. Sissy stopped a security guard and asked him to call the security manager. She used his name, but it went by me. My hearing was slurred. He spoke into his radio and within half a minute a balding guy appeared. He had an erect, military bearing, which was ruined by the stomach bulging out of his cream uniform.

'Mrs Smith?'

'Andrew. How are you?'

'Fine. Thank you.'

271

Andrew smiled warmly. Sissy kept her face grim but nodded appreciatively. He took her hand in two of his and squeezed it. Sissy introduced me. He shook my hand and then motioned for us to follow him. He led us to an elevator and from there to the fourth floor and on into an office. A bank of video screens, forty-eight in all, dominated one wall. Three security men sat before them, watching intently.

Sissy shook her head. 'Sure looks like my idea of hell, watching those things all day. Television's bad enough.' One of the men looked round. 'No offence,' she said.

'No offence taken, ma'am,' he said, and returned to the screen.

'Don't worry about them, Mrs Smith,' said Andrew, retreating behind a mahogany desk. 'They watch them for no more than thirty minutes in any one hour. And they can be fun.' He waved his hand at a couple of chairs and we sat. 'Any more than half an hour though, and they start to miss things. Proved by the experts. We have them all on rotation. We run a book on the shoplifters. Arnie over there holds the record. Seventeen in one day. Can I get you a coffee?'

Sissy shook her head. 'Any chance of a Coke?' I asked. Andrew pushed his swivel chair backwards about five yards and opened a fridge masquerading as a cupboard. I could have put my head in it and gone to sleep. He pondered the contents for a second, then glanced round at me.

'Diet?'

I shrugged. Not one of my better shrugs. I had some worries about my head falling off and rolling across the floor towards him with my tongue hanging out. Andrew propelled himself back to his desk and reached the can across to me. I flipped and guzzled. I cleared half the can, stifled a burp and said: 'Sorry. Dehydrated. Long flight.'

He nodded. Sissy gave me the eye, then turned back to the security chief. 'You have some news for me.'

'Yes. Of course. I'm very glad you called, very glad. I would've called earlier – but I lost your husband's number. Lost his damn name too, to tell you the truth. Damn near tore the office apart trying to find it, but no luck. It gets hectic in here, lady, as I'm sure you'll appreciate. How is he, by the way?'

'He's dead.'

'Ah.' His mouth widened slightly, his eyebrows arched, like he was waiting for a punch line. Sissy's face remained sombre. 'Oh,' he said simply, 'I'm very sorry.'

'Thank you. He was murdered. Working on this case. So I'm sure you'll appreciate the urgency of the matter.'

'Yes. Of course. He was a nice guy. Very thorough. You can always tell an ex-cop, can't you?'

Sissy nodded. 'The shirts?'

'Yes, of course. The shirts. Your husband was here enquiring about purchases made by a Mrs Mary McMaster. Purchase by way of a Visa card. Three shirts, and a pair of sunglasses.' Sissy nodded. Andrew opened a drawer and produced three white shirts. He pushed them across the table towards Sissy. She didn't move for them, so I leant forward and picked one up. 'These shirts were returned the day before yesterday. Too small. Exchanged for larger sizes. They hadn't been opened.'

'Do you know who by?' I asked. 'Was it a woman?'

'No. It was a man.'

I passed the shirt to Sissy. She turned it over in her hand without looking at it. 'How did this come to your attention?' she asked. 'There must be ten thousand transactions here every day.'

'More than that. Good luck plays the major part in it. The shirts were returned to customer services and set to one side for return to stock control. As it happens the employee who originally sold the shirts, and was aware of my enquiries about their original purchase, came on duty shortly after. We move our staff around all the departments, so it was your good luck that she happened to come on to customer services at that time. She recognized them. So she brought them up to me. A very efficient girl.'

'Can we talk to the cashier who received the shirts in the first place?' I asked. 'Get a description.'

Andrew smiled. 'Oh, I think we can do better than that. How would a name, address and photograph do?'

Sissy matched the smile, and raised him half a dozen teeth. 'You're not serious?'

'Absolutely. I don't think the guy you're after is one of life's smarter cookies. For one thing, he made no attempt to disguise himself, so we have him on video. We can't cover every part of the store all the time, because it's so damn big; our cameras flit from point to point, but we keep one permanently on the customer services department because that's where most of the attempted frauds are mounted. Once I'd found the video of him returning the shirts, I tracked back through the other tapes in the store covering that particular time period. Took me an hour or two, but once I get started on something there's no stopping me. Found him eventually in the women's lingerie department. Bought some pretty hot stuff as well. And he used a credit card.'

'What a wanker,' I said, mainly to myself, but it came out as normal.

Andrew glanced over. 'I'm not sure I know the term, but I get your drift.' He opened a file on his desk. 'Guy's name is McLiam, Marcus McLiam, has an address in Brooklyn Heights. We showed the tape to our employee in the lingerie department. She remembered him vaguely. Remembers he was talkative, without ever really saying anything. Know the type? Had an accent, but she couldn't really place it. Thought it was maybe Irish or Scottish. Said it was harsh, grating on the ears, sounded like he was complaining, when he wasn't.'

'Northern Irish,' I said.

'Could be.'

I turned to Sissy. 'Is this what's called hitting pay dirt?'

'Oil. Gold. Owning an ostrich farm. All rolled into one. We're on our way.'

It seemed important not to rush into anything, to call a time-out to consider. I needed to get my brain into gear. Sissy's friend Duncan owned a fast-food place behind Macy's. It was crowded but we still managed to talk international terrorism with raised voices over doughnuts, coffee and Coke, without anyone batting an eyelid.

After the initial euphoria, and still with the hangover, I tried to deflate things, just a little. Whatever way you looked at it, it was a good break, but just how good?

We had the name and address, plus two slightly blurred stills from the video cameras. The guy looked pretty young; short dark hair, moustache, pug nose, wide-set mouth; he wore a khaki jacket, what appeared to be black jeans. We watched the video through four times. He smiled a lot, didn't look nervous at all; I had to admire it, I would have been nervous being in the lingerie department for perfectly legitimate reasons.

'Okay,' said Sissy, 'so it doesn't say very much about the calibre of the opposition.'

I nodded. The head stayed on. 'Your husband once told me he'd never met a smart foot soldier yet. Maybe he had a point.'

'He knew what he was talking about. The question is, though, was it a foot soldier being stupid, or something else? Was it overconfidence? Or something to throw us off the trail?'

'Stupid isn't a word you would normally associate with the IRA.'

'But isn't that the point? The IRA have called a ceasefire, haven't they? And they never operated on the US mainland anyway. So we're probably looking at some maverick outfit. And there's no shortage of radical Irish groups in New York.'

'And how would you know?'

'Starkey, there are radical groups for every nationality. Scratch a New Yorker and there's an emigrant's fury just dying to get out.'

'Yeah, someone left the melting pot on the boil.'

A pained expression crossed her face. She opened her mouth to say something, but some half-digested doughnut got in the way. She coughed, swallowed, her eyes watered a little. Undeterred, she took another bite.

'I'm sorry,' I said, 'you've obviously been busy. Busier than me. No, I know the IRA didn't operate over here. A few arms deals maybe. But no terrorism. Mostly because they didn't want to affect Noraid's fundraising activities by carrying out anything that might be regarded by the public as an atrocity. But not everyone's happy with the ceasefire. Maybe not even the IRA. They could be looking for a way to creep back into action. Or what about all those gunmen who aren't finding it easy returning to normal life? And organizations like Noraid are still raising money. Where does that all go if the war's over?'

'Re-education? Community work?'

'Possibly. Or funding a kidnap and blackmail. It's hardly an atrocity, unless you're the one's been kidnapped. There are endless possibilities. Maybe they've formed a new stupid wing. Most terror groups have them. I'm sure we would have found the Stupid Sons of Muhammad if we'd looked long enough. Marcus has done something that's almost too stupid for words. That's what bothers me. We could be reading too much into it.'

I took a bite of a chocolate doughnut. Washed it down. I looked at the photos of McLiam. He looked so normal. That was the problem with back home. The psychos looked normal, and vice versa.

Sissy picked up one of the photos and studied it. 'He could be entirely innocent. Maybe the shirts were just dumped some-where and he found them, decided to trade them in. Maybe they were given to him by someone involved in the kidnap-ping, someone trying to help out an impoverished relative.'

'He can't be that poor. He used a credit card.'

'You never been poor and used your credit card?'

'Point taken.'

'There are other possibilities of course,' said Sissy.

'I know. I was trying not to think about them.' It was too close to home. 'That Mary is having an affair with this guy. That she's decided to dump Bobby.'

'But she's only been in New York a few days. That's quite a jump.'

'It happens. Besides, maybe she knows him from Belfast. Maybe he followed her over. Proclaimed undying love. She moved in. He returned the shirts, bought her sexy underwear.'

'What about the threats then?'

'Could be genuine. Could be they're trying to make some money off Bobby.'

'Wouldn't she be better waiting until the fight was over? Divorce him then, take him for every last cent?'

'They've no kids, she's run away – be long-drawn-out, she

mightn't get much in the end. Better to get your money up front, in one big pile.'

'But there haven't been any demands for money.'

'Not yet. He could be the genuine article, a terrorist she happens to have fallen for. He's carrying out the blackmail, plus whatever else might be in store, and he gets to sleep with the kidnap victim as well. Best of both worlds. It's happened before.'

Someone tapped me on the shoulder. I jumped. Spilt my Coke. A heavily built bloke in a trench coat raised his hands in apology. 'Easy there, bubba,' he said.

'I'm sorry,' I replied, wiping at the Coke as it dribbled down my coat, apologizing as we British Irish do for things we haven't done. It comes from an inferiority complex caused by being inferior.

'Let me get you another.'

'Never worry. I was nearly finished.'

'Sure?'

'Certain.'

'Okay. Sorry again. The reason I touched you, I'm meeting a girl tonight, first date, y'know? And I couldn't help over-hearing you discuss the plot of that movie. It sounds intriguing. I have Irish roots, y'know? From County Cork originally. Say, isn't it dreadful the way everyone's killing each other over there at the moment?'

'We have a ceasefire,' I said.

'Whatever, sounds like an incredible movie – where'd you see it?'

I looked at Sissy. She rolled her eyes. 'Private screening,' I said.

'Really? You in the business?'

I nodded.

'That's a shame, sounds like a good night out. What's it called? I'll watch out for it.'

'Born on the Twelfth of July.'

'Born on the Twelfth of July. Cool. I'll remember that.'

'Good.'

'Who stars?'

'Who else? Sylvester.'

'Sylvester? Cool. Sounds great.'

'And Tweetie Pie.'

His eyes narrowed. Then he laughed and slapped me on the shoulder. 'Aw, you guys!'

He turned and left Duncan's, still chortling.

I shook my head. 'Americans,' I said.

'Include me out,' said Sissy.

28

Sissy practised the sophisticated surveillance techniques of her late husband. The fishing boat, having been rescued from Harlem, was now restored and lurked in a mildly dilapidated section of what was once known as Brooklyn's Irish quarter. Times had changed, ethnic boundaries had shifted or been stolen, and it was now merely a place where no quarter was given. Sissy was big enough and threatening enough not to have to worry about giving quarters, or halves or three-quarters, and I was wasted enough to look like I'd taken a quarter, or a half, or the whole rock. We were left alone. Sissy munched on a doughnut. I munched on my fingernails. Together we weighed down the hood and watched a brownstone building on the corner of the block, a four-storey effort that had seen better days. I'd checked the names earlier; McLiam was listed on the third floor.

Two hours we sat there. It was pleasantly warm if you were well wrapped up. It was a run-down area, but it wasn't Harlem. People came and went. No one bothered us. We didn't see McLiam. We didn't even see anyone who looked particularly Irish. No pointy green hats. No shaggy horse tied up outside. We just watched and waited.

Eventually I said: 'Well, I guess the party's not at McLiam's.'

'Seems not.'

'We should try some thunder and lightning.'

'Mmmmm?'

'Ring the bell and run away. See who comes out.'

She didn't think much of that idea. I didn't think much of that idea, but it was better than sitting for another couple of hours waiting for McLiam to make a move. So I sauntered across the road and rang the bell. There wasn't any need to run away. There was no response. No muffled reply over the intercom. No anxious glances out of the windows. I nodded across the road to Sissy, then pressed the button beneath.

'Yeah? Who's that?'

Young voice. Teenage. Chinese struggling to go American. 'I'm looking for Marcus McLiam.'

'Upstairs.'

He clicked off. I pressed again.

'Yeah.'

'Hi. Yeah. Marcus McLiam. He's not in.'

'Can't help that.'

'I know. I'm sorry. Do you know where he is?'

'Try the office, man.'

Click. Buzz. 'Sorry. One more question . . .'

'Fuck, man, I'm doing something here, you the fuckin' cops or what?'

'Immigration.'

'He works on West 42nd. Beside the Port Authority. Irish place. Norda. Nerda. Something like that.'

'Noraid?'

'Yeah. That's it.'

'Okay. Cheers.'

Click. I crossed back to the car. I told Sissy about my chat. 'You think we should take a look inside?'

She looked up at the apartment, then shook her head. 'Let's tackle the man himself. I like the immigration line. That should open a few doors for us. Tell me about Noraid.'

Sissy nosed the car back out into the traffic while I fumbled about for some info on Noraid. There wasn't much. It was a name everyone back home knew, but nobody knew much about, save that they were sympathetic to all shades of militant Irish Republicanism.

'They raise money amongst the Irish community here for those suffering under the British jackboot back home. For the poor, for the political prisoners. They set up tours for New York's second- and third-generation Irish who see the old homeland through shamrock-tainted glasses. They pay big money, spend a week getting a terror tour of the North, Guinness, folk music, meet a couple of ex-terrorists out because of the ceasefire who fill their thick skulls with tales of sticking it to the Brits. A bit of a thrill for armchair terrorists. Then they write their big cheques and feel good about doing something for the cause. Noraid has been making its money exploiting sad old Yanks desperately looking for a culture to cling to, using that money to finance the senseless murder of people back home. They've been nothing but apologists for a gang of murdering cut-throat bastards, they wouldn't know the real Ireland if it came up and spat down their throats. I'd say they're panicking because the war's theoretically over. They've made a nice wee living from it and now they're scared that's going to change, so maybe they're doing their little bit to help it start up again. Bastards the lot of them.'

'So you've no strong feelings one way or the other about them,' said Sissy, piloting the car back up onto the Brooklyn Bridge.

'No,' I said.

We decided to approach Noraid separately. Strategy. I went first. Maybe it wasn't a good idea. I felt a little tense. Rather than cleansing the soul, my little rant against Noraid had served to crystallize my dormant feelings towards them. Once again I had forgone my chosen stance as the detached journalist; I wasn't even semi-detached; I was a journalistic chalet bungalow, well built down below but with a lot of empty space up top.

It was a slick, modern office, laid out much like a travel agent's, with the staff on one side of a counter and a wide range of brochures on display for the public to leaf through or lift on the other. I browsed for a couple of minutes; there were two fellas behind the counter, both busy on phones. One nodded over and held up two fingers. I didn't take it as an insult, though I was prepared to. About half the brochures depicted the Ireland of postcard and Hollywood, the rest the heroic struggle of the downtrodden. There were plenty of pictures of gunmen in silhouette, of dead hunger strikers and civil rights marches. Not too many of kids with their heads blown off.

The fella who'd signalled came off his phone and approached the counter with a grin and an apology. I moved towards him. I smiled back, but steely with it.

'Afternoon,' I said.

'G'day,' he replied.

'Australian?'

'Sure am.'

'Immigration,' I said.

He stiffened. 'Identification,' he said.

'Boy, you're defensive.'

He put his hand out. 'Identification.'

I laughed, winked, leant forward. 'I'm interested in immigrating here. I was told you might be able to help me out.'

'We're not that sort of an organization.'

'Just the basic details. How to get a Green Card, that sort of thing.'

'We're not that sort of an organization.'

'Whaddya mean, you're Noraid, aren't you?'

'Sure.'

'That's like Traveller's Aid, isn't it? You help people from Northern Ireland out when they're on holiday, don't you?'

'No, sir, that's not us. That's not what we do.'

'Well, what do you do, if not that?'

'We're a pressure group. We're trying to bring about a united Ireland. You've come to the wrong place.'

'You can't get me a Green Card then?'

He took a deep breath. His eyes flitted behind me as the door opened. Sissy's thundercloud shadow passed over me as she sauntered towards the brochures. 'No, sir, we can't.'

I nodded. He looked back at his colleague, but he was still on the phone. 'I was misinformed then,' I said.

He nodded. 'You must have been.'

'I was told to ask for Marcus McLiam. You're not him. He's Irish. I think he's Irish. Can I speak to him?'

'Marcus isn't here today.'

'But I was told to ask for him.'

'Marcus isn't here today.'

'When will he be back?'

'I can't say.'

'Can't say or won't say?'

'Sir, if there's nothing more I can do for you, I've work to do.'

'Sorry. Don't let me keep you.' I stood back, ready to go, then stopped. 'Just one thing. How come an Australian is working in an organization dedicated to the armed struggle in Ireland?'

'Easy, sir. I like to help out where I see injustice.'

'Have you ever been to Ireland?'

'No. I hope to go soon.'

'Well, I hope you do.' I grinned and put my hand out

to him. After a moment's hesitation he reached over and we shook. 'And I hope you take your fuckin' blinkers off when you do go, you interfering Australian shite.'

I let go of his hand and made for the door. He was round the counter and after me in a second. Then I stopped, stood my ground. I wagged a finger at him. 'You touch me, I'll sue your ass off!' I shouted.

He was a big fella, all muscle and teeth, but he stopped, surprised that I wasn't still running. I glared at him. He was weighing it up in his mind. When you're in America you can always keep someone at bay with the threat of a good lawsuit.

His jaw set firm. 'Leave the building, sir, or I'll be forced to call the police.'

'I'm leaving. Just making a point.'

'Well, make it somewhere else.'

'Do you have a Green Card?'

'As a matter of fact I have.'

'What about him?' I nodded back to his colleague.

He didn't know. 'Of course he has,' he said.

I tutted. 'I'm giving you due warning. I'll be back tomorrow. You better have your documents sorted or you're on the boat. Understand?'

'I'm calling the cops.'

I turned to Sissy. She had a brochure open. 'And what the fuck're you looking at?'

'Excuse me?'

'I said, what the fuck are you looking at?'

Her mouth dropped open. 'I . . .'

'Okay! That's enough!' Australia stepped forward, fists bunched. I opened the door quickly and jumped out onto the sidewalk.

He stopped in the doorway. We looked at each other for a few moments. Then I shrugged and said: 'Good night.' I turned and walked on up the street. I didn't bother looking back.

There was a McDonald's three blocks up. I bought a cheeseburger and a Diet Coke for myself and two cheeseburgers and fries for Sissy and found a table upstairs. She arrived in five minutes and slipped into the two seats opposite me. I pushed her food across to her. 'Successful?' I asked.

She nodded and unwrapped a cheeseburger. She bit into it. Chewed. Swallowed. Took a sip of Coke.

'You seemed to enjoy that,' she said.

I shrugged. 'You have to take your enjoyment where you can these days. Anyway I don't see why I have to be pleasant to people who support terrorism.'

'It doesn't do any harm if you get vital information in the process.'

'Did you get vital information?'

'I did.'

'Well, then? What's the problem? I had my fun, we got our information. I mean, I hate Noraid anyway, but I especially hate Australians who work for Noraid. What business is it of theirs to stick their noses into other people's problems?'

'You might say the same about me.'

288

'You're getting paid for it.'

'So is he.'

'I doubt it. He looks like a volunteer. Jesus, you'd think Australia had enough problems of its own without . . .'

'Starkey, will you calm down?' She reached across the table, put her hand on my arm. 'No need to get excited. I understand, you're patriotic in your own way, it's natural to get a little upset . . .'

I laughed. Grimly. Feeling slightly stupid. 'I'm sorry. It's not your fault, I shouldn't take it out on you. I'm the least patriotic person I know. I shouldn't let it rile me. I don't give a damn whether we end up in a united Ireland or not. I just have a thing about terrorists. And people who suck up to them, like Noraid.'

'You've a chip on both shoulders.'

I nodded. An entire pastie supper, in fact, but I didn't expect she'd get that one; if she did, she'd probably eat it. 'We're getting away from the point here. What happened in there?'

'You got him in quite a state, Starkey. Came back to the counter all mumbles. I asked him if he was okay. He apologized to me, for you, and for him. We chatted for a while about how many crazy people there are in New York. Then I could see the look coming into his eyes, you know, the look that says, what's this black person doing in this Irish place?'

'Like me in Harlem.'

'Like you in Harlem. So I asked what time Marcus would be

back at and he said why, and I said, well, I got an urgent message for him; he said what about, and I said, well, it's personal, but it concerns my daughter. He weighed it up for a little, then said sorry, but Marcus was off work. I asked where I could contact him; he said I couldn't. I said why not. He said he wasn't allowed to give out personal information about employees. I said, well, son, you'd be looking for personal information if your daughter was pregnant, and he said, oh. Anyway, we chatted a bit, I asked him if he had a girlfriend, said he had; I said, well, how would you feel if she was pregnant, but she wasn't able to tell you, because she was scared you wouldn't want to know, because you maybe didn't want children, and she wasn't sure you wanted a long-term relationship with a black woman.'

'Ever think of writing a soap opera, Sissy?'

'No. Shut up and listen. He said he didn't even know Marcus had a girlfriend, but then he didn't see much of him outside of Noraid. Said he understood my position but that there wasn't much he could do. He hated to say it, but now that he thought about it, maybe Marcus had an inkling something was up, because he rushed into the office yesterday and said he wouldn't be in for a while, he was going on vacation. Said it left them short-staffed, but there wasn't much he could do, because they're all volunteers. So off he went on vacation. Yesterday. Missed him by a day.'

'No idea where he went?'

Sissy slurped up on her Coke, swallowed. 'Princetown,' she said, cool as you like.

29

The fishing boat wasn't up to it, so we travelled by Greyhound. It was a nine-hour trip, scooting quickly up the road to Providence, Rhode Island, stopping for a bite to eat at a depot outside the city, and then meandering at a more leisurely pace through the myriad small towns on Cape Cod before rolling into Princetown.

The bus was half empty. Sissy took up a pair of seats and a lot of time talking about her life. I sat in front of her, and before we were a couple of hours down the road I had a sore neck looking back at her. Once in a while she would lose her train of thought and stare out of the window, and I knew she was thinking about her husband. I wondered if she knew he was capable of snipping someone's fingers off with a set of rose clippers. It wasn't the sort of thing that generally cropped up at the dinner table. The thing was, I supposed, you never really knew what your partner was capable of. I had never thought Patricia capable of conceiving a child by another man. I had never considered that Mary McMaster might wear sexy underwear for another man. I had never thought that a Harlem man might worship Barry Manilow or that a self-confessed scaredy-cat might take part in a daring rescue mission. I had never thought very much at all, in fact.

'He's not very open-minded, is he?' Sissy was saying.

'Mmmmm?'

'Your boxer. He's hardly Mr Liberal.'

'How do you mean?'

'He's perceived as being a racist.'

I shrugged. 'He's misunderstood.'

'If he does lean a little to the right, Princetown'll be an eye-opener for him.'

'In what way?'

'You've never heard of it before?'

I shook my head. 'I know about Cape Cod. Playground of the rich and famous, isn't it? The Kennedys and all that.'

'Sure. But Princetown itself. You know that after Frisco and Key West, it's the gay capital of America?'

'You mean, jolly, happy-go-lucky . . . ?'

'Starkey, you know what I mean.'

'Yeah. Okay. But it's a holiday resort, isn't it? It'll be empty this time of the year.'

'I doubt it. It has a large all-year-round gay community. A lot of writers and artists. Hardy perennials.'

'Okay. So he'll be welcomed with open arms. He can become a gay icon.'

'Maybe. If he chooses his comments more judiciously than he did when he spoke about black people in New York.'

'You heard about that?'

'We all heard about that, Starkey.'

'Like I say, he's misunderstood. Don't worry about him. He's only got a few days until the fight. He'll be busy training, getting psyched up, he won't have time to mix with the locals. And even if he does, he's well aware of the damage ill-considered comments can do. And he won't even want to. He's a well-balanced guy. He's got no problems with blacks or gays or Catholics or Muslims. All he wants to do is get his wife back, fight for the title, become champion of the world. He doesn't want to offend anyone.'

A salty rain was blowing in off the Atlantic when we finally reached Princetown.

Sissy had picked up a guidebook on our stop in Providence and spent the second half of the journey regaling me with stories from the town's old whaling days, of its literary past and present, and then, as our hunger grew, she switched to the restaurant guide and taunted me with a walk through dozens of lobster restaurants and Portuguese bakeries. I was stiff, tired, hungry and prepared to eat well, relax and immerse myself in a bit of culture before turning to the fight game and its attendant problems. I'd just lifted our bags out when Stanley Matchitt walked up and stuck his hand out. I shook it warily.

'Hey, Starkey,' he grinned, 'you should see this place. Nothing but fucking poofs everywhere.'

'Really.'

Sissy appeared at my shoulder. Matchitt looked surprised. Then embarrassed. 'Hello,' he said, and put his hand out. Sissy shook it. 'You won't remember me,' he said.

'Of course I do. You're Stanley. I never forget a handsome face.'

'Aw, shucks,' said Matchitt. He bent and picked up her bag.

'Why, Stanley,' I said, 'you've become a gentleman.'

Turning, his mouth contorted Popeye style, he whispered, 'Fuck up, Starkey,' and then led us to a large red car. Matchitt said it was an S-class Mercedes Benz. I took his word for it. It was certainly plush. Sissy and I got in the back. It was a bit of a squeeze.

'So,' I asked, as we cruised gently through the town, 'what's new?'

This time it was a more sombre, thoughtful Stanley Matchitt. Once or twice in the mirror I saw his eyes flit to Sissy. She didn't notice. Her eyes were fluttering. Mine weren't far behind. It had been a long old trip.

'Not much,' said Matchitt.

'Nice car,' I said. 'Whatcha do, nick it?'

A little smile. 'Poodle's. He has a certain style.'

I nodded. 'How's the contender?'

'He's okay. Sleeping like a baby when I left him.'

'You mean he'll wake every four hours screaming to be fed.'

'Something like that.'

'What about the kidnappers?'

'No word.'

I'd told Geordie McClean about Marcus McLiam and his vacation in Princetown. I'd held back about the lingerie. It didn't seem especially relevant. Maybe he wore it himself. I wasn't sure if he'd relayed the information to Matchitt. It wasn't my place to keep him informed.

'I'm sorry about your husband, Mrs Smith,' said Matchitt. Sissy shuddered awake. 'Uuuuuuh, yes. What?'

'I'm sorry about Mr Smith. How he died.'

'Thank you.'

'There's not much I can say.'

'I understand.'

'But if I can be of any help . . .'

'Thank you. I appreciate your concern. I'm coping fine.'

'Stanley is famous back home for the depth of his compassion,' I said.

'Starkey . . .'

'There are many widows who can testify . . .'

'I'm sure you've grown accustomed to Starkey's sarcasm, Mrs Smith.'

Sissy smiled kindly at me. 'It has a certain charm, Stanley.'

'Charm wasn't the word I was thinking of, Mrs Smith . . .'

'Sissy, please . . .'

'Sissy, yes, of course.'

We were only three or four minutes out of town when Matchitt turned the car into a wide driveway. He pulled up well short of an impressively large log cabin as two figures in black held up their hands to the car. Matchitt zipped his window down and stuck his head out. 'Only me,' he said.

One of the guys, big, bald, I recognized from the board meeting back in the Mirage with Poodle Clay. He nodded and waved us on. Matchitt rolled the car down until it rested just in front of a small verandah. A man was rocking gently in a chair, his shaggy hair silhouetted against the interior light, his face dark but for the red point of a cigarette. As we got out, the security guard approached Stanley and nodded his head towards the verandah. 'Reporter arrived. Says he's from the *Daily Mirror* in London.'

'What did Geordie say?'

'He's gone out.'

Matchitt nodded. He turned to me. 'You handle the press still, Starkey?'

I shrugged.

'You handle the press then. I'll get Sissy organized.' He opened the boot and yanked out her bag. He left mine. Then he put a guiding hand on Sissy's arm and piloted her into the cabin. I lifted my own bag and stepped onto the verandah. The man stood up and extended a hand. I shook it. It was a sign of maturity that I was becoming depressingly familiar with.

'Richard Curtis, *Daily Mirror*,' he said. He spoke around his cigarette.

'News or sport?'

'Sport,' he said, a little too quickly.

I nodded cynically. It wasn't much different from nodding

normally. It was the slight narrowing of the eyes that made all the difference. Maybe he missed it in the half-light, or maybe he missed it because his eyes were slightly narrowed as well. 'You're Starkey,' he said. I nodded. 'I've heard the name in Belfast. Am I the first?'

'Here?' I shrugged. 'Far as I know. You have your scoop. What're you after?'

'A word with Bobby.'

'I'm given to understand he's asleep.'

'You could wake him.'

'I could. I won't.'

'I've a deadline.'

'So has Bobby. He needs his sleep.'

'Just a quick word.'

I shook my head. 'I'm sorry. Come back in the morning. I'm sure he'll oblige.'

'The others will have caught up by then.'

'Maybe. Maybe not. You'll have to take your chances.'

'Aw, come on. I've travelled a long way. Give me something. Some background. Anything.'

There was a hint of desperation in his voice. He had a scraggy, unkempt look about him, a paleness that spoke of worry and debt. I'd seen his kind before, the ageing journalist battling to keep his place on the tabloid front line, resisting to the last the inevitable move to the sub's desk. It was a young man's game, and sometimes it wasn't a game at all. I felt a bit sorry for him.

'Listen,' I said, 'I'll see if I can get you a word with Jackie

Campbell. He'll fill you in on how the training's going, okay? It's better than nothing. Then come and see me tomorrow and I'll sort something out with Bobby, okay?'

'Great. Yeah. Sure. Appreciate it, Dan.'

I told him to wait where he was and went inside to look for the elderly trainer.

Davy Crockett wouldn't have known what to make of the log cabin. Six bedrooms. TV/cable. Jacuzzi. Imaginary log fire. Everything over the top of the range. Sissy was already plonked on a massive settee. She smiled over. 'Where's Stanley?' I asked.

'He's fixing me some coffee,' she said and pointed across the room.

I followed her finger to the kitchen. He was pouring two cups. 'Domesticated as well,' I said.

He smiled.

'What is it, Stan, guilt or infatuation?'

He stopped smiling. 'You open your mouth again, Starkey, you're a dead man.'

I slapped him playfully on the shoulder. 'Och, Stanley, I'm only raking.'

'And you're a sarky cunt too.' He lifted the cups and headed for the lounge.

'You seen Jackie?'

He nodded backwards. 'Outside.'

A large marquee had been erected in the backyard. It billowed gently in the sea breeze. I made a mental note not to let Sissy into the yard in case she snagged it for a dress.

Jackie was inside, tightening the ropes on the ring. He was alone. 'Hey, Jackie,' I said.

He turned. The eyes tightened.

'It's me. Dan. Starkey.'

As he ventured closer, recognition dawned.

'How's it going?' I asked.

'Could be better. A hundred per cent better.'

'I heard you weren't too fussed on the training facilities.'

'The training. The town. The people. This place ain't normal. You know I saw two men holding hands down the street today? And they were both wearing high heels.' He shook his head sadly. 'In my day . . .'

'I hear you had some new sparring partners flown in.'

'Had to. The others were useless. Or dead. Dead useless. The new ones'll not last the pace either. Not the mood the big man's in.'

'That's a good sign, isn't it?'

'I suppose. We'll see.'

'Jackie, would you do me a favour?'

'Within reason.'

'There's a reporter outside. Interested in your career, and how things are going for the fight, would you have a word with him? Just quickly. He's from London, made a long trip.'

He tutted, but said he'd do it. I walked him out to the verandah. 'One thing, Jackie,' I said, before letting him loose, 'keep it brief, and stick to the boxing.'

'That's two things,' he said.

30

Lack of alcohol. Sea air. Extreme weariness. A huge feathery bed. They all combined. I slept like a drugged baby.

The clatter of a team breakfast brought me round, but it took a while to claw my way out of a satisfied slumber and by the time I made it as far as the kitchen there was only a scattering of messed dishes left, plus Stanley and Sissy chatting over coffee. Stanley and Sissy. It had a bit of a ring to it. Like an old music hall duo. One of those knife-throwing acts perhaps. Stanley knew a thing or two about knives.

I wished them good morning and we exchanged pleasantries for a while. No one had been thoughtful enough to furnish the fridge with Coke. There was some Gatorade, and it tasted like it. Matchitt was in a tracksuit. He'd breakfasted early and gone out on a run with McMaster. The big bloke was already back in the ring. I walked on through to the marquee.

Of Wee Sweetie Mice and Men

Bobby McMaster was covered in a fine sheen of sweat, but he wasn't blowing too hard. He was punishing a blubbery-looking white guy. Jackie Campbell shouted encouragement, slapping his hand down on the ropes for added emphasis. Then he called time and the hired help lumbered across to his corner and slumped down on the stool. McMaster leant on the ropes and waved over. He manoeuvred his gumshield out of his mouth and held it awkwardly between his gloves. 'How goes it in the city?' he asked. Jovial almost, like he knew the wife was alive and all he had to do was hang on in there and she'd be returned.

'Fine,' I said.

He nodded across to the other side of the ring. Three overweight men in scruffy city suits sat on fold-down chairs, arms crossed, notebooks out. 'The baying horde has caught up,' he said.

I circled the ring and introduced myself. Two were from New York, one from Boston. There was no sign of the guy from the *Mirror*, or the rest of the British pack. They'd all arrived independently in the early hours of the morning and got lodgings in town. They'd been tipped off as to our location. I wasn't surprised. It was a difficult thing to keep quiet. There wasn't much point in denying them access either; it would be more of a distraction to have them camped outside. We chatted about boxing while they kept an eye on McMaster's movements in the ring. They seemed pleasantly surprised by him, not so much by his shape and condition, which still needed a little work, but by his enthusiasm.

Surprised, but not convinced. 'Keep that up,' said Larry Fortenz from the *New York Times*, 'he'll maybe make it into the third round. Now there's not many get that far. I saw Tyson yesterday. I've never seen him look meaner. Like someone's done a good psych job on him.'

Bernie Gold of *Boxing World* nodded in agreement. 'You won't be needing the undertaker so early. But you'll still be needing him.'

Buoyed by their enthusiasm, I went to find Geordie McClean. He was lying on his bed talking animatedly on the phone, trying to rescue some of the endorsement deals McMaster had signed prior to the allegations of racism. He gave me the five-minute sign. I returned to the makeshift gym. McMaster had despatched his white opponent within three rounds and was now pulverizing his second opponent of the morning. He had him pinned in the corner and was steadily, unspectacularly ploughing body shots into him. He tried covering up, crouching low, but he couldn't quite do it; McMaster's blows just pile-drove through him and eventually he sank to one knee. McMaster gave him a playful tap on the head and returned to his corner.

'That's ma boy!' shouted Jackie Campbell. 'Three more rounds, we'll call it a day, Bobby.'

The third and final boxer of the morning had been limbering up at the back of the marquee, facing away from the ring. As his fallen companion bent awkwardly under the ropes to exit, he turned, then stepped forward and, placing one gloved hand on the top rope, he propelled himself up and over with the agility of a featherweight. As he landed he fixed his feet firmly on the canvas and glared across the ring at McMaster. His head was shaved close, emphasizing the meanness of his eyes. Although he was a good six inches shorter than the contender he made up for it with a taut, compact body. Like Tyson, he had no neck. He had a thick body, a thick head, and all of it looked dangerous. He slapped his gloves together. Let's get it on. McMaster smiled at him.

Bernie Gold shouted across the ring, 'Hey, Jackie, where'd y'get the bull?'

Jackie shrugged and rang the bell. He stepped down from the canvas and lifted a clipboard, then ran his finger quickly down a list. 'Mo Barkley out of New Orleans,' he shouted across the ring.

McMaster moved forward. Barkley advanced to meet him. McMaster stuck out an exploratory left jab. Barkley moved left easily and slapped it away as he went. He circled. McMaster stuck out another. Then another. Then followed it with a right which bounced off Barkley's shoulder. Barkley bunched the shoulder up disdainfully and pushed out his own jab, McMaster shrugged it off, then moved forward again. Barkley stepped back – no, he appeared to step back, he rocked back on his heels, then pulled forward and crashed a left hook up through McMaster's defences. Bobby's head shot back and for a moment his eyes glazed and his legs wobbled. But for the headguard he would have gone down. He staggered back to the ropes. Barkley closed in. This time an overhead right. McMaster retained enough sense to move left and under and pulled a hook into Barkley's unprotected midriff. Barkley grunted, stepped back, then ducked low and moved in again, elbows out wide, and fired an uppercut to McMaster's jaw; Bobby moved slightly, just enough to commute the death sentence. I stepped up to the ring and held tight onto the top rope. The other reporters clambered after me. 'Gee,' said one. That was the sum of the press analysis. Jackie Campbell, sprightly beyond his years, moved around the ropes until he was behind Bobby, then slapped his shoulder. 'Move! Move! Move!' he screamed. McMaster didn't have time to worry about advice. The blows were raining in. Three or four landed. McMaster got one back. Three or four landed. McMaster got another in. 'Move! Move! Move!' Campbell shouted again. McMaster shuffled a little to his right. Barkley let go a fairground left that knocked him back to stage centre, and the blows started raining in again. 'Jesus Christ!' Campbell screamed. McMaster was wilting.

And then the bell rang. Campbell looked up. McMaster looked up, then leant back as another hook raced up towards his chin. Just in time. He bent forward and shoved Barkley hard in the chest with both gloves. His sparring partner, surprised, tumbled backwards.

'Quit at the fuckin' bell!' McMaster snarled.

'Whatcha ring it for?' Campbell demanded.

Geordie McClean stood in the corner by the bell. He looked tense. He lifted his hand to his ear. 'Call for you, Bobby,' he said. 'It's your wife.'

Barkley had raised himself to his feet. He slapped his gloves together again. The glare was still there. McMaster matched it for a moment, then shook his head and spat out his gumshield. He started to say something to McClean, but Geordie shushed him, nodding across at the reporters. McMaster ducked under the ropes and headed for the kitchen.

'Fortuitous call,' said Bernie Gold, laconically.

'Saved by the wife,' added Larry Fortenz. They looked pleased with themselves. They returned to their seats and started making notes.

McClean jumped down from the ring. His face was red. 'Everyone has an off day,' he spat and followed McMaster.

Mo Barkley ducked under the ropes. He picked up a towel and rubbed his face. Then he held out his gloves for Jackie Campbell to untie.

'Hey, Mo,' shouted Bernie Gold, 'where you been hiding?'

Mo shrugged.

'Doing anything on St Patrick's Day?' shouted Larry Fortenz. 'I hear Tyson's looking for an opponent.'

Mo shrugged again.

Fortenz walked round to Barkley and ran an approving eye over his body. 'New Orleans, is it? Whose gym?'

Barkley barely opened his mouth. 'I don't talk to the press,' he said. The glare was still there. Maybe he was born with it. Born angry. Not a bad thing for a boxer.

'So? Talk to Bernie then, he barely qualifies.'

Bernie groaned. 'You crack me up, Larry, you really crack me up.'

Jackie Campbell pulled the gloves off, then handed them back to Barkley. 'Well done, son,' he said.

Barkley nodded and walked off. He disappeared through the marquee flaps. Campbell watched him go, nodded himself.

I nudged his elbow. 'Good, wasn't he?' I said quietly.

'Good?' he snapped. 'Brilliant. Too brilliant.'

Stanley and Sissy had some fresh coffee. Nice.

I shook my head at her. 'Shouldn't you be out . . . sleuthing, or something?'

Sissy looked lazily up. 'Sleuthing, Starkey?'

'Yeah, well, whatever the fuck you do.'

Matchitt said: 'Watch your tongue, Starkey.' But he didn't look up. He looked at Sissy. She smiled warmly.

Jesus, I thought. 'More sleuthing, less smooching, we might get something done around here,' I snapped.

Matchitt looked a tad embarrassed, just for a second, then his upper lip curled back in anger, but Sissy shushed him. 'While you been sleeping, Starkey, I've been working. Sleuthing since dawn, honey.'

'Yeah? You realize there are terrorists on the phone in there?' She nodded. 'I mean, shouldn't you be doing something about it?'

'I am doing something.'

'It looks like it.'

'I told you about the sarcasm,' said Matchitt.

'You're not getting paid . . .'

'I'm not getting paid full stop. Dimes and quarters, Starkey, dimes and quarters. If I turn her up, I turn her up, okay?'

'Yeah. Okay. Right.' I nodded. Classic Coke withdrawal symptoms. They knew all about withdrawing Classic Coke. Or was it Coke Classic? 'Sorry,' I added.

'For your information I've been to see the local police and they're not averse to helping out. There isn't much happens round here besides a couple of queens fighting it out on a Saturday night, so a heavyweight contender and a kidnapping kind of shook 'em up. So now every call coming in is being monitored and traced. Every hotel and guesthouse within a twenty-five-mile radius is being checked for McLiam.'

'Very good,' I said. Matchitt nodded at me.

'The problem is,' Sissy continued, 'they're mostly small, privately owned establishments, no one really seems to have a list of them all, and there aren't that many cops in town, so it might take a bit of time.'

'That's understandable,' I said.

'So, I've organized all that, and still have time for coffee. What've you done, honey?'

'I've made some notes,' I said.

'Class,' said Matchitt.

'It's what I'm paid for, Stanley. I still haven't quite worked out what you're being paid for. Bag carrier, is it?'

I walked on through; Matchitt's glare burnt holes in my back, but I was tough and could take it. He didn't think the glare was enough. He came after me and hauled me back by the arm.

'Every day you push me that little bit closer, Starkey.'

'Closer to what, Stanley?'

He let go. He stepped back. I tensed, ready for the punch. I'd slip to the floor and feign unconsciousness. It was a good way of getting sympathy. It didn't come. 'Your problem, Starkey, is you think you're God's gift. God's gift to everyone. And you know what you really are? God's unwanted gift. You're that big fluffy jumper someone gets at Christmas. You're God's outsize shoes.'

I walked on. He turned back. We were never going to be friends.

Bobby McMaster was sitting on the bed in Geordie McClean's room. He cradled the phone under his chin, but the call was over. McClean stood before him. They looked round as I entered.

'Well?' I said.

McClean stepped over and closed the door. 'You know what they say about walls?'

'It was them, wasn't it?' I said. 'Wasn't just an excuse to get out of the ring?'

He shook his head. 'Them. Mary too. She sends her love. That's about all she said. I shouldn't complain. At least she's still alive.'

I looked at McClean. Grim-faced. 'What's the crack then?' I asked.

'Simple enough. They've decided to hold on to her for a while longer.'

'We knew that.'

'And they have a couple more demands before they let her go.'

'Such as?'

McMaster finally replaced the receiver. He swung his legs up onto the bed and lay back. He folded his hands behind his head. 'You know I was asked to lead the St Patrick's Day parade through New York? They want me to make a speech on the day calling for a united Ireland and demanding that the armed struggle be taken up once more against the British oppressor.'

'You've started down that road,' I said. 'You may as well continue. Then they let her go.'

'No. Then I fight for the world title, and they want to call the result.'

'So they want to make a little money as well.' I shrugged. 'What do you think? They call the round you go down in, is that it? Don't they understand it's not up to you? They would have been better kidnapping Tyson's wife, getting him to take the dive.'

'It's not like that, Starkey. They want me to win the fight. They say it'll do wonders for their publicity. They want me to win the title or they'll kill my wife.' He snorted again, shook his head. 'Rich, isn't it? I was starting to think I might do all right against Tyson, and then I nearly get my lights punched in by some cheap wanker from New Orleans. In a couple of days I've to beat the Terminator or my wife dies.'

I leant back against the door. 'They wouldn't settle for an honourable draw, would they?'

'Nice thought,' said McMaster, 'but even that's a bit beyond me.'

There was a knock on the door. I pushed off it and opened it a crack. Sissy was there. I opened it wider, ushered her in and closed it again.

'The local police got back to me,' she said. 'Didn't get enough time on the call to trace it all the way. They're not used to this sort of thing. But they got the general area.'

'Good!' said McClean, slapping his hands together. He bent forward and punched McMaster lightly on the leg. 'It's a start, Bobby. We'll get the bastards yet. Just a matter of narrowing it down.' He turned back to Sissy. 'Whereabouts?'

'New York,' said Sissy.

'Whereabouts in New York?'

'New York.'

'That's it?'

'That's it.'

'Jesus.'

31

McMaster said he didn't feel up to getting back into the ring with Barkley. Speaking to Mary had cast him into a gloom. A cynic could have blamed this on getting beaten up by his sparring partner, but there were no cynics around, unless you counted the three reporters scribbling and the manager biting a hole in his lip.

I patted his shoulder and asked him what he wanted to do. He said he fancied a walk round the town. I said why not? Let's go. A bit of peace and quiet. Of course he was depressed about his wife. Who wouldn't be? And who wanted to climb into a boxing ring in that frame of mind and get beaten up for nothing, when he could hold off for a few days and get beaten up for a million dollars?

I had thought just the two of us might go. I would be his shoulder to cry on. He could pour it all out the way one man can only do to another. I wouldn't even think about shame-lessly exploiting it in my account of his title challenge, although I wouldn't be held responsible for my tape recorder inadvert-ently switching itself to record. But it wasn't to be. Because McMaster was going, Matchitt insisted on going along to guard him. And because Matchitt was going, Sissy decided to go as well. Geordie McClean said he was fed up arguing on the phone with dim Americans and reckoned a break would do him the world of good. And just for good measure a couple of Poodle's boys came as well. We sneaked out on Jackie Campbell, snoozing on the lounge sofa, like children running out on a gruff grandparent. We crowded into a couple of cars, the Mercedes and a smaller, blue effort, and made for town.

It was all very pleasant. We parked in a large, mostly empty seafront car park, and at first the sharp wind off the bay took our breath away. We turned towards the slight shelter of the main street and began sauntering along, stopping here and there to admire the picturesque wooden storefronts. My attempts at companionship thwarted by the greater group, I let McMaster walk ahead. Poodle's boys, Zack and Jack they said in the car, crop hair, ever-present sunglasses, kept a little behind him, but didn't approach. I walked with Geordie McClean. Matchitt and Sissy brought up the rear. It was a dysfunctional family outing.

Geordie seemed pleased to be in the open air. 'It's fuckin' freezin',' he growled, his hands sunk deep into the pockets of his cashmere coat.

'Never mind,' I said, 'spring's on the way.'

'That's a big fuckin' relief,' he said, hunching his shoulders angrily.

'Howdya think the big man's taking it?' I asked.

His eyes swept up to McMaster, then across to me. 'How would you take it if someone kidnapped your wife?'

I nodded. Someone had kidnapped my wife. It was getting fashionable.

McMaster walked into a bookshop. Our little troop gathered outside to wait for him. The shop was called Rubyfruit Books. He wasn't inside for more than thirty seconds. When he emerged his face was bright red, and it wasn't down to the sea air.

'That,' said Matchitt, with admirable restraint, 'is a bookshop for fruits.'

'So I discovered.' McMaster pulled the hood of his tracksuit up around his head and led the party off again.

'Anything you want to tell us?' Matchitt called from the back, as we resumed our previous formation. He sniggered. McMaster shouted something back, but it was lost in the wind as the street bent back towards the bay.

I pulled the collar up on my jacket. 'Do you feel safer here, Geordie, away from the city?' I asked.

He looked up the street. At the pleasant country stores, their little dolls'-house gardens, at the white wooden town hall and library. He shook his head. 'Not a lot, no. It's like fucking Amityville. I don't know why I let Poodle talk me into this.'

'You still want to go home?'

He shrugged. 'We've come this far. I suppose it can't get

much worse. Maybe it'll even get better. Maybe we've turned the corner.'

'We have. Into an icy wind.'

'Thanks. You've cheered me up no end.'

'Stanley and Sissy seem to have hit it off well,' I said, nodding back.

McClean tutted. 'That's what I like to see, a nice respectful period of mourning.'

'Mourning has broken, as the song says.'

'I suppose we must take love where we find it.'

McMaster entered a bakery and we gathered together again in the shelter of a striped awning. Even Zack and Jack, normally so unnaturally erect, looked a little diminished in the cold. McMaster emerged clutching a paper sack.

'Hot pastries, anyone?' he asked and held it up like a trophy.

We crowded round. Matchitt sniggered again. 'Didn't you get any fruitcake?' he asked.

McMaster gave him a sarky smile and passed the bag round. We got a bun each. Hot and sticky and sugary and nice. Sissy got the smallest of the lot. She looked a little disappointed. Matchitt tore his in half and offered her a share. She made a bit of a show of saying no, then accepted it with a smile. McClean turned to me and rolled his eyes. I rolled 'em back.

McMaster wasn't finished with his surprises. 'I have seen the future,' he proclaimed, reaching into his tracksuit and pulling out a folded leaflet, 'and the future is whale-watching.'

'Aye, fuck,' said Matchitt.

'Yup. Whale-watching.' He unfolded the leaflet. He winked at Matchitt. 'An afternoon on the high seas getting back to nature. Seeing the most majestic of God's creatures in their natural habitat. For only fifteen dollars each. Plus five dollars for harpoons.' The contender cackled. His first proper laugh in quite a while. 'Who's game?'

'It'll be fuckin' freezin',' said McClean.

'So. Are ye a man or a mouse?'

'Mouse. A house mouse.'

'Starkey?'

I shrugged. 'It's not out of season?'

'Nah. They're there all year round. I asked in the bakery. In fact they're easier to spot. Less tourist boats to annoy them. You're game?'

I shrugged again. 'Yeah. Sure. Why not?'

'What about it, Stanley?'

'Nah. Geordie's right. It'll be freezin'.'

McMaster shook his head. 'The boat's heated. Says on the leaflet.'

'Be warmer than this then,' said McClean.

'Who wants to see a bloody whale anyway?' said Matchitt. 'I seen Orca.'

'Aye,' said McMaster, 'Orca Killer Plastic Whale. See the real thing, Stanley, while you can. Marvel at the majesty. Enthuse at their intelligence.'

'Yeah,' sneered Matchitt, 'I'd love to see them use a knife and fork.'

'I'd love to see you use a knife and fork,' I contributed.

Matchitt turned quickly. Sissy put a restraining hand on his arm. 'I'd love to see a whale,' she said.

His eyes softened.

'Stanley doesn't like the sea,' I said.

'I've nothing against the sea.'

'And he doesn't like boats.'

'I don't mind boats.'

'Well, why not then?' she asked. 'It'll be wonderful.'

'I'm just not that interested in whales.'

She squeezed his arm. 'It'll be fun.'

'Hey, Stanley,' said McMaster, 'says there's a bar on the boat.'

Matchitt gave a half-hearted shrug.

'Come on,' said Sissy, tweaking his face.

'I might just sit in the bar. I'm really not that interested in whales.'

'That's okay.' She smiled warmly. He smiled warmly too, but he had anxious eyes. You recognize anxious eyes in my trade. Anxious eyes, subdued mouth, effervescent lips. Everything that goes towards giving an unhappy man a face like a Lurgan spade.

McMaster nodded at Zack and Jack. 'What about you guys? Coming whale-watching?'

They didn't need to look at each other. 'We go where you go,' said Zack.

Geordie slapped McMaster on the back. 'Lead on then, Captain Ahab.'

Sissy still had Matchitt by the arm. 'It'll be fun,' she said again.

'Sure.'

'Looks like Snatchit Matchitt's back in business,' I said.

Anxious eyes gave way to murderous eyes. 'One day I really will kill you, Starkey.'

'You kill me now, Stanley.'

Sissy tweaked his cheek again. 'You really are so sweet,' she said.

Captain Frank Tilson was an old sea mongrel. He was past sixty. He'd spent twenty hard years on whalers. Now he and his son ran a whale-watcher. He sailed her, his son Junior gave a running commentary. Junior was into conservation. Frank said he was into conservation too, but he didn't sound very convincing. Their boat, the *Charles W. Morgan Jnr*, had seen better days.

'They won't see nothing for a while yet,' he said, nodding forward, ''less they get excited by dolphins.'

'They'd get excited by fish,' I said. He laughed. McClean, McMaster and Sissy were up front, catching the sharp wind full in the gob, eyes peeled. McClean, caught up in the excitement of the journey, seemed to have forgotten about the cold. Junior was behind them, talking thirteen to the dozen about the life and times of the whale. I wasn't particularly interested. A whale was a whale was a whale. Matchitt wasn't much interested either. He sat behind me, cosied up to a heater and sipping miserably at a bottle of whiskey he'd found in the fridge. He offered me some. I turned it down. We'd been under way for forty-five minutes. Forty-five minutes away

317

from Zack and Jack. We'd left them standing at the jetty. Captain Frank wouldn't let them on board. Said the boat was too small. They only used a small boat in the winter season, and our group was two too many. He was only observing standard safety procedures. It could have been racism, but who was to say? There seemed to be plenty of room, but what did I know? And he didn't object to Sissy. 'Away back up to the house,' McClean had said, 'and man the phone. You know Jackie Campbell's as deaf as a post.' They accepted it with quiet resignation. Sissy, I suspected, would have torn his head off, but she was unaware. She'd been first on board and had already bounded well up the deck in search of her first whale.

'You do this all year round, Frank?' I asked.

He nodded.

'You think we'll get our money's worth?'

'Most always people do. Once we hit the shallows, there'll be plenty to see. Minkes mostly.'

'Monkeys?'

'Minkes. Minke whales. The lesser rorqual if you want to be specific. Junior there's the specific one.'

Junior was drawing a picture in the air. Sissy nodded. McMaster scanned the sea ahead. 'He seems greatly into saving the whale,' I said. 'What about you, poacher turned gamekeeper, aren't you?'

By all rights he should have gotten a wistful look in his eye, the memories of daring deep-sea adventures should have raced through his mind, battling, conquering, being conquered by the master of the ocean. Instead his eyes had a cynical glint. Cynical like a man robbed of his one true career by do-gooders. 'Poacher turned cab driver.'

'Save the whale,' I said, 'for supper.'

'Sounds about right.'

Matchitt jogged my elbow. 'Are we nearly fuckin' there yet?' I shrugged. 'And what's this about monkeys?'

'Minkes,' I said.

His voice was already slurry. Probably the arrhythmic sway of the boat wasn't helping his sobriety. 'Big fuckers, are they?'

The language seemed not to worry Frank. The whaling fleet probably knew about cussin'. ''Bout thirty foot. The females are slightly bigger.'

'Story of my life,' Matchitt gurgled to himself and stepped out from the cabin.

'Actually,' said Frank, 'they're not that big. Just about the smallest whale there is. We didn't even used to bother with them much out on the whalers. Folks on the coast did, mind. Friendly old souls, the minkes, used to sail right up to the boats to say hello, get a harpoon for their troubles.'

Matchitt stepped back in as the vessel banked up. He looked a little green. 'Is it getting rougher?' he asked.

'Wind'll drop soon, son,' said Frank.

'Aye, aye, Captain,' said Matchitt. He moved up to the wheel. He bent and examined Frank's trousers. 'Say, Captain, what's that round your belt there? Can I see it?'

'Pizzle,' said Frank.

'Pizzle,' said Matchitt.

'Pizzle,' I said.

Without looking down, Frank unclasped a whip from his belt and handed it to Matchitt, who turned it in his hand. Flexed it once. Twice. Three times. He looked impressed. 'Whatcha need a whip for?' he demanded.

'Show,' said Frank.

'Could do with one meself.' He cracked it again. I stood well back. 'Round up the usual Fenians!' he shouted and threw it out again. He cackled. 'Can I buy it off of you?'

Frank shook his head. 'It was my father's.'

Matchitt turned it over in his hand. 'What's it made of anyway? Cowhide? Sea cow?'

'Whale's penis.'

Matchitt dropped it. 'Ugh,' he said as it hit the floor.

I pushed the handle with the toe of my shoe. 'Seriously?' I asked.

Frank nodded. Ugh, I thought. Matchitt returned to his seat by the heater and took another pull on his bottle, then scowled back at us. 'No wonder they're endangered, people keep cutting their dicks off.'

'Sure, Stanley,' I said.

Frank had a smile fixed on his face. Not so wide that Matchitt could see it, but a thin, hint-of-tooth grin that slit his face like a bowie knife on an old tawny saddle. 'Tough guy,' he said.

'He has his moments,' I said.

32

'Thar she blows!'

The cry came from the most unlikely of sources. While we clustered up front, eyes narrowed against the spray, he had gone to be sick over the back security rail, hunched down as so many of his victims must once have hunched waiting for the bullet – if they were lucky – but now he stood proudly erect, one chubby hand pointing out over the waves, the other clamped tight to the rail.

Eyes turned, feet moved, Frank cut the engines. Junior put his hand up to stop us rushing. He didn't want to capsize the boat.

'Over there!' Matchitt shouted again. We stopped for a moment, following the direction, but whatever it was, we lost it in the chop.

Sissy pressed against Junior's outstretched hand. 'Please!' she wailed.

He stood firm. He shouted, but it was a kindly shout bred of years of dealing with excited tourists. 'Take it easy! There'll be plenty more!'

Frank stood in the cabin doorway. His face was a mask of steady stoicism. He too had seen it all before. Made his living by killing them. If he still got a rush from the first sighting, it didn't show.

We split up, filed down either side of the cabin. Sissy reached him first. 'What was it like?' she squealed.

'Big.'

'Where?'

'I . . .' He pointed again, not quite so certain.

'She'll have dived,' said Junior. He raised a pair of binoculars to his eyes and scanned the horizon. 'They don't stay up very long. But she'll be up again in a moment. Did she blow?'

'Yeah! Of course she did!'

Junior didn't look convinced. 'I didn't hear anything,' he said quietly.

Sissy put one hand on the rail, the other on the back of Matchitt's jacket. 'This is so exciting!'

McClean shouted, pointed left.

'That's her!' shouted Matchitt.

Something black showed through the spray.

'It's a minke!' McMaster guldered.

Junior lowered his glasses. 'If it is,' he said, 'it's driving a speedboat.'

'You what?' I said.

Junior smiled and nodded. 'Easy mistake to make.'

'Fuck,' said Matchitt.

Now we could all see it, a long, blue-black boat, three people on board, cutting through the waves at speed, about three hundred yards to our left.

Sissy tutted. 'They'll scare her off.'

'On the contrary,' said Junior, 'she'll probably hang around. They like the boats, like to come and play. Good for us. Not so good for the minke in the old whaling days.'

The speedboat passed on. Sissy waved at the crew. They didn't seem to notice. Matchitt went back to the cabin for a drink. Sissy went with him. McMaster and McClean returned to the prow. Frank returned to the wheel and restarted the engine.

Junior leant on the rail. I leant with him. 'You ever get tired of doing this?' I asked.

He shook his head. 'I love it.'

'What about your dad? He used to hunt them, didn't he?'

'Of necessity. It was his job. We live in more enlightened times now.'

'I doubt if he looks on them as enlightened.'

Junior smiled. 'You'd be surprised. He puts on a bluff old act.'

'He does it well.'

'Well, we're in the tourism business. It's not Disneyworld, but every little bit helps.'

'A bit of hype. Just like in boxing.'

'Sure. He snarls and growls once in a while, but there's no killer instinct in him. He did a job once. On a whaler. Now he doesn't have to any more. Who would choose to kill a majestic creature like the whale if they didn't have to to survive themselves?' He raised his glasses again and began scanning.

I shrugged. He had a touching faith in human nature. McMaster was just doing a job. A job for which he needed the killer instinct. It was a pity Matchitt couldn't box for toffee. 'Who indeed?' I said and spat into the water, a nasty habit, but someone has to do it.

I spat on a thirty-foot whale.

I stepped back. Sleek. Silent. Beautiful. I didn't know what to say. I pointed.

Junior didn't notice.

'Whale,' I said.

'Mmmm?' Junior dropped his glasses and looked at me.

'Whale,' I said, and pointed again.

He just caught the tail end as it dived. 'Whooh!' he said. 'Snuck right up!' He turned back, shouted: 'Cut the engines! Sighting!' The thunder of footsteps. 'Take it easy!'

They came from different directions, but in a hurry, the boat banked a bit, then settled. 'Where?' squealed Sissy, the first to arrive.

'Gone under again.' Eyes intent now on the water about a hundred yards ahead. 'But she'll be up in a moment.'

We followed his gaze. The engines died. Frank appeared in the cabin doorway. Matchitt pushed past him, clutching the bottle of whiskey, and made his way along to Sissy. 'Lost the speedboat then?' he growled.

And up she came.

'Jesus,' said Matchitt.

'Okay!' shouted Junior. 'It's a minke okay! It's a female! Slightly longer than the male! See the pronounced dorsal fin! The white band round the pectoral fins!'

She slipped under the waves again.

'Gee!' said Sissy.

'Beautiful,' said McClean.

'There's another!' shouted McMaster, pointing right.

'There's one!' shouted Sissy, further right.

'There's stacks a them!' shouted Matchitt.

They seemed to be everywhere, but there were only seven or eight. All close to the ship, all diving and surfacing independently but hinting at a secret link, like they were all part of one giant creature wriggling about us. A great blue worm. They were astonishing. Incredible. Fandabbydozey. Junior kept up the running commentary. 'The minke feeds mainly on krill. That's a small, shrimplike crustacean. If they're in short supply it has been known to take small fish. It's sometimes mistaken for the killer whale. They're both about the same size.'

'Oooh,' cooed Sissy, 'there's so many of them!'

'Don't be misled by the numbers, ma'am. The minke is an endangered species. There are thought to be only around fifty thousand of them alive in the world today.'

'Fifty thousand!' roared Matchitt. 'Fuck, that's millions!'

'It's really not . . .' began Junior and then stopped. Matchitt had produced his gun.

'I really think . . .' said Junior.

'Fifty thousand?' said Matchitt.

'Yes, sir . . .'

'One wouldn't make any difference then, would it?'

He turned and walked unsteadily back towards the prow, bottle in one hand, gun in the other. Junior followed. I went after him. McMaster shook his head disdainfully.

'Stanley?' said Sissy.

'Just the one!' Matchitt roared again. He stopped and pulled the gun up. The nearest minke to him was about thirty yards out. He steadied his aim as best he could, then fired twice. Junior and I both ducked down. We couldn't see where the bullets landed. Lost in the waves. The minke dived. Matchitt let out a roar of laughter and moved on up the boat. He took another swig as he moved. Then stopped and pulled the gun up again. Junior moved for him, but Matchitt swung the gun round on him.

'Leave me alone!'

Junior raised his hands. 'Just give me the gun, sir.'

'Fuck off!' roared Matchitt. He loosed another couple of bullets. 'Last of the big game hunters!' he shouted and cackled again. 'C'mon, Moby, show your head!'

'Stanley!' I shouted. 'They're not even Fenian whales!'

I don't quite know why I said it. Don't know why I was sticking my neck out for a bunch of dopey, blubbery mammals. Matchitt turned the gun on me. His eyes were wide. Nostrils flared with excitement. Blood lust, maybe. Maybe I had gone a joke too far.

'Now here is an endangered species!' he shouted. 'The lesser-known crap reporter. Do you want put out of your misery, son?'

Sissy appeared behind me. 'Stanley, put the gun down,' she said.

Matchitt shrugged. 'Ach, Sissy, love, I'm only raking. Do you want a go?' He waved the gun at her.

'No, Stanley. This isn't a good idea.'

Junior went to move forward again. Matchitt trained the gun on him.

'All in my own time!'

'Okay! Okay!' said Junior. 'Take it easy. Just put the gun away. Nothing more will be said. Just put it away.'

He crept forward another foot or two.

'I'm fuckin' warning you!'

And then there was a crack and I ducked involuntarily, in the same instant looking for the splash of blood, and it was a second before I realized that the yelp of pain came not from Junior but from Matchitt, that the gun was skidding across the deck and Frank was standing across from us with his whip in hand. It was incredible. It was like a scene from *Raiders of the Lost Ark*, if it had been made on a very small budget.

Matchitt stood in shock. He cradled his hand. Junior ran and picked up the gun. Frank just shook his head and returned to the cabin.

Sissy stepped forward and put a hand on Matchitt's shoulder. 'Oh, Stanley,' she said. 'A little too much whiskey.'

McMaster pushed through. 'You are one stupid cunt, Stanley,' he said. 'Excuse the language, Sissy.' Sissy nodded. Then McMaster threw an excellent left and Matchitt fell like a sack of Comber spuds.

McClean came up, turned to Junior. 'I'm very sorry about this.'

'I should report it.'

'I'm sure we can sort something out.'

Junior nodded. He glanced back at the cabin. 'We'll talk,' he said.

McMaster and I pulled Matchitt up and dragged him to the cabin. We lay him down on a bench. He was out cold. We stood over him for a moment.

'Poor Stanley,' said McMaster.

'Which do you think he'll boast about in the future?' I asked. 'Being knocked out by the future world heavyweight champion, or being disarmed by a whale's penis?'

'Future world heavyweight champion?'

'Yeah, well.'

'Och, Starkey, I didn't know you cared.'

'I'm subtly trying to build up your confidence, Bobby. Don't get carried away.'

'I'll try not to.'

Then there was another crack, a deeper, duller crack which shattered the window behind us. The crack of a bullet. We hit the deck. Frank shrank behind the wheel. Sissy let out a scream. Another crack. Another.

'Jesus,' moaned McMaster, 'they're shooting back!'

I crawled forward to the wheel. Frank and I both cautiously peered out. Sissy was lying up front. She looked okay. She was pointing at Junior. He lay opposite her, on his belly. There was an ugly red patch on the back of his shirt. Frank moved for the door.

'Stay here,' I said, holding him back. 'Look after the boat.'

'It's my boy.'

'We'll sort it out.' I looked back. McMaster was on his feet. 'Come on, Bobby, let's see what the stupid git did.'

'He stuck the gun in his jacket and the bastard went off, that's what he did,' he said quietly.

I turned my head from Frank and gave McMaster a wry smile. 'Three times?' I said. 'Accident prone, isn't he?'

McMaster gave me a wry smile. 'And Kennedy committed suicide.'

Crack. Shatter.

We hit the deck again. 'They *are* shooting back!' McMaster yelled.

I cautiously pulled myself up and looked out, this time away from the boat. Out to sea where the speedboat had reappeared. It bobbed quietly about fifty yards away. Three men stood behind the wheel. They had rifles aimed at us.

I ducked down again. 'Jesus,' I said, 'there's pirates out there.'

329

Frank inched his head above the shattered window. McMaster looked too.

Another three or four rounds were loosed.

'What the fuck do they want,' McMaster wailed, 'fish?'

I looked out again. They'd restarted their motor and were moving towards us.

'I don't suppose we can outrun them,' I whispered to Frank.

He shook his head. 'No chance. I must go to my son.'

I held him back again. 'There's no point in you getting shot as well.'

The shout came from close at hand, maybe fifteen yards, but it sounded weak against the volume of the water. 'Everyone out on deck! Where we can see you. Put your hands up!'

I looked out again. They were coming alongside. One gun was still trained on the boat. One man was steering. Another was preparing to board us. I recognized him. He was a reporter. The reporter who'd first accused McMaster of racism.

'If I'm not mistaken,' I said, 'we're about to be boarded by a Son of Muhammad.'

'Oh shite,' said McMaster.

33

'Martin,' I said, reaching over the side of the boat and grasping the reporter turned terrorist firmly by the hand, 'how are you?'

Although the reporter turned terrorist club is a small and exclusive one he gave no indication of recognizing a fellow member, or perhaps that recognition was coded in the disdainful scowl his face seemed to wear so naturally as I pulled him up onto the *Charles W. Morgan Jnr*. I'm a recent recruit and not greatly au fait with the rituals of the club, so I might have been reading him all wrong. He relaxed his grip and thumped his black boots onto the deck.

'Keep well back,' he growled.

We kept well back. Martin King wore camouflaged fatigues. Camouflaged for jungle warfare. Not for naval combat. For that he would have needed a nice blue and white ensemble and a seagull's-nest hairdo. Still, maybe I was being picky. Maybe he hadn't been in the club that long himself.

He produced a pistol and waved it in our general direction. 'You armed?' he asked.

I shook my head.

'What about the Irish snake?'

I nodded at McMaster. 'That'll be you.'

'We've no weapons,' said McMaster.

King nodded. With the sound of the speedboat and the sound of the sea, they probably hadn't heard Matchitt's attempts at whale murder. He looked at the wheelroom. Captain Frank was in the doorway. 'Come out here where I can see you,' he said.

Frank stepped out.

'Further.'

Frank took another step. As an act of defiance it ranked pretty low on the scale, but it rankled King.

'Come out here now!' he yelled. Frank took two steps. 'Raise those hands!'

Frank raised them slowly. King searched me, then McMaster. Then he stepped up to Frank and pulled him forward roughly by his collar. Frank's hands bunched into fists, but he didn't use them. King ran his hands quickly around his body. They eyeballed each other the whole time. Then, satisfied, he turned to Sissy.

She stuck a finger out at him. 'You think you searchin' me, honey, you gotta another thing comin'.'

'I trust you, sister.'

'I ain't your sister.'

King smiled coolly. 'Yes, you are, sister, you just don't know it yet.'

'You don't know fuck, honey.'

'We'll see.' He nodded towards Junior, still lying motionless on the deck. 'What about him?'

'Well, he ain't seasick,' said Sissy.

'Dead or alive?' King snapped.

'I don't know. I haven't had the chance to check.'

'Well, check, sister.'

Sissy blew some air, then crossed to Junior and knelt beside him. She touched the back of his head, whispered something, waited a moment then rocked him gently by the shoulder. 'Honey, you okay?' she asked.

Junior gave a little moan. Sissy rolled him over and he let out a bigger moan. 'Sorry,' she said gently, resting his head in her lap.

'At the risk of jumping your gun,' I said, 'I'd say he needs urgent medical attention.'

'As will you, smartass, you keep opening your mouth.'

I shrugged.

'Okay. Now you can give my comrades a hand up. And take it easy. I'm right behind you.'

McMaster and I moved up to the security wire and ducked under it. The speedboat had drifted off a little. The two remaining Sons still stood with their sights trained on the *Charlie W.* King signalled for them to draw closer. One dropped his rifle and restarted the engine, then slowly manoeuvred her in. The water was pretty much calm, but it was still awkward as the two vessels bobbed at different levels. A rope was thrown on board and we tied her up, but pulling the two of them up was still all about timing and it was the sea setting the clock. Frank and Junior could have done it in half the time, but one couldn't and one wouldn't.

One Son reached up, the other held his gun. I nearly got him, but the boat sank down. With the next swell I grabbed his hand, but then the boat was pulled hard away until it strained against the rope.

The boat moved back in. Rose towards me again. 'Third time lucky,' I said.

The Son nodded, reached up. I grasped his hand. The speedboat rose again. I started to pull, but he hesitated. Something didn't feel right. An odd rhythm between us. The speedboat continued to rise. And rise. It was above the level of the *Charlie W.* and I thought, Jesus, we're going to be swamped. But it wasn't a wave at all. The Son, eyes wide in panic, let out a scream and let go. He toppled back. His companion was thrown back against the side of the speedboat; one gun clattered on the deck, the other went overboard. Up the boat went still and then suddenly it was thrown upside down and both Sons were lost in the mad swirl of wave and chop and suck as the speedboat was swamped. Going down too was the long sleek form of the minke which had spoilt the boarding party. It came, it sank, it left.

'Jesus H. Christ,' said McMaster.

'I thought that might happen,' I said, and looked back at Martin King. His mouth was hanging open. He probably hadn't considered the possibility of a whale upsetting his master plan, a common mistake amongst the less professional terrorist organizations. He raised his gun and pointed it at us and his mouth opened, but he didn't know what to say. He darted forward. We moved aside. He looked overboard. One Son, the one I'd tried to help on board, had reappeared and was desperately treading water. The other hadn't. The speedboat, still tied to the *Charlie W.*, resurfaced.

'Throw him a rope, a vest, something!' King barked.

'Throw it yourself, homeboy,' Sissy barked back. I thought this was maybe pushing the bravado thing a little far, but when I looked at her I could see her point. She held Matchitt's gun against the side of King's head. 'Now, how about you give your gun to that nice man there, honey?'

King handed me the gun. I thanked him. Frank came by. King turned. Frank cracked his knee into King's groin. King collapsed. Without speaking Frank hurried across to his son.

McMaster shook his head in disbelief. 'That,' he said, 'was crazy.'

'Absolutely,' I said.

'Incredible,' said Sissy.

'You going to put that in your book, Starkey? Getting saved by a whale? You think anyone would believe it?'

'Would you?'

'Not if I hadn't seen it with my own eyes. You think I

could maybe get a minke to cruise by when Tyson's about to get into the ring?'

I shrugged. 'You could ask.'

McMaster bent down and lifted King to his feet by the hair, then walked him, still half-doubled over, to the cabin. As he got to the door, Geordie McClean emerged. 'Where the fuck were you?' McMaster snapped.

'In there, planning when to strike.'

'You mean you were hiding.'

'Yes. Someone had to do it.'

McMaster peered into the gloomy interior of the cabin. 'What about Mr Security?'

'Still in cyberspace.'

I looked back out to sea. The Son was looking a little tired. 'Do you want to come on board?' I called.

'Please,' he yelled.

'You promise not to kill us or try to convert us?'

'Please!'

I threw him a rope. It fell a little short. I dragged it back in and threw again. This time he grabbed it and I pulled him towards the *Charlie W*. He was heavy and tired. I needed Sissy's help to pull him on board. We put him in the cabin with King. Frank came through and radioed ashore for medical help to be standing by.

'How is Junior?' I asked.

'I don't know. Alive.'

Sissy went to sit with Junior. Frank started the engine and turned the boat round.

'Now what?' said Geordie McClean.

'Maybe we should have a chat with our friends here,' I said, 'see if we can get this mess sorted out.'

'I thought we had sorted it out,' said McClean.

McMaster shook his head. 'If they're prepared to do something as dumb as this, there's no telling what else they might try. Maybe we should talk to them one on one? It can't do any harm.'

I'm always wary of things which can't do any harm, but he had a point. We hadn't tried any direct negotiations with the Sons of Muhammad. We'd left that up to Poodle Clay and it was patently obvious that he wasn't getting anywhere.

King sat on the bench beside the comatose Stanley Matchitt. He was bent forward, his hands pushed between his legs massaging his groin. McMaster shook him lightly by the shoulder, then hunched down in front of him. 'Still sore?' he asked.

'What do you think?'

'Yeah. Well. I thought we should have a chat.'

'About what?'

'About the mess we've got ourselves in.'

King shrugged.

'We got off on the wrong foot,' said McMaster.

'You attacked my people.'

'I didn't. Or if I did, I didn't mean to. What I said, what I said wasn't meant to offend anyone. All I said was I'd never seen so many black people before. I was just making an honest observation.'

'Yeah. Sure. And we all look like Al Jolson.'

'I shouldn't have said that. I'm sorry. It was said in the heat of the moment. There really aren't any black people in Ireland. It hasn't anything to do with racism. It's just the way things worked out. I mean, if you went to China, what would you say? You'd say, I never seen so many Chinamen before.'

'I don't judge a man by the colour of his skin.'

McMaster tutted. 'I'm not saying . . . look, I'm really not a racist. Back home in Ireland we've just come through a religious war, you know? I'm a Protestant, but I'm married to a Catholic. Do you know what I'm saying? I don't care about religion, I don't care about race. Everyone should be left alone to live their own lives. That's what I believe in.'

'Like the people you had murdered in the Shabazz.'

'That shouldn't have happened. I know that. We're all very sorry. My wife has been kidnapped. We presumed youse had her. We were wrong to presume.'

'That don't bring those people back.'

'I know that. I'm sorry. If I could go back in time and change things, I would. I really would.'

'So what you expect me to do now? Tell my people the Irish snake is sorry, and just forget about it? No way, man. No way. I'm sorry about your wife, but that ain't our problem.'

'So this is just going to go on and on until you eventually find some way of killing me, is that it?'

'That's it.'

'There's no room for negotiation?'

'No.'

McMaster shook his head. He turned to the other Son, shivering in his sodden fatigues. 'What about you, treading the same line?'

He nodded. 'We all true believers.'

'So you think Muhammad is guiding you?'

'Yeah. Of course.'

'He led you to Princetown. He got you a speedboat.'

'Yeah. Of course.'

'He led you out over the sea to exactly the spot we were at.'

'He sees everything.'

'And then he ordered a whale to capsize your boat.'

The Son looked quickly at King. King remained impassive. 'That was just bad luck.'

'You really think that?'

'Course I do.'

'You know what the chances of a whale capsizing a boat are? You know what the chances of a whale capsizing a boat while an act of piracy is going on are? We're talking millions, billions and trillions to one here. You don't think maybe Muhammad was trying to tell you something?'

'Man, it just happened.'

McMaster turned back to King. 'Is there nothing I can say that will change your mind?'

King shook his head.

'I don't understand you at all. You're the one accusing me

of being racist, and yet it's you, with your every word, is the racist one. You just won't listen to reason, will you? You have it in your head that I'm some kind of devil and I must be killed.' They regarded each other for a moment, unblinking. 'Or do I have it wrong,' McMaster continued, 'you realize that there's nothing wrong with me at all, but you've made your mind up and you'd lose face if you back down. That's it, isn't it?'

A cocky smile slipped onto King's face. 'You're scared, man.'

'Of course I'm scared. It's not much fun living in fear of your life.'

'You're scared even though you're calling all the shots. You got the guns, man, yet you scared to death of us. May as well just kill yourself now, 'cause we'll get you eventually.'

'Can't you just accept an honest-to-God apology? Look, I'm sorry any of this ever happened, I spoke out of turn, I want to forget about it. I'm sorry about the attack on the Shabazz. If you want I'll organize a fund for the families of those that died. That would help, wouldn't it?'

King slowly shook his head. 'You're dead, man.'

McMaster matched him. 'I've done everything I can to appease you.'

'It's easy for you to be gracious, you got the gun, man.'

McMaster looked round at me. 'Gimme the gun,' he said.

I gave him the gun. He reached it handle first to King. King took it warily.

'If you don't believe that I'm being honest about all this then go ahead, shoot me. You're going to get me eventually. May as well do it now.'

'Are you sure you wanted to do that?' I asked.

'They should trust me,' he said.

They looked at each other for several moments. King broke off the stare, glanced at me, then back at McMaster. He clasped the gun in his hand. His finger slipped onto the trigger. His brows furrowed. He looked at his comrade, who looked extremely confused. Then he nodded slowly. Maybe he had misjudged the Irish snake. Maybe he had been careless with his words. Maybe the attack on the Shabazz had been a ghastly mistake. Maybe he really was willing to make amends. Or maybe not. He raised the gun and shot McMaster between the eyes.

34

Or he would have if I hadn't removed the bullets.

My inspired moments are few and far between. Once I'd lobbed the keeper from thirty yards in a school football match. I'd never heard of Dr Feelgood, but I bought *Stupidity* entirely on spec and it is still one of the finest albums ever made. And even if I had later thrown it all away, I had once been inspired enough by love to propose to Patricia. Removing the bullets was my fourth moment of inspiration. I'd seen too much violence, I'd seen too many tables turned.

King pulled the trigger three times. McMaster blinked three times.

King dropped the gun. 'Can't even commit suicide honestly,' he sneered.

'I didn't know.'

'You knew.'

McMaster picked up the gun. 'You would have been perfectly happy to splatter my brains all over this boat,' he said.

King nodded. 'It would have given me no pleasure. But I would have done it.'

'No matter what happened to you as a result?'

'I would have taken the consequences. Just as you clearly were not prepared to take the consequences of giving me the gun.'

The contender handed me the weapon. I handed it to Frank, who, if he was aware of any of the drama being played out behind him, didn't give any indication. He accepted the weapon wordlessly and stuck it into his waistband. His eyes flitted from sea to son, son to sea.

'And now what do you expect the consequences to be of trying to shoot me?' McMaster was asking.

'It doesn't matter. I tried. I failed. I'll try again. If not me, someone else.'

'I don't like you zealots. You're never wrong.'

'I would disagree.'

McMaster turned to me. 'See what I mean?'

I nodded. 'You can thank me later,' I said, 'for the bullets.'

McMaster stood again. He pulled King up by the hair and led him out of the cabin. Then he threw him overboard. As he went, King looked a little surprised.

'Do you want to go for a swim?' McMaster asked.

The remaining Son shook his head.

'Do you think I'm a racist?'

The remaining Son shook his head.

'Are you just saying that because you don't want to go overboard or are you genuinely convinced that there was no racism involved in any of my comments?'

The remaining Son nodded. Then he shook his head. He was a little scared and a little confused. 'Martin was our leader. He was always the most committed. Without him, I don't know what will happen. I just wanna go home, man. I wasn't cut out for this.'

McMaster nodded. Who of us are? Which of us is?

'Are you a man of honour?'

The Son nodded.

'What're you going to say about the death of your leader?'

'He drowned.'

'Accidentally.'

'Accidentally.'

'You won't change your mind once you're back with the rest of the Sons?'

'Man, there ain't that many of us left. Just don't throw me in the water again. I never liked the water. I won't breathe a word. Honest.'

Matchitt began to blink back into reality. He heaved himself up off his back with a woozy groan. His eyes slowly focused in on the Son. He rubbed the point on his chin where McMaster had whacked him. I left the cabin. McMaster could explain how we came to have an extra man on board. Once I started talking about the intervention of the whale Matchitt would think I was winding him up.

Sissy was sitting beside Junior. He had a coat round him now. He was unconscious and very, very pale. Sissy dabbed at his forehead with a tissue, then looked back out over the waves. 'How long do you think he'll survive back there?'

I shrugged. There was no sign of him. 'Depends. On whether he can swim. On the water temperature. Whether the whales are peckish.'

'They don't eat humans.'

'No, but they'll have a bloody good suck at you.'

'Don't, Starkey. It isn't funny.'

'Of course it's funny.' And it was. Looked at from afar. 'What a way to go, eh? We defeat a terror group and discover Bobby McMaster's killer instinct all in one go. It's magic. These chapters just get better and better.'

'You're going to write about this?'

'Of course.'

'But he'll be charged with murder!'

'Not if he's dead, Sissy.'

'You think the Sons of Muhammad will get him in the end?'

'No. But Tyson will.'

I was being pessimistic, of course. I was tired. We were all tired. Two people had died. One was seriously injured. We'd been saved by a whale. I needed to lie down somewhere, contemplate the craziness of the situation. The meaning of it all. If there was a meaning. I needed a drink. Just a beer. Instead, Matchitt joined me.

'Sore head?' I asked.

He nodded vaguely. 'Seems like I missed the fun.'

'Yeah.'

'Saved by a whale and all.'

'Yeah. After you tried to shoot them.'

'I didn't really. I was only raking. I wouldn't shoot a whale.'

'You gave a good impression of it.'

'That's half the secret of this business, Starkey, giving a good impression. Or a bad one.'

'I'm sure the whale could tell the difference.'

'Obviously he could. He came and helped.'

'At least he was around to help. Not out cold.'

'I can't be blamed for what happens when I'm unconscious.'

'Of course you can, Stanley. You can be blamed for everything. I imagine even Sissy blames you.'

Matchitt looked up the deck to where she sat with Junior. Sat with Junior, but with her eyes on Matchitt. For a second they held each other's gaze, hers stern, his myopic. Then she smiled. He squinted. Maybe he thought he was seeing another whale.

'She's smiling at you, Stan,' I said.

'Gosh,' he said. It was a most unexpected word for Matchitt to come off with. Fuck, yes. Cunt, yes. Gosh, no. His face, at least beyond the bruisy blotch McMaster had inflicted, was red. He forgot I was there. 'Isn't she lovely?' he said quietly, unintentionally, to the air. He nodded in response to his own question and then suddenly shook his head. 'See you later,' he said and moved on up the deck.

Darkness was falling when we finally cruised back into Princetown harbour. The sprinkly lights of the town were welcoming, the flashing neon of the police cars not quite so. An ambulance was there too. Junior was unloaded. He was still unconscious. We tied the boat up for Frank while he went with his son to the nearest hospital. We didn't ask where that was. We were too tired. The cops wanted to question us there and then but Sissy was able to persuade them to follow us back up to the house. The Son was handed into their custody. He didn't say anything, but he looked relieved to be back on dry land.

McMaster stared morosely out of the window as we drove back to Poodle's house. His wife's abduction seemed to hit him hardest in the dark. She was hundreds of miles away. A prisoner. Injured. Dying. Maybe just crying. It wouldn't have taken much to push McMaster towards tears. A word, maybe. Some sympathy. I left him alone. I fell in and out of sleep. I dreamt about snuggling up in bed with Patricia. About us both wearing pyjamas. We never wore jimjams. Pink jimjams. With little whale motifs on the front. Those were exactly the type we never wore. And it was lovely. And warm. And then she got out of bed and they weren't jimjams but maternity smocks and I was confused because I wasn't pregnant and I tried asking her but she told me to be quiet because Tony was in the next room and . . .

BANG!

'Whaaaa?' I reared up in the back seat. Dark. We were pressing slowly through a forest, a loud, windy, branch-shaking forest . . . that wasn't . . . The trees were people and as the lights from the house and camera lights penetrated my sleepiness I realized that they weren't just people, but protesters with placards clattering against the car and journalists thrusting at it and screaming questions.

'What the fuck is this?' McMaster said, irritated more than angry.

'Looks like the Sons or Brothers or whatever the fuck they are are still keen on lynching you,' said Geordie McClean. 'Maybe they haven't heard about the whales yet. Or maybe they have.'

BANG!

Another hardboard clatter. I jumped away from it. The window stayed intact. A twisty-ugly face pressed against the glass, screaming, then pulled away. Others clustered in around the car. Flat hands drummed down on the roof. The noise was deafening. I leant forward, peered through the windscreen. I took a closer look. There was one crucial difference.

'Bobby,' I said, 'they're all white.'

'It's not snowing.'

'No, I mean, their skin. They're not Sons or Brothers. Look at the placards . . . they're . . .'

'Gay,' said Zack, pulling open the passenger door and then standing guard on it with his gun drawn. 'They been here the last hour looking to lynch you, Mr McMaster, sir.'

McMaster jumped quickly from the car. A roar went up from the crowd. There looked to be about a hundred of them. Jack opened the back door and me and McClean jumped out. Matchitt and Sissy pulled in behind in a taxi. It got clattered with placards as well. Matchitt jumped out and shielded Sissy while she got out, then shadowed her to the house; McClean followed. McMaster stood in the porch shaking his head as two police cars pulled into the yard.

'Fascist!' someone called

The call was taken up. 'FASCIST! FASCIST! FASCIST!'

A woman tried to push past Zack. He held her back with one massive hand. She stuck a microphone between his arm and chest. 'Bobby!' she called. 'Any reason for making those comments?'

McMaster shook his head and entered the house as camera flashes zapped around his head.

I stood on the steps for a moment while the crowd started their fascist chant again. Six of the eight police went to help Zack and Jack slowly push the protesters off Poodle's property while the other two entered the house. I followed the thin blue line up the yard, then got Zack to bring the woman who'd shouted the question at McMaster back into the yard.

'Hi,' she said, chirpy pleased that she'd been picked out of the throng. 'Colette Chisolm, KWIJ.' She pushed the mike into my face.

'Dan Starkey, wit and raconteur. Please don't record anything for the moment. Tell me what this is all about and then I'll see about a quote.'

Her face was red and puffy from the wind, but she had an innate prettiness that reminded me of someone. Patricia maybe. Auburn hair, pushed untidily under a scarf, the way hair hadn't been untidily pushed under a scarf since the fifties. She nodded and withdrew the microphone.

'They're protesting . . .'

'They being . . . ?'

'The local gay community. I don't believe there's any specific gay organization involved, it's a spontaneous protest against Bobby McMaster's presence here in Princetown . . .'

'But they're not, like, gay followers of Muhammad . . .'

'No. Of course not. They're just upset at the comments made by Mr McMaster . . .'

'About black people?'

'You know what I mean . . .'

'I don't. Honestly.'

'About the gay community . . .'

'But he hasn't said anything.'

'I'm afraid he has. We picked up the story from NBC in New York. They picked it up from . . . who was it . . . ?' She pulled a notebook out of a pocket, and flicked back a couple of pages. 'Yeah. The *Daily Mirror* in London. He, uh, described Princetown as . . . let me see . . . Pooftown by the sea . . . I never seen so many poofs in one place . . . it makes me sick . . . not a man amongst them . . . they should all be taken out and shot . . . or have their dicks cut off.'

'And that upset them? Bit sensitive, aren't they?'

'Can I quote you on that?'

350

I'd forgotten she was American. I shook my head. 'I'm sorry. I didn't mean it like that. I can tell you for a fact that Bobby McMaster did not say anything like that, nor would he. Neither has he spoken to a reporter from the *Daily Mirror*.'

'But the *Daily Mirror* despatch, according to NBC, was from Princetown. Said he was the first reporter to catch up with the McMaster camp.'

'Yes. There was a *Daily Mirror* reporter here. But he didn't speak to Bobby. You have my word on that. I don't know who he spoke to, but it wasn't Bobby McMaster. For the record . . .' She raised her mike with the polished speed of an ageing gunman. 'Bobby McMaster has made no comments about Princetown to any member of the press. He has been made perfectly welcome here in the run-up to his world title fight, and has received support from both the gay and straight people of the town, and hopes that he will continue to receive that support. He acknowledges the *Daily Mirror* in London has a right to go after a story, but believes that it has been badly misled by someone outside the McMaster camp. Bobby will be happy to meet with representatives of the local gay community so that he can get this sorted out and he can concentrate fully on the fight. It's only a couple of days away, y'know?'

I ran a finger across my throat and she switched off the mike.

'Thanks,' she said.

'No problem.'

'Any chance of a word with Bobby?'

'Not yet. But hang around. I'll see what I can do.' I looked back up the drive. Zack, Jack and the cops had managed to lock the gate and were now walking back down towards the house. The top of the protesters' heads and the banners were visible above the gate, bobbing about like they were floating on an ocean of hate. 'They're in an ugly mood, aren't they?'

Colette nodded. 'Could get nastier yet. What will he do now?'

I shook my head. 'Well, if they don't accept his denial, he'll just have to come out and kiss and make up.'

I smiled at her, then turned for the house. I had to find a septuagenarian with a colostomy bag called Jackie Campbell, then beat him up.

35

Jackie Campbell sulked in his locked room for forty-five minutes, and then only came out because someone threw a rock through his window which narrowly missed scalping him. He came flying out of his door with a torrent of vitriol and was only persuaded to shut up when Geordie McClean slapped him.

I'd given off to him already about yakking to the *Mirror*. McMaster had given off to him. Even Matchitt had yelled at him. Yelling at an old man is like yelling at a child. It seldom works and it doesn't make you feel any better. Only violence makes you feel better, but guilt stops you hitting a child, and guilt usually stops you hitting an old man, especially an old man whose grip on life, or sanity, or both, is widely regarded as meagre and that only because of his passionate devotion to both Bobby McMaster and the possibility of a world title.

So the slap, and it was a good slap, came as a bit of a shock to Jackie and to the assembled team. He shut up. Geordie looked shocked himself, and suddenly very embarrassed. Everyone felt embarrassed. There was silence for a few moments, relative silence, what with the blare of the TV and the fascist yells from outside. Jackie Campbell stood slop-shouldered, hand to face, looking at his gutties.

McClean stomped off out of the room. Then he stomped back in and stood before Campbell. 'You okay?' he asked.

Campbell nodded. He didn't look up. 'They tried to kill me,' he said meekly.

'I'm sorry,' said McClean. 'I shouldn't have done that.'

'Don't matter,' said Campbell. 'They smashed the window.'

McMaster came forward and put an arm round his trainer. 'Hey, old man, you okay?'

'Yeah. Sure,' Campbell said vaguely, then shuffled across the room towards the kitchen. 'I'll find a brush,' he said.

We looked helplessly at each other as he left the lounge.

Geordie McClean shook his head. 'Shit,' he said, and went after Campbell. 'The things I have to do,' he moaned.

The police still wanted to interview McMaster about the shooting on the boat and had been growing increasingly impatient, so I finally got them into a bedroom with the contender and left them to it. Matchitt and Sissy sat side by side in the lounge, watching the TV and occasionally giggling in each other's ears. I got a cup of coffee for Colette, who'd remained impassive throughout the tantrums, although her sparkly darting eyes betrayed her profession and barely masked the fact that she was enjoying herself. The reporter accepted the coffee gladly, holding it in two hands, sipping with her head held low to the kitchen table.

'Wonderful,' she said.

I smiled. 'Thanks. First cup I ever made.'

She grinned. Nice grin. Capped teeth. Fillings visible further back. 'Things seem quite tense round here.'

'Never tense enough for coffee,' I said. 'Coke – now that would be a saviour. We could give it to Jackie Campbell. Apparently it adds life.'

She grinned again, but it was a grin of perplexity. I let it ride. We chatted for a while. With my customary charm and guile I persuaded her to go outside and speak to the protesters, and she returned within ten minutes with their hastily elected representative. Name of Nathaniel Price. Tall bloke, cropped red hair and pale skin that would frazzle in summer. He wore a green parka, a short moustache and an expression of benign exasperation. Like, how dare we? But he didn't seem like a bad chap. Probably none of them were, individually, just dangerous in packs, like cigarettes. I made him a coffee too.

'We seem to have a problem,' I said, handing the cup to him. He sat at the table beside Colette.

Price nodded. 'Several.'

I gave it to him straight. 'Look, I'm sorry any of this has happened. So's Bobby.'

'So are we. But it's not the sort of thing we can ignore. Not on home turf.'

'Sure. I understand that. But let me assure you, Bobby didn't make any of those comments. They were made by his trainer. He shouldn't have made them. He wasn't speaking on anyone's behalf. He's an old man, he has an old man's prejudices. The *Daily Mirror* decided to run them as Bobby's comments. There's not much we can do about it, 'cept apologize, and sue their asses off. That's how simple it all is.'

He looked at Colette. 'You believe him?'

She looked at me. Sucked at her lower lip for a second. 'Yeah. I think I do. They gave the old man a roasting. He admitted it. Stormed off, locked himself in his room. Yeah, I believe him.'

'Can you call the protest off?' I asked. 'We only have one more day here before the fight. Bobby needs all the peace and quiet he can get.'

Price stood up. 'Okay. I'll see what I can do. Maybe some tickets to the fight might help.'

'Wouldn't that seem like we were trying to buy you off?'

'Yes.'

I shrugged. 'I'll see what I can do.'

We shook hands and I walked him to the door. I returned to Colette. 'Are negotiations meant to be this simple?'

She lifted her empty cup and put it in the sink. 'No,' she said.

'No demands. No threats. You think maybe they have a hidden agenda?'

'I think maybe they're cold.'

*   *   *

356

Of Wee Sweetie Mice and Men

An hour later things were looking a little better. Three-quarters of the protesters had accepted our explanation and gone home. The rest hung around outside, occasionally mustering a half-hearted chant between them that didn't carry much further than the front yard. Sissy took several flasks of coffee out to them and got chatting and before long they were all getting on famously, though they were still reluctant to move on. When Sissy came back in she reckoned they'd be no further threat and went on to bed. Matchitt went to bed too, though I didn't see which door he went in. Zack and Jack made themselves a belated supper in the kitchen. I stood talking to McMaster for a while, then stood on the verandah while he went out front by himself, opened the gate and walked across the road to the protesters. When he rejoined me twenty minutes later, they had started to move off.

'Why, you old charmer,' I said.

He shrugged. 'They didn't expect me to come out in person. You don't get to meet a star of my magnitude every day, y'know. We had a chat. I asked them to move on. Was friendly. Was natural. They appreciated that. There's still a few militant ones. Maybe when they go home and think about it they'll decide I am anti-gay and come back with a vengeance.'

'And are you anti-gay?'

'No, I'm Auntie Lily.'

'Could you explain that one?'

'It would take too long.'

'I'm sure it means something.'

'It does.' He smiled and clapped an arm round my shoulder. 'You think Jackie's okay?'

'As ever he will be.'

'That was quite a whack Geordie gave him.'

'Yeah. Surprised me.'

'Surprised Jackie.' McMaster examined his fingernails on my shoulder. I looked too. Short-short. 'The pressure's getting to Geordie,' he said quietly. 'He still wants to go home. Today didn't help much.'

'Yeah. I know. Still, if we survived today, we can survive anything, can't we?'

'You'd think that,' he said, then gave a slight shake of his head. His voice faltered. 'I was out enjoying myself with the whales, and Mary's still being held.'

'I would hardly call it enjoyment, Bobby.' I punched him lightly on the shoulder and gave him my best reassuring smile. 'Don't worry, mate, she'll be okay. All you have to do is betray Ireland again and beat Tyson.'

McMaster sniggered. 'I've stopped thinking about it, Dan, because it's all so crazy. I mean, you couldn't invent something like this, could you?'

'I could.'

'I know I'll wake up on the morning and there'll be a school of dolphins outside protesting about Stanley shooting at the whales.'

I nodded. There probably would be.

*   *   *

In the morning, standing by the kitchen window, I said to McMaster: 'Hey, Bobby, there's a whole pile of dolphins outside with placards.'

'Fuck off, Starkey,' he said and prowled off towards the marquee. He wasn't always in good form in the morning. Maybe he was missing his guitar.

'Positively Wildean this morning, cont,' I shouted after him, but he ignored me, as all good men do. I'd driven into Princetown first thing and bought a crate of Coke. I felt great.

Breakfast finished, and the can thrown in the bin, I followed McMaster through to the marquee where Jackie Campbell was taping his hands. Overnight a dozen more reporters and a couple of camera crews had arrived and it was fairly buzzing at the ringside. The three recently imported sparring partners sat quietly at the back of the marquee.

'Last few rounds till Tyson then, Bobby?' I said.

McMaster nodded. Campbell looked up. 'He doesn't need them.'

'Course I do.'

'I'm the trainer. You don't need them.'

'So stop me.'

'That'll be the day.'

'You don't think he needs them?' I asked.

'He doesn't need them against yer man over there.'

'Barkley,' said McMaster. He nodded back up the marquee. Barkley nodded back and slapped his gloves together. Then he stood and approached the ring. He bounded over the top rope, as before.

Campbell finished his taping, then helped McMaster pull the gloves on. 'Thinks he has something to prove,' he said grimly.

McMaster bent under the top rope and stood opposite Barkley. He slapped his gloves together too.

'You could ask Geordie to stop him,' I said.

Campbell shook his head. 'He might slap me again,' he said and turned quickly for the bell so that I couldn't see from his eyes whether he was being sarky or genuine. You couldn't tell from his voice. It was too age-gravelled to register nuance. I hoped he had sarky eyes.

Campbell rang the bell and the boxers advanced. I stepped up to the side of the ring. Video cameras were snapped on. Photographers crowded up. Reporters loosened their ties. They'd been primed for some action. McMaster obliged early, a big haymaker with his right which grazed Barkley's ear; Barkley veered left and brought up his own right which McMaster blocked well, before jabbing into his sparring partner's face. Barkley grimaced and stepped back, but it was another of his fake steps and McMaster still wasn't wise to it and he caught a left uppercut as he moved in.

Bernie Gold stepped up beside me as the boxers broke off and began to warily circle each other. He had a copy of his magazine, *Boxing World*, folded in a chubby left hand. He leant on the top rope and watched the fighters. 'Looking good,' he said after a little, the words escaping out of a gap in the side of his mouth which looked like it was waiting for a pipe. I nodded. 'Bobby's not bad either,' he added, and his mouth thinned out into a sly smile.

'Not convinced yet, Bernie?' I asked.

He shrugged. 'I was talking to Barkley last night,' he said, his eyes still fixed on the fighters.

'You got him talking? Fancy himself now, does he?'

'No. No, not really. He has the boxer's habitual self-confidence, of course, but he doesn't have any immediate plans to take on the world. Not until he gets the plaster off, anyways.'

That brought my head round. 'Bernie,' I said, 'there's something you aren't telling me.'

A grin swept his face. A scoop grin. A bad poker player's grin. 'Yup,' he said and stepped back from the ring. He waved a finger at me to follow him and led me to the back of the marquee. We sat down on a bench while Jackie Campbell screamed encouragement at his fighter.

'Bernie,' I said, 'enlighten me.'

Bernie pulled out a box of cigarettes and offered me one. I shook my head. He put one in his mouth and lit up and took a long drag, then breathed out through his nose. 'Timing,' he said, 'is what I haven't got. Me and your boxer, maybe. Anyways, I wanted to do a background piece on Barkley, 'cause he's a new one on me. But he wouldn't even tell me what gym he works out of in New Orleans. Still, it was simple enough to trace his registration back and I finally tracked him down to Buster Duva . . . you hear of Buster?' I shook my head. 'Yeah. Buster – had three or four world champs back in the fifties, nothing much since, but still runs a good gym, though he's not as young as he was . . . Anyways, I get him on the phone and I start enthusing about Barkley and he's surprised, seeing as Barkley's not only overweight, washed up and generally bad news, but that he busted a hand the week before in an undercard scrap in Chicago. That he's back in New Orleans and not likely to be near a ring for a few months . . . He gave me his number, I called him up, and, true enough, he has bust a thumb and he's out of commission. He's eating pizza, enjoying a Bud and watching some baseball.'

I looked back up to the ring. Barkley had McMaster in a corner, and was pounding in the shots.

'Who he?' I asked.

'Who indeed?' Bernie smiled again.

'You know, don't you?'

'I can hazard a guess.' He unfolded his magazine and opened it to a centrespread. The pages were headed BOXING WORLD'S TOP TWENTY CONTENDERS and there were mug shots of that many fighters. Only one of them was white, and he wasn't Bobby McMaster. 'I was just mulling over it this morning. That guy in there's obviously a quality boxer, and despite Hollywood and St Patrick, they just don't come from nowheres. If you're any good, *Boxing World's* heard of you. Take a look at number eleven there, Dan.'

I took a look. Number eleven was called Marcel Blackwood. I'd never heard of him, but then there were a lot of people I'd never heard of. I looked at his eyes, looked at his face.

'This is going to sound awfully racist,' I began, and the ghost of Martin King swam over my grave, 'but . . .'

'No, look – see that healthy head of hair?'

'Yeah . . . ?'

Bernie moved his thumb and index finger down the page, n-shaped, and slotted them in around Blackwood's head. He looked up and smiled again. 'Now tell me that isn't Mo Barkley.'

'That isn't Mo Barkley.'

It wasn't, of course, it was Marcel Blackwood, and Marcel Blackwood, head shaved, moustache gone, was in the ring giving Bobby McMaster the hardest fight of his career just when he needed to be tapering off with some light sparring.

I patted Bernie on the shoulder. 'Nice job, Bernie,' I said. 'You could have saved it for yourself.'

He shook his head. 'We printed a week ago. Gotta get the sales in before the fight. No use to me – and I wouldn't give it to those other mothafuckas.' He nodded across at the rest of the pack. 'I'll maybe get some priority access to Bobby after this, eh?'

'Absolutely,' I said, and made for the ring.

They were into the second round now. Barkley had McMaster back in a corner again and was raining in blows. Three from Barkley, one from McMaster, three from Barkley, a scream from Jackie Campbell, one from McMaster, one from Barkley, a worried-sounding yell of encouragement from Geordie McClean and a camera flash, then one from McMaster and two more from Barkley.

McMaster tied Barkley's hands up, Barkley stepped back, pulling his gloves away. McMaster lumbered forward, low, looking for the uppercut; Barkley took another step back, ready to plunge his right in above McMaster's suspect defence.

'Nice going, Marcel,' I said quietly.

If you weren't listening for it, you mightn't have heard, but there's something about hearing your own name which defies volume. If you weren't looking for it, you mightn't have noticed, but Blackwood froze.

A slight stiffening of the limbs. A flutter of the eyelids. The merest of glances away from his opponent. A slight lowering of the guard. But enough.

Bobby McMaster fired up the sweetest left hook of his career. Blackwood's head shot back, sweat and blood sprayed across the ring, his legs buckled and he hit the deck.

A whoop of delight went up from Jackie Campbell and he bustled in under the ring towards his fighter. The cameras flashed. The reporters buzzed. Bobby McMaster looked puzzled for a couple of seconds, then casually raised his arm and smiled for the pack.

36

Matchitt raised his glass and angled it towards me. 'To Bobby, may he win the title,' he said, with surprisingly little hint of malice.

I raised mine somewhat reluctantly. 'To Bobby,' I said, 'may he live to tell the tale.'

We clinked, he a little too hard. Most of the other customers looked round. Matchitt grinned beerily. 'To the Sons of Muhammad, fuck 'em, well and truly laid to rest.'

'Fuck 'em,' I agreed and we clinked again. He a little too hard, again. He was probably trying to break the glass. He was in belligerent form. He wasn't entirely comfortable in the Lobsterolla restaurant either. Neither was I – with him, and to a lesser extent, with it. It was a pleasant enough little establishment, located several blocks from the wind-battered Main Street, but it seemed to wallow in its own pleasantness.

It was the sort of self-confident eating establishment which knows that it's described in tourist books as a hidden treasure or as favoured by the locals. No frills. The year-round staff, instead of being money-grabbing slumming students, had an air of self-importance out of proportion to the quality of the menu, and the food, while properly prepared instead of hurried through for the tourist crowds, was presented in such a dead-on way that it suggested that the chef had perfected a humane way of boiling lobster.

Just the two of us, and a couple of lobsters, sitting at a corner table, a candle between us. Matchitt in a red cap-sleeve T-shirt and a black Harrington jacket with tartan lining, 501s. Me in a leather jacket, black jeans, Tintin T-shirt. Just the two of us, left behind in the exodus from Princetown.

The jet had come in the early evening, piloted by Poodle Clay himself, anxious to bring us the good news that he had made a deal with the Brothers and Sons of Muhammad. He blustered about a bit, but at the end of it all, what he had secured was a promise to withdraw their death threat against McMaster in exchange for a hefty loan to rebuild the Shabazz and financial support for the families of those who had died in our abortive raid. This, while welcome news, was like shutting the bar door after the drunks had staggered. Poodle, to his credit, was only a little taken aback to discover that we had already foiled two plots by the Sons to scuttle McMaster's attempt on the world crown; one literally, although we were a bit vague about the whale.

Martin King, idealistic but fatally flawed – couldn't swim

for toffee – was indeed the kingpin of the Sons, and his death had robbed the terrorists of their driving force. Marcel Blackwood on the other hand was a talented boxer with a cocaine problem. He was still ranked number eleven in the world, but was about to be kicked off the ranking list and banned for testing positive for drugs after his last fight. In the way of many criminals in adversity, he had suddenly discovered religion. Cynics might view his sudden conversion as an attempt to lighten his punishment not only in this world but the next. However, cynics might also note gleefully that instead of choosing Catholicism where he might have gotten away with a few Hail Marys and the issuing of the Holy Pin for his condom collection or Mormonism where the tea bags might have been out the window and the Donny and Marie bootlegs in, Blackwood plumped for the family of Muhammad. The Brothers decided his act of contrition ought to be to knock spots off Bobby McMaster, with the aid of an extremely close shave and a little subterfuge. Blackwood, grasping at straws, a notoriously difficult thing to do in boxing gloves, went for it, but thanks to the brilliantly incisive yet subtle intervention of a young journalist had not been able to succeed with the fiendish plot.

There wasn't much we could do with Blackwood. He had no career left. The Brothers would disown him. McMaster's uppercut had speeded up the process, begun by the cocaine, which would eventually lead to his head caving in. His new-found devotion to Muhammad was not such that he found it impossible to curse the Brothers up and down for leading him into such a ridiculous scheme, so ridiculous that it had come within seconds of working. No, there wasn't much we could do. He cursed them, he cursed us, he packed up, he moved out. Matchitt followed him out to the gate, and gobbed on his back. Sometimes words don't say everything.

'So, Stanley,' I said, sipping my beer to give the appearance of both gentility and a recent vacation from total abstinence – it was my eighth, but only the staff knew that – 'your sudden fall from grace, are you reconciled to it?'

'I've had no fuckin' fall from grace,' he replied testily. He had not made any attempt to conceal his intake, and was mostly pissed.

'You're not on the plane, Stanley. You're meant to be his number one man.'

Matchitt ran a finger across his nose, then sniffed up. 'There wasn't room. You should know that. You're sitting here.'

'At least I was offered a seat.'

'Aye, sure.'

I had, in fact, been assigned a seat, but had given it up to Bernie Gold. A promise, was, after all, a promise. McMaster was, however, adamant he didn't want Matchitt on the plane. His old mate had just gone too far with the whales and now, with the Sons off his back, he felt he no longer needed the specialized attention Matchitt gave him. 'Stanley,' he said, 'is a liability,' though he didn't say it within earshot.

Another time, another place, and I suspect Matchitt would have gone for him anyway; insisted on a seat or offered violence. But when he heard that Sissy hadn't blagged a seat either, he seemed content to remain for an extra night and bring up the rearguard with his new-found companion. Sissy, surprisingly, had rejected the offer of food and was out on patrol with the local cops in one final effort to track down the mysterious Marcus McLiam. If he was in town, and it was becoming increasingly unlikely, then the chances were that he was about to leave, to follow the McMaster camp back to New York. Princetown, luckily, was on the end of a peninsula and there were only a limited number of exits from the town. The police had thoughtfully set up check-points on all of these routes and were confident of catching him if he was there to be caught.

'Of course, I don't think he's here at all,' said Stanley.

I nodded. 'Probably not.'

'A red lobster. Designed to confuse us. Nobody's fault. Not Sissy's.'

'I agree. Disinformation. He's in New York. Has been all the time.'

'Or he's here. Just to keep an eye on us. Lying low the whole time. Disguised.'

'As a local.'

'As a poof.'

A couple of heads turned. I smiled apologetically and whispered, 'Between you and Jackie, all the slabbering youse do gets Bobby into some trouble.'

Matchitt sat back, threw up his hands. 'Whaddya mean? What slabbering?'

'You on the boat. Jackie to the *Mirror*. Loose talk. Costs lives.'

'Bollocks.'

'And now in here.'

'Whaddya mean?'

'In here. Just now.'

'Just now what?'

'You said it. Poof. You said, poof.'

'So what?'

'It was just a poor choice of word, given our surroundings.'

'No, it wasn't.'

'It was. A poor choice. There was no need for it.'

'All I said was poof.'

'It's a derogatory term.'

'No, it's not. I'm calling a spade a spade. A poof a poof.'

'Stanley, you don't understand . . .'

'I understand perfectly. What exactly are you objecting to, me calling a poof a poof, or me calling a poof a poof in a place populated by poofs?'

'Both.'

'So it's just the term poof.'

'Yes.'

'What would you have me say, fruit?'

'Stanley, how would you like someone to call you a mind-less bigot?'

'To my face?'

'To your face.'

'I've no objection, if they don't mind taking their chances.'

'You're talking violence.'

'Maybe.'

'Because it's a term you don't like.'

'Maybe.'

'So what if people don't like being called poofs. Are they right to offer violence?'

'But they are poofs. That's my point.'

'And you're not a mindless bigot?'

'Clearly not.'

'Can you prove it?'

'Well, I'm having this argument, so I'm not mindless. And I've formed a close friendship with Sissy, so I'm not a bigot.'

'You're a selective bigot, then.'

'No. I'm not a bigot. I've nothing against poofs.'

'So why call them poofs?'

'Because it's what they are.'

'But it's not what they like to be called.'

'How do you know, Starkey?'

'Of course they don't, Stanley.'

'But how do you know?'

I sighed. 'I'm sorry I brought this up.'

'But seriously, how do you know?'

'Stanley, let's drop it.'

'You're admitting defeat?'

'No, Stanley. I'm just bored.'

'You're beaten, mate.'

Stanley shifted his gaze across the room to a line of waiters who were chatting by the kitchen doors. His eyes flitted from one to the other. Five or six of them. He nodded slowly.

'See the third one along?'

A tall guy, short hair, designer stubble. I nodded.

'He's a poof.'

'Stanley, I'm not interested.'

'No, but he is, he definitely is.'

Matchitt raised his hand and waved across to him. He noticed immediately and came across.

Matchitt smiled. 'We'd like to see the sweet trolley,' he said.

'I'm sorry, sir, but I didn't serve . . .'

Matchitt pulled a twenty-dollar bill from his wallet. 'I'd like to see the sweet trolley,' he repeated and handed the waiter the note.

'Very good, sir,' he said, accepting the note quickly and crumpling it into his trouser pocket. He left us for a moment and returned pushing the sweet trolley ahead of him. 'Tonight,' he said, 'our specialities are Pecan Pie, Strawberry Pavlova, Black Forest Gateau or Key Lime Pie. I would particularly recommend the Black Forest Gateau.'

I nodded. I gave him an appreciative grin, then concentrated on the contents of the trolley.

'Are you a poof?' asked Matchitt.

'Stanley . . .'

'I'm only asking.'

The waiter leant forward slightly. His eyes crinkled up. 'Excuse me?'

'I asked if you were a poof.'

The waiter straightened, then looked from Matchitt to me.

'Pay no attention,' I said. 'I'll have the Black . . .'

'Are you a fuckin' poof or what?'

'Sir, I . . .'

'Are you a fuckin' poof or what?'

'I must object to your . . .'

'Are you a poof?'

'Sir . . .'

'Are you a poof?'

The waiter looked anxiously back towards the kitchen. His voice rose a little in pitch, and was all the more potent against the embarrassed silence which had descended on the restaurant. 'Sir, I should advise you that if you wish to cause a scene, I am a karate black belt.'

'Aye, and I've a black belt on me trousers and DMs on me feet. So are ye a poof or not?'

We were joined by the maître d'. Tall. Balding. Carried himself well. 'Is there a problem, gentlemen?'

'This . . .' began the waiter, but his superior raised a finger to his lips.

'Sir?'

Matchitt pointed at the waiter. 'I was merely enquiring if your waiter was a poof.'

The maître d' stiffened. 'Sir?'

'Is he a poof?'

The maître d' turned back to the waiter. 'That will be all, Thomas,' he said gruffly. 'You may return to the kitchen.'

Thomas nodded and walked quickly away, eyes front. The maître d' placed two hands on our table and leant forward. 'Gentlemen,' he began, but looked directly at Matchitt, 'I'm afraid I must ask you to leave the restaurant. I really cannot allow my staff to be insulted in this way.'

'I only asked if he was a poof. Is he?'

'No, sir, he isn't.' His eyes bore angrily into Matchitt and his mouth curled up in distaste. 'But I am. Now I regret to say I must ask you to leave the restaurant. Immediately. We really can do without custom like yours. Please leave now. Or I will have you removed.'

Matchitt snorted. 'Aye. You and whose army?'

The maître d' placed a hand on Matchitt's shoulder. This was not a good idea. Matchitt, as if capitulating, shrugged lightly, but then quickly slapped the hand away. Surprised, the maître d' stumbled forward. Matchitt rammed a fist into his stomach as he came towards him. He let out a startled, winded gasp and sprawled across the table, sending our plates flying in the process. He lay there for a second as Matchitt and I both pushed our chairs back and stood.

'Stanley, you stupid cunt,' I shouted.

He stuck his fist out towards me. 'Hold onto your horses, Starkey,' he snapped and bent towards the prostrate figure.

The maître d' coughed twice, then tried to raise himself. Matchitt helped him up.

'Are you all right there, mate?' he asked.

He coughed again. 'Yes . . . I . . .'

'You really don't like being called a poof, do you?'

The maître d' shook his head.

Matchitt turned to me. 'You were right, Starkey,' he said, then thumped the maître d' in the stomach again. He gasped, folded down. Matchitt stopped him falling by holding him up by one ear. Then he walked him forward and buried his head in the Black Forest Gateau.

I stood with open mouth. Our fellow diners sat open-mouthed. A broad grin sliced Matchitt's face. 'God, Starkey,' he said, 'you were right all along. The poof is in the pudding.'

He cackled.

I shook my head. I grabbed my coat and made for the door. Matchitt grabbed his and followed. 'You stupid bastard,' I shouted.

'Hahahahahaha,' said Matchitt.

We made it as far as the car. I fumbled with the keys for a minute, while Matchitt pulled impatiently at the passenger door, still laughing his head off.

Then there was the hurried scuff of many footsteps on gravel, and six gay waiters beat the tripe out of us.

37

We ran for our lives.

No, we limped.

No, that suggests one good leg each. We lumped. We lumped for our lives.

We lumped and screamed and bled and when finally they gave up the chase we collapsed on the beach where the bitter wind whipped through us and blasted sand into our bloody crevices.

The pain, the sand, the wind, the drink, the hangover. All in one. And yet he slept. Matchitt on his back, snoring loudly, eyes fist-puffed, nose black-blood-hardened, looked almost happy, happy with the thrill of the assault. It wasn't the winning that mattered, it was the taking part.

I hated him.

I had always disliked him, but now I hated him. He

represented everything I hated in a human being: a swirling, bigoted condescension, a nationalism born of old wives' tales and ghetto prejudice, in love with the glamour of confrontation, an enemy of compromise, an insecure, incomplete man with ambitious delusions of mediocrity. And he got me into fights.

There was a faint moonlight poking through the clouds and the wiry rattle of yachts in the bay; behind me, the modest lights of Princetown in its winter slumber; in front, way out in front, the Atlantic and Ireland and home. Where was Patricia now? Was there room in her turbulent mind for me? Two minds now, one barely formed, one set hard. She was at home contemplating new responsibilities; I was on a bitter-cold beach contemplating recent irresponsibilities; she was at home remembering the beauty of a relationship which had led her to conceive; I was cursing an ill-conceived relationship with a murderer thrust upon me by circumstance I had courted. Matchitt snored.

I sat shivering for I don't know how long. Maybe an hour. My head pounded. My nose cracked and bloody. My lip thick and unwieldy. In the ice-windy, throbbing darkness I made promises to myself that I knew I would not keep, the same promises, the promises Patricia had grown tired of. Everything would be different, but everything would be the same. There was a frightening inevitability about it.

After a while the water began to lap gently at my feet and the thought came to me that if I slipped into that water I could float gently out into the ocean and home to Patricia, that the waves would carry me to her, or that a whale would nudge me across and I would step out at the mouth of the Lagan and find her waiting for me, our baby in her arms. And I would say to her, I love you, please forgive me, and she would smile and the three of us would scrum together, then walk through the city to our home. I smiled at the sea, black and welcoming, but the wind threw sand in my eyes and burnt them. I worked my fingers into them, and the tears ran down my face and I shook my head and knew that I would not be able to swim home to Ireland, that I couldn't swim and hated the water, ever since at school I had put my learner's armbands on my feet and nearly drowned. I moved back, pushing achily through the sand. I looked across at Matchitt. His DMs were already partly submerged.

It came to me then that his accidental death by drowning would be no great loss to mankind. One small step, in fact. I could just get up and tie his laces together and then lump off into the distance and leave the waves to gather him up. Perhaps he would float out to sea and be washed up somewhere further along the coast, his corpse bloated and picked at by seagulls. But it wouldn't happen like that. When the salt water trickled into his nose he would splutter into consciousness and he would see me grinning from the top of the beach and he would stagger after me through the streets and eventually he would catch me and kill me, for that was his nature.

I stood up. I creaked. I shuffled across to him and kicked

him. He didn't respond. I kicked him harder. Nothing. His breath was raspy, but undisturbed. I bent and grabbed the neck of his jacket and dragged him up the beach. It took a long time. He was heavy, I was weak. It took fifteen minutes, punctuated by kicks and curses, to get him up onto the boardwalk. I flopped him down again and he rolled over. 'Thanks,' he mumbled, and slept again.

I cursed him and walked away.

It was late. The bars were shut, the streets empty. I walked the drink-sodden walk of the drink-sodden with added sand-soaked grit-shoed lumpness for comfort. I needed a hot bath and some love. A bath and some hot love. Even a shower and someone to pat my head and tell me everything would be okay and that, yes, the tide had washed Matchitt away, but it was a forlorn hope. I trudged into Poodle's yard and rang the bell; I'd had a key, once, but it was long gone. Sissy answered the door and I needed her face to be anxious yet welcoming, but it was stern and war-set. She was fully dressed, which I thought was a bad sign.

'Morning,' I said, and I wasn't far off the mark.

'Where the hell have you been?' she rasped.

I shrugged.

'Where's Stanley?'

'Nevil Shuted.'

'What?'

'On the beach.' I laughed and cracked my lip. I felt the blood trickle. 'We got in a fight. He's okay. Sleeping it off. Nice to know you're concerned.'

'I'm not particularly. You should be. We have a visitor.'

Goody, I thought. Just what I needed. Another twist. 'Who is it? The Duke of Marlborough?'

'Take a look, Starkey.'

'Just tell me, Sissy.'

'Take a look.'

'I'm not in the mood for surprises.'

'He's locked in the front room.'

'He's stuck?'

'He's locked. You'll see what I mean when you open the door. He arrived after ten and I thought it wouldn't do any harm to lock him in for a while. I thought Stanley would be back sooner. He banged and wailed for a while, but he's been quiet these last few hours.'

'Maybe he climbed out the window, Sissy.' I tutted. 'This is stupid.'

'There's bars on the windows – Poodle's a rich guy, remember.'

I shrugged. 'I doubt if they make much difference. Sure the whole bloody place is made of wood. A medium-size rodent could gnaw its way out in half an hour. Can you get me some headache pills?'

Sissy paid me no attention. She nodded at the door. 'I don't think he's armed,' she said.

I turned the key in the door and we entered.

'Hello,' I said to the figure in the corner, 'we come in peace.'

'Hello,' said Marcus McLiam with a scowl the size of

Scotland. 'Do you mind telling me what the fuck you think you're playing at?'

In the flesh he didn't seem any more threatening than Martin King. Small, wiry, well dressed in an overawed Irishman-on-holiday kind of way. His accent was pure earnest patriot Belfast. He didn't appear to be carrying a gun and I wasn't close enough to check out the lingerie angle. 'We haven't met,' I said, 'but I've seen your video.'

He screwed up his eyes. 'What the hell are you talking about? Who the hell are you? And what the fuck did yees lock me in here for?'

'You called for us, mate, it's what you want that interests us. We were just showing you a bit of Belfast hospitality. You got it easy, there's boys in Beirut got chained to a radiator for five years for walking into the lion's den, y'know?' I sighed. I was babbling. I was half drunk. I was half sober. I was sore. I'd had my fill of crap terrorists. I wanted to lie down and dream of good things. 'And if you've come with more demands,' I snapped, 'you're too late. They've left for New York.'

'Demands for what?' He shook his head and looked at Sissy. 'Is Mary with them?'

Sissy gave him the eye.

'Fuck,' he said.

'You've released her then,' I said.

'What?'

'You decided to let her go after all.' I tutted. 'Better late than never, I suppose. What a pity you let it happen in the first place.'

He raised a finger to me. I suppose it was meant to be threatening. It wasn't. It was a couple of bones and some pale flesh. Threatening only to another pale bony finger.

'Listen, mate,' he growled, 'I don't know what kinda drugs you or your woman are on, and I don't much care, but I just came looking for my sister. I didn't expect to get locked in a fuckin' room for four hours and then get talked shite to.'

I looked at Sissy, who had retained a diplomatic silence throughout, although her mouth had now dropped open a little. In that respect, it matched mine. I put my hand up to him, palm out. Placatory. It worked. He removed the finger. 'Who's your sister?'

He looked from me to Sissy, and back. 'Mary, of course.'

'Of course,' said Sissy.

'Mary McMaster?'

'Yes. Mary McMaster. I just called to see where she was, I didn't expect all this shite.'

'You're Mary McMaster's brother?'

'Yes!'

'But . . . but . . . your surnames aren't the same.' It sounded crap, and it was.

He gave me the look. 'Of course they aren't.'

I shook my head. 'I mean, her maiden name's Wilson, yours . . . I mean, you haven't got a maiden name but your surname's McLiam . . .'

'How the fuck do you know that?'

'We know all about you – Jesus! We've been trying to track you down for the past three days!'

'Me? Why the . . .'

'Because we thought . . .' began Sissy.

'Because you kidnapped Mary!'

'Aye, I'd do that to my own sister!'

'Right! Right.' I put both palms up. 'Let's calm this down and get it sorted out.'

He nodded, raised his own palms a little. 'Okay. Okay.'

'You're Marcus McLiam.'

'Yeah.'

'Not Marcus Wilson.'

'Yeah.'

'Yeah?'

'I'm Marcus Wilson.'

'Not Marcus McLiam.'

'Yes. Marcus McLiam. And Marcus Wilson.'

I looked at Sissy. Her eyes widened a little. 'Am I missing something here?' I asked.

'Honey,' she said to, well, Marcus, 'you talking in riddles.'

A little light dawned in his eyes. 'I'm sorry. Yes, I am. I'm so used to it myself, I sorta think everyone else is used to it too. Yes, sorry. Yes, my name is Marcus Wilson. Yes, I am Mary's brother. I live in New York. I work for Noraid – you know Noraid?'

'We know Noraid.'

'Working for Noraid, I use the Gaelic spelling of my surname. So I'm Marcus McLiam.'

'Ah,' I said, 'and so the penny drops.'

McLiam nodded. 'But how do you know that I'm McLiam?'

'We watched you return Mary's shirts to Macy's. Or at any rate we watched you on video. Traced you through your credit card. But you'd left for Princetown.'

'But why watch me at all?'

'We thought you had her.'

'Had her?'

'Had kidnapped her.'

'But I'm her brother!'

'We know that now! Jesus! Look, Mary disappeared in New York, we followed up every lead we could. One of them took us to Macy's, we saw a tape of you returning some shirts she had bought. We traced you to Noraid . . . meanwhile the first of the demands from the IRA had come in.'

He looked a bit doubtful. 'The IRA?'

'Well, someone like the IRA. We aren't really quite sure.'

'You're serious?'

'Yup.'

'But . . . how? Christ, why?'

'You really don't know?'

'Of course I don't fuckin' . . .'

'So how did you come by the shirts?' Sissy asked.

'Well, Mary gave them to me, of course!' He blew out some air, shook his head a little, then went and sat on a chair in the corner of the room. 'Look, to tell you the truth,' his voice quieter, even a little shaky, 'Mary and I haven't got on for years. I've always been quite political, back home,

384

then when I moved to New York I started working for Noraid. But I was never into terrorism. Maybe you won't believe it, but there are some of us aren't. So anyway, Mary comes to New York, comes to see me, brings me some shirts as a peace offering. She always thought I dressed like a tramp. Gave me tickets for the fight. We got on okay. I hadn't seen her for years – maybe we'd both matured a bit . . . look, I'm sorry if this sounds like *This Is Your Life* . . .'

'Never worry . . . I'd like to know . . . right up to the mystery guest at the end . . .'

He gave me a wan smile. 'Look, she went back to her hotel, didn't want me to go because I'd never got on with her husband. Religion, politics, you know how it is. She promised to come back and see me, never did. I thought, well, there you go. Maybe I'm not forgiven. I'd grown a bit since the last time she'd seen me, shirts were a bit small, so I took them back to get something bigger . . . something a bit more fashionable, if you must know.'

'And some underwear.'

'Underwear?'

'Ladies' stuff. Y'know. Each unto his own.'

'Right sure. For my girlfriend. Does it matter?'

'No. Of course. Just polishing off a red herring. Go on.'

He paused for a moment.

'Go on, honey,' Sissy encouraged.

'I got worried about her when I started hearing about the death threats against her husband. I was concerned for her safety, okay? I went to see her, but she wasn't there. Next thing I know everyone's left for Princetown. I'd been given some time off work anyway, so I thought I'd travel up, see if I could keep an eye on her, from a distance, like. Only I haven't seen her once in three days, and I'm worried, so I thought I'd insist on seeing her . . . and I get locked in this fuckin' place . . .'

'And that's the honest-to-God truth?'

'Honest to God.'

'And you know nothing about the IRA kidnapping her.'

'I don't.' He shook his head slowly, then raised his hands to it and slowly rocked it. 'Fuck it,' he snapped suddenly, 'what a bloody eejit I am. They get me out of work, give me holleys when I've no time due to me, just so as I'm offside when they kidnap my sister. My own sister!' His eyes peeked out from between his fingers. 'Fine fuckin' reward.'

'Honey,' said Sissy, stepping forward and putting a sympathetic hand on his shoulder, 'you wouldn't have any idea where they might be keeping her, wouldja?'

'I don't,' he said, and then added slowly, 'but I've a good idea who might.'

38

It was 5 a.m. Still dark. Freezing. We swung by the beach to see if we could pick Matchitt up, but he was nowhere to be seen. There were some vague footprints on the sandswept boardwalk roughly where I'd left him, heading out along the coast, but none of us were Indian tracker enough to say whether they were his or not. Sissy called to him a few times from the shelter of the car, then reluctantly nosed the Mercedes out onto the main road and out of town. Soon we were cruising down the peninsula and off Cape Cod. She didn't speak until we hit Rhode Island, and that was only to ask, 'Do you think he's okay?'

Of course he was. Matchitt could survive a direct hit with a nuclear warhead. Unfortunately he was also the kind of man could attract a direct hit with a nuclear warhead. Sissy couldn't see that, or wouldn't. I'd hoped maybe the incident with the whale had opened her eyes, but it had only narrowed them in the manner of a mother scolding a loved child. There would have been something nice about their fawning over each other if only I hadn't known Matchitt to be such a psycho, and but for the fact that her husband was only recently cremated.

We drove with speed and were blessed with a noticeable lack of highway patrol. Possibly they were all Irish and already half drunk for St Patrick's Day, or maybe we just had the luck of the Irish, that luck which had already made my research on a sporting biography so varied and interesting.

We had debated briefly what to do about McLiam's information. McLiam had joined in. Already he was one of us. There was no reason not to trust him. He knew enough about Mary to match what I had gleaned from her for her role in my biography of her husband, and I was prepared to accept him at his word. He just seemed trustworthy. Sometimes you have to go on your instincts, like Napoleon into Russia.

Our first decision was not to tell anyone else. To let McMaster go through with his speech and the parade, not to get him any more excited than he already was. If we got Mary out, well and good; if McLiam, through no fault of his own, led us on a wild goose chase, then no one would be any the wiser and McMaster would still have a chance of getting his wife back. All he had to do was beat Tyson.

Our second decision was to cancel the jet. It was to pick us up at 10 a.m. at Princetown airstrip, but McLiam reasoned that a hell-for-leather drive back to the city would give us an hour's start on the search for his sister. Sissy wanted to wait for the jet. No, Sissy just wanted to wait. To give him another chance to turn up. We outvoted her and she reluctantly agreed. We called the pilot, told him we preferred to drive. He didn't sound unduly suspicious. It was St Patrick's Day.

While Sissy drove, McLiam and I lolled in the back of the Mercedes. I slept on and off for the first couple of hours as the headache pills kicked in. Each time I opened my eyes McLiam was staring out of the window. I felt a trifle sorry for him. I knew what it was like to be missing a loved one, even a loved one you didn't get on with half of the time.

We stopped briefly outside Providence for breakfast. Sissy loaded up on Egg McMuffins. I got some Diet Coke and chocolate. McLiam had nothing.

'Worried?' I asked as we climbed back onto the highway.

'What do you think?'

I nodded, half apologetically. 'She'll be okay.'

His eyes flared angrily for a moment, then he let out a sigh and asked in a voice of strangulated calmness: 'What possible basis have you got for saying that?'

I shrugged. 'I was just saying.'

'Well, don't. It's stupid.'

'I was just trying to cheer you up. Sorry I spoke.'

'Cheer me up by all means. But don't say something so blatantly bloody stupid. She'll be all right . . . Jesus.'

'Okay. She won't be all right. They probably have her head on a spike even as we speak. Popehead.'

'Oh, that's not childish.'

Sissy glanced back: 'Please, guys.'

We fell silent, spent the next ten minutes looking out of our respective windows at the drab countryside. 'Sorry,' I said eventually.

'Yeah. Sorry,' he said.

'That's more like it.' Sissy's eyes caught his in the mirror. 'Don't worry. She'll be okay.'

McLiam snorted. 'Ha-ha,' he added.

Sissy smiled broadly. The McMuffins had cheered her up. 'How come you managed to avoid all the cops in Princetown?' she asked.

'What cops?'

'The cops we had out searching every hotel and guesthouse in town.'

'Didn't see a thing, mate. I saw plenty of you lot though. I was on a bike outside the house three or four times a day hoping to catch Mary.'

Sissy shrugged. 'I didn't see you. But then all you white guys look the same to me.'

'Aye,' I said, 'all but one.'

'You trying to say something, Starkey?'

'Nah.'

'Sure?'

'Absolutely.'

If I hadn't known that Americans don't understand sarcasm, I would have sworn that mirrored smile she gave me was a sarky one. Maybe I was rubbing off on her; maybe Matchitt was.

I offered McLiam a conciliatory slug of Diet Coke. It was pretty much flat anyway. He refused, but smiled. 'Thanks,' he said, 'I don't.'

I tutted. 'Mother Nature in her purest form,' I said, and showed him the carton. 'All they add is phenylalanine, caramel, aspartame, phosphoric acid, sodium citrate, caffeine and citric acid to the carbonated water. It adds life, y'know?'

'And teaches the world to sing in perfect harmony.'

We fell silent for the next few miles, lost in the drum of the heavy rain against the windscreen and the steady rhythm of the wipers. It reminded me of home. Dull. Wet. Widespread terrorism. The old dependables.

'Right now they're painting their faces green in New York,' McLiam said presently.

'Mixing the green beer,' added Sissy.

'And preparing to talk the biggest load of auld shite about the auld sod this side of the United Nations,' said McLiam.

'It is shite, isn't it?' I said.

'Complete and utter shite.'

'Shite. Shite. Shite. Shite.'

'And more shite.' He nodded enthusiastically. 'If St Patrick was alive today . . . he'd be about thirteen hundred years old. But he'd still recognize shite if he heard it, would St Patrick.'

'Wouldn't buy you a pint, though. He was Scottish, wasn't he? Tight as fuck.'

'Scottish? Welsh? English? Who knows?'

'So Noraid must hate St Patrick's Day then, seeing as how it represents the first British colonization of Ireland.'

'Bollocks. He's an honorary Irishman. Like Jack Charlton. He did us proud.'

'How, threw out a few snakes?'

'Made Christians of us.'

'Christianity breeds contempt.'

'Familiarity.'

'Whatever. We would have been better off as heathens.'

'Catholic heathens or Protestant heathens?'

'Now there's a point.'

'Y'know,' he said, a little smile creeping onto his face, 'Noraid'll make more money today than it does in the next six months. A lot of drunks'll get whimsical over their Guinness and start writing cheques. Christmas for us really.'

'So you actually encourage the talking of shite.'

McLiam nodded.

'And you still feel the same way, now that they've kidnapped your sister?'

'They didn't kidnap her.'

'They bloody did.'

'Noraid didn't. The IRA did. Or their close cousins.'

'Marcus, it's all the bloody same.'

'No, it's not. Noraid are a legitimate pressure . . .'

'Balls. They're terrorists, just as much as Sinn Fein, just as much as the IRA . . .'

'The Army, the RUC . . .'

'You're getting away from the point. Your own people set Mary up. They got you out of the way, and they kidnapped her, they've maybe even killed her. There must be an acute sense of betrayal lurking in there somewhere.'

'There is. Of course there is. But looked at objectively, if it's the IRA it's not such a bad move. I mean, what better opportunity to get some publicity on the world stage.'

'I wish I could say I admire your objectivity.'

'I'm not saying that I am . . . I'm just saying that if I was, that's what I'd see.'

'What I see is your sister kidnapped by a lot of murdering bastards.'

'To a certain extent I can see that as well.'

'I mean, it's going to come out in the end one way or the other that what McMaster was saying was a result of blackmail, so where's the gain?'

'Ask the terrorists.'

'I'm asking you, you're Noraid.'

'I'm not Noraid. I man a desk in a little office. I do a job to help the folks back home. I don't run the show. You think if I ran the show I'd have pulled something like this against my own sister?'

I shrugged.

'Thanks,' he said.

'I'm sorry. I don't know you well enough to say you wouldn't. No – I tell a lie. I honestly don't think you would do something like this against your own sister. But I'm not entirely convinced you wouldn't do it against someone else's sister. I've been up against enough zealots in the last few weeks not to rule anything out, Marcus.'

'I'm no bloody zealot.'

'Aye. Sure enough. Top of the mornin' to ya, St Patrick.'

'I'm no bloody zealot.'

'Aye.'

We spent fifty miles or more in renewed silence. Sissy hummed along to a Doris Day tape. Then some Sinatra. A little Waylon Jennings, though not little enough. The rain let up, the traffic began to get heavier as we approached the urban sprawl of New York.

'I used to read your columns when I lived at home,' McLiam said.

'Really?'

'Yeah.'

He drummed his fingers on the window and feigned interest in the back of Sissy's head. He waited. I took a sip of Diet Coke. It hadn't improved much. All it needed was a million bubbles and eighteen heaped spoonfuls of sugar. Maybe one day my teeth would thank me, and then they'd lock me up.

'So what did you think of it?'

'Of what?' he asked, dragging it out deliberately.

'My column.'

'It was okay. For what it was.'

'Thanks. What did you do for a living?'

'Nothing. Nothing much. I was at Queens.'

'Studying what?'

'Politics.'

I snorted. Not a pretty sound, but I'm not a pretty person.

'And you still joined Noraid? Did you miss all of your tutorials?'

'Starkey, we're all entitled to our views, okay?'

'No, we're not. You shoot people who don't agree with yours.'

'We don't. We're a political pressure . . .'

'Shite.'

Sissy caught my eyes in the mirror. 'Are you two having fun back there?'

'Bags,' said McLiam.

'We nearly there? If we don't get there soon Marcus may lay claim to articles two and three in my suitcase.'

Her brows bunched up. 'I don't follow.'

'Americans,' I said.

'Americans,' said McLiam, laughing. He put his hand out. I handed him the Diet Coke. He rolled down his window and threw it out.

After due consideration, I said: 'What the fuck did you do that for?'

'That was an act of sheer bloody nastiness,' he said.

'Was it meant to prove a point?'

'No.'

'It was meant to show that the Irish Republicans take anything they want, and destroy it, wasn't it?'

'No, it was meant to show that you've been cradling that bloody carton for two hundred miles and it was starting to annoy me. I did you a favour.'

'Aye.'

'Aye.'

As we hit the first traffic jam of the morning I closed my eyes and thought for a moment of Patricia. Imagined that I was travelling in a car to try and free her, not Mary. 'She's a strong girl, isn't she?' I asked.

'You think so?'

'She gives that impression. Feisty is a word that comes to mind.'

McLiam shrugged. 'I don't know. Maybe she is. It's difficult to tell in a family situation, brothers and brothers, brothers and sisters, they're always battling it out . . . they can be so different with other people.'

'These people that have her, that you think have her, would they harm her? Would they harm her even though she was your sister?'

McLiam nodded his head slowly. 'They wouldn't give it a second thought.'

'And do you still support what they do?'

'Passionately.'

39

'Hi, Mal,' I said, a foot in the door as soon as it opened, 'thought you'd be out with the troops.'

Malachy Doherty didn't know me from Eve, but he knew Marcus McLiam all right. His jaw moved, but nothing came out. His eyes blinked helplessly. His sudden metamorphosis from a sun-shy sickly white to bright-pink burny was more suited to a chameleon in a strawberry blancmange than a born-again Irish patriot in a Manhattan brownstone. He stood in the doorway, a blue towelling dressing gown tied loosely about his waist; it did little to hide the bulging breasts that dominated his scraggy-haired chest. He was round. He was fat. His bulk suggested not so much a taste for the good things in life as a taste for the big things in life. Given better circumstances he might have given Sissy an admiring glance as she pushed past him, but he was too shocked to admire anything.

He stood to one side as McLiam and I entered behind Sissy. She had her gun drawn. It was a revolver of some description and it had once been Stanley Matchitt's. Big. Nothing dainty like you'd find on a Southern belle or a riverboat gambler, but something that could blow a fist-sized hole through your heart. She checked each room while I stood admiring the decor and McLiam stared at his colleague.

'But Marcus . . .' Doherty began, his voice a rare mix of fear and hangover, his brow heavy under a sudden sweat.

Before he could finish McLiam raised a hand to silence him. 'Mal, don't start off a conversation with a "but", you know an excuse is bound to follow.'

'But . . .'

'You're not listening to me, Mal. There are no excuses.'

I looked at my watch. 'Parade's about to kick off,' I said to McLiam. He nodded. We'd already skirted the parade route at speed, already been annoyed by the shrill of fife and cat-strangling me-me men.

Sissy returned to the lounge. 'No sign of her, 'less she's a heavy smoker, room in there's turned gold with the nicotine.'

McLiam shook his head. 'She doesn't smoke.'

Sissy poked the gun into Doherty's chest. 'You should listen to the Surgeon General. Smoking can seriously damage your health. So can this, and it's cheaper. Now where's the girl?'

Doherty raised his hands.

McLiam snorted. 'No need for that, Mal, I doubt you're carrying a concealed weapon and I've seen more threatening pieces of cheese.'

Doherty shook his head and dropped his arms. Sissy removed the gun muzzle from his chest; a little red impression showed through his wiry hair. 'I'm sorry, Marcus,' he spluttered quickly and rubbed his hand across his damp scalp. 'It wasn't my idea.'

'Where is she?' McLiam snapped.

'It's more than my life's worth, Marcus.'

'Cliché,' I said.

'Just give us the address,' said McLiam, and poked him in the chest.

'I'm a dead man if I do,' moaned Doherty.

'Cliché,' I said.

'Honestly, Marcus, they'll have my guts for garters.'

Now that was a line I could relate to. McLiam appreciated it too. He grabbed Doherty's cheeks and began to twist them. Up. Down. Across. At home it was a method of torture known for obscure reasons as the L-pan and practised widely by small boys denied access by virtue of age and poverty to more sophisticated means of inducing pain, terriers who could only dream of one day being rich enough to afford a Black & Decker for the instant removal of knee-caps. L-pans, though, were just as effective. In half a minute Doherty was on his knees groaning. McLiam gave another twist for good measure. 'C'mon, Mal, save yourself some pain. Where is she?'

Doherty finally raised a hand. 'Okay! Okay!' he squealed, and McLiam let him go. He fell forward onto his elbows, then slowly righted himself and raised two hands to his cheeks and began to massage them. 'Jesus,' he said, 'Jesus Christ Almighty.'

McLiam stood over him. 'I work with you, day in, day out, for the greater goodness of Ireland. I buy you drinks, you fuckin' old soak, keep your arse out of trouble and then you do this to me.'

'I'm sorry, Marcus. They made me.'

'The big boys made me do it,' McLiam chided.

'I swear to Christ.'

'Sure, Mal. My sister, Mal.'

'I know, Marcus, I'm sorry. They swore nothing would happen to her. Nothing has happened to her. She's okay, she's just . . .'

'Being held hostage. Lovely. So give me the address. Tell me who has her. Tell me the plan . . .'

'I don't know any plan, Marcus. Look at me for Christ sake, do I look like someone they'd explain their plans to?'

I nudged McLiam's elbow. 'Never trust a man with a low opinion of himself.'

McLiam gave me a little smile. 'That has all the hallmarks of a brand new cliché.'

I shrugged. I tapped my watch again. 'We'd better move.'

McLiam put his hand out to Sissy. She gave him the gun. He handled it gingerly.

'Know what you're doing, son?' I asked.

He nodded. 'I watch a lot of films.'

'Aye.'

'And I meet a lot of shady characters.'

'Aye.'

He placed the gun against the back of Doherty's head. 'I'm a pacifist by nature, Mal, you should know that. But family's family, so speak now or Starkey here'll be for ever holding your tongue.'

Doherty swallowed hard, his eyes fixed on me, big bulgy eyes like someone had once tried to strangle him, then lost interest, but the eyes had stayed out in shock. 'Those guys arrived a few weeks ago . . .' he spat out. McLiam pushed the gun further into his head. 'Jesus, Marcus, I'm tellin' ya . . . those guys, the three of them, they arrived from Derry . . . you met them, everyone was running around after them . . . you met them, Mar—'

'The councillors, the Sinn Fein councillors?'

'Aye, call them what you want . . . I thought maybe they were out trying to buy guns . . . it happens from time to time . . .'

'They were here to lobby . . .'

'Aye, so they said. Someone told them about your sister . . .'

'Someone?'

'I was drunk . . . I was just talking . . . I didn't think . . .'

'You never do . . .'

'I didn't mean anything by . . .'

'You never do. You just sold me down the river in an orange crate.'

'I was just chatting. Just slabbering. You know how it is. Then they got nasty. Started slapping me about. Wanted to know everything I knew about her . . . I mean, what did I know? I talked to you some, you told me some more . . . they took it from there. I didn't know what they were going to do. But Jesus, Mal, I was scared. I couldn't warn you. They said they'd . . .'

'So where is she?'

'I don't know. I wasn't part of it.'

'Well, where are they? It amounts to pretty much the same.'

'They wouldn't keep her where they were staying.'

'Says who?'

'Jesus, Marcus, they wouldn't be that stupid.'

'Of course they would. We're Irish, we're supposed to be stupid. Now where the fuck are they?'

'As far as I know they're still in their hotel, but I don't know anything for sure, I locked myself in here as soon as the whole thing started. I wanted nothing to do with it. I'm just sorry I couldn't tell you, but it was more than my . . .'

'Which fucking hotel?'

'The Mirage, it's . . .'

'I know where it is,' I said quickly. I still had a couple of their towels stuffed in my rucksack. 'We all stayed there first time round in New York.'

'If they have her in the same hotel, they have a nerve,' said Sissy.

'It's not likely, is it?' McLiam asked. 'The same hotel?'

'Likely?' I said. 'Likely doesn't come into it. Nothing likely has happened since I arrived in this stupid country. But is it possible?'

'It's possible,' said Sissy.

'To keep someone hostage in one of New York's most prestigious hotels for . . . what, over a week?' McLiam asked.

'Honey, for the right money, you could keep an elephant hostage in one of New York's most prestigious hotels.'

'Or a whale,' I said.

McLiam pulled the gun away from Doherty's head. 'Okay. All we can do is find out. What about Sad Sam here?'

Doherty's head swivelled back towards McLiam, eyes pleading. 'Go and get her back, Marcus. I won't say a word.'

'Won't and can't are quite different things, Mal.'

'I swear.'

'That carries a lot of weight, though not as much as you. Mal, you have fucked me over something shocking, and I'm telling you now that if I ever see you again I'll kill you. Do you understand?'

Doherty nodded. His dressing gown was soaked with sweat.

'Okay,' said McLiam, handing Sissy her gun back, 'we're off.' He wagged a warning finger at Doherty. 'If you warn them, we'll know, and we'll come looking for you. You understand?'

'Of course. I won't say a word. I swear to God.'

'Swear to whoever the fuck you want, but do it quietly. They hear anything at all, you're a dead man.'

'I swear to Christ.'

'Okay,' said McLiam, 'let's go.'

'Good luck,' said Doherty, still on his knees, as we headed for the door.

'Aye,' said McLiam.

Outside, the party had started, the celebration of everything Irish carried out with such tack and misplaced nationalism that it made me proud to be British, though only just.

Winter might have been heaving its last bad breath along the streets of the city, but the city was fighting back with an early spring of its own creation. Everything that could sprout green did. Doors were painted. Bunting hung. Shamrocks, deprived of their natural environment, sprouted instead from ten thousand lapels, a heaving mass unconsciously celebrating the holy trinity and slowly dying at the same time. On a corner we passed one of New York's finest mounted on a green horse. Green beer sloshed already in the gutter. Old men pondered on when to get teary-eyed for maximum effect. German barmen sharpened their Irish accents. In side streets a thousand kilties squeezed their bagpipes. Noraid rubbed its hands and prepared to count the cash. It was, as Oscar Wilde had said, although it was one of his less widely quoted epigrams, a lot of shite.

And we were stuck in the middle of it. We could only get the car so far. Too many streets were sealed off for the parade, a parade which would be led by Bobby McMaster. The ex-Loyalist thug from Crossmaheart would force a smile and wave at ten thousand born-again Republicans and then spit out through gritted teeth a speech to inspire more terror in the country of his birth. Then he would fight the most dangerous man on earth for a cheap belt for his waist and the life of his wife, or, more likely, face humiliating defeat in the ring, and the murder of his beloved.

If we hadn't known better we might have thought that the police were deliberately blocking off every street we chose to drive along, always just staying a block ahead of us. Finally Sissy could take the car no further. She pulled up behind a line of cars. Twenty yards up, a police crash barrier blocked the road. Before she could reverse half a dozen vehicles crammed in behind us. She blared her horn and screamed out of the window, but to no avail.

McLiam and I got out of the back. Sissy slapped the wheel, cursed, then clambered out.

'Are you not going to stay with it?' I said.

'You stay with it if you want to.'

'But . . .'

'It's not my car. Poodle Clay can afford a thousand more.'

'Okay.' McLiam had already broken into a trot. 'Hey!' I shouted. 'Hold on!'

He turned back and waved me on. I shrugged at Sissy. 'We'll have to run.'

'What're you implying?'

'I'm not implying anything. I just said we'll have to run.'

'I can run with the best of them.'

'I'm not doubting that you can, Sissy.'

'Will you fuckin' hurry up!' McLiam screamed. He was already a hundred yards down the road.

I started running. 'Find McMaster, Sissy,' I shouted back, 'stick with him.'

She shouted something back, but it was lost in a blast of car horn.

Within a couple of blocks I had caught McLiam. He may have had the enthusiasm of a do-gooding pacifist but he also had the stitch of a couch potato. I eased up beside him.

'You don't get enough exercise,' I said. His face was puffed red and he'd already broken into a thick sweat.

'Thanks for the tip,' he said between gasps, but they were determined gasps, he kept his rhythm, kept his pace.

We reached 42nd Street. The neon hadn't dulled any in respect for St Patrick. We pushed through the crowds, already ten deep, onto Broadway, then ducked under the crowd control barriers and started running again. A cop shouted at us. We ignored him. He lifted his radio but then dropped it as someone else ducked under the barriers and attempted to cross the road.

Up ahead, the Mirage.

'What's the plan then?' I asked between puffs.

McLiam shook his head. 'This is all new territory to me. You done stuff like this before?'

I laughed. 'Sure.'

'What do you recommend then?'

'We just run right up to reception and ask for the Hostage Suite.'

'As simple as that?'

'Of course.'

'And you remembered to get the gun off Sissy?'

'Shite,' I said. There was always something.

40

Finding their suite was a cinch, for American hotel staff are nothing if not helpful. Gaining access to it was another matter entirely.

For a start, they had posted a guard outside it. We weren't too put out by that, as it kind of indicated that there might be something inside worth guarding, like a damsel in distress. Luckily he was stationed two-thirds of the way up a very long corridor and gave no indication of noticing us as we hesitated and then passed by its mouth.

We stopped about twenty yards further up. I leant against the wall; McLiam stood in the centre of the corridor, fingers bunched into fists at his sides.

'Recognize him?' I asked softly. Everything else was quiet and my voice fell into step with it. It was a time for some contemplation after running ourselves ragged and then wheezing through the lobby. When we had first arrived in New York, the Mirage had seemed so bright and welcoming, but those had been largely carefree days, before the Sons, before the kidnap, and now the corridors seemed darker, shrunken almost.

McLiam shook his head. 'Too far away. Doesn't look familiar though.'

I shrugged. 'Doesn't matter much. He's still in the way. What'll we do?'

'Besides calling the police?'

I nodded. 'I've never been one for brave or selfless acts. But I think this one's down to us.'

McLiam nodded too. 'Aye. But I'd feel a lot better about a brave or selfless act if I had a gun. We're completely weaponless, aren't we?'

'I've a blue biro. And a rapier-like wit.'

McLiam sniggered. His fists relaxed for a moment. 'Aye, and I have my lethal left foot.' He swung it out, arching it mock professionally. 'We could challenge them to a game of football, I'll score the goals, you write a damning report.' He dropped his foot again, shook his head slightly. 'God, this is stupid. She's in there and we're out here doing nothing.'

'We're not doing nothing and it's not stupid. We're the only two doing anything. We're not the bloody SAS, Marcus, we haven't always got to have a master plan.'

'I know. I'm sorry, it's just . . .'

'There's always the old dependable.' He looked up,

hopefully. 'Room service. Just go right up and bluff our way in. I'm sure we could liberate some uniforms from somewhere.'

'Aye.' Disdainful. 'You've been watching too many old movies.'

'If I'd watched too many movies, I would have extricated myself from this one before the first reel was up. Okay, room service wouldn't work. Just a thought.'

'We could just walk right up. I'll tell them it's my sister they're holding, and we'll take it from there.'

'You mean negotiate for her release?'

McLiam nodded. 'Talking never hurt anyone.'

'Rubbish. You can't talk to terrorists. They give you peace with one hand, then change their names and punch you with the other. Violence is the only thing these people understand.'

'I'd beg to differ, if my sister wasn't in there with them.'

And then I spotted something, and inspiration flowed again. I grabbed McLiam by the shoulder. 'We smoke them out,' I said.

'We what?'

'Smoke them! Smoke them out of their lair!'

'Starkey, settle down. Explain.'

'The fire alarm.' I pointed along the corridor to a red square on the wall and the fire extinguisher beneath it. 'Smash it and wait for something to happen.'

He shook his head. 'They'll just phone downstairs, find out nothing's wrong.'

'We'll make something wrong. They'll clear the building, they're obliged to. Rules is rules.'

'They'll poke their heads out, see nothing's wrong, and stay put.'

'Not if they see smoke.'

'What're you suggesting, lighting a pipe or burning the building down?'

'Burning something.'

'Starkey, there's at least eight hundred rooms in this hotel. Could be two thousand or more people in the building. You can't just set fire to it.'

'I can set fire to part of it. It's in a good cause.'

'Is that really the best you can come up with?'

I nodded enthusiastically.

'God help us then,' said McLiam.

But he went along with it, because he knew that it was an idea in a vacuum otherwise free of ideas. We returned to the lobby. We bought three copies of the *New York Times* and a lighter. We returned to the thirteenth floor. The guard was still in the same position. The corridors were still quiet. I set fire to the Mirage Hotel.

It wasn't a major fire. A boy scout with a water pistol could have brought it under control, but it did the trick. McLiam smashed the alarm, the alarm went off. Fifteen seconds later, as I held the burning newspapers up to a smoke detector, the sprinklers came on. I dropped the papers and stamped on them.

We ran back to where the corridors intersected and turned towards the guard. He was standing facing us, looking helplessly up at the ceiling as the sprinklers soaked him. We started banging on doors.

'Fire! Fire!' McLiam shouted.

'Everyone out! Everyone out! Head for the lifts!' I shouted.

'What's going on!' the guard bellowed along the corridor. Plumes of smoke snaked round the corner behind us.

I looked up towards him. 'Fire! Fire!' I shouted.

'Everyone out! Everyone out!' yelled McLiam.

The guard turned and opened the door to the suite. He closed it quickly behind him. We kept yelling, but skipped up half a dozen doors.

One of the first doors we had banged on was yanked open and a middle-aged man in a dressing gown peered anxiously out. 'Is there a fire?' he called up to us.

'Fire! Fire!' yelled McLiam.

The man closed the door behind him and stepped out, wincing as the first sprinkles landed. 'Where do I go?'

'Take the lift!' I shouted.

'In a fire? Aren't you suppos—?'

'Take the fucking lift!' I yelled.

He turned quickly. Up ahead several other doors opened.

'Fire! Fire!' I shouted.

'Everyone out! Everyone out!' yelled McLiam.

There were a dozen people in the corridor then. Damp people hurrying along, but calm enough with it.

We came inevitably to the door of all doors. We listened

for a second. Raised voices. Indistinct though, with the hiss of the water and jabber of the evacuees.

I nodded at McLiam. He winked back. I banged on the door. 'Fire! Fire!' I yelled.

'Everyone out! Everyone out!' shouted McLiam.

Someone tapped me on the shoulder. I turned. An elderly nun. 'Is this the way to the lift?' she asked.

'Fuck away off!' yelled McLiam. 'Sister,' he added.

She took a step back and then followed everyone else.

I banged on the door again. 'Get out now!' I yelled. 'The roof's coming in!'

The door was pulled open. The guard. Behind him two men. Between them, supported, Mary McMaster, head down, pasty-faced, wasted.

'We're coming!' shouted the guard.

McLiam raised the fire extinguisher he'd been cradling all along and unleashed it full force in the guard's eyes. It wasn't much more than soapy bubbles, but he recoiled like it was acid. He staggered back, and McLiam hit him with the cylinder across the top of the head and he fell.

'Drop her!' I screamed.

Wide-eyed, shock-faced, they dropped her like a sack of potatoes. McLiam threw the cylinder at them. They veered off.

I ducked down into the room and ran my hand inside the guard's jacket. A gun. I pulled it out and shot the television in the corner of the room. The tube exploded. Both men dived for the ground and covered their heads. 'Don't shoot,' said one.

'We can explain,' said the other.

McLiam looked at me quickly, chest panting, surprised both at the suddenness and completeness of our victory.

I shook my head and smiled, breathing hard as well. I closed the door. He ran to his sister and lifted her up. I trained the gun on her captors.

'Are ye all right?' he asked, holding her under the arms and gently shaking her.

'Uhhhhhhh,' she said and her head flopped sideways. There was a suggestion of a smile on her lips, although it could easily have been a precursor to a particularly nasty drool. McLiam was happy, she was alive, she was in a stupor, but she was alive. Even if she did start drooling, it was a drool of the living. Drooling has never really caught on as a fad, or at least not in the same way as, say, skateboarding, although it's a lot cheaper and you don't have to wear kneepads, but at least if you can drool you can breathe, and if you can breathe, you're alive, and that was all we had hoped for.

'We were just trying to help Ireland.'

'Because Ireland won't help itself.'

'The IRA's gone soft.'

'As margarine.'

'We didn't mean any harm.'

'Or not much.'

Their names were Sean Mac and Brendan McFarlan, as if it mattered. They were Sinn Fein councillors; both had been quartermasters for the Provisional IRA in the good old days, a couple of months before. They had come ostensibly to publicize the cause of Republicanism in the States, and had managed to bluff their way into the country on false passports. Pro-Irish as it is, the States has never been particularly fond of IRA terrorists or Sinn Fein politicians. Publicizing the cause didn't take much of their time as they spoke mainly to the converted. This left them plenty of time to set about their real agenda, buying guns to open up a new front back home, or would have if they hadn't got talking to a drunk Noraid official who'd told them about a certain boxer's wife. And so the plot had unfolded. They'd nabbed her in the hotel lift, marched her up a couple of floors and kept her locked and mostly drugged in their suite ever since. They were quite talkative, really. The gun in Sean Mac's ear helped. Standing them both in front of the window and threatening to blow them out of it was an added incentive.

McLiam worked on his sister. She looked ill. The drools hadn't really developed. He slapped, he tickled, but he didn't get a great deal of sense out of her. She lay sagged and sallow on the settee.

'What the fuck did you use on her?' McLiam growled.

'Nothing lethal,' said McFarlan, medium height, middle-parted hair, business suit. 'I don't know what, exactly. A doctor gave it to us. A sedative or something. She comes out of it after a couple of hours. She'll be okay.'

McLiam looked daggers at him. 'She'd better be.'

'I'm sorry,' said Mac, smaller than his comrade but looking much the same. 'We wouldn't have hurt her.'

'You have hurt her. Look at her. She doesn't know where the fuck she is.'

'I know, but . . .'

McLiam wagged a finger. 'You've hurt her!'

Mac nodded apologetically. He tried to give me a reassuring smile. I had the gun.

McLiam shook his head. 'When I think of all the work I put in for you bastards, Jesus . . .'

'No man, no woman, is more important than the cause,' said McFarlan. He was quoting something, someone, but he said it without conviction, quoting from duty rather than belief.

'So you're quite happy to lay down your life for it?' I asked.

McFarlan nodded slowly. Mac looked quickly at his companion, then at McLiam and his sister. 'We just wanted to raise some money, get some publicity. We wouldn't have killed her. Jesus, mate, it was the ideal opportunity. And we could hardly ask you, could we? You weren't likely to agree, were you?'

'It's always nice to be asked. Especially when we're supposed to be on the same side. You never know what I might have suggested. Kidnapping the manager. Kidnapping the trainer. Kidnapping Starkey here.'

'Thanks,' I said.

'I'm serious.'

'I know.'

'And now you've fucked it up.'

McFarlan nodded.

'What'll the boys back home be thinking when all the bad publicity comes out?' I asked. 'Damage limitation strategy already established, is it?'

Mac looked at McFarlan. McFarlan looked at Mac. They both shrugged.

'They don't know anything about it, do they?'

McFarlan shook his head. 'It was our idea.'

Mac stared at him. 'It was your idea,' he snapped.

'You went along with it.'

'You made me.'

'I did not. You suggested the drugs.'

'Only because you wanted to cut her ear off and send it to them!'

'You fuckin' liar!'

'Fuckin' liar yourself!'

'Children, please!' I shouted.

They looked at me.

'Sorry,' said Mac.

McFarlan nodded.

I looked over at McLiam. 'Any improvement?'

He gave a little shrug. 'Difficult to tell. We should get a doctor.'

I reached for the phone. 'What should we do with them?' They twitched nervously against the Manhattan backdrop and shifted their attention to McLiam.

'Maybe this is the time to call the police.'

'Now that we've done the rescuing hero bit.' I smiled. Mac and McFarlan visibly relaxed.

And we had done it. Mary McMaster was alive. Everything was working out. Maybe we could all live happily ever after.

'I'll call Bobby. Let him know she's alive.' I checked my watch again. The parade would be mostly over and he'd be repairing to Madison Square Garden for the weigh-in and press conference at which he had been ordered to promote Republicanism. 'Maybe we can stop him before he makes a fool of himself on international television again.'

'Ahm,' said Mac.

'Shut the fuck up,' snapped McFarlan.

'You shut the fuck up for a change!' shouted Mac. 'I'm sick and tired of you getting me in the shite! You shut up! We tell them now and maybe we can do some good . . .'

'Keep your fuckin' trap . . .'

I butted Mac with the muzzle; he fell back and let out a little scream of fear, forgetting for a moment that there was glass between him and the ground thirteen floors below. 'Tell us what?'

'Keep your fuckin' . . .'

I hit McFarlan hard on the nose with the handle. He turned away, cupping his face in his hands. Blood squeezed between his fingers. It was good to see someone else's nose bleed for a change.

'Tell us what?' I asked again.

Mac looked a little sheepish. 'You won't shoot me?'

'Tell us what?'

He looked quickly at his comrade, then at McLiam. He didn't look at me at all. 'We have a man shadowing McMaster on the parade. He'll be at Madison for the weigh-in by now. He's in radio contact with Damien . . .' He nodded at the unconscious figure of the guard sprawled across the floor. 'Checks in every half-hour. His instructions were to shoot McMaster if something went wrong, if he couldn't make contact.'

'And when was he supposed to call?'

Mac looked at his watch. 'Five minutes ago.'

41

There were firemen in the corridors. Policemen in the lift. 'Smoke inhalation!' I shouted as we helped Mary through the door and punched for the lobby. 'There's others along the way!' I coughed for good measure. The cops nodded and hurried on. It was no time to get into complicated conversations. They'd find McFarlan and Mac trussed together with their own ties soon enough.

McLiam cradled Mary against his chest, one arm round her, one hand stroking her brow. She wore a grimy white shirt and crumpled Levi's. She was soaked. We all were. I drummed my fingers impatiently against the lift doors.

'We can leave her in the lobby,' I said, 'make a run for Madison. It's only a couple of blocks.'

McLiam shook his head. 'I'm not letting her out of my sight.'

'We haven't time, Marcus.'

'I'm not letting her out of my sight.'

The doors opened. A fat guy in a Republic of Ireland T-shirt blocked our way. He clutched a beer glass to his chest, then suddenly thrust it towards us. 'Happy St Patrick's Day!' he yelled, spraying us with spit.

'Fuck away off,' McLiam growled and pushed past, pulling Mary with him. She was starting to move under her own steam, hesitant Bambi steps which weren't helped by being hurried along, but a good sign nevertheless.

'Happy St Patrick's Day!' the drunk yelled again, his face resting against the back wall of the elevator.

'Senpadrik,' Mary mumbled.

'It's okay, love,' McLiam said.

We left the hotel and threaded our way through the traffic jam outside. The blare of horns was music after the bagpipes. I took one of her arms, McLiam the other, we lifted, then skipped her towards Madison Square Garden.

It took us ten minutes where it should have taken five. We should have left her, but I could see his point. We laboured up the steps into the ticketing area, then moved left to an escalator. I fished out my press pass, but there was no need for it. The human tidal wave of support which had surged around McMaster at the head of the St Patrick's Day parade had followed him to Madison and washed away the security put in place for the weigh-in and press conference. At the top of the escalator we turned right into the Sports Bar and a chaotic pre-fight celebration. Maybe three hundred singing

Irishmen were congregated there, swamping the television cameras which had been set up with the expectation that the most hectic event they would have to cover would be the ritual eye-balling between champion and challenger. The news teams didn't quite know what to make of the horde of drunks singing 'Here We Go Here We Go Here We Go Here We Go Here We Go Here We Go-o' again and again. McMaster was at the top of the room on the left of the scales, flanked by Geordie McClean, Jackie Campbell and Sissy Smith; he looked tense, and slightly embarrassed. To the right of the scales Tyson shuffled tentatively from foot to foot; Don King had an arm round him. A dozen or more of his entourage were grouped about him, looking nervous.

'Gentlemen, please!' The master of ceremonies wore a white dinner jacket. He looked like Bogie in the latter stages of a terminal illness. He tapped the mike again. The singing abated a little. 'You were good enough to keep order for the weigh-in, now if we could just extend that into the press conference – I'm sure you'd all like to hear what the boxers have to say.'

'BOBBY! BOBBY! BOBBY! BOBBY!'

'EARWIG JOE EARWIG JOE EARWIG JOE!'

'Gentlemen, please!'

'TYSON'S GOIN' DOWN, TYSON'S GOIN' DOWN . . .'

'Please!'

'UP YOUR HOLE WITH A BIG JAM ROLL, DO-DAH, DO-DAH . . .'

McLaim set Mary carefully on a seat at the back of the

bar, made sure she was comfortable. 'Maybe he's been scared off by the crowd,' he said.

'Maybe.' We both scanned the throng as best we could, but it was like looking for a needle in a box of needles. We'd a rough description of one Denny Doyle, a shooter hired in from some quasi-Irish Mafia in New Jersey, but it could have fitted most anyone of vaguely Caucasian appearance.

McLiam put his hand out. 'Gimme the gun,' he said.

'What for?'

'I'm going to tell Bobby that Mary's all right.'

'You need a gun for that?'

'Jesus, Starkey, there's an assassin up there somewhere. Now gimme the gun.'

I fished it out of my pocket and handed it to him. He clasped it in his hand. This time there were definitely bullets in it. He nodded and turned. He started to push his way through.

Mary slipped off her seat. 'Sanpatrik,' she mumbled.

I pulled her back up. She slumped forward and went to sleep on the table.

McLiam was making good progress towards the front. A reporter was speaking to McMaster, but he wasn't miked up and his question was lost in the hubbub. I could hear McMaster, though, breathing heavily into a hand-held mike and nodding slowly. Geordie McClean bent forward, straining to hear the question himself. Behind him Sissy suddenly looked left and broke into a smile. I followed her gaze. Stanley Matchitt was edging along the back of the bar towards her, his face puffed up; he saw suddenly that Sissy had spotted him and he grinned. Then something else caught his attention.

McLiam broke through the line of questioners.

Matchitt recognized the face.

Matchitt saw the gun.

Matchitt pulled at his jacket and produced a gun. He raised. He fired. Everyone started screaming. McLiam fell. Pandemonium.

I raced forward. Everyone raced backwards. They took me with them.

I forced my way back. Tyson had been lifted bodily by his team and rushed out a side door.

McMaster pulled himself up from the ground, pushing McClean off his back.

Matchitt held the gun out in front of him and slowly advanced on McLiam. His eyes were wide with excitement, the tip of his tongue just showed red between his swollen lips. 'You okay, Bobby?' he said breathlessly. McMaster nodded and bent down to McLiam. Matchitt knelt beside him.

'I . . .' he began.

'STANLEY!'

Sissy's voice, shrill, panicked . . . a man in a green football jersey stepped out from behind a camera and raised a gun. He fired once. Matchitt fired twice. The man fell.

'Two outta two!' Matchitt yelled.

Then he fell over and Sissy screamed.

* * *

The rage of volume: the silence within. I sat at the bar sipping beer while all around the reality of human drama was played out as on a television screen; I had my seat and my remote control and my beer. Barely moving, I could flick through a dozen channels, I could be alternately fascinated and repelled, brought close to tears and bounced edgily along the rim of laughter.

I flicked to the panoramic shot, where the panic had given way to panic control and military administration: police, paramedics, journalists, boxers, sports officials, all carrying out their appointed tasks with single-minded efficiency.

Then close in to Mary McMaster rising unsteadily from her table at the back of the bar and shuffling forward.

To Bobby McMaster, suddenly looking up from tending Stanley Matchitt, seeing his wife, seeing the pale apparition that was his wife moving unsteadily through the confusion. He rose quickly, but then stood mesmerized. Her eyes, unfocused still, were nevertheless drawn hypnotically to him. He stepped over Matchitt, stepped over McLiam, and she fell into his arms. He let out a little moan and tears jumbled down his face.

I flicked to Marcus McLiam, flat on his back, eyes open, blinking, his shirt blood red, a paramedic talking to him, reassuring him. McLiam's eyes swivelled back until all I could see were the whites and I feared for a moment that he had died, but all he was doing was looking at his sister in a safe embrace with her husband.

To Stanley Matchitt, head cradled in Sissy's lap, blood burbling from his swollen lips, a priest bending over him, giving him the last rites, the Catholic death passage that was anathema to him but which he was incapable now of resisting.

To Sissy, her large fingers easing through his, about to lose another man.

Untended, flat on his back, eyes wide and lifeless, the assassin from New Jersey.

Geordie McClean sat at the end of the bar, eight empty seats up from me, shaking his head.

And I looked at myself, alone in the eye of the hurricane, unharmed but not untouched, unloved but not unloving. I found myself shaking my head in time with McClean. Maybe he was thinking the same thing. This wasn't real. None of it was. Not the Sons of Muhammad. Not the Brothers of Muhammad. Not Irish freedom fighters. Not the deaths, none of the deaths were real. Not this carnage. Certainly not the whales. It was all television. All fiction. Meant to be enjoyed by someone else. Real life was about being married and having children and going shopping and betting on the Grand National and carving the Christmas turkey and losing your keys down the back of the chair; it was about trousers that no longer fitted and toilets that wouldn't flush and songs by embarrassing relatives who thought they were Johnny Cash. We were living an elaborate fantasy and we would wake to a bowl of Frosties and a glowing electricity bill. We'd go, 'Jesus, that was a bit lifelike,' and give our wives a hug. Except I didn't have a wife, and Stanley Matchitt, King of the High Seas, had just died in front of me.

I got my old room back at the Mirage. It wasn't exactly like going home, but I was content with it. I bought a lot of beer and watched a lot of television. Bobby McMaster figured heavily. Duvet coverage.

It was quite a story. Kidnap. Murder. Scary black men. Drugs. Rescues. Whales. Noraid raided by the FBI, but still fighting the good fight. Geordie McClean was trying to sell the film rights almost before they'd taken Stanley Matchitt to the mortuary. But to sell the film rights there had to be an end to the story, and the end wasn't the reunion of Bobby McMaster and his beautiful wife, it was the union of Bobby McMaster and Mike Tyson in the ring.

There was some talk about cancelling the fight. Out of respect for the dead. But as with all sporting tragedies, the potential for money making proved too great; they wouldn't cancel it, they would postpone it for five days to give everyone time to recover, and then stage it as a tribute to the heroism of those who had died and those who had been injured. Sport would be the winner. And if everyone made a little extra money then, well, hell, there you go.

McMaster hosted a press conference the day after Matchitt died. He stood with his arm round Mary, her face beaming, his face beaming too. He called for peace and reconciliation in Ireland. An end to terrorism. The restoration of democracy.

From being the racist, gay-bashing, terror fan, he was now the hero, the lone voice of sanity in a world gone mad. I didn't begrudge him it, I was happy that everything was working out. I just didn't feel a part of it. I sat in my room and I drank my beers and I watched the television.

'Were you ill-treated by your captors?' a reporter asked Mary.

She squeezed her husband. 'I can't remember. They kept me drugged. I'm just glad it's all over.'

'Has this put you off New York?' called another.

'It's put me off being kidnapped,' said Mary. Everyone laughed. I thought back to Paula, the stripper. She'd said something similar. Does this put you off men? Only the type that would come to a place like this. Was she at work at this very moment, fulfilling a fantasy for a fistful of dollars? I should go and see her. Say goodbye to her. Because it was time to go. Time to go home and pick up the pieces. Forget about the book. Think about putting my life in order. Quitting the booze once I'd said farewell to the temptations of New York. Enjoy the bright nights of the summer sober for a change. Win back Patricia.

'What about Mike Tyson, Bobby, has he spoken to you about all of this?'

McMaster shook his head. 'Not directly, no, but he sent me a nice note.'

'What'd it say?'

'I'm not sure. The crayon was all over the place.'

And I blinked, and I blinked again, and I could hear five

hundred people in the press conference blinking, and everyone at home blinking and I could hear the cash registers jangling again as Bobby McMaster told the world once more that he was only joking and that he had the highest regard for Mike and he was looking forward to fighting for the heavyweight championship of the world.

42

The TV threw its dancing shadows across the room. I watched the boxers, I sipped. The phone rang. Cameron calling me from home. Three hundred years before, he had asked me to write a book about a fighter.

'How's it goin'?' he asked cheerfully, like he didn't know about all the people who'd died.

'As well as can be expected.'

'Sorry I haven't been in touch, but I'm sure you've been busy. You realize the demand for this is now going to be phenomenal, Dan?'

'I'm sure it will be.'

'Just a matter of writing it now, eh?'

'Yeah.'

'The quicker you deliver, the better. There'll be a bonus if it's within the month.'

'Great.'

'You'll be ringside later?'

'Not quite.'

'They promised ringside.'

'Yeah, well.'

'I'll phone Geordie McClean. Remind him.'

'It doesn't matter. Don't worry about it. I'm closer than ringside.'

'Good. Great then. How's Bobby looking?'

'He's looking good.'

'Sparring well?'

'Yeah. I suppose so.'

'You reckon he'll sneak it?'

'No.'

'Are you okay, son? You sound a bit tired.'

'I am a bit tired.'

'You've had some excitement then?'

'Some.'

His voice slowed, dropped a pitch. 'Trauma, Dan?'

'Yeah. Trauma. You could say that.'

'They say the best thing is just to get back on the bike, Dan.'

'I've no stabilizers.'

'You don't need them, Dan. You're a hardy perennial, son, you've come through worse.'

'You think?'

'I know.'

*   *   *

Forty-five minutes before the fight, Bobby McMaster called. 'Where the hell are you, mate?' he growled. Distantly I could hear the songs of drunken Irishmen.

'How the hell did you track me down here?'

'Dan, it really didn't take Sherlock Holmes. How come you haven't been around?'

'I've been busy.'

'Doing what?'

'This and that.'

'You were supposed to be doing press for me. Public relations.'

'My contract ran out on the seventeenth. The St Patrick's Day Massacre.'

He was quiet for a moment. They were on to 'Danny Boy'. 'Hit you hard, did it?' he said softly.

'Didn't hit me at all. That's what worries me.'

'Affects us all in different ways, Dan. You should have come around.'

'Like I say, I was busy.'

'I needed your confidence-building wisecracks.'

'Sure.'

'C'mon, Dan, lighten up.'

'Shouldn't you be psyching yourself up or something, Bobby? You're getting in the ring with Tyson in a wee while. You shouldn't be wasting your time talking to me.'

'Ach, sure, it's only a fight.'

'Aye.'

'It is, Dan. The real fight's over. I got my wife back, and

I didn't have to lift a finger. You did the real fighting. You and Stanley and Sissy and her husband and Marcus.'

'And a whale.'

'Yes, and a whale.'

'We'd probably all be dead, but for the whale.'

'But we're not. We're alive. We've got the rest of our lives.' He sniggered. 'Well, you have. I'm about to get duffed up by Tyson.'

'Good crack about the crayon.'

'Yeah, thought that would go down well. I didn't want anyone to think I was getting soft.'

'And "We can work it out."'

'Yeah. Lennon can't sue. I doubt if McCartney can be bothered.'

'Are you really not that fussed about the fight?'

'I'll go in and give it my best. What more can I do?'

'It seems stupid to have gone through all of this shit, only for you to get killed in the ring.'

'That's the old Starkey confidence booster I was missing.'

'Yeah. Well.'

'Will you not come down?'

'A bit late now.'

'Starkey, it's only down the road. You know it's only down the road. Now get your arse down here. Jesus, Dan, I've got Jackie Campbell nodding off on one side of me and Geordie McClean tearing his hair out on the other. Even Sissy's moping about, one hand out for her reward, the other drying her eyes. I need someone with both feet on the ground.'

'I'm half pissed.'

'So am I.'

'You serious?'

'Come and find out.'

'Liar.'

'Come on down.'

'If I'm not there, Bobby, I'll be watching. And the best of luck. Give a good show.'

'I'll see you in a minute, Starkey.'

I had a shower and a shave. The supporting bouts were coming to a conclusion. Between rounds the cameras cut to the dressing rooms. Tyson's exuded quiet confidence tinged with menace, McMaster's fidgety nervousness. McClean in a monkey suit. Jackie Campbell, in a faded blue sweatshirt and mangy-looking bobble cap, silently taped McMaster's hands. I put on a shirt. Buttoned the top button. Toothpaste. Mouthwash. I sat on the bed and stared at the screen. Ten minutes to go. I closed my eyes.

. . . Jesus Christ! McMaster staggered back . . . fifteen seconds left of the third . . . weaved from left to right . . . bounced back from the rope . . . Tyson was there . . . ducking down . . . bringing up the right . . . Jesus Christ! . . . the sickening crack . . . the tearing of flesh and bone . . . McMaster's head snapped clean off at the neck . . . it bounced twice across the ring . . . screams erupted . . . his torso remained erect, pumping blood . . . fists swinging out at a stunned Tyson

. . . his head came to a rest . . . his eyes stared . . . tongue hanging out . . . mouth open . . . screaming silently . . . Jesus Christ!

I shuddered, opened my eyes. Someone was knocking at the door. The national anthems were just finishing. McMaster had chosen 'God Save the Queen'. As much for Matchitt, I thought, as for himself.

I stepped backwards, my eyes still stuck to the screen. I opened the door.

'Mmmmmm?'

'Hello, Dan.'

I stared for a second. Then I reached across and touched her arm. Made sure that she was real. 'Patricia,' I said.

'Surprised to see me?'

'Surprised. Pleased. Jesus Christ. Come in.'

I guided her in.

She nodded at the screen. 'I thought you'd be at the fight.'

I shook my head. I pushed some old clothes off the bed and sat her down. 'I couldn't,' I said.

She nodded, slightly, smiled. Jesus, that smile. I hadn't forgotten it. But dreams and life are so different. I nearly reached up and touched it.

'But . . .' I started. I looked at the screen. The first bell.

'I got your letter.'

'But . . .' I looked at her face. Blooming . . . but with love or baby or both?

'I know, love, it was stolen. The man that stole it from

you read it. He wrote me a note. Said it reduced him to tears. Said it changed his whole outlook on life. Said he only had fifty cents and a pair of shoes to his name, but he was going to spend what he had making sure the letter got to me. Said he was going to forsake a life of crime and join a Christian commune.'

'Jesus Christ,' I said.

A roar went up from the crowd. McMaster had staggered Tyson. He took two unsteady steps back, then lumbered forward, attacking again.

Patricia looked back from the screen. 'And I read it too, and it moved me to tears.'

I gave a little shrug, and a boy's smile. 'Maybe it was meant to,' I said.

'You were always a brilliant writer.'

'But not a brilliant person.'

'Dan, we're all different. None of us is perfect.'

'Are perfect.'

We smiled. A great smile.

The bell for round two. McMaster was slow off his stool. Tyson was three-quarters of the way across the ring. The referee held him back until Jackie Campbell was out under the ropes. And the war began again.

'So you came to see me.'

'I thought you'd have been back before this. That's why I didn't come immediately.'

'I got delayed.'

'I know. I didn't know whether to come.'

'I'm glad you did. At least I think I'm glad you did. Are you the bearer of tidings of great joy, or am I about to get kicked in the balls?'

Patricia put a hand on my knee. 'I wouldn't travel three thousand miles for that, Dan,' she said. 'I've been stupid.'

'We've both been stupid.'

'I've stopped seeing Tony.'

'He wouldn't leave his wife.'

'No. He would have left his wife. I decided to stop seeing him. I didn't love him.'

'And what about the baby?'

She patted her stomach. 'He's there. She's there. Waiting.'

'I'm glad you're keeping her. Him.'

'I'm glad you're glad.'

The bell for round three. The Irish contingent sang their heads off. The noise was phenomenal. Tyson and McMaster met in the centre of the ring, arms flailing. A left hook from the champion just caught McMaster as he slipped sideways and knocked him well off balance. He staggered across the ring, Tyson followed him quickly, another two, three blows. McMaster bounced off the ropes, threw a left of his own, Tyson ducked, threw in another left, then a right, McMaster ducked down, then pushed Tyson back, threw out a straight right, connected. The Irish roared.

I put my arm round her and we kissed. A soft kiss. A first kiss. I pushed the hair out of her eyes. She held my chin in her hand. Kissed the end of my nose.

'I've been so stupid,' she said.

'You believe anything in that letter?' I asked.

She shook her head. 'Of course not.'

Round four. Tyson had him in the corner. Lefts and rights to the body, one to the head, lefts and rights to the body, one to the head. McMaster's head sagged . . . the referee took a close look over Tyson's shoulder . . . McMaster shot a left hook up through Tyson's fists that rocked the champion's head back . . . he followed up with a left to the ribs . . . roar of the crowd . . . Tyson bunched down . . . McMaster encouraged . . . stepped forward . . . dropped his defence . . . let go with a head cleaver . . . Tyson moved sideways . . . fired over a left . . . connected perfectly . . . and McMaster went down.

'Jesus!' I said.

'Is it over?' said Patricia, gripping my arm.

'I don't . . .'

The referee was standing over him, counting off on his rubber-gloved fingers . . . then he raised his arms and crossed them quickly and Tyson threw up his arms in triumph and the ring was invaded.

I lay back on the bed. My shirt was sticking to me. I let out a sigh.

'I'm sorry,' said Patricia.

'Not your fault.'

'Did he do well?'

'He did well.'

I pushed myself up on my elbow. They had McMaster on his feet. Mary was in there with him. She had her arms round him. He was crying over her shoulder.

'Very well,' I said.

She lay down on the bed beside me and we watched the screen for a while. Tyson and McMaster embraced in the centre of the ring. Then Tyson went to the ropes and waved at the crowd and a cheer went up. Then McMaster joined him and the cheer became a roar and there was a lump in my throat and I didn't know whether it was for Bobby McMaster or for Patricia. In fact, I did know. It was for both of them.

'You know,' she said, 'we were always chalk and cheese.'

I stroked her hair. 'Weren't we just.'

'I never liked boxing.'

'You liked tennis.'

'I liked tennis and swimming and golf.'

'Yeah, golf. I could never understand why you liked golf. So slow.'

'Relaxing. So relaxing. That's why I liked classical music.'

'I liked some of it. Mozart. Beethoven. Couldn't stand Dvořák.'

'I liked beans on toast.'

'I liked beans with toast. I liked the mopping up operation.'

'I hated that. And I hated the way you burnt the steaks.'

'They were well done. Yours were still alive.'

'They were rare, as they should be.'

'You insisted on tea with everything.'

'You drank Coke till your stomach rusted.'

'Coke adds life.'

I shook my head slowly. She turned slightly and looked up at me.

'Why did we ever get together?' I asked.

'Because I fell absolutely and completely in love with you. And I still absolutely and completely love you.'

And that set me off.

Mystery Man

Bateman

He's the Man with No Name and the owner of No Alibis, a mystery bookshop in Belfast. But when a detective agency next door goes bust, the agency's clients start calling into his shop asking him to solve their cases.

It's not as if there's any danger involved. It's an easy way to sell books to his gullible customers and Alison, the beautiful girl in the jewellery shop across the road, will surely be impressed.

Except she's not – because she can see the bigger picture. And when they break into the shuttered shop next door on a dare, they have their answer. Suddenly they're catapulted along a murder trail which leads them from small-time publishing to classical music to Nazi secrets and serial killers . . .

'Funny as well as gripping' Ian Rankin

'Bateman has a truly unique voice . . . he is a dark and brilliant champion of words' James Nesbitt

'Witty, fast-paced and throbbing with menace' *Time Out*

978 0 7553 4675 2

headline

Now you can buy any of these other bestselling
books by **Bateman** from your bookshop
or *direct from his publisher*.

FREE P&P AND UK DELIVERY
(Overseas and Ireland £3.50 per book)

Orpheus Rising	£7.99
I Predict A Riot	£7.99

Mystery Man Novels

Mystery Man	£7.99
The Day of the Jack Russell	£7.99
Dr Yes	£7.99

Martin Murphy novels

Murphy's Law	£7.99
Murphy's Revenge	£7.99

Dan Starkey novels

Belfast Confidential	£7.99
The Horse with My Name	£7.99
Driving Big Davie	£7.99

TO ORDER SIMPLY CALL THIS NUMBER

01235 400 414

or visit our website: www.headline.co.uk

Prices and availability subject to change without notice.